Beyond Her Words

BINK CUMMINGS

~BINK CUMMINGS~

ISBN-13: 978-1519122896
First Edition

Copyright © 2015 by Bink Cummings

All rights reserved. No part of this book may be reproduced or transmitted in any form or by any means, electronic or mechanical, including photocopying, recording or by any information storage and retrieval system, without written permission from the author, except for the inclusion of brief quotations in a review.

Editor #1- Kristina Canady
Editor #2- Genevieve Scholl
Beta Team – Jay Samia, Mary Bevinger, Teena Torres, Dyana Newton, Zetta Via, Jezebel, Pixie, Tamra Simons, Sue Banner & Michelle Follis.
Cover Artist - Bink Cummings
Photo provided by- BigStock
Chapter Titles © Acme Labs
-This novel is a work of fiction and is not associated with any motorcycle clubs or persons.

Shout Outs

When an author spends hours, days, weeks, and months writing a book, it's emotionally taxing. It's frustrating, yet rewarding. It's a piece of our hearts and our lives that are poured into the pages for you to read. It's not just a book; it's a small sliver of us—a piece of our hearts.

During the process of writing Beyond Her Words, I was blessed with a brand new beta team. From the beginning, I had been scared to bring anyone into my inner sanctum, but as the time has progressed, I have slowly allowed my walls to come down. Jay was the first, who is my PA, beta, Vp, and real sister 'til the end. Then after opening my clubhouse on Facebook, I was blessed with hundreds of beyond amazing sisters who have not only come into my life but climbed into my heart.

Among those beautiful women, there were a few that I felt I got to know a bit more by their constant interactions in the group. They really tried to be a part of something that's greater than just myself—our Sacred Sisterhood. Which is how those few select sisters were bought into my beta team. This isn't a team where they just read my book at the end. They read along the way, gave opinions (sometimes daily), and really make the hard work I put into my novel extra special.

So without further ado, I want to shout a huge thank you to…

Mary, Teena, Tamra, Zetta, and Dyana (my beta bitches)—you have been my never-ending cheer squad, my sisters, my pick me up, my mentors…and for that, I will be forever thankful. Love you, bitches!

Sue: Thank you for all of your kind and helpful words- It made all the difference.

Kristina: (my editor): Thank you for pouring your time into the book to make it that much better. I know we had time constraints, but we made it work and I am grateful for your dedication and honest, no holds barred, opinions—it was exactly what I needed from you and you delivered. I hope to work on many more books together… You're awesome!

Genevieve: (my editor): Thank you for your quick, precise work. Your swift and clean proofreading, along with mild editing was exactly what I needed and I am thrilled to have worked with you on this project. I hope to work on many more.

To Jay: (My PA): I just have to say your loyalty knows no bounds and your support could never be beaten by any other author's PA or sister. I'm proud to call you a part of my life and the clubhouse. Love ya, VP!

To Pixie, the never forgotten stepchild: I love you bitch. You're my rock, my biggest cheerleader, my sounding board, and a huge but lovely pain in my ass. I'll love you forever. You're never gonna get rid of me, even if I have to cuff myself to you when we're old and in wheelchairs. Haha- Sucks for you.

To Jezebel: My sassy mouthed sister with a perverted mind and an even bigger heart. I love you, hooker. You're always there to pick me up, tell me when I'm being a dumb bitch, and have my back when shit gets real—loyalty to the end. Sorry to tell ya, but Bulk is just gonna have to get used to sharing, because I'm here to stay. We've been sisters for what feels like forever, and until the Lord takes me, I'm glued to your hip. Get used to that shit.

~BINK CUMMINGS~

Scottish Word Index

This book contains Scottish words and phrases. The ones included in this index are the ones chosen to be incorporated in this book to authenticate the character(s) without overwhelming the readers.

Scottish - American

Aboot - About
Arse - Ass/Butt
Aye - Yes
Bonnie – Beautiful
Cannae- Can't
Didnae – Didn't
Dinnae – Don't
Dunno – Don't know
Na – No
Tae – To
Wee – Small
Ye – You
Yer – Your
Ye're – You're

CHAPTER 1

"We're not in Kansas anymore, Viola."

I firmly grip the steering wheel of my restored '69 z28 *Camaro*—Viola. She's my pride and joy. Leaning forward in my seat like an old lady, I try to gain visibility through the torrential downpour. My windshield wipers swish maddeningly back and forth, doing little good. Brilliant streaks of light flash through the murky sky, quickly followed by a heart-stopping *boom*. A knot forms in my throat and I swallow hard, trying to dislodge it.

This storm's the worst I've driven through, and it's right above me, creeping at a snail's pace, looming overhead. It's like the darkness that is my life. It's lurking around every corner, between every nook and cranny, waiting to swoop in and sip the happiness from my marrow like a fine wine. I won't let this storm win, though; not this time, not again. Tenth time's the charm, right? Or maybe it's the eleventh? Crap, I dunno. But for my sake and sanity, I hope so.

Strong wind wickedly batters the sides of my car, swerving it to the left. I hold on tighter to the wheel, keeping the tires on the road. I can do this. I know I can. I can find a place, any place, along this never-ending country road to get gas and suitable shelter. My body needs a break and a place to rest my tired head from this hellacious storm.

After eight hours of driving straight through, with the exception of two shitty pit stops, my patience is wearing thin. But, the more pavement that rolls under my tires, the faster I get away from Jonathan and his sick, addictive behavior. Why I'd spent the past six months hoping he might be *the one* to cure me, I can't be sure. Loneliness, maybe? Stupidity? This inherent need to help people? I have no clue. I just know that yesterday was the last straw.

At thirty-two, I'm too gosh damn old to put up with men's bull-honky. Guess that's what I get for dating younger men. This time, it was only by four years. But in women's years, it might as well have been ten. When they say women mature faster than men, no truer words have ever been spoken. I'm just glad I didn't waste another six months trying to help him cure his alcohol addiction, which regrettably transposed his dependency to me and everything I do. I became his need. His drug of choice. For a woman like me, that doesn't mix. I can't fill that tall order, no matter who the man is. I don't have it in me. My soul's too damaged; my heart too broken.

Through my water-logged vision, the broken sign swings from a pole on the side of the road—Miller's Gas Station, one mile. I pray this gas station is still in operation. I'm pushing less than a quarter tank in an engine that devours gas and need to fill up.

Quickly, I steal a glance at my passenger side floorboard. The box holding my potted garlic bulbs is still keeping them safe; no soil has been spilled. I blow out a relieved breath and focus my eyes back on the road.

Those garlic bulbs are the only thing I have left from my grams' garden. They're my most prized possession, aside from the two rings I wear on my left hand and my beloved car. Who knew so much love could be wrapped in these otherwise insignificant possessions? Not me. Not until everything was stripped away, and all I was left with were these objects, the clothes on my back, and a dirty box of old photographs.

Red lights flash up ahead in a store window—*OPEN*. A single uncovered pump sits in the middle of a gravel drive. The price for unleaded fuel is written in white on the shop's window. Unable to pump gas in these conditions without drenching myself in the process, I idle to the front of the rundown gas station. There are no marked parking spots, so I make my own. Through the rain I see a short, older woman curiously peer out of a window with a shotgun in her hand. I can tell she wants me to see it when she raises it above her head and shakes it a few times to get her point across. I'm not going to mess with her, but I suppose she can never be too careful out here.

A gust of wind jostles my car as the storm boisterously ensues from above. I lean over my shifter and grab my purse from the floor. Reaching into the front pocket, I fist the crinkled wad of cash before turning off the car and tossing my keys on the passenger seat.

Leaning back into the soft leather, I try to relieve the tension in my back and numb butt. A tired groan escapes my lips as my eyes scan the lot, waiting for the rain to slow so I can go inside. At the back of the rural property sits an older and heavily rusted mobile home. Parked beside it sits a flashy motorcycle with a blue tank and a red pickup truck. Must be where the owners live. Though I'm pretty sure the woman in the window, who's still staring at me, won't be riding that bike anytime soon. Although I could be wrong—wouldn't be the first time or the last.

Shoving the money between my legs, I absent-mindedly pick at my nails and wait for the storm to slow. It has to let up sometime; it can't last all dang day. Figures, I'd be the one to get caught up in a storm on my drive to the East Coast. I don't really care, though. I just have to get away from small towns, and, more importantly, away from lazy, crazy, or drug addicted small town men. Men who are pros at bullshitting their way into your pants right before they try to stake claim over your heart. Not like I'd ever give them that. You can't give them something you don't have.

Which is the main reason why I'm sitting here in this gravel lot right now, staring out my window, daydreaming and talking to you. You're the only real person who I've got to listen to me anyhow. Men surely don't care what comes out of my mouth if they're not getting the candy in my pants, and usually not even after that. Trust me—us girls gotta stick together. Chicks before dicks. All for one and one for all—you know, all that female power bull-honky. If that actually exists. Does it? I dunno. Probably not.

Not like I think you'd like me anyhow if you got to know me. Nobody does. I'm easily forgettable. I mean, what can you do when you're the person that nobody sees? The tomboy; the girl with grease on her face and dirt under her nails? How do you cope with boys seeing you as one of them, not a person with XX chromosomes? How do you handle all the women being jealous of you because you're one of the guys? Like that's something to strive for. It's not. I'm the living, breathing proof.

I've spent too much time wishing I could tell people, and make them understand, that two people molded me into the person I am. Two people who really cared. Two people who were just as odd and backward as I am. And that those two amazing people are dead, buried, and never coming back. *Ever.* It's a harsh reality I am faced with, day in and day out. Something that wrecks me on a daily basis, leaving me only a tiny sliver of my former self—a hollow shell.

Both of my people tragically died four months from each other to the day. Both of them ripped from my soul, leaving me to painfully wander the world alone. That was ten years ago. And I've been adrift, floating haplessly through a meaningless life ever since. Living a shoddy existence, where I roll into a town just as quickly as I roll out of it, never staying more than a year or two at most.

Ten small farming communities in ten years. Places where you're guaranteed to be an outsider since you weren't born and raised there. Places where you become the dull gray stone in the vast sea of pearly white. Or more specifically, the sloppy, introverted, vertically challenged, backward tomboy, who could always understand cars and vegetables better than she could ever understand a living person. Especially females, who are notoriously focused on the glitz, the glamor, the 'something better'—the end game. Rings, weddings, babies, dresses, being sickly thin, and wearing gobs of makeup. All of those things I've never understood. Or maybe I did once, but not anymore. That part of me withered away and died long ago.

Well, I suppose I should stop being a Debbie Downer and make a run for it. The storm has settled for a moment and the clouds have parted in the sky. Beams of vibrant sun are casting down on Mother Earth, breaking through the dreary for a moment.

I grab the cash between my legs, throw open my weighted car door, and make a break for the entrance. The door chimes as I dash inside and shake off like a dog. My hand runs through my long, wavy hair, damp from the rain.

"Can I help ya?" the older woman asks with a smoker's rasp, standing behind the counter with her shotgun left lying in front of her, next to the register.

The noise of the weather forecast is broadcasted over the surround sound speakers, as heavy winds shake the windows. Air whistles through poorly sealed seams, and water drips from the leaky roof into buckets on the cracked linoleum floor. On a deep inhale, I'm assaulted with the cheap tang of lemon cleaner, and worse—the unmistakable scent of mildew. I try not to judge or crinkle my nose in disgust, because I've smelled worse. Lived in worse. Survived worse.

Meeting the woman's eyes, I flash her a friendly, closed mouth smile. "I need to fill up," I point to my car outside, "and I could use a little break from riding so long."

She leans against the wall behind her, covering a beer poster, and crosses her arms over her chest. "You been drivin' long?" She jerks her chubby chin my way.

"Eight hours." I wade further into the store. The shelves are minimally stocked and the prices, as I figured, are outrageous. Beggars can't be choosers, though, so I snatch a handful of candy bars and a few bags of chips, paying special attention to the expiration dates. There is no way I'm paying almost two dollars for a bag of candy if it's expired. All of them, except the *Baby Ruth*, are fresh, so I put that one back and continue my inspection of snacks for the long ride ahead.

"Where ya headed?" she snoops, just as a siren broadcasts over the speakers, immediately followed by a tornado warning.

"Is that a local station?" I ask, choosing to ignore her question.

"Yeah," is as much as I get outta her.

"Should we be taking cover?" From my experience, most warnings are more of a safety precaution. However, this woman appears unfazed by the whole thing. She doesn't seem to care that the rain is beating the windows like they owe it money. Or that I can see huge branches flying like feathers through the front lot.

I wince, sucking in a sharp breath when a broken branch barely misses my beloved Viola. At my sides, I fist my hands, still full of candy, and clench my teeth. My car shouldn't be out in this weather. It's not letting up; it's only getting worse. If she gets the slightest scratch, I'm going to lose it. I've kept her pristine for almost fourteen years. I can't allow a storm like this ruin her custom paint job. It'll wreck me.

The sky's black now, matching my heart. Can you see the low hanging clouds and the streaks of lightning slash through the sky? It's beautiful, in an End of Days morbidity, don't you think?

A deafening *boom* and sizzling crackle of thunder shakes the windows. I move closer to the back of the store, just in case one of those flying branches decides to do the swan dive and impale the glass.

I spare a brief sideways glance at the woman. Her bushy brows are pinched and her aged lips pursed as her eyes fix on the storm brewing in Mother Nature's cauldron. She makes a disgruntled noise in her throat.

My eyes fly wide when I catch sight of an iron gate tumbling like a weed down the country highway. "Holy crap," I mutter to myself, following the gate's path until it's out of sight.

"It's gettin' nasty out there," she comments. "Owned this place for thirty-five years and she's still standin'." Her hand proudly slaps the counter and it startles me. I fidget, dropping my unpurchased candy to the floor, and my heart leaps into my throat.

Bending down between two shelves to pick up my mess, I hear the first crack.

"Damn it!" she barks.

I forget the candy and shoot upright just in time to catch another branch collide with one of the store's windows, cracking the pane like a spider web. The rain hardens and the roof groans under pressure. I warily watch the paneled ceiling and send a silent prayer to my grams, God, and Brian, to keep me safe and the roof from buckling. If anything goes, my fear is that'll be the first to collapse.

The older woman leaves her post and scurries past me to the back wall of the store. She presses herself against it, between stacks of unpacked goods. I follow right on her tail and slide up beside her, my back flush against the wall. "Is this the safest place?"

"The store room has too much glass, so yes." Her voice wavers.

Uh-oh, that's not a good sign.

CHAPTER 2

The leaded darkness drowning me slowly drains away. My temples pound with the steady beat of my heart. The smooth cadence pulses in my ears as a nearby machine beeps the same methodical rhythm. My dry tongue runs over the back of my teeth, and the metallic tang of blood claims my taste buds. I try to swallow and internally wince from a sharp stabbing sensation in my throat.

I can almost reach out and touch the lethargic fog that muddles my brain. It's like a thick, warm blanket suffocating my senses—dulling them, forcing the world to slow and my muscles, that I know are there, to feel weightless, boneless. Unable to pry my anchored eyes open, my mind irrefutably shifts, delving into the deepest, darkest, most sacred recesses of my mind. A place where pain consumes my soul, swallowing it whole. A place where I drown in long lost memories that should stay buried. I can't go through this again. I don't want to see them. I can't do this. Not here. Not now.

Yet, I drift...

A memorable light flickers in my brain as a movie that I wish would disappear forever starts to play. It's a movie of that day. The day that changed my life forever. A day that has imprinted on my soul, branding its mark indefinitely. *A mark* I wish I could carve out of my soul like a festering sore.

My thoughts continue to reel…

Why is my brain doing this to me?! If this is what dying feels like, I'd rather go quickly. *Take me, God, if you must, just don't play this memory. Any day but that day. Please. I beg you. If you're listening, take me into the light but leave this behind, all of it.*

"*Magdalene.*"

Dear Lord, no! I can hear her voice again. She's speaking. Can you hear it, too? She sounds so sweet, doesn't she? That's my grams.

The pounding in my head throbs harder and my chest aches as the movie blasts to full color and I'm transported back in time. A scarred piece of my heart tears open.

"Magdalene, honey, can you tend the garden this mornin'?!" My kooky Grams yells from the bathroom down the hall. "I've gotta do the wash and redd up the kitchen so we can make jam this afternoon."

Early to bed, early to rise makes a man healthy and wise, my Grams has always preached. By seven a.m. she's already half done with the day's chores before she bothers to rouse me. If I'd had it my way I'd sleep till noon, but grams always has other plans. On a lucky day, she'll let me sleep till eight. Today isn't one of those days.

"Sure, Grams!" I holler from my shoebox bedroom.

Shuffling off my twin bed, I stifle a yawn and slump the three steps to my grandpa's old army trunk to grab clothes. Throwing back the creaky lid, I snag an old t-shirt and a pair of cutoff jean shorts before removing my pajamas. Tugging the outfit on, I quickly move to slide on my mud-encrusted flip-flops and head down the stairs. I am through the kitchen and out the backdoor before Grams leaves the bathroom.

Outside, the garden is just waking for the day. It is what Grams calls the magic hour. The most special hour of the day where the garden soaks up the most water before the sun rises high in the sky. It's the only time she swears the plants can listen to us speak to them. I've always thought it was a silly superstition, but my grams lives by her kooky traditions, so I do, too.

Birds chirp in nearby trees, and the wind whips through the cornfields that encircle our small slice of country heaven. Strolling over to the well spigot that incessantly drips, I attach the garden hose that lies coiled like a snake at the base. Five pumps to the lever and the water begins to siphon out, trickling from the hose nozzle and into the grass. Soon, it will pour, so I act fast and lug the hose across the grass to our garden – one of my favorite places in the entire world.

As the crops thoroughly soak up the water, I run my fingers over their green, thriving leaves as I sing to them off-key. A dog barks in the distance, growing nearer between the excited noises. A commanding voice trails close behind. "You damn dog! Get back here!" The voice drifts on the wind.

My ears perk, listening, and I stop watering long enough to see a floppy eared coon dog shoot out of the tall corn, heading across our yard. Suddenly, instinct takes over and I kneel.

"Hey, boy," I call, clucking my tongue.

The hound dog catches sight of me and swiftly changes his trajectory, barreling toward me full speed ahead. Lurching himself into my chest, he knocks me flat on my butt in the freshly watered garden. Sticky mud squishes under my weight, coating my thighs, calves, and feet in the nutrient rich detoxifier.

A startled laugh ignites in my belly as the sweet dog begins to excitedly bathe my chin in his sloppy kisses; wearing off any upset that I might have felt about him tackling me. Lifting my hand to his head, I scratch behind his ears— which only makes him vibrate with further elation. My brilliant laughter continues to grow with each sloppy stroke of his tongue. I can't help it. It has been far too long since we've had a dog on the property. Our property that's now overrun with barn cats. Cats, only my grams loves. In town, they don't call her the crazy cat lady for nothin'. It's a name she wears proudly.

"Rock! Bad dog!" A male's voice cuts through my merriment, simmering it to a low chuckle.

"Rock!" The man calls again. Only the dog doesn't respond; he keeps ravishing my chin in his kisses like it is a delicious salt lick, and I let him.

Feet stomp across the hard grass behind me, then stop. Just as I turn my head to find him, he speaks, "Ma'am, I'm so sorry..." The words die on his lips when I catch sight of the young man standing in a crisp white t-shirt, and tight Wranglers *on the edge of the garden, tugging the hose into the grass before it makes a pond in the lettuce patch. My eyes lift to meet his, and I swear I feel my heart expand and contract while also losing my ability to breathe.*

His eyes are the most beautiful greenish hazel I'd ever seen. His hair, so blond that it could be white, lies in a mess of sexy waves on top of his head and spills over his forehead. My cheeks flush under his gaze, which appears to be assessing me just as I am him.

The captivating trance breaks all too soon when the realization hits that I am soaking in a mud bath, wearing cut-off shorts that expose too much of my thick thighs. The scorching heat of my embarrassment creeps down my chest and washes over my body. I'm a disaster, and can't even imagine what my hair must look like—a curly wadded mess probably.

Sickness curls in my stomach as I shy from his gaze and push the dog from my lap. Turning onto my knees while ignoring my butt being on open display, I stand up, trying not to get my hands muddy. I can feel my thighs jiggle the entire way and pray he doesn't notice.

Just look away. Look, away.

Mustering fake courage, I straighten my spine and turn a bit sideways to glance at the young man. He's knelt, petting his dog, with eyes on me and his lips curled into a smile. An unknown sensation whirls in my belly as I try to smile back. Although, I know my smile is lopsided and can never compare to his.

He stands, and his dog nudges at his ankle for more attention.

"Hey, I'm Brian." He dusts his hand off on his jeans before extending it to me.

Flicking my eyes downward, I look at my hands once more and pray for them to magically be dirty. No such luck.

Maybe I should've dipped my hands in the mud so I wouldn't have to touch the cute guy. Dagnabbit!

Slipping off my flip-flops, I wade barefoot through the mud and to the grass before I take his proffered hand into mine. "I'm Magdalene." I shake it once and let go as if it's burned me. It had. And what his proximity is doing to my heart and senses as the wind wafts his clean, masculine scent into my face, is freaking me out.

An awkward silence settles over us. He shoves his hands into his pockets, and Rock circles us, stopping to sniff Brian's boots before he circles again.

"Sorry about the mess," he finally says, nodding to my legs, then tries to meet my eyes once more. I look at the grass instead and wring my hands in front of me to keep myself occupied so I don't run inside. It's not like I want to be rude, but I have no idea what to say to him. Although, I certainly don't want him to leave. He is really cute and is the first boy who has actually talked to me in a while.

"It's okay," I mutter shyly under my breath.

"You home for the summer?" he asks.

What kind of question is that?

I shift uncomfortably, staring at my toes, thinking that I am lucky they are covered in mud so he won't notice how awful the chipped polish is. "Um, yes, I'm always home."

"Oh...ahh... you go to college 'round here?" He is fighting for words as if he's nervous. Though, he has nothing to be nervous about. I know he has to be much older than me and probably used to all the girls throwing themselves at him. He's too cute for that not to happen.

His bizarre question strikes me funny, so I bring my head up and frown at him. "College?" My brow cocks in question.

"Yes. You're what? Nineteen? Twenty?"

What? Now why on earth would he think that?

I watch his eyes momentarily dip to my chest before returning to my face.

Oh, my boobs, of course. Always those. Is that all boys notice when they see me?

My rare temper flares, and I blurt out, "I'm fourteen!"

Brian gasps loudly, which is quickly followed by a coughing fit as he chokes on his spit and takes a staggered step back, pounding his chest with his fist. The distance feels like a swift slap in the face as a boulder settles on my self-esteem, sinking it deeper.

Nervously, I run a hand through my messy curls. "Listen, Brian, don't worry about the dog. Now, please excuse me. I have more chores to do." I turn to leave, even though I don't have anything else to do except get washed up.

Three steps forward is all I manage before a warm hand settles on my shoulder, halting me and spinning me back around.

"Sorry, Maggie." He chuckles nervously. "Guess I've been apologizing a lot today." He grins, and my insides warm at the sight. "I just moved to the farm next to yours with my dad. I'm kinda new 'round here. Not making a very good first impression." His hand shakes, as it slides through his loose waves. I think my knees might give out at the sight. He is too cute and way too close for comfort. I take a step back.

"Who's your friend, Magdalene?" My grams' voice cuts through the yard, and I peer over my shoulder to see her wearing her usual—a farmhouse apron and calf length dress. She smiles at us from the back door.

"I'm Brian, ma'am." He waves and bows his head in greeting—a true country gentlemen.

"Well, Brian, looks like my granddaughter had a fight with some dirt and a garden hose." They both

snicker at my expense, and I grumble under my breath. "So why don't ya come inside for some tea while she washes up?"

Brian and Rock slip past me, heading for the farmhouse, and I turn around to watch them meet my grams at the door.

A pang of agony lances through my heart and my pulse skyrockets.

This is a memory—a dream. I can't go into that house. I can't. Please, God, stop this now. No more. *If I go in there, I'll see them laughing at the kitchen table.*

My grams loved Brian from the start, just as I did. He was the boy next door. My farmer boy who came from a broken home, whose mother didn't want him just as my mother never wanted me. Brian was sixteen when I first met him. He was my everything, and now he's gone.

No more of this. I can't bear another second.

Clenching my teeth 'til it hurts, the vision finally recedes and the pain fades. It's replaced by the comfort of an old friend— loneliness. Loneliness and I have become best friends over the years. He's been my constant companion. The only one I can count on.

Slackening my jaw, I try to swallow again. The pain is so raw that I whimper, blowing out a shaky breath through my nose.

Dear God, why does my throat hurt like this?

Where did this happen?

Where was I last?

The....

A burst of recollection jolts my mind like a light breaking through the lifting fog.

The gas station...a wicked storm...me and a woman hiding in the back...glass shattering...tiles falling all around...the roof...

My temples seize and a lancing pain streaks through my brain. I try to cry out, but it's muted—nearly silent.

Locked, frozen in agony, I struggle to breathe. Panic ruptures deep within.

Please... this can't be my last moment.

A coarse voice echoes in my ears, cutting through my thoughts. "Fuck!" it booms.

Comfortingly, a rough heat presses to my forehead, slightly relieving the misery. I inhale sharply, and the pain in my throat ignites into a burning throb. More pain soon follows in my arms, trunk, and legs, as this dense fog blanketing my mind fizzles to nothing.

Like an angel sent from heaven to ease my suffering, the rough-comfort caresses the top of my head and the span of my forehead before slowly sweeping down my nose to the tip and back up again, soothing me.

My panic begins to mellow. The throbbing in my ears floats away.

That's when I first hear it...

A voice... The hot breath of another, fanning my face as it gently hums, "Shhh, wee lass. Shhhhh, it's all right."

The rough-comfort lowers, brushing across the apples of my cheeks and down to my lips. They part in welcome, and the grizzly angel fumbles over his methodical words.

All too soon, the sweet caress is wrenched away when an authoritative female voice snips, "You're not allowed in here. It's past visiting hours."

A string of sharp foreign-tongued curses quickly follow, and an argument erupts.

I try to listen and dial back into reality, but the sudden burning in my forearm and awful taste in my mouth robs me of all thought. Pain ceases as a warm, fuzzy fog settles over me and my mind blanks.

Night, night.

CHAPTER 3

"Sir, we've had this talk. Our privacy laws state that if you are not family, you are not allowed to stay," a man argues.

"Ye think I give a fuck?"

"Sir, please don't make me call security."

The weights hooked to my lids ease off as they begin to open and I glance around. Dim light filters into the room through drawn shades. A tan couch along the wall of windows is littered with unkempt blankets; a leather vest hangs on its arm. An IV machine next to my bed pumps a clear liquid into my arm. I'm in a hospital. Not sure where or why, but I'm in one.

Sluggishly, I turn my head to scan the opposite side of the room. By the door, an argument ensues between a male nurse and a.... *oh my bejesus*...he's... Hell, I don't even know what to say.

Can I be sure this is happening; right here, right now? There's no way men like that exist in the real world.

Briefly, I close my disbelieving eyes and open them again. Yes, that man is standing right in front of the hospital door. I've never seen him before, I can tell you that much. 'Cause trust me, if I had, I'd have remembered him. He's gargantuan. His heavily tattooed arms that stretch the sleeves of his navy t-shirt have to be the size of my thighs. Okay, maybe not quite that big, since my thighs are huge, but you get the point.

What I really don't understand is what Thighs-for-arms is doing in my hospital room, arguing with a nurse. Did they just filter in from the hall?

I open my mouth to ask, except a string of unintelligible squeaks tumble out. My eyes spring wide at the strange noise coming from my lips. I try again and fail. My voice...it doesn't work! Reaching up to touch my throat, I stop and look at my arms. They're both casted from the elbow down, allowing only my fingers to move freely.

I frown.

What happened to them?

The gruff clearing of a throat brings my head back up to see that both men have stopped arguing and are now facing me. Two sets of eyes assess me with concern. Or the giant's does.

Is the nurse still here? Not sure. I can't see anything except this scary man before me, as he stands with hands fisted at his sides, lips unemotional.

Just when I thought he couldn't be any larger, I get the frontal view. The fully clothed one, that is. Not that I'd want to see him naked or anything. So get your mind out of the gutter.

If it's possible, I think my eyes have morphed into saucers, ready to bug out of my head, as I blatantly absorb all of him. I know that it's rude to stare. But I can't control it even if I tried. I've never seen anyone like him before.

The cropped, rust-color hair on his head matches perfectly with his neatly trimmed goatee. Though a dusting of gray mixes pleasantly with the ginger hair, adorning his chiseled chin and jaw. My eyes lift to meet his, and I gasp a sharp, noiseless breath. The teal of his eyes – look at them; they're gorgeous. Unlike any color I've seen before—orange around the center, and bursting out to a cool teal. The brightness somehow reduces the harshness of his brooding expression, pinched brows, and mature eyes. Although, the lines at the corners of his eyes somehow give him a softness on an otherwise daunting face. One that's full of sharp, masculine lines, and a dark expression that seems right at home.

Someone speaks, but it doesn't register when my eyes dip lower, taking in his corded neck that seamlessly matches his wide, linebacker stature. His meaty pecs are on full display as his shirt stretches across them. I can practically hear the cotton groan in protest. Lower, the shirt clings to his thick abs, and his waist tapers into a pair of jeans that hug a set of long, muscular thighs.

I blink again, momentarily holding my eyes shut before opening them. There's no way this is happening. I have to be dreaming again.

In through my nose and out through my mouth, I breathe. Shaking my head, I try to clear it and wake myself up. The stiffness forces me to grumble in discomfort. It didn't work. The man is still standing here, unmoving, like a marble statue, erected straight out of the floor.

"Miss," a soft male voice slices through the air.

Finally, I'm able to hear again, and sweep my eyes left, where the nurse stands.

I try to reply 'yes?' But another squeak tumbles out instead.

Not again.

The nurse strolls to my bedside, a fake smile in place. I know that smile. That's the same smile they used when my grams lay in bed, rotting away to nothing but skin-and-bones as cancer gnawed the last months of her life away.

"Can you talk?" he asks.

Trying again, nothing comes out. I die a little on the inside when I have to shake my head to answer him.

A fleeting frown passes over his features before his fake smile reappears.

My arms are in casts. My voice doesn't work. What else is wrong? Do I dare look at my legs? They feel heavy, but I'm too afraid to peek under the blankets. Tears prick the back of my eyes and I bite my lip, desperately trying not to cry. The tingling in my nose tells me the waterworks aren't far off. I can't remember the last time I felt this broken. That dream didn't help either. Neither is this scary man who's standing in my room, watching me. It's all too much.

My lip trembles, and I close my eyes, inhaling deeply through my nose as I press my head back into the mattress. Viola…my garlic…the storm. What happened to them? An elephant starts to crush my chest, and my pulse skyrockets. Sweat begins to drip down my forehead and cheeks. My breathing accelerates, coming out in short bursts.

For a split second, I hear an argument erupt once more, but I soon blank out, as the world crushes me. My car, my garlic, my pictures, my…. my…Oh god! My arms…my voice…Brian…Grams…

A hiccupped cry rips through me and the tears start to flow. I never thought life could get worse, but it has.

Without cause, my mind races through meaningless thoughts...I shouldn't have left Johnathan. He loved me. He did. He'd said as much when he asked me to marry him the day before I skipped town. In the parking lot of the jewelry store, over the console of his *Lexus*, hand in mine, he'd proposed. It wasn't a scene out of a romance novel. It was reality. Four simple words, and a kiss on the cheek. I faltered, fumbling over words, and finally said that I need time to think it through. Although, I knew I didn't need any time. I was trying to be polite, letting him down gently. Or, the only way that I know how to let a man down—quick and painless. Running away, it's better than arguments, which will turn to bitter hate in the end. Johnathan didn't deserve that. He didn't deserve me. How could I marry a man when he didn't even know my name? Rebecca, he called me, and never questioned it. Not once.

No one knows my name. A new place, a new identity, a new hair color. The day I'd left, I stripped my hair of all color. I missed the strawberry blonde, just as much as I missed my name. Magdalene, or Maggie, for short. Brian first started calling me that, and I've never heard another person say it since. I've been a Misty, a Johanna, and once at a bar, a man had asked if I was a Sally. I'd said I was, his eyes lit up, and we ended up dating for three months. For a fleeting moment in time, I became his Mustang Sally. That is, until one night when we fought because I refused to kiss him. That's not something I do. *Kiss.*

I've only ever kissed one man in my life, and I plan to meet the Lord staying that way. Loyal to the core, to the only man I've ever loved. The only one who ever meant anything to me—my Brian.

Muffled noises clash just as the memorable burn and horrid taste in my mouth returns. Thankfully, the elephant climbs off my chest as the fog I thought I'd beaten, descends upon me once more, a murky darkness slowly following behind.

Nighty, Night.

CHAPTER 4

Why do doctors always speak to their patients like we have advanced medical degrees? Or they do the complete opposite, and treat us like imbeciles?

Doctor Whatcha-ma-callit is doing the former as he stands astutely at the foot of my hospital bed, reading my chart from a tablet in his hand. What I've gathered thus far from this titillating experience is that he's a *big city* doctor. One that stooped to country town level when he was drugged, cuffed, and dragged to this hospital in order to work his one-of-a-kind miracles to save me. Yeah, he doesn't have a "God complex" at all. Nope, not a bit. Internally, I roll my eyes at the thought.

It's not like I asked to be here. I didn't ask the storm to conjure, or a ceiling to fall on me. It happened all on its own. And, I certainly didn't ask to have a blah-blah-blah fractured wrists. Or, a femur somethin' or other, which I'll be getting a cast on in the next two days. Oh, and let's not forget a temporarily paralyzed voice, thanks to a blunt object doing something blah-blah-blah to the nerves in my neck. In layman's terms: I was stabbed in the neck, which caused my voice to stop working until the nerves heal. Thank heavens Doctor-Snooty-pants thinks healing is a probable outcome. You know, since his bagillion medical degrees tell him so. I'm hoping the mothership calls him home soon to the planet Uranus, where he belongs. He's driving me crazy.

Oh…and, how could I forget? I've suffered a mild laceration on my back that needed thirty-something stitches as well as a concussion that's now stable. Basically, I'm more screwed than a two-bit hooker wearing crotch-less panties in a whorehouse. However, I'm not getting any pleasure out of sitting here listening to this man talk. I'm not sure if it's his insensitive attitude or cocky voice that is making me more annoyed. I'm gonna have to say both. It's grating on my nerves.

"Do you have any questions?" he asks, lifting a bushy brow my direction.

Yes; I have plenty of them, but I guess he forgot my voice doesn't work. He's a genius, can't you tell?

I nod, answering his question, and as a reminder, I point to my throat. It doesn't take but a second to click before he frowns and scans the room for something to write on. Every surface is bare, aside from a small daisy bouquet in the corner.

A soft knock at the door disrupts his search, and the door swings open. Vibrant curls of red poke around the corner, attached to the head of a beautiful young woman.

Ignoring the doctor, she smiles at me with eyes that light up. "Is it okay to come in?"

I don't know who she is. Maybe a nurse? Regardless, I nod once. Why would I care if she came in? I already like her better than my current visitor.

Not wasting any time, the petite redhead wades further into my room and comes to stand next to my bed. Crossing her tiny arms over her chest, she glares at my doctor, cocking her head to the side.

Yes, I definitely like her better.

"*Now,* you decided to finally show up?" She tosses her attitude out in spades, her sweetness a distant memory.

Both the doctors' eyes and my own spring wide at her tone.

"*Well?*" she adds.

Quickly, to regain his composure, the doctor straightens his spine and returns Red's heated glare. "I'm only allowed to speak to—" his eyes snap to my chart and back up again, "Miss Murdock's immediate family," he finishes arrogantly.

Red flips her long hair to the side. "Well, I'm her daughter," she retorts smoothly, like it's the most natural thing in the world.

The doctors disbelieving eyes drop back to my chart. A smug smile curls at the corners of his lips when he gazes back up, meeting her eyes. "I doubt that, little girl. She's only thirty-two, and you're what?" He's baiting her. Dang, he's good.

Red scoffs, affronted, and if I had to guess, her eyes are rolling, too. I know mine would be.

Putting on one heck of a show, she slides closer to me and sets her hand on my shoulder. I don't know why, but I allow it, and even smile up at her to keep our little charade going.

"Doctor, are you telling me that my mother having me when she was a teenager bothers you?" She pauses a beat, then snorts, "*That's rude,*" before her gaze drops to me and winks so the doctor can't see her.

"I'm sorry I wasn't here sooner, *Mom,*" she says, oozing sincerity.

A laugh almost escapes my throat at her brilliant performance; although, I try to look at her like a mother would her daughter—lovingly. The better the show, the faster the doctor will leave.

Out of the corner of my eye, I watch him sway uncomfortably before clearing his throat.

Red glances back at him. "How much longer does she have to stay here?" she probes, asking a question I was wondering myself.

"Just to be safe, I'd say another week."

"Another week?" she groans. "She's already been here twelve days."

Twelve days? I've been here *twelve* days? How could that be? This is the first time I've been awake for longer than a few minutes. Last night—well, I think it was last night—Thighs-for-arms was here. Or was that a dream, too? *Crap*, I don't know. It all feels like a muddled blur of time merging, layering on top of itself. Nothing's crystal clear. Except for right now—right now, I feel clearheaded.

"It's just a precaution. Your...*mother*," he emphasizes, "has suffered multiple life-threatening injuries. And we wouldn't want her to sustain further injury, now would we?" His tone drips with sarcasm.

Red silently shakes her head, agreeing.

"Great." He smiles shrewdly. "Now, she should be safe to go home in seven days. Though, she's going to need physical therapy down the road after her arms and leg heal."

Shouldn't he be telling me this and not her?

"Not a problem. We'll take good care of her," she replies.

I'm not sure if she's being serious or just playing her part. By the way her hand grips my shoulder, I want to believe her. Although, it can't be true. I've just met her, and nobody cares that much about someone they've just met. Just like no man I've dated, aside from Brian, could handle me all broken like this. They'd have cut and run at first sight. Not that I can blame them. I'm a mess. And, my world has just gotten more complicated. As if it wasn't already jacked up enough in the first place, let's add voiceless and bedridden to the list.

"I'm sure you will." Doctor Jerk-off bobs his head in her direction. "Now, if that'll be all. I'll see you in seven days," he finishes, and doesn't even wait for a reply when he turns to leave, shutting the door in his wake.

Once he's gone, Red and I expel sighs of relief.

Giving my shoulder one final squeeze, she removes her hand and steps away to take a seat on the plastic chair next to my bed.

"Sorry about that." She smiles at me, tugging a phone from her pocket, and shooting a quick text before lifting her eyes to mine again, her smile still in place.

Out of politeness, I return a smile. Like my grams always used to say—*Smile even if it hurts, life can always get worse*. Granted, I'm not quite sure how much worse it can get at this point. But I'll smile, anyway; closed mouth, as always.

"I'm Bridget, by the—" a loud ruckus ignites in the hall outside my room. "Uh-oh, he's here already." Is all Bridget's able to convey before my door is thrown open by a massive man with shoulder length blond hair, wearing a black vest adorned with an array of colorful patches.

"Woo-wee! Our girl's awake!" he hollers excitedly in his thick country accent.

With eyes burning holes into mine, he blasts me with a smile so bright that it could light up the *Empire*

State Building. Crimson dots my cheeks, heating rapidly under his jubilant stare.

Our girl? What does he mean?

I don't have long to ponder the idiocy when the hulking, blond God makes a beeline for my bed, and doesn't stop there. Not waiting for proper introductions, he yanks me against his massive body, enveloping me in a crushing hug as he peppers kisses atop my head.

By default, my face is now stuffed to his thick chest that smells like leather, the outdoors, and spicy man. It's addictive. At this moment, I'm not sure if I should be appalled and push him away, or let him attack me with more happy kisses. I choose the latter—although, there's no way I'm returning his affection. The odd closeness forces an uncomfortable knot to form in my throat. Honestly, I can't remember the last time someone hugged me.

To my left, Bridget barks an amused laugh. "Magdalene, meet Thor. You're the one who saved his grandma."

Ah, now all this is starting to make sense. His grandma must have been the woman who owned the gas station. The moments before we were trapped are a bit hazy, but I remember throwing my body over hers when the ceiling began to crumble. It fell on us, and ultimately trapped us under its soggy weight. Seconds following our entrapment, the windows began shattering one-by-one, and something heavy landed on me, knocking me unconscious. That's the last thing I can remember.

For a fleeting moment, guilt curdles in my stomach for not asking about the older woman sooner. Though, it rapidly disperses when I remind myself that I've only been coherent for less than an hour…I think.

I'd only been awake a few minutes when a nurse first entered my room, and left just as quickly to fetch the doctor. That's when Doctor Personality had graced me with his arrogant presence and Bridget saved my hide. I definitely owe her one.

"Thank you," Thor utters between kisses.

Thor. That's a strange name to give your child. Here I thought Magdalene was weird.

A disgruntled grumble reverberates in the room just before Thor is yanked backward. "Leave the lass be," a familiar grizzly voice commands.

I watch with wide eyes, as Thighs-for-arms manhandles Thor by the scruff of his neck, shoving him onto the nearby couch with a satisfied growl. He's also wearing one of those black vests, dark washed jeans, and a white t-shirt that clashes beautifully with the dark ink encasing his muscled arms. If I didn't know any better, I'd say my mouth is watering a little. It's not, though. No way.

Thor scowls like a scolded child and slaps the giant's hands away. Leaning back on the couch, he crosses his arms defiantly over his thick chest. "Don't you fuckin' touch me like that again, Smoke," he snarls.

Smoke snickers under his breath in response, his mouth remaining impassive.

"Magdalene." A tiny hand fleetingly touches my arm, tearing me from this need to stare at Thighs-for-arms.

What is it with this guy? There's something different about him that I can't put my finger on. Maybe it's the hair, or the tattoos, or maybe his height. I don't even care that he's scary looking, or broody. He's different than anyone I've ever met before. A quiet, dominate presence that makes you feel scared and safe all at the same time. It's disconcerting.

Yep, Magdalene, you're definitely losing your marbles. Wouldn't you agree? I mean, would you stare at him, too? Or am I going crazy?

With a deep inhale to calm my thoughts, I revert my attention to Bridget, who's smiling at me—again. Does that girl ever stop?

"You still can't talk, can you?" she asks, calmly.

I shake my head in reply as Thighs-for-arms grumbles under his breath across the room, and I try to ignore the sound.

"Do you wanna talk about what happened? Do ya remember anything?" This girl is beyond sweet, which oddly matches her appearance. Petite and thin, with long, bright-red hair that tumbles down her back in tight curls. Glancing to meet her eyes, I gasp in recognition. They're teal with the same orange burst around the center.

Needing an answer, I point to her before swinging my finger to Smoke, who's leaning against a wall with his arms tucked across his broad chest. Deep down, I know I shouldn't pause to linger on him, but I do. *Corrupt Chaos MC* is embroidered on a patch that's stitched to his vest, and stacked below it, another reads *Treasurer,* followed by *Kentucky Chapter* at the bottom. More colorful patches litter both sides of the supple leather, but I'm unable to read them. A grizzly noise emanates from the object of my distraction, forcing me to lift my eyes to his stony face. Powerless to control this strange sensation in my gut, I meet his hard, assessing gaze. My insides quiver.

It's unmistakable. Bridget has to be his daughter, or maybe his sister. They look too much alike.

Beside me, Bridget makes a tiny surprised noise in her throat. "Magdalene, this is my dad, Lachlan." She pauses, her tone growing firmer. "*Dad*, meet Magdalene; the woman you saved."

The what!?

'*You saved me?*' I painfully attempt to blurt. Regrettably, a string of ugly squeaks tumble out instead.

Embarrassment singes deep, making me drop my eyes to my lap as I wrap my fingers around my damaged throat. How stupid could I have been? Try to talk? I knew I couldn't. I shouldn't have tried. Why did I try? Now *everyone* knows how ridiculous I sound. Now, I'm not only the ugly, ridiculous, fat girl that's injured. I'm the ugly, ridiculous, fat girl who's injured *and* can't speak.

Good god.

Biting my lip to the point of drawing blood, I swallow down my rising emotions. I'd cried the last time I saw him. I can't do that again. This isn't the time to feel sorry for myself. This is the time to be strong and put on a brave face, even if all I want to do is crumble inside. I can do this, just like I did when Brian died, and again when my grams withered away to nothing. Ten times in ten years, I've gathered enough strength to run from those men I could never love. I was strong enough to reinvent myself then, and I will be strong enough to dig through the mud and the muck now. *I'm a survivor.*

Tossing my emotions to the side, and brushing off the singe of embarrassment, I ready myself for the next journey in my life. Licking the tang of blood from my lip, I inhale one final breath through my nose and blow it out of my mouth before raising my head proudly to face Bridget. God knows, I can't face Thor or Smo— Lachlan, right now.

Reaching out my hand to Bridget, I gesture to her phone. Without hesitation, she gives it to me and I pull up a text screen so we're able to communicate the only way I know how.

Thank you for saving me, Lachlan, is the first thing I type, then hand it back to Bridget for her to reiterate out loud, which she does.

I spare a sideways glance to gauge Lachlan's reaction. He nods his head once in acknowledgment, but says nothing.

Thor adds his lively two cents instead. "He's a firefighter, so it's his job. Although, from the way I hear it, there was blood everywhere when he dug ya out from under that mess. My grandma was still awake, ya know. She said she kept tryin' to talk to you, and make sure you were still breathin'. If it weren't for you, she'd be dead. So the way I see it, I owe you big time. Anything you need. A place to stay—"

Thor's word vomit is suddenly cut short when Lachlan makes a scary noise in his chest that sounds a lot like a growl.

Goosebumps sweep down my arms and legs.

"What the hell's your problem, brother?" Thor barks.

My eyes stay solely focused on Bridget.

Don't glance over. Don't glance over.

"*Huh?*" Thor goads. "I just asked you a question."

An even deeper, scarier noise thunders in reply. There is no way I can watch this play out now. Lachlan's face will probably end up giving me nightmares. As if he isn't already big and scary enough as it is. Add the sounds of a predator and he could easily be deemed the devil himself.

Those noises, can you hear them? His breathing's a low, purring growl like a dog ready to attack. I've never heard anything like it. Are you frightened, too?

I gulp and watch Bridget's face turn grim. "Dad." She speaks softly. "Dad."

The grizzly sounds dissipate, and I visibly watch Bridget relax back into her chair, eyes closing with relief for a moment before she expels a sigh and speaks once more. "The doctor said that Magdalene could go home in a week."

Her head turns to Thor, but I don't follow her gaze. "Dad and I have been talking, and I've set up the spare room next to mine for her. Mom will be gone a lot, so it's not like she's going to care if she's there or not. But, you know you're welcome over anytime. We've always got a fresh stash of Aunt Whisky's cookies to munch on. I know how much ya love those." Bridget winks, grinning friendlily.

He's marr—

"Aye," Lachlan mutters strangely, stealing my thought.

"All right, that's cool with me. But my offer is still gonna stand," Thor replies.

Throughout all of this discussion, the three of them are so caught up in their part that they haven't even bothered to ask me my opinion. Don't they think that I might be uncomfortable crashing with a bunch of strangers? Not that I'm unappreciative for the indirect offer. But I need to have control, and they're robbing me of that.

Snapping my fingers, I point to the phone in Bridget's hand. She hands it to me, and I type out another message before giving it back.

Don't want to be rude, but I don't know any of you. You're talking as if this is all set in stone.

Bridget reads the message but doesn't reiterate it aloud. "You're right; you don't," she replies kindly. "I didn't even think about that. We've been so caught up in getting you healed and making sure you were never alone, that I never thought to talk to you about it."

I nod in understanding, and smile closed mouthed.

"I'm Lachlan's and Meredith's daughter, Bridget MacAlister. It's a pleasure to make your acquaintance," she extends her hand to me, giggling. I briefly shake it.

Setting her dainty hand back into her lap, she continues, "I'm seventeen, a senior this coming year. And my dad, as Thor said, is the one who found you. He's a fireman and a....well...I'm not sure how much you know about motorcycle clubs."

The word motorcycle club has me shifting uncomfortably in my reclined bed, which seems to amuse Thor when he barks a laugh, and Lachlan when he snorts his amusement.

Great.

Bridget simply smiles and rubs her hands over her dress covered thighs. "Not much, I take it?"

Rapidly, I shake my head and frown.

"I figured as much. So..."

For the next fifteen minutes, Bridget runs down all that I need to know and understand about motorcycle clubs, or more precisely, the one her dad is part of.

I'm schooled about patches and vests, which are considered their *colors*. The brotherhood. Their club,

Corrupt Chaos, which is actually a club for military veterans, and her uncle, by marriage, is the club president.

Thor and Smoke, as they are known by their *road names*, remain quiet through the whole ordeal. As Bridget, who seems to be highly versed in the MC lifestyle, runs through the basics with their approval. I'm not sure why she is telling me all this. Though, I'm guessing it has to do with making me comfortable enough with the prospect of moving in with people I don't know. People who are part of a *motorcycle club*. Which still has me freaking out a little.

"Do you have any questions?" she finishes, and I shake my head, still trying to digest what she'd said.

"Oh," she adds, lifting her hand to smack herself in the forehead with a giggle, "and one more thing: Casanova found your car outside the gas station and had it towed over to our house. The only thing Dad touched was your purse, for identification purposes. It's parked in our barn now."

Right now, I'm too afraid to ask about my car's condition, so I'll wait to see it for myself next week.

Scrubbing my hands over my face, I yawn and sink into my hospital bed. Is it wrong that I feel exhausted already? All this talking, listening, and thinking has my brain working on overdrive. Just when I thought I'd be living somewhere in New York by now, here I am in some small, Kentucky town. My visitors are agreeable enough, which is a bonus, I suppose. Although I can't help but wonder if all of this is just a nightmare that I'll eventually wake up from.

Closing my eyes, I tilt my head back, and Bridget comments, "All right, guys, I think it's time for you to head out. Magdalene's getting tired. I'll take tonight's shift."

Tonight's shift? Opening my eyes, I tilt my head to the side and regard her with pinched brows.

She catches my questioning look and explains, "Dad's been staying most nights when he's not working. But, a nurse last night kicked him out, so I came up here instead. He's not much company now that you're awake."

Lachlan scoffs under his breath, and she continues, undeterred. "He's quiet 'round most people. I'll stay if that's all right with you?"

Someone to stay with me in the hospital? I'd much rather have Bridget here. Her dad…he's…he's not someone I want staying the night with me. I know that much. I'm just glad she offered instead of inviting herself; even if they've been doing it since I was first admitted. Not that one can complain when comatose.

A single nod is my reply to her before I reclose my eyes, trying to become invisible. Or, for it to convince the men to leave without me having to be rude.

What I really want to ask is why they're so nice to me, and why are they trying to take care of me? I just don't want to ask with either men present. I'll ask Bridget later when both large, room-swallowing men aren't present.

The longer I quietly lay here, listening to their heavy breathing and inhaling their distinct scents, the quicker the walls close in. Suffocating me. Making me antsy. Claustrophobic. I've never been this way before.

Their presence is making my skin tingle and my insides squirm. I can feel their eyes pinned on me. Staring at one hot mess.

Why won't they leave?

Minutes slip by, and the heat from their stares begins to scald my flesh as I pretend to be asleep. Keeping my breathing even is the hardest part, when all I want to do is pant for breath while my heart continues to hammer uncontrollably in my chest. The knot that forms in my throat ... I can't even swallow, in fear they'll notice I'm awake.

"Dad," Bridget whispers.

"Aye?" he replies just as quietly.

What is it with his voice, his tone, his accent? It's different.

"You both know you can leave me with her."

"I'm not leavin' till he does," Thor whispers.

"Nothing is going to happen to her when you're gone, Dad. The worst is over. You stopped the bleeding. You plugged the hole in her neck. You saved her life already. There is nothing left to save. Go home. Get some sleep. Let the dog out. Mom should be home by now."

Plugged the hole in my neck? Stopped the bleeding? I can't even imagine the sight he must have seen. Maybe I've traumatized him. Although, I highly doubt that. He doesn't seem like a man to be easily traumatized.

And Bridget's right; there is nothing more to save. Physically, I will heal, and emotionally, I'm not troubled by the damage inflicted. I've been through much worse. What doesn't kill you makes you stronger. Right? Just another bump in the road. Another shitty hand dealt. Yadda-yadda-yadda.

All I know right now is that Lachlan and Thor need to go home. I'm not going to be able to fall asleep until they do.

"Dad." Bridget's voice is firmer this time.

"I know, I know, wee daughter," he mumbles.

Wee? Where do I remember that from? The angel who touched me that night. Whoa, wait, that was him? He caressed me? No! That can't be right. Can it? Crap...

Quickly, I toss those thoughts over the ledge before that strange feeling in my stomach gets any worse. It's bad enough with them staring. Knowing, thinking, guessing that he might have...you know. That's... I don't know what that is. But it's not helping the sensation in my stomach, I know that much. I'm just going to pretend it was a real angel.

Couch groaning, heavy feet shuffling, and a bunch of hushed whispers say their goodbyes. My hospital door opens and closes, then a single pair of feet stride across the linoleum.

The couch groans for a second time. "I know you're awake, Magdalene," Bridget comments playfully.

Not wanting to open my eyes or acknowledge her keen senses, I continue to pretend, and soon my pretending slips into the real thing.

"Goodnight, Magdalene," are the last words I hear before I drift into sweet oblivion, where those cunning teal eyes are sure to follow.

Goodnight, Bridget.

CHAPTER 5

I'm. In. Hell. And, about to break free.

There're no butts about it. I'm living in the undeniable, bedridden-depths of flesh, eviscerating hell. Shimmery golden flames lick the walls while the Devil cackles in the background.

This dream I thought I'd waken from isn't a dream at all; it's my afterlife. Where I'm damned to an agonizing eternity in...what again?

You guessed it.... H.E.L.L.

Or, like my grams used to call it, H-E-double-hockey-sticks.

Do you wanna know why I'm here?

You nodding?

Good.

Other than the fact that God has decided to make me pay penance for whatever reason by being tormented daily. The executor? A singular, room swallowing, broody, self-confidence murdering, gargantuan, who openly refuses to take a hike in order to give my mind, body, and soul, a moment's rest.

The worst of it all?

He's here every single gosh-frickin' day, almost all day. In the mornings when I wake up, he's always sitting on the couch in my room, sipping fragrant coffee from a white Styrofoam cup, looking grouchy as he stares a hole through my head. On a rare occasion, I catch him playing with his phone, which never lasts long. Then, if he doesn't have to work, he spends every waking moment in my room, never leaving, as he slowly kills me with his soul-sipping silence.

Have you ever peed in a bedpan with a stranger in your room? It's bad enough doing it with a nurse present. Add Lachlan, and I'm in H.E.L.L. Or, how about changing out of your hospital gown while your nurse helps you wipe down with baby powder scented wipes? Then washes your hair in this weird contraption that you know they must use in old folks homes. It takes embarrassing to a whole new level. Sure, he is polite enough to close his eyes and turn his head without me having to throw a paper ball at his thick skull and reminding him to do so. But he's still present, still listening to me pee, change, and wipe the bed-ick off my dry skin.

I can't wait to slather myself in coconut scented body butter again, or brush my teeth in the sink, or shave, or roll on quality deodorant again. Those small things that you take for granted are definitely things I will never take for granted again. Peeing in a toilet is a luxury I can't wait to partake in. Two-ply toilet paper—another luxury I'm dying to use. This bedridden stuff is no joke.

Oh...and god forbid the tattooed, rusty-haired ginger has to speak to lowly ol' me. Well, aside from listening to me urinate. I'm pretty sure I've yet to see him staring without his eyebrows pinched in a scowl. And, just when you think his face is permanently frozen in that position, Bridget shows up and washes the scowl clean off his face. Oh...I'd also like to point out—I don't even think he knows how to smile. Which is odd, considering how much his daughter is smiling all the time, day and night. Smile, smile, smile—It's as sweet as pie.

Bridget. That girl…she's a godsend. My saving grace. A guardian angel. She also visits the hospital every day and inadvertently keeps my sanity intact. Especially since mind-numbing TV isn't really my thing.

I can't tell you the last time I watched a movie or TV show; it's a hard thing since technology has never grown on me. It's too disconnected.

All I ever had growing up was farmer vision on my grandma's old box TV. You know the one where you had to get up and use a dial to change the channel? That's the one. Our phone, too, was an ancient, cream rotary that hung on the wall in the kitchen. Heck, I'd never been to a movie theater till Brian took me when I was sixteen. Even then, it didn't hold much appeal. We made-out through most of it, anyhow.

To put it plainly, my grams was old school. We baked, canned, raised chickens, and grew our own fruits and vegetables. When the housework wasn't keeping me busy, I was reading. Classics, cookbooks, romance novels—you name it, and me and my grams devoured it. *Stephen King* was her favorite author, while I could never settle on just one.

Then, when I got older, you know, after Brian came into my life, cars, and more specifically, their engines, became my new passion. Still are to this day. There's nothing sweeter than the scent of grease as you rebuild a transmission.

Put it this way: there are some women who use Yoga to achieve their Zen; then there's me. Where jamming to classic rock or country music while bent over the hood of a car, wrenching, gives me that same peace.

I'm not really sure why I'm rattling off all this nonsensical crap to you. Guess I'm just trying to pass the time in the elevator on the way down to the car before I can break out of this joint. And more importantly, so I'm not stuck in a room with *him*, nearly twenty-four hours a day. The first night awake was my reprieve. Since then, I've been accosted by his presence, his manly scent, and more disconcertedly, his shrewd, calculating eyes. I can't wait to have some alone time away from them.

Ding. The elevator doors chime open.

Bright light casts through the tall, hospital windows as a nurse wheels me across the tiled lobby. Mechanical doors slide open, granting us exit to the fresh outdoors. The final door zips shut behind us, allowing me to fully inhale a deep breath of crisp summer air. The hint of fresh-cut grass and flowers drifts on the slight breeze, wafting through my hair. Closing my eyes for a moment, I relish in my newfound freedom.

"You ready?" the nurse asks.

I nod my reply for the millionth time this week, and she rolls me forward.

Straight ahead, Lachlan stands next to a black SUV in the direct sunlight. Highlights of brilliant red dazzle in the rays, mingling with the darker rust of his hair. It's even lighter than I thought, and his goatee has gone untrimmed today. That's unusual for him.

Approaching the back passenger side door, he holds it open as the horn beeps. I turn my attention to the driver seat where Bridget is waving animatedly with a giant smile. "Hurry up, slow poke. Let's get you home!" she hollers.

The nurse rolls my wheelchair next to the vehicle and sets the brakes before rounding to the front. I'm not much help with a cast that goes all the way from the top of my thigh down to my foot, leaving my knee and ankle joints immovable. Not to mention the forearm casts I'm wearing like they're the newest fashion statement. *Bleck.*

It's not too hard to hobble into the SUV with the help of my nurse. My leg stretches through the middle two seats, and the nurse waves a quick goodbye before Lachlan pushes my door shut. Through the tinted window, I catch him sneak a peek my way and try to ignore it.

Suction from the back hatch opens and closes while the giddy Bridget sings along with the radio. Her excitement makes me grin.

Soon, the vociferous rumble of a motorcycle springs to life at our rear.

"Looks like Dad's ready," Bridget remarks putting the SUV in gear.

Buildings and stoplights swiftly turn into vast fields of farmland as we cruise out of town. The loud motorcycle tore off not long after we left the hospital, which has allowed me to breathe easier. Bridget's spent most of the drive singing to a country radio station, tapping her hands on the steering wheel in time to the music. Even though she can't carry a tune in a bucket; I'm adoring her spirited rendition of *Carrie Underwood*'s; *'Good Girl'*, while resting my head against the soft, tan leather of the SUV's seat.

Bridget makes a right onto an unpaved side road. Tall flourishing trees line either side of the vehicle as we slowly creep down the bumpy gravel drive. At the end, the tree line breaks into a clearing, and I sit up to peer around the passenger seat. Straight ahead there's an old, single-story, brick house with white shutters and a magnificent wraparound porch. The picture is topped off with stark white rocking chairs, and lifeless flower boxes attached to the railings. From the looks of them, the flowers died years ago and now they've become a cemetery for dead annuals. It's depressing.

"We're here," she singsongs, cruising along the wide driveway, around the side of the house, and down an incline. At the bottom, she parks and cuts the engine.

Staring out of my window and up at the single story house, I notice a walkout basement. A large wooden deck built off the main story serves as shade over the lower concrete patio. Lounge chairs and a rocker welcome guests, while the large, sliding glass door provides a wide entrance into the basement.

"What do ya think?" Bridget chirps from the driver's seat as she opens her door. Inside the house, a dog barks his welcome.

Unable to reply to her without a phone or pad of paper, I grin and unlatch my door.

"Let me get your wheelchair." She climbs out of the truck and slams her door shut. The gravel crunches under her shoes as she walks to the back of the SUV and opens the hatch. Bridget grunts from strain, hefting my wheelchair out before she recloses the back.

Carefully, I twist so my leg hangs out of the door as I ready to transfer into the chair. It's time to welcome myself into this new house, and my journey to recovery. I just hope we can make it inside without incident. Wish us luck. We're gonna need it.

CHAPTER 6

Lachlan

Dad, tomorrow I'll drive Magdalene home in the Tahoe while you pick up her medicine. Sound good?

Yesterday, Pip had texted that tae me when I was watchin' the lass learnin' tae get in and out of her wheelchair on her own. Bloody painful tae watch when I could do that for her myself.

Now, I'm sittin' here on my *Harley* outside the pharmacy, waitin' on her scripts tae get filled. I dunno why I listened tae Pip, when all I'm doin' is worrying if they got home all right. What if she couldn't get the lass inside?

Tuggin' my phone from the front pocket of my jeans, I shoot Pip a text.

Are ya home yet?

Maybe I should call. Waitin' on this textin' business will fuckin' put me into an early grave. As if I'm not old enough already.

Grumblin', I give Pip time tae respond and scan the lot, watchin' the cars roll through. It's a bonnie day out tae ride. Not a cloud in the sky. It'd be an even better day if I could keep my head clear, but it's too busy with these fuckin' thoughts I shouldn't be thinkin'.

A young blonde woman slows her car as she passes. Her lusty eyes burn through my leather cut and t-shirt as she goes, wonderin' what I look like underneath. A foul taste raises tae my mouth. Na American woman wants tae see what's in these pants. That's for fuckin' sure.

A shiver of self-loathing pricks my skin.

I knew I shoulda had Pip get the meds. I dinnae like tae be out on display. Too many eyes, too many people.

My phone vibrates, and I lift my sunglasses tae check the screen.

It's Sniper callin', so I answer.

"She at the house yet?" he blurts before I get a chance tae say hello.

"Aye, I think so. Pip hasn't texted tae confirm."

"You didn't drive her home yourself?" He's stunned. Shoulda known he would be.

Uncomfortably, I scrub my palm over my face with a groan. Bloody hell, I knew I shoulda driven her home myself.

Guilt spears my gut, and I sigh, heavily. "Na, Pip wanted tae bring her." That's such a damn lame excuse. Why'd I even admit tae that?

Sniper snorts. "Fuck, brother. First, your wife has ya by the balls. Now, your daughter does, too? Are you sure ya ain't a woman and Whisky's the man of the family? That sexy, ginger-bitch has been bustin' my goddamn balls about this Magdalene shit all fuckin' week."

If any other bastard talked tae me this way, he'd be eatin' his teeth for breakfast. But, seein' as though Sniper's not only my brother-in-law and best friend, he's also the club's president, I generally cut him some slack. And, I know how much my sister can be a pain in the arse.

"What she doin' now? She been talkin' tae Pip aboot this, too?"

If Whisky has dragged my daughter into this, I'm gonna be bloody pissed. She had tae learn the hard way last time when she started tellin' Pip stuff about her mother and me. Once I'd found out, I told Sniper and he'd paddled Whisky so hard, she couldn't sit down for a week. *Good.* Lesson learned. Hope it stays that way. If not, I suppose it'll be time tae teach her another lesson.

"I don't think so. She said she wants to meet her—,"

Without warnin', my body tightens in defense and a fearless growl rips through me, cutting Sniper off.

Why does this keep happenin' tae me? Closing my eyes, I shake my head, angry with myself for doin' it again. Sniper's the last person I have tae act that way with.

"Whoa, brother, chill. I told Whisky she had to talk to you first. She's too busy with the bakery, anyhow. But, I'm warnin' ya: if you don't want her makin' a surprise visit, call her and tell her what's doin'. You know your sister; she's gotta know everything."

That, she does. Stubborn lassie.

He continues. "Oh, and before I forget, club cookout next Sunday. Bring Meredith and Pip,"

Ha, bring Meredith. That's—

From my left, a woman yells my name, severin' my thought. Tiltin' my head tae the side, I watch Carrie, the firehouse dispatcher, walkin' my way.

"See ye Sunday," I mutter tae Sniper, and end the call before he gets a chance to reply.

"Lachlan," Carrie purrs, smilin' up at me as she stops next tae my bike, her hefty purse slung over her wee shoulder.

"Hey," I greet.

She's standin' too close for comfort. And there she goes with twistin' that hair again. Every time I see her, she's playin' with it. "What're ya doing here? I thought you were on vacation. I haven't seen you in a few weeks. The boys down at the firehouse said you were taking some time off," she says.

Why do I always get stuck in these awkward situations? Years ago, I tried havin' a conversation with the lass. Didnae work. Like most Americans, she can barely understand a bloody thing I say unless I talk very slowly and try tae pronounce my words clear enough. It's my deep voice and thick accent that throws 'em off. I know that. So I've stopped tryin' tae engage before they start lookin' at me like I'm a foreigner, or talkin' tae me like a wee lad. Or, worse, when the lassies ignore the ring on my finger and beg me tae talk more. Na matter what, I'm uncomfortable.

I've got plenty of stories, but I suppose ignorin' Carrie ain't the polite thing tae do. Better keep this short.

"A family friend got injured, and I'm carin' for her." *Aye, nice and slow, Lachlan.* I think that came out clear enough.

"Aww," Carries gushes, her eyes lightin' up.

Bloody fuckin' hell. Maybe I shoulda lied. She's wettin' her lips now, steppin' a wee bit closer. Why do women always act like this?

My phone vibrates again, and I glance at it. Liftin' the edge of the sunglasses, I read the screen. *Pip.*

Tae give me a sec, I hold up my finger tae Carrie. She gets the point.

She's in her room now, getting settled in. Pirate's taken with his new best friend. I took her to the barn to show her, her car. Don't want you to worry, but she cried a lot. I couldn't get her to tell me what was wrong, but she was really upset. Mom's home now, too, and I'm staying in the basement with Pirate and Magdalene until you get home to take care of it. If you're still at the pharmacy, could you bring home some popcorn, too? Maybe a girl's night will cheer her up.

I have the sweetest daughter in the world. I dunno how I got so lucky.

I reply, *Picking up scripts now. Be home soon with popcorn. I'll deal with Mom when I get there. Daddy snuggles.*

Instantly she sends me one back. *Thanks, Dad. I love you, too.*

Glancin' back up, I catch Carrie checkin' me out, and quickly dismiss the nasty feelin' it gives me.

"Got tae jet." I swing my leg over my bike, dismountin'. And my manners elude me as I stroll past her into the pharmacy. I'm a man on a mission. Dinnae have any time tae waste. Gotta get my arse home.

CHAPTER 7

Why was I so anxious to leave the hospital? Why did I come here? I shouldn't have come. First, I saw my car and its horrific condition and lost it right there. I tried to be strong and hold back the tears, but I couldn't do it. My eyes were bawling before I could stop them. Poor Bridget watched my physical pain unfold, and didn't know what to do. The only positive thing about seeing the mangled mess, covered in dents, scratches, with nearly every window broken, was my garlic bulbs. Somehow, they were saved by the grace of God, and remained on the passenger floorboard; a little jostled, but seemingly untouched. Like divine intervention had kept them safe. I cried like a baby because of that, too. *Pathetic.*

Bridget retrieved my suitcase from the dented trunk while I tried desperately not to puke from all the crying. Once the floodgates opened, they wouldn't stop.

Today was almost as heart-wrenching as what I endured eons ago when I actually knew what real joy and happiness felt like...

Many, many, years ago, I was forced from the only home I'd ever known. Physically, I was kicked out of my grams's house with nothing but the clothes on my back, my garlic bulbs, a few pictures, and my car. Thankfully, it was in my name or my mother would have demanded that as her inheritance, too. God knows she took everything else of which her grubby paws could stake claim.

I hadn't even seen her since I was six, which was four years after she'd dumped me on my grams's doorstep and drove away— never looking back. That's how my grams always told the story, anyhow.

At the age of six, the only time I remember meeting mother-dearest, she had come for money. My grams wanted custody of me, so they swapped. Five thousand dollars; that's what I was sold for. Then, years later when my grams tragically died, I had assumed she had a will, leaving her household to me. Boy, oh, boy, was I sorely mistaken.

Two months after my grams was laid to rest in the cemetery next to my grandpa, her dearly departed husband that I'd never met, my mother showed up, staking claim of the property and everything in it.

Apparently, it had taken her two months to get the paperwork filed and the court system to grant her sole ownership of the estate. And just like that, a local sheriff's deputy and my mother took away everything that I'd ever loved. Brian was dead. My grams, too. I was given fifteen minutes to vacate the premises with whatever belongings that were mine, and fifty dollars to my name.

Now look where I am. I'm lying in a downy, full-sized bed that isn't mine; cuddled up with a spotted, one-eyed mutt named Pirate, who also isn't mine.

The only things that belong to me are the two rings that were given back to me at the hospital today with my things, which were stuffed into a plastic hospital bag with my tattered clothes, and the tiny burgundy suitcase that I've had forever. Oh, and the garlic bulbs that I left sitting on the living room end table where the sun could hit them just right. And, let's not forget the beat-to-hell car that's no longer drivable and parked in an old pole barn. My life has turned from depressing and lonely, to downright pathetic. Ashamed, is putting my predicament mildly.

Want to hear the worst thing? Are you listening? Right above us, on the main floor, there is a massive argument erupting between Lachlan and his wife, Meredith. She doesn't seem pleased that I'm here. Want to know how I can tell? Listen to her words. In the past five minutes, I've been called a lazy bitch, a moocher, a selfish whore, a liar, and my personal favorite: a cock-sucking club-slut just looking to break off a piece of Lachlan's ugly dick. Yes, you heard that right—*Ugly dick.* A wife just screamed that at her husband, all because he brought me home to live in their basement with their daughter.

It's not like I want to eavesdrop. And if I had a pair of earplugs right now, I'd probably be using them. Wouldn't you?

It's not easy being here, but I have no place to go. If I broke down and called Johnathan, my last boyfriend, I'd be stuck with an obsessive man, who's probably a little bitter about my sudden departure. And I can't survive in my current condition alone. I'm seriously screwed.

As hard as it is for me to admit, I have no other place to go, except maybe Thor's. I'd be out in the world on my tuckus. I owe Bridget and Lachlan my life for going out of their way for me. I've never had anyone do that before, not even grams or Brian. They never had to handle me this way.

A soft knock sounds at the door and Pirate perks his head off my stomach. Both of us watch Bridget enter the room, face grim and colorless. I don't even have to ask what's wrong; she's heard the whole argument, too. It'd be impossible not to.

"I'm so sorry," she apologizes glumly, and Pirate makes a tiny noise before laying his head back on my stomach. I pat him affectionately, and he snuggles deeper.

Frowning, my bottom lip poking out, I wave off her apology. It's not like the poor girl can help the fighting. Neither of us can fix what has already been done.

"You stupid son-of-a-bitch! You tell me we don't have enough money for me to buy a case of wine! Yet, you can have little Miss Moocher live down there with our daughter? How do you know she's not a serial killer, Lachlan? Huh?!" Meredith screams, and more growled accented words follow. Lachlan doesn't yell, so I can barely make out a thing he says. I'm almost relieved by that.

"Oh! Big shot! Just because you bring in all the money, you get a fucking say in whether or not you bring home another stray?! I put up with that stupid mutt for two years now, shedding all over the goddamn place. Now you bring a slut home? Is she gonna shed all over my carpet, too? You selfish bastard!"

I try not to let the hurtful words of a bitter woman cut deep, but they do. She's never met me. She doesn't know me. I know that. But it doesn't change how profoundly her words sink. They seep into the gashes and settle, pooling into the recesses where my self-confidence should live, yet doesn't. I wish I was stronger than this. I wish I could say it doesn't affect me, but I'd be lying to you, and myself.

Bridget wades further into the room and sits on the edge of the bed. Her hand comes to rest on the top of my leg. I'm not sure who is hurting more right now, her or me. It can't be easy listening to her parents duke it out over a stranger and money. I only pray that Bridget doesn't end up hating me because I appear to be driving a wedge between her parents.

My stomach jerks at the thought.

God, I'm doing that, aren't I? I'm doing this to them. If I'd never come home with them, none of this would have happened. I should call Thor and take him up on his offer. It couldn't hurt. And, maybe it would make that sullen face, on the most beautiful girl on earth, go away. I hate to see her sad. It's like kicking a puppy; the worst thing in the world.

Lachlan came home shortly after I'd stopped wallowing in self-pity. I heard his motorcycle pull up; the screen door open, and close. He and Bridget had exchanged a few pleasant words in the kitchen before he'd taken the stairs to the main floor. It wasn't long after that Meredith's screaming match had begun. The funny thing is, even in anger, I don't think I've ever screamed at a single person. That's not who I am. Why people believe that they can get their point across that way, I can't comprehend.

"My mother…" Bridget swallows hard and shakes her bouncy curls; her hand absentmindedly running up and down my sheet clad leg. "I'm so sorry, Magdalene. They're not gonna stop anytime soon. Do you want to get out of your room and sit in the living room? Or maybe the back patio? You hungry? Need to use the restroom? Anything you need..."

With each emotional word, I feel myself crumbling inside. What a broken girl. A broken girl that I did this to. My heart shatters at that thought. *Yes*, I need to call Thor.

Bringing my hand up, I point to Bridget then bring my hand to my cheek like I'm talking on an imaginary phone.

"You want my phone?" she asks.

Regrettably, I nod, and she slips it out of her pocket then hands it to me.

I know it's rude, but I scan through her contacts until I come across some strange names. Whisky, Sniper, Casanova ... I click Thor when I find it and tap *send message*.

Thor, this is Magdalene. I know it might be too late, but I was hoping you could come pick me up at Lachlan's...Smoke's...house tonight. I don't think I can stay here. If this is an inconvenience, I apologize. Please let me know.

Grimly, I smile at Bridget and pull up another texting screen to explain what I just did.

Once finished, I hand her back the phone and she reads the message. Her eyes then lift to meet mine. "You can't leave. My mom and dad aren't like you think. This isn't because of you."

My brows quirk up in skepticism. It has everything to do with me. How could it not?

She wages on. "My mom and dad aren't like most couples. I thought they were for the longest time. Last year, my aunt Whisky filled me in on some things. So please don't think that it's about you. It's not. It's more about my dad and money. Trust me."

A woman's high-pitched screech has my eyes tipping toward the ceiling again, as a set of heavy stomps move across the floor above us, rattling my bedroom's light fixture.

"Lachlan MacAlister, where in the fucking hell do you think you're going?! Don't you walk away from me, you selfish bastard!" Lighter stomps retreat in the same direction as Lachlan's. A door is slammed, and the heavier stomps grow near, clunking down the stairs to the basement. Crap! They can't fight down here, too. The other was bad enough.

A thump resonates upstairs. "You fucking bastard! Locking me out of my own basement! I want to see my daughter!" Meredith shrieks, amending my assumption.

Is it wrong that I want to smile because he locked her out of her own basement? An evil cackle mocks her in the depths of my mind. It's a little payback for calling me all those cruel names. I know I won't forget those anytime soon. Forgiveness is a trait I should probably work on.

The sound of boots amble across tile near our door and stop right outside. A string of unintelligible curses roll off Lachlan's tongue. My heart revs into overdrive and dampness slickens my palms. I think I'm starting to sweat. The knot in my throat expands, making it harder to breathe.

Pirate and I jump when a hefty fist bangs on the door before it swings open. Quickly turning my head, I rest my cheek flat on the pillow. Standing in the doorway, shirtless, Lachlan heaves for breath, as his I-can't-believe-they-really-exist abs ripple between laden inhales and rushed exhales. Sweat beads at his temples before sliding down the edges of his reddened face and dripping off the tip of his stalwart chin. If I didn't know any better, I'd say he'd just run five miles.

Cuffing his hands on the sides of the doorframe, his massive biceps swell and his shoulders hunch in palpable tension.

Bridget watches her dad, her hand still resting on my calf, serving as a lifeline. "Dad," she mutters.

Lifting his head to meet his daughter's eyes, he grumbles and severely frowns, his eyes sinking into sadness. Even the teal seems to dull in color. "I'm sorry, Pip."

Pip? I've never heard that before.

"Da—"

Bridget's words are severed when Lachlan's eyes cut to me, instantaneously switching from sadness to anger. They narrow and his breathing accelerates. Mine does, too. A strange sensation flutters in the pit of my stomach. I'm not sure if I should be terrified or something else entirely.

His intense eyes tell a story that I can't pinpoint. Are they saying he's mad about the fight I caused between him and Meredith? Or that it's time to go because I've overstayed my welcome? The flutter in my stomach turns acidic, and I bite my lip, feeling nausea rise.

Lachlan's fat tongue sweeps his bottom lip. I shiver at the sight, and goosebumps prick my skin.

"Ye…are…not…goin'…tae…*Thor's*," he speaks slowly.

The shiver intensifies at his potent words.

I'm not deaf nor dumb, so I'm not sure why he thinks he has to talk to me so slowly. Like I'm a child, unable to comprehend. Maybe it's to rein in his anger? And...how does he know about Thor, anyhow? I sent that text less than ten minutes ago, and never received one back.

Lachlan's eyes briefly sweep to Bridget, conveying something I can't read before they swing back to me.

"Dad said you can't go to Thor's," Bridget reiterates.

I know that's what he said, but what I don't understand is why, or how he even knew. What the heck's going on? Shouldn't we be talking about Meredith, and the horrible things she said to him? Like calling him a bastard? Which he most certainly is not. Or saying his cock is ugly. Let's not forget the million other ruthless jabs. I'd be willing to bet he didn't call her a single bad name.

Gah! The more I think about her mouth and the things she said, the angrier *I* become. How dare she?! What kind of woman speaks to her husband that way? Bitches, do. Oooo, crap, I can't believe I said that about another person. She deserves it, though. If I had my voice back, I'd love to give her a piece of my mind. Maybe I'd even have the audacity to call her a bitch to her face. That would feel *so* good. I know I'd feel guilty about it later, but it would definitely be worth it. Don't you agree?

This must be what true anger feels like... *Wow.* I don't think I've felt this since the day my mom stole grams's house right out from under me. And, even then I was still more distraught than mad.

"Magdalene, did you hear what I said?" Bridget grabs my attention.

Yes, of course, I did. I nod my reply and gesture to her phone, as my other hand continues the rub Pirate's lazy head.

After she hands it to me, I sluggishly type. *I heard what your dad said the first time. Though, I'm not sure why he thought he had to speak to me that way. I'm not deaf nor dumb. Just a mute for the time being. And he didn't say I couldn't go to Thor's; he said I'm not going. What I want to know is why, and how he knew I'd texted Thor in the first place?*

Handing the phone back to Bridget, she reads it aloud.

Lachlan doesn't smile, but he does snort in amusement as he removes his hands from the door frame and crosses them over his chest, making his pecs and forearms pop even more than they generally do.

Desperately, I try not to look at him, and stare at the white door instead. It's easier and much less embarrassing. If my eyes are allowed to roam where they want, they won't be able to control themselves once they gaze upon him in *that* position. I can't help it. He's way too much man not to take a gander at. Yes, he might look like he could dismember me with the snap of his fingers and bury my body in the backyard. Heck, his facial expressions have me thinking he's plotting that exact same outcome—*Dispose of the fat girl.* But, that still doesn't change the fact that he's a massive, virile man with intricate tattoos that mysteriously travel to places I haven't seen. And, he has this gruff voice that is not only scary, but also warm, and dare I say it? *Sexy.*

Oh. My. God. I'm now going to H.E. double-hockey-sticks. I said it. I called it...*sexy.* Please, please, please don't tell him or anyone I said that. I feel guilty enough admitting it. What if he knew? Or by some off chance Bridget found out? I'd just die. Okay, it's official, just forget I even mentioned it and let's get back to this bipolar conversation we are all trying to have with me.

Out of the corner of my eye, I catch Lachlan cock his head to the side. I know his eyes are on me. I can feel them. Just like I've been able to feel them every single day for a week. They *burn*.

"Lassie, can ye understand me when I talk like this?" he asks, using what I assume is his normal voice.

I nod, understanding him completely. It's not without a little difficulty, but it's not that hard either.

He continues. "Good...Thor texted and I told him tae fuck off. Yer not gonna tae be stayin' with him in that trailer when yer gonna be stayin' right here with us."

Holy moly, I think that's the most I've ever heard him speak at once. I couldn't place what his accent was before. Now, I'm pretty sure it's either Scottish or Irish. Though, it's not sing-songy enough to be Irish. But I could be wrong.

However, I do know that the tattoo knots that sleeve his entire arm are Celtic, which could mean either. I wish I could ask, but that might be considered disrespectful. And after the argument with his wife, disrespectful is the last thing I want to be.

So I'm going to do the only thing I can at this point—ignore him ordering me to stay here whether I like it or not. His way might have been kinda nice, but if I actually start to think about him controlling the situation to this level, I might become angry again. And we all know that won't get me far. Except maybe outside, huffing a wheelchair up an incline that I'm fairly certain I couldn't manage. Yep, I'm screwed. I said it once, and I'll say it a thousand more times. S.C.R.E.W.E.D.

Rolling my head to the opposite side, I pretend I'm exhausted. Although, that couldn't be further from the truth. I just want him—well, the shirtless version of him, out of my room. He can come back later when there are fewer muscles, and tattoos to look at. It's too hard to think with him in that *condition.*

That doesn't mean my mind isn't deviously putting pieces together of what I briefly saw. I'm pretty sure he has a small patch of hair on his chest, and possibly a faint line of it trailing down those rippling abs. I couldn't bear to dip any lower in fear that my body might burst into flames of mortification. No one should ogle a man. At least not someone that looks like I do. Skinny supermodels with bodies that men like him drool over, sure, they can ogle him.

But, it definitely shouldn't be someone that looks like me. I'm barely above five foot, and my hair has been in a continual state of curly disarray since I left Johnathan. I don't even know how to wear makeup, except lip gloss and mascara, and I wouldn't know the first thing about eyeshadow or eyeliner. Now, don't even get me started on clothes. I can't remember the last time I wore a single digit size, or something that resembles feminine. Heck, my panties are plain white cotton. I'm *that* boring.

Lachlan and Bridget carry on a conversation like I'm invisible. It doesn't last long and is pretty anticlimactic; something about his sister, Whisky, his wife, and some other odds and ends. I'm too busy pretending to be falling asleep to really listen. I've had enough listening for today. Meredith made sure of that.

My mind drifts...

I can't help but wonder what this Meredith looks like, and how long it will be before I'm forced to come face-to-face with her. What do you think? Want to make a wager?

Taking Lachlan's appearance into consideration, and how much Bridget looks like him, I bet that his wife is short and petite like Bridget, since Lachlan towers well over six foot. I bet she has blue eyes and blonde hair, too. And, she's probably thin as a rail with huge headlights, and a killer butt. I wouldn't be surprised if his sister is the same way; except maybe taller and a redhead. Lord knows their family won the genetic lottery. Mine surely didn't. Not everyone can be blessed with good looks. At least I have nice headlights, and my butt isn't too bad, either. A little thick and juicy maybe, but I have to live with it, so I might as well embrace these curves.

Before too long, Lachlan exits and I barely hear him leave. Bridget sweetly pats my calf and bids me a goodnight before she exits, too. At last, I'm alone with a lazy, floppy eared dog as my companion. Pirate's an excellent buddy. He's lazy and doesn't talk. Plus, he doesn't have a calculating eye or body that....well...let's not think about that, shall we? I'd much rather forget what I saw.

I'll catch ya later.

CHAPTER 8

The genius, blood-pumping beat of *Disturb*'s; '*Get Down with the Sickness*' echoes off my bedroom walls, waking me.

Groaning, I stretch my arms high to feel that delicious pull in my biceps and shoulders. Pirate, my best mate, lifts his head off the pillow beside me and snuggles closer; his wet nose rooting into my armpit.

Silent laughter wracks my body, and I push his head away. Grumbling his disapproval, he rolls back on his pillow, and I reach above me to wrap my fingers around the new bar Lachlan installed yesterday. Using my upper body strength, I bring myself into a sitting position, both legs tucked under the covers, my butt numb.

It had taken me close to ten minutes to get up yesterday. I haven't admitted that to anyone. Though, Lachlan must have known because I now have this chain bolted to the ceiling that hangs within arm's reach. It's a godsend.

Throwing off the covers and scooting to the edge of the bed, I swing my legs off before grabbing my wheelchair's arm. I know it's not the easiest or the most graceful maneuver, but I successfully transfer myself into my wheelchair without incident. Blowing out a relieved breath, I release the brakes and roll over to my dresser where I tug a folded dress off the top and drop it into my lap.

I'm not really a fan of dresses, but Bridget made it clear yesterday that it's too difficult to dress me in much else. I've even decided to forgo panties in the meantime. I never liked them much, anyhow.

The music grows louder when I roll out of the bedroom, and into the bathroom. As I use the restroom, wash my fingers, and brush my teeth, the song switches to *Buckcherry*'s *'Crazy Bitch'*. Spitting my toothpaste into the sink, I wipe my mouth off and begin lip syncing. After rinsing the paste down the drain and drying my hands, I steal the handheld mirror off a bathroom shelf and give myself a look-see.

I gasp at the horrid sight. My hair's a fluffy mess and I look *meh*. Snatching a hairband off the shelf, I secure my curls in a low ponytail. The dryness of my lips forces me to borrow a tube of lip balm and run my newly washed finger over the top to gather a dollop. I generously apply the strawberry flavored balm to my lips. Before exiting, I shove my blue dress into one the shelves for me to change into later after I wash up.

Yesterday was my first full day here at the house, and my initial go at doing things on my own. It sucked. I ended up needing Bridget's help more times than I care to admit. She made me lunch, and dinner since I'd slept through breakfast. Lachlan had been down here when I'd woken and wheeled out of the bedroom. He and Bridget must have been in some sort of private conversation, because when I interrupted them, they stopped talking entirely. Although, Lachlan did stay until he finished his mug of coffee. Then he disappeared out the back door, and the only other time I saw him was when he came back to install that magical contraption above my bed. I thanked him with a tight smile, and he grunted indignantly. So much for communication.

Pirate, my bum mate, is still sleeping in my bed when I roll past my bedroom door and into the open living room/kitchen space. The outside of the house automatically brings thoughts of country living. However, inside this live-in basement, you are transported to a serene beach bungalow. How in the world Bridget managed to transform this into such a tropical oasis, I'll never know.

Stark, white stone tiles run the length of the entire floor. The walls are painted the palest of blues. From the couch to the end tables and chairs, all the furniture is a dark, chocolate rattan, cushioned in plush tan fabric with light blue throw pillows. In the kitchen, there's a bistro set with wrought-iron chairs and an exquisite mosaic tabletop with a curved base. It's one of those tables you see and wish you owned yourself. It's *that* amazing.

The song switches, and *AC/DC*'s '*Thunderstruck*' roars to life outside. It somehow feels louder, as if the vibrations are beating off the sliding glass doors, making them hum.

Thanks to some masterful rearranging, I roll straight through the living room to the doors. White linen curtains cover the wide glass, and I shuck a portion of them back before sliding open the door. The high-intensity music ricocheting off the house blasts me in the face. It steals my breath and I wait a moment to catch it again.

With a little oomph, I force the wheelchair out of the doorway and onto the patio. And fumble as I close the door in my wake.

It's much earlier than I suspected. The sun is just beginning to rise to mid-morning, as a muggy dampness hangs in the summer air, fanning over my skin in the gentle breeze. I roll myself forward, set the brakes, and cast my eyes over the expanse of the backyard that stops on the edge of a rising cornfield. It feels like its own little world out here. Peaceful and still, with the exception of the music that's pumping from the old pole barn at the corner of the lot. The wide doors are retracted, somehow funneling the music louder. Or maybe it really is that loud and the person listening is partially deaf. I can't be sure.

Rob Zombie's '*Feel so Numb*' is next on the powerhouse playlist, and is followed by six more adrenaline doused songs. My good, uncasted foot bounces to the beat and my mind blanks, soothed by a symphonic music high. A peacefulness cruises listlessly through my blood, calming and warming me from the inside out. This is the same sensation I've always embraced when I'm wrenching under the hood of a car. My Zen.

Minutes blend into eternity, and I fall deeper into a mindless lull; my heaven on earth, far away from racing thoughts and soul-eating torment. It's pure bliss.

All too soon, my serenity is cut short when the music is turned off, and the sound of feet moving across the yard has me opening my eyes. Lachlan....*he's*....I snap my eyes shut before I can process another thought.

Christ almighty.

What was I thinking? I should have known this would happen again. My jaw clenches and my stomach dips at the image scorched into the back of my eyelids. Lachlan, coming toward me, in nothing but a pair of black exercise shorts, overused *Nike* shoes, and he's shirtless—again. His healthy skin gleams with sweat in the early morning sunlight. Those impossible muscles are twisting and contracting beneath his flawlessly inked skin. The hair that I thought I'd seen a few nights back has now been confirmed, as it, too, glistens with sweat, matting to his broad, meaty pecs and abs.

I *still* cannot believe real men can actually look like that. My stomach and nether regions squirm at the thought.

Sheesh, what's wrong with me?! I've slept with plenty of handsome men. Some thin, some fat, and some in between. Some had muscles, and others were flabby; all of them had varieties of hair colors, tattoos, and heights. They were always younger than me, aside from Brian. Hey, don't judge. I never said I was a saint. I do have itches that need to be scratched, sometimes. And those men served a purpose.

However, I've never in my entire existence seen a body like that, other than on magazines at the store like *Men's Health.* And if I'm honest, those men don't hold a candle to Lachlan. What does that say about him? I don't have a clue. Except that I'm in serious trouble if he keeps running around here shirtless in front of me. I can already feel my cheeks heating at the prospect of it; and I don't want to objectify him by staring at his pecs, abs, and...um...other places. It's rude, and worse, it's embarrassing. Yes, it's his house and I don't have a say, but that doesn't change how it affects my mind...or body.

Please tell me I'm not the only woman on the face of the planet who's ever felt this way. Shy, scared, uncomfortable, and about a million more words could explain how I'm feeling right now.

Okay, Magdalene, you need to get a grip, stop breathing so dang heavy, and hope that he doesn't want to chat.

I slow my breathing. In through my nose and out through my mouth. Sighing in relief, I slouch in my chair and my head lulls back. *Much better.*

The crunching of footsteps cease nearby. "Ye want me tae help ye into the chair?"

Do you want to go put a shirt on over that chest, please? I dare to beg.

Keeping my eyes closed, I shake my head in reply and he grumbles.

"Ye want me tae get ye some lemonade?"

I shake my head again. I don't want anything from him. He's already done plenty. Why won't he leave?

Those eyes again—they're on me, burning away. At least I have my hair back and look a little more presentable this morning. The dress Bridget helped me into last night is a pale yellow, and hits me just below the knee. Which is above the knee when I'm seated. Speaking of Bridget—where in the world is she, anyhow? Maybe she's still asleep? Hum…

"Lachlan, baby, I'm going to be leaving soon. Can you please come up here and give me a kiss goodbye?" Meredith purrs seductively from the deck above. My insides jolt at the sound, rolling and swirling in disgust.

She's a real piece of work. A piece of work that's married to a man that looks and acts like him. He's got a huge heart; it doesn't take much to figure that one out. What does that say about her? I suppose she must be pretty great, too, if he's married to her.

Internally, I kick myself for thinking polluted thoughts about her. I'm the mean one here—shame on me. I really have to stop judging her. Lachlan's wife is probably an amazing woman; she'd have to be to snag him. Women would give their right arm to be with a man that looks like him. Add that voice, and niceness, then subtract his broody scariness, and someone would give their left arm, too. I'm not saying I would, but could easily see it happen; wars have been started over much less.

Lachlan clears his throat before he replies, "Aye, I'll be up in a minute."

"Okay, babe," she comments and a door is shut, leaving us alone once more.

A blanket of silence settles over us.

I squirm in my chair, feeling the heat of his gaze. I don't know where his eyes are roaming, and I don't want to. This dress has a built-in bra that doesn't really help when you have headlights as big as mine. I've got cleavage, a lot of it. Even though I really wish I didn't. Not here, not now. Maybe when I'm in the bedroom with a man, it does serve as a benefit. It forces their eyes away from the less desirable parts of me and draws them to the more pleasing ones. If you could actually consider boobs to be that pleasing; I don't. Not really. But I'm not a guy, so I can't really speak for them.

I'm rambling, aren't I? Oh, fudge sticks.

Lachlan cracks the silence with his grizzly voice. "Mags, I'm gonna take care of that," he grunts under his breath and then continues, "Then I'm comin' down here and puttin' ye in that chair so we can share some lemonade. Aye?"

Gah! Didn't he realize I already said no to both of those things? What's wrong with him? He can't force me to do something I don't want to. And I really don't want to be alone with him more than necessary. Doesn't he get that without me having to spell it out for him? I should go wake Bridget up. I hate to say it, but she makes the perfect buffer.

Hands briskly land on either side of my chair, jostling it. My eyes burst open, coming face-to-face with Lachlan's—his mouth mere inches from mine. I didn't even hear him move.

The mint on his breath wafts over my face as he exhales heavily and licks his lips.

Lord almighty!

My heart leaps into my throat, and a shudder wracks my body. I know he can feel it through my chair. My cheeks blaze with uncertainty, fear, and maybe a little something else.

He's too close.

Releasing the arms of my chair with a low grunt, he runs his thumbs over the apples of my cheeks. A hard expression locks his features and his thumbs lower, trailing along my jaw to the tip of my chin. Those teal eyes drop to my lips, and I'm not sure if this is real, or if I just passed out and I'm dreaming.

Lachlan flicks that pink tongue over his bottom lip once more; his eyes zeroing in on my mouth, causing the hairs on the back of my neck to stand at attention.

Nope, definitely not dreaming.

Lachlan really needs to back up. I lift my hands to push him away, but stop when I realize I'd have to touch him in order to do that. I. *Can't.* Touch. Him.

"I gotta gift for ye," he whispers in that same grizzly, skin prickling tone that's laced with the most beautiful accent.

I feel something happen between my trembling thighs. A tingling. Did my lady parts just pulse? Please, no. Too close, too much man, too-too-too much of everything. He needs to move away. Move away now. I can't take this.

Squeezing my eyes shut from sensory overload, and possibly a mild heart attack, I try to drown him out. He growls his displeasure, making the shaking in my thighs travel up my spine, and branch out to my arms. My breath sputters erratically, forcing me to breathe through my mouth—silently panting.

Lachlan's searing thumb traces even lower; dipping down the slender curve of my neck to the hollow of my throat. I lose my breath entirely. "Ye cannae bloody talk tae me, Mags."

That nickname...he said it again. *Mags*. I run my sweaty casted palms over my shaky thighs. The brief distraction steadies my irregular pulse. I'm finally able to exhale and gulp down a fresh lungful of air.

"I wanna hear ye speakin'. I wanna see ye walkin'. But for now, I'm gonna leave ye here, bring back yer present, and we're gonna spend the day layin' in the sun, sippin' on lemonade. Dinnae try tae run from me, lassie. I won't take na for an answer." With each gruff word, Lachlan's accent thickens and I have to listen harder to understand him. His thumbs swirl at the base of my neck, stroking my sensitive flesh, entrancing me.

A wetness dampens my inner thighs and I quake, squeezing my eyes tighter. I just have to get through this. He'll go away soon. Bridget will be a buffer. Just a few more minutes. I can do this. I know I can power through it. If only my stomach would stop with the fluttering.

Lachlan pulls away with a long groan, and I expel a rushed exhale. Relief washes over me, ebbing the tension away.

"I'll see ye soon. Dinnae go anywhere," he orders earnestly, an edge in his tone.

And just like that, he's gone, moving away. I wait to make sure he truly left before prying my eyes open.

Would you care to tell me what the heck just happened?!

Oh boy....

He touched *me*. Touched...me. *Me*. He. Touched. Lordy, my brain can't even wrap around that crazy thought. I can still feel his phantom fingers caressing my skin.

I have to stop thinking about it or it's going to make things worse.

Staring across the gravel drive, my eyes settle on an old tree standing alone in the middle of the yard. Abundant leaves fill its branches, as a squirrel barrels down its side and is followed by another chasing him. Around the trunk they race, tumble, and play. Then back up the trunk they go, getting lost in the foliage. I smile at the sight. It's simple and peaceful, just like the MacAlister's home.

By focusing on the tree and following its beautiful lines, a sense of tranquility shoves all those other feelings to the back of my mind. I have to focus on something else, 'cause if I actually think, I'll be wondering what Lachlan is doing upstairs with his wife. Is his tongue plundering her mouth? He looks like a man who plunders, a lot. Maybe he's taking her against the wall in a scorching hot quickie? Isn't that what men who look like him do? Maybe the other night wasn't a fight at all, maybe it was their own form of foreplay. It didn't seem like it at the time, but what else would you call it if he's up there with her now, *'kissing her goodbye'*? After all, she did speak sweetly to him. Which indicates they made up. Right?

I must've been staring off into space far too long, because the next thing I know, the screen door is opening. Glancing over my shoulder, I hope to see Bridget. Instead, I get Lachlan carrying a clear pitcher of lemonade in his hand, with two glasses tucked under his big arm. Thankfully, he's changed, his goatee has been trimmed, and his hair's even wet.

How long have I been out here? Long enough for him to plunder his wife and take a shower? Maybe he had to wash off all that post-coital...aftermath. My stomach recoils at the thought.

Gosh, what is up with me today? Do I have a burr up my butt, or what? Of course, it was to shower off his workout and the sex with his *wife*. Why shouldn't he be allowed to plunder her? She's his *wife*. No matter how many nasty things she said about me, she *is* allowing me to sleep in her house. Sure, I'm a stranger she doesn't know and has shown little interest in meeting, which I can't say I'm too broken up about.

Frick....I've got to stop thinking.

Lachlan seems to understand my thoughts without knowing it, because he sets the glasses and lemonade down on the concrete. Then, one second I'm sitting in my chair, and the next, I have beefy arms *touching me,* lifting me way too easily and sitting me on the lounger; where my casted leg can stretch outward and my back can sit up. I'm too stunned to make a sound or put up a fight, so I don't. I just stare and frantically try to keep my dress down, so my *parts* aren't suddenly exposed.

I exhale, not realizing I had held my breath that entire moment. My fingers remain curled around the base of my dress, holding it down with arms of steel. I can't believe he just did that. Lifted me like *that*.

Once I'm over my initial shock and my heart calms, I turn my head and glare at him. Which turns out to be a wasted effort since he doesn't even notice. He's already seated himself beside me on another lounger, having pushed my wheelchair out of arm's reach, leaving me once again, helpless.

Pouring some lemonade into a glass, he hands it to me. I unpeel my fingers from the hem of my dress and wrap them around the cold glass. Taking a sip, I gently balance the glass on my lap, before carefully setting it on the ground beside me. Out of the corner of my eye, I watch Lachlan settle into his lounger, crossing his bare ankles and tucking a hand behind his head before he takes a deep breath and releases it on a sigh. I'm not sure if it's an, *I just had great sex* sigh, or an *this is nice sitting out here* sigh, or possible *I'm beat* sigh, and I'm not going to ask to find out.

He takes a sip of his own lemonade and rests it beside him on the ground, the glass clinking and scratching against the concrete. My attention reverts to the yard and that same tree, ignoring his proximity.

"Ye comfortable?" he asks sweetly.

Nodding, my eyes stay cast forward, and my heart beats faster just because he's talking to me. I'm used to men speaking to me at work. I've worked at nine different auto repair shops, so it comes with the territory.

It's always small shop-talk. And the men I dated, those small town countrymen I told you about, they would talk some. But mostly, I don't talk, so they don't talk; and they seemed perfectly content with that as long as they got some *candy* every now and again. I couldn't tell you the last time a man has sat next to me without an alternate agenda on his mind. And I definitely can't remember a time, if ever, a man asked me if I was comfortable.

"If ye need tae use the bathroom, I'll help ye get inside," he tacks on. This time, he sounds more uncomfortable with that prospect of helping me to the toilet. Not that I'm too keen on the idea myself. I'm not. Not at all.

To keep things unruffled, I nod again, watching a bird dart out of the tree and over to the forest at the edge of the property. Even though I really want to tell Lachlan he can help me to the bathroom, *over my dead body,* but, the man did save me from that very thing. Saying what I want is a bit too morbid, not to mention, rude. So I don't. I go with the flow. Which is something I'm not very good at.

I like to hold the control—all of it. I like my ability to pick up and leave whenever it suits me. I like being unattached, unburdened, and unemotional. It serves its purpose in life. The less you care, the less you feel. The less you let bother you, the better you are. Emotionless. Which, as of late, has been the complete opposite of what I've been experiencing. I don't know what's come over me. The near death experience, maybe?

I was always the type to go to work, drive Viola home to whatever fully furnished apartment I was renting at the time, cook dinner, shower, go to bed—

wash, rinse, and repeat. Then, the boyfriends came; and trust me, they always did. Working at a repair shop in some small country town, I was bound to catch the eye of some halfway nice guy who had a job, drove some sort of truck or motorcycle, and found me cute. They'd hit on me a few times, then ask me to dinner. The same old story every time—wash, rinse, and repeat.

Beside me, Lachlan sits in companionable silence, both of our eyes cast forward over the beautiful land. The sun rises higher in the sky, beating down on my legs while the rest of me stays shaded by the deck above. Quietly, we sip from our lemonades and just *be*. There's something perfect about it.

I haven't sat and enjoyed life this simply since my grams was alive. We used to perch outside on our front porch, rocking in our rocking chairs, drinking ice water and soaking in nature's beauty. Sometimes we'd talk. Sometimes we didn't. Sometimes we read. Sometimes we shucked corn. And sometimes, we peeled apples. Always on our porch, and in those two rocking chairs. Always together. Even in her last days of life, I wheeled her to the porch and there she'd rock in that rocking chair, as it creaked methodically over the oldest of floorboards on our whitewashed porch, and I'd read to her.

Four months to the day that Brian tragically died, she died in that chair. Skin and bones, oxygen tank at her side, those little things stuffed into her nose. A hospice nurse sat inside the house, playing on her phone to pass the time. We knew cancer wouldn't take long to eat away at her organs. Stage Four lung cancer had metastasized, and spread to every vital organ of her body before we caught it. There was nothing we could do, and nothing she wanted to do. She wanted to die at home. She wanted to die just like she did, looking over the yard with me reading *'The Stand'* by *Stephen King* to her. It was peaceful, and in its own way, beautiful.

"I love the way you read to me as the birds sing...I can smell the roses, Magdalene. You'll pick some for me, won't you, honey?" my grams whispered softly.

Wrapping her innocent request around me like a warm blanket, I nodded, "Yeah, Grams, I'll pick you some roses."

Although I knew I couldn't. The roses weren't even in bloom. The birds weren't singing in the trees. I knew that God was right there with us, knocking on our door. And all my grams could do was rock slowly back and forth with a little smile on her face, as the good Lord took her. Her eyes closed for a moment, and when they didn't open again, I knew she was gone. I sat and watched death claim her frail body, seconds passing rapidly. Then, I set the book on the porch railing before I went to her and kissed her forehead, saying my final goodbye to the most amazing woman I'd ever known.

A tiny tear slips down my cheek at the thought. Ten years ago it happened, and this is the first time I've felt anything similar to the peace I used to have, rocking on my grams's front porch for all of those years.

"Ye all right?" Lachlan whispers softly beside me; he must have been watching.

I turn my head and smile sadly, nodding my head. '*Yes*,' I mouth.

Lips pressed together, Lachlan's eyes catch mine and hold them, his hand slipping into his pocket. Whatever he grabs, he lays in my lap. "For ye." His gaze flicks to the item, and I glance down.

A phone. And it's not just any phone. It's an *iPhone*—*an iPhone* with a blue and white daisy case.

Lachlan reaches into my lap and slides on the screen with the flick of his finger. I jump at his sudden movements, yet he doesn't say a word.

The background of the phone is daisies, too. How did he know those were my favorite flower? They were at the hospital, too. A small vase of them had died and we threw them out before I left. Still, they were there for days. I had figured they were from Thor, or maybe Bridget. And since they came with no card, I had settled on one of those two people. Maybe I was wrong about that, too.

Lachlan reaches into my lap again and presses the contacts button. I don't jump this time. Though, I'm not entirely comfortable about this either.

"Yer new phone. Pip's, Whisky's, and my number are in there. Ye got any family tae add, ye can. It's yers tae keep."

I turn my head and look up at him to see if he's kidding. He's not. His face is fierce, unnerving. Pretty much what his face always looks like.

Our eyes lock again, and he jerks a nod at the phone still sitting on my lap, untouched by me. "Ye understand what I just said, lassie?"

I understand him perfectly fine; which means I think he's lost his flippin' marbles, too, handing me an *iPhone* with a daisy case and expecting me to take it. Nails meet coffin. That's the first thing a gold-digging moocher would do, accept an *iPhone*. Well, I'm not one of those women. I refuse. Whether he's being nice or not, or if this is a test, I can't accept the gift.

Picking it up between two fingers like it's diseased; I toss it back into his lap and cross my arms over my chest. My eyes cut to the tree again, face tight.

Lachlan growls, yes, *growls*, his dislike. "The fuck?" he bites off.

Yes, what the fudge? I would like to know the same thing.

The phone is tossed back into my lap again, and this time I toss it right back at him, releasing a satisfied *humph*, as I re-cross my arms over my chest.

"Ye care tae tell me what crawled up yer arse and died?"

I would if I had a *voice* that worked! I'd be happy to tell him all about it.

Firstly, he's nice enough to let me stay in his house with his daughter and his wife. And possibly the best dog I've ever met in my entire life. And that is saying a lot, because I loved Rock, Brian's old coon dog. Secondly, he saved my life. That's a huge thing that I can never repay; just like I can never repay his kindness for letting me stay here. There are just some things money can't buy. Kindness is one of them.

Lachlan's kindness is irrefutably endless. I know he gave Bridget money to buy the clothes for me. The food I ate for dinner last night. Let's not forget my ruined car taking up space in his barn. Or, that weird chain hanging from my ceiling that has a bar attached to help me get out of bed in the morning. And that's the short list.

Now, the last thing I am going to do is accept an expensive cell phone from a man I barely know. Who has already shown me more kindness in the few weeks I've known him, than most people do in their lifetimes. Granted, most of the time I've actually known him, I was drugged. But that doesn't mean he wasn't sitting in my room, burning holes through me with those penetrating teal eyes. Or grumbling for whatever reason, which he seems to do a lot.

Lachlan seems to get my point, or at least I hope he does when he gets up, grabs the empty pitcher, and goes inside. I sigh guiltily, feeling terrible for possibly hurting his feelings.

A couple minutes later, Lachlan returns with a bottle of sunscreen tucked under his arm, and a refilled pitcher of lemonade. He must really like that stuff. I've only had one glass.

Lachlan refills his cup, chugs it down, and refills it again. Then he sets it down, along with the pitcher, next to his chair before grabbing the sunscreen and snapping open the cap. He steps around his lounger and stops at the end of mine. Squeezing some lotion into his hands, he slathers them together, coating them in white, and leans down. I barely get a chance to let out a terrified squeak when he touches my leg, running his hot, rough hands up my calf to my thigh. I grab the hem of my dress to keep that from coming up, too.

Oh.

My.

God.

His hands knead in the lotion, taking away that creamy white color. My heart rate goes from zero to a million miles an hour at the feeling, and even more so at the sight. His corded forearms contract as his palms and fingers not only rub in the lotion, they massage me, too—digging in deep, but not enough to be painful.

I go ramrod straight, and hold my breath the higher he creeps, not paying any attention to my reaction. It's like he doesn't even care; he's too intent and focused on my leg for anything else to matter.

Lachlan then lifts my leg, bending it at the knee, and I stuff the dress between my thighs, covering my nether region. *That was a close one.*

He massages the lotion into the back of my thigh, and gets so close to the crease where my butt meets my leg that I think I might actually faint from his touch. More wetness pools between my thighs, forcing me to inhale deeply, praying I don't smell myself. I don't.

Squeezing more lotion from the bottle, he scoots up the lounger between my legs and gently tugs one of my arms, massaging sunscreen into the cast-free parts. I can't decide if I should push him away, slap him, or let him keep going. It feels so good I instantly start to become noodley as the cranked tension in my muscles floats away. People would pay loads of money for a massage this good.

Staring straight ahead, I try to keep from looking at his face. Which leaves me with an up-close eyeful of his black t-shirt covered chest. The shirt leaves very little to the imagination, like most of his clothes. I don't know if it's intentional or not, but Lachlan's clothes hug each muscle like they're best friends. They don't drape like most men's; instead, they hug and cuddle the muscles in a way that make most women drool and all men envious.

Lachlan finishes my quasi-massage, sunscreen rubdown and drops back into the lounger beside me. This time the satisfied sigh that escapes his parted lips I know isn't about sex; it's about something else entirely. And I like that, since I know it has nothing to do with Meredith.

Lachlan doesn't bother lathering himself in lotion as he relaxes back, and I close my eyes, relishing in the sun's warmth beating down on my legs.

Our companionable silence ensues.

I nod off for a few, and when I wake, Lachlan is still on the lounger beside me, both of his massive arms tucked comfortably behind his head, and he's wearing a pair of sunglasses.

I glance down and gasp. That damned phone is in the top of my dress, nestled between my breasts. That stinkin' jerk!

This time I don't even think when I yank it out, slide on the screen, and find his number so I can give him a piece of my mind.

How dare you! Putting a phone, I don't want, between my boobs. That was rude! I don't want the phone. I'm not a moocher. I don't need your money or your pity. I just need a place to crash. And seeing as though you refused to let Thor come to get me, I guess I'm stuck here.

I click *send* and throw that damn phone between my thighs; it bounces on the cushion for a moment before settling there. Clenching my jaw, I wait to see if Lachlan even has his phone with him.

Seconds later, I find out that he does when he removes one hand from behind his head, tugs the phone out of his cargo shorts pocket, and lifts his sunglasses to read the screen. He rumbles a deep noise in his throat. Out of my periphery, I watch his giant thumbs type away on his matching *iPhone* that has some sort of blue and black armor case on it.

My phone vibrates and I pick it up to read his message.

I slipped it there so you're forced to keep it. I didn't touch your breasts. I wouldn't do that. And just so we're clear, I don't think you're a moocher, whatever the hell that is. And I don't pity you. Pity is for the weak, not the strong. You're not weak. Trust me. I've seen plenty of weak fuckin men and women. You don't seem the type. I don't know your story. Not gonna make ya tell me either. But I have to go to work tomorrow for a twenty-four-hour shift, and you might be here alone most of the day. Pip is helpin my sister with her shop. I don't want you out here alone, without a fuckin phone. If you fell or something happened, I'd feel like bloody hell. So take it...Please.

I read the message once. Then I read it again, trying to read between any lines, and realize the *please* was tacked on at the end for a purpose. Like it was forced, and he's losing patience.

I return a message.

Your wife thinks I'm here for money, and because I'm lazy. I don't think it'd be right to take the phone. And what shop? You don't have to answer if I'm being too nosy. I'm not trying to be. I'm just trying to get better and get out of your hair.

I need him to understand where I'm coming from. We haven't had any time to actually talk. This is the first time, ever. Since I can't speak, this texting thing is much easier. I just hope my voice doesn't take too long to heal or I might have to learn sign language. What good that'll do me I dunno, since people I know would have to know what I sign. This is just too dang complicated. I hate even thinking about any of it. Sometimes, I wish I could just go back to Johnathan and forget this whole thing ever happened. Then, perfect days like today happen where I get to sit outside, in peace, and let the world fade away. Those are the times I wish I could freeze and make them last forever. Minus the phone in my boobs.

Reading my message, Lachlan shakes his head and grumbles something under his breath as he types.

Ask whatever ya bloody want. I'll tell ya no if I don't wanna answer...My sis owns Whisky's Corrupt Confections. It's a bakery. Since Whisky's got two sons and no daughters, she taught Pip to bake. She's worked there every summer since we moved here. That's why I was at the hospital more than her. If she'd had it her way, she woulda quit Whisky's and lived at the hospital with you...but we cut a deal. She works, I take time off. I had the vacation time, anyhow. Worked out.

Is it weird that I'm trying to read his message like he'd talk? Spellcheck seems to ruin part of that charm. But I'm trying.

My fingers go to work.

You took time off to stay with me? Why? Wasn't Thor's grandma the one who owned the gas station?

I click send.

This time, Lachlan is quiet when he reads my message and types his response.

The dog scratches at the door from the inside. I receive Lachlan's reply just as he leans back to slide the door open a hair, and close it once Pirate meanders outside. The pup stops on the patio in front of us, looks between Lachlan and me, and does a long stretch before trotting out into the grass, wagging his accidentally cropped tail.

That poor dog has been through the wringer. He's missing an eye, a tail, and has a spot on his back that's devoid of fur. Though, you wouldn't suspect he'd ever went through any trauma by the way he acts. He's the happiest and sweetest dog I've met. And I've met plenty of dogs. Most of the men I dated had one or two. It must be a guy thing.

I finish watching Pirate trot around the yard like he owns the place before glancing at my phone.

Thor lives with his grandma in that trailer outside of her station. He needed to be there to look after her, and you needed someone to look after you. Since I was the one who found ya, I figured it was the right thing to do. Your blood bein on my hands and all...can't get much more personal than that. In church, Sniper brought the shit up. I put in my two cents. Thor added his. I got the votes, and that's why you're here.

Another comes straight after.

I've got almost a month of vacation time saved. I rarely use it. Seems like as good a time as any to take a couple days off. Don't ya think?

I'm not sure if I'm more shocked by the amount he's texting or what he's trying to explain. But, I'm confused about one giant thing.

Church? Sniper? Votes?

An amused grunt is rumbled beside me and I try to ignore it.

My phone vibrates with another incoming message.

Church is biker code for meeting. Sniper, my club Prez, brother-in-law, and best friend. Votes...know that democratic thing where everyone chooses what they want and the most votes win. Sound familiar?

Well, well, well, isn't someone being a snooty jerk today.

I know what votes are, I reply.

Then why ya asking me what they are?

I was asking what they were for.
I can't read your bloody mind, lassie.
He's got me there. He can't.
Fine. What kind of votes? What's the purpose? Explain, please. If you're allowed to.

I remember Bridget's brief, but somewhat thorough rundown of MC basics, and few of their rules. One of which was, 'club business, stays club business'. Ergo, he might not be able to discuss it with me since it was part of this *church* meeting. Which seems like sacrilege if you want my opinion.

Sniper and Cas wanted to know what we were gonna do with the lassie that saved one of our own. Don't take that shit lightly. Thor put in he wanted ya under his roof. I made a bid that ya stay here. Brothers decided to take it to a vote. I took the cake. The end.

Beside me, Lachlan dusts his palms together making a *'swish' 'swish'* sound. I get it. *The end.* He's washing his hands of it.

Lachlan

Remind me tae thank Pip later for the dress she picked out for Mags. So much exposed, freckle-kissed skin, and the sun keeps bringin' more of 'em out. Dinnae want her tae burn, though. The SPF 50 I massaged in should keep that from happenin'.

I finish dustin' my hands as a gesture tae my message, and out the corner of my eye, watch Mags finish readin' it. A tiny grin quirks at the corner of her pretty pink lips.

Wish that day had gone down as simple as I'm explain' it tae her. Ain't gonna tell her otherwise. Na. She dinnae wanna know aboot Thor and I aboot rippin' each other's heads off. Arsehole thought he could take the lassie home tae that piece of shit trailer he's livin' in. I ain't got nothin' against people livin' in trailers unless those people think they're gonna take what's mine and force it tae live there. Then I've got a problem.

At church, Sniper threw the gavel, shuttin' our arses up. I was just aboot to jump across that table and kick the livin' shit outta Thor for thinkin' he was gonna take her home. If it weren't for Sniper, I would have.

"You two, shut the fuck up, sit your asses down, and stop acting like two horny teenagers fighting over some pussy," Sniper commanded, and I growled at him for referrin' tae Mags as pussy. Lookin' at the lass, ye'd know she's a bloody lot more than that. Thor wouldn't know that, now would he? He just wants tae dip his wee cock in her. Dirty bastard. "Let's just throw a quick vote so you two assholes stop. We've got more important shit to deal with. Thor, tell us why you think Magdalene should stay with you?" Sniper was bein' diplomatic, and I bloody well hated it. I knew I shouldn't have let Pip text him when Mags woke up. Good thing we were ridin' together at the time, not far from the hospital, or Thor woulda been there without me.

Thor puffed out his chest, and slapped his hand on the clubhouse table, tryin' tae look like a badass. I thought he looked more like a bleach blond pansy arse. "I want her at my house 'cause she saved my grandma. It's the best way to pay her back. I take care of her, she gets better, then we're even," he said.

Not even fuckin' close. I saw how he was lookin' at her in the hospital, like a walkin' boner. Thinkin' with his cock. That's all the bastard does. Na way was I gonna allow him tae take her home.

Once Thor finished his bullshit explanation, I was shakin' full of adrenaline. My body was wound so fuckin' tight and ready tae fight that I barely heard Sniper callin' my name. My jaw ached from grindin' me teeth, leerin' at the lyin' bastard.

"Smoke," Prez snapped, punchin' me in the arm.

My leer swung tae Sniper. "What?!" I bit off in a growl.

Sniper grinned at me before lookin' back tae Thor. "Ya sure you wanna go down this road with Smoke?" he tested. "Hear she's a babe. But I gotta tell ya, brother, Smoke's gonna make your life a livin' fuckin' hell if you push this. The man carried her outta that store with his finger pluggin' a hole in her neck. Ya best think long and hard before you try takin' a dog from his bone."

Thor shook his head at our Prez, then turned his attention tae me, glarin' through wee eye slits. "Ain't your bone, brother. She's family now. Saved my grandma, the woman who's like my fuckin' mother. I'm not backin' down. We vote this shit. Winner gets the girl."

It. Was. On!

"Aye." I nodded sharply, my lip curlin' in pure aggression, nostrils flarin'.

"Smoke, tell us why Magdalene should stay at your house?" Sniper asked on an eye roll. He'd already said from day one that he'd give me as much time as I needed tae take care of the lass. He'd help me if I asked, and

keep Whisky off my arse aboot it. I knew I had his vote in the bag. Only ten more tae go.

Shovin' my chair back, I stood and planted both my fists on the tabletop; flexin' my arms as I leaned on 'em. I hated speakin' in front of the brothers, since part of 'em couldn't make out a bloody thing I said. I'd have tae use Sniper tae translate the rest.

"Magdalene's gonna stay with me." I swung my fist tae pound my chest, before addin', "Pip's been at the hospital bondin' with her." My eyes circled, sweepin' the table, briefly lockin' eyes with each brother I passed. I was gonna get my fuckin' point across one way or another.

I kept at it. "I got a house. I work two days a week. Pip wants tae help. And I dinnae care if ye vote I get tae keep her or not, she's stayin' with me. She's got her own room, and I've got the money tae take care of the bloody rest. The lassie almost died in my arms. I'm not aboot tae let her outta my sight."

Finished, I sat down and waited for Sniper tae translate. Then the votes came in. I won unanimously, aside from Thor, that is.

My phone vibrates, and I lift my sunglasses tae read her message.

Thank you.
Bloody hell.

Mags

Finishing my last text, Lachlan groans lowly. The sound does something funny to my belly. Abruptly, he slides off the lounger and walks barefoot across the sharp gravel drive to the yard, where he paces with his back to me. Pirate takes this opportunity to rub against Lachlan's bare calves for attention; even though Lachlan ignores him.

Step-step-step, pivot, turn, step-step-step, pivot, turn.

Watching Lachlan's long powerful strides over and over, he completes the same pattern, head down, hands fisted at his sides. I can't help but wonder if I said something wrong? My gut tells me I haven't crossed any lines, so I stick with my gut and stare out into the green, wide-open yard, and the man who seems to swallow the whole world so the only thing I can focus on is him. The way his calves flex with each purposeful step. The way his forearms tense and loosen with the clenching and unclenching of his fists. Briefly, he stops midstride to crack his neck then continues pacing.

Soon, Pirate joins his owner, heeling without being told to do so. Together they stride, man and dog.

Maybe this is his way to sort things out in his head? To clear it? I know my brain always clears itself best when riding in Viola. Music playing on the radio, the open road, high speeds, the wind whipping though my hair with the windows down, the smell of fresh air, and my favorite part: the feel of the shifter sliding into gear with each punch of the clutch. There's nothing like it. It centers your mind; shoving away all the crap life throws at you, whips it out that window, scattering it along the empty road. A distant memory on the wind. *Bliss*.

Leaving Lachlan to his devices to workout whatever demons he has, I gracelessly roll across his lounger and lift the lemonade pitcher from the other side. Shuffling back into my seat, I place the pitcher between my bare legs. It's cold to the touch and I shiver, silently giggling at the condensation dripping down my inner thighs. It feels great in this heat.

Grabbing my cup off the concrete beside my seat, I pour myself a full glass. Taking Lachlan's visual advice, I chug it down. A little bit escapes the sides of my mouth; with another giggle, I wipe it off using my bicep and continue until I'm finished with the entire glass. Then, I pour myself another before I set the pitcher and cup back down.

Glancing back up, I catch Lachlan's eyes trained on me from across the yard. I can't actually see them since they're shielded behind a pair of black shades; making him appear scarier, tougher, and somehow manlier than he already is. If that's even possible. However, I can feel them. Those teal eyes are like lasers. I've never, in all my life, been able to feel a person's eyes on me—only his. It's bizarre, yet, intriguing, like a phantom flame branding your flesh from afar.

Unconsciously, I wet my lips, fiddling with my hands in my lap. My fingers accidently bump my cellphone and peer at it. I've got a text from him.

Next time ya want some lemonade, make sure you're coverin yourself.

Holy. Hot. Damn.

A rush of crimson bursts from my cheeks, spreading downward, as my stomach takes a dive. I keep my eyes averted, staring at my lap and those words; tracing each letter repeatedly. *Make sure you're c.o.v.e.r.i.n. yourself.*

Cheese and rice, how much did he see? All of it? A little? Did he watch the entire show? Or did he look away? How much did I expose?

Without sparing a glance, I peck out a short message with trembling fingers.

What'd you see?

I gulp nervously and press send. My teeth move to saw my lip, gnawing at the inner corner.

An instant response. *You don't wanna know.*

Yes. I. Do,

Ya sure?

Yes!

All of your bottom.

What the heck does that mean?

All of what? My bottom, as in my butt? Or as in other parts, too.

Your butt and...other.

Oh. My. God. Take me out back and shoot me now!

First, I'm worried he might see me exposed when he moves to me to the lounger. The second time, when he's massaging the sunscreen in. Then, here I go stupidly exposing myself. This no panties thing is a bust. I've got to start wearing them again, even if it does feel good without them, and they are a pain to change with this cast on. There's too much to worry about. And, I haven't shaved down there in almost a month; I know what it looks like—a jungle. I'm just thankful he was *that* far away and that my curtains match the drapes, if you know what I'm sayin'.

Shooting a glance over my shoulder, I search for my wheelchair. It's too far for me to reach, so I fire Lachlan another message. I have to get away from him, and the only way to do that right now is to bite the bullet and have him bring me my chair.

Can you bring me my wheelchair?

Why?

Frowning severely, I shake my head in frustration.
Because I want it.
Why?
To go inside.
Why do you wanna go inside?

Why does it matter if I want to go inside or not? Aren't I allowed? Is this school and I have to ask for a hall pass to get outta class? Gah!

You know why. Now, please…
Because I got a wee glance at your parts?
No.
Because I saw your arse?

Oh, for the love of god. He's such a pain. Of course it's because of that! I'm lying through my teeth—or my fingers, as it seems.

No. I just want to go inside.
Why?
Because I have to use the restroom.
No, you don't.
Yes! I. Do!
No, you don't, or woulda bloody said that from the get-go, lassie.

You know what? I'll pee right here and I'll make you clean it up.

Ha-ha, now what's he gonna say? Not that I'm going to urinate on the lounger. My threat is weak at best. But he doesn't know that.

No, ya won't. You were embarrassed about pissin' in the bedpan at the hospital. You're not gonna do it there.

Lifting my head, I glare at the stubborn know-it-all with my lips pursed. He's standing directly across from me, staring right back, shades still cloaking his eyes.

Briefly, I peek down to text, but return my glare once I hit send.

Mr. Know-it-all, huh? Am I a baby now? Need to be put on a schedule to know when I'm allowed to eat, drink, sleep, and use the potty? Why don't ya type one up so I know what I'm allowed to do and when?

One second, Lachlan is lifting his shades to read my reply, the next he's sauntering across the gravel barefoot, with Pirate following in his wake. Without a word, he grabs my wheelchair and rolls it to my seat. Bending at the waist, he doesn't seek permission before scooping me up, and gently setting me in it. I don't fight him, because I'm too preoccupied with trying to keep my dress from riding up again, and clutching my new cell phone to my chest. Once he's righted me in my chair, he wheels me to the door, slides it open, pushes us through, and pulls it shut again. Still, without making a sound.

Now inside the small basement apartment, Lachlan briskly pushes me across the tile to the bathroom, where he reaches over me to shove the door open before rolling me inside. And he doesn't stop there. Setting my brakes before I get a chance to, he steps in front of me, and lifts me once more. I let out a startled squeak, and my body jerks when I realize he's going to set me on the open toilet to pee.

As soon as my bottom rests on the cold seat, Lachlan releases his hold and exits the bathroom, quietly shutting the door as he leaves.

"Pee," he instructs gruffly behind the door.

All right, all right, I will.

Minutes tick by and I still can't pee, knowing he's outside the bathroom door listening. I can hear him breathing.

Since I have nothing better to do, I text him to pass some time.

If you'd leave, I'd be able to pee. Please go back outside.

I'm not going back outside. You needed to pee. So pee. Bridget won't be home till late. So, I'm gonna fix you some lunch, give you your pills, then we're gonna relax and enjoy the bloody day. Aye?

Insert the biggest eye roll in the history of the world, and add a long silent groan of defeat. That's what I'm doing right now, staring at his message on my screen. It's like those happy little daisies on my case are taunting me—*Neiner-neiner-neiner, you're stuck in hell.*

I'm totally losing it.

What choice do I really have at this point? Bridget has apparently gone to her aunt's bakery, and I can't run away from him. So I'm only left with one option: suck it up and deal. But the whole time he's around me, all I'm going to be thinking about is how much he actually saw.

Lifting my dress, I inspect that part of myself. It's just as bad as expected. The strawberry blonde curls of female mockery have got to go.

Foregoing the reason Lachlan deposited me on the toilet to begin with; I grab my wheelchair, heft myself into it with a bit of difficulty, and set about my exploration of the bathroom. Inside cupboards, drawers, and under the sink, I search for a shaver. I don't care if I have to dry shave with a little bit of water, this hair's going bye-bye.

Ah, found it. A new, disposable razor in one of the many colorful tubs of girl crap under Bridget's sink. Generally, when I shave this part of myself, I sit on the edge of the tub; it's easier to rinse that way. And, that is exactly what I'm going to do, if I can manage to sit outside the tub without getting my hands or leg wet. Strict orders from my doctor and nurses, *'don't get your casts wet'*. I won't.

Shucking back the tropical shower curtain and stuffing my phone between my breasts, I set my wheelchair brakes and maneuver myself to the edge of the tub. If my doctors saw me now, I'm sure they'd be screaming for me to stop. But I need to clean myself, and I need to get this done and out of the way or I'm going to keep obsessing over it.

Casted leg out straight, other bent for balance, my bare butt sits on the ledge of the white porcelain tub. It's freezing, and I shiver as goosebumps fly down my legs.

Pooling my dress around my waist, most of it draped behind me, I make use of the coconut body wash and add a tiny drop to my mound. I get a little water from the faucet on the tips of my fingers, and I massage it into my parts, through my cleft, and all around, getting a tiny lather. It's not the best, but it's better than nothing.

Quickly, I run the shaver through the fine hair and rinse it in the tub between passes. It doesn't take long to complete. Just when I'm about done, the door cracks open. Panic fires through me, and I seize my dress, shoving it back over my lady bits. Lachlan's head pokes around the corner, spotting me, and his brows pinch together, eyes narrowing.

"What the hell are ye doin'?" he scolds.

I lift the pink *Bic* to show him as my eyes lock on his.

"Ye shaved down there?" He jerks a nod to where my hand is clutching the base of my dress.

I bob my head in reply.

"Are ye shittin' me?" he bites off.

Frowning, I shake my head. Why would I lie about shaving? That's stupid.

"Ye doin' that because of earlier?" He wades further into the bathroom, dragging my chair away. The wheels don't move because they're locked in place, so a loud screech echoes in the room as they skid across the tile. I wince at the noise.

Lachlan moves to stand in front of me, towering far above, shaking his tilted head, lips tight. His teal eyes are on fire.

"Why would ye do that? Women dinnae need tae shave down there." He gestures with his eyes to my parts.

Is he kidding me? Don't all men expect that? Not that I care what he expects. He's a married man, after all. But I do care how I feel. I like to be clean down there, and shaving is just something I've always done. Even us backwoods country girls can shave, too. I enjoy the feeling, and it's not like I shave everything. Not that you really care to know that as you're sitting here with us, listening to this whole thing play out. You're probably shaking your head, wondering why in the hell you're here listening in the first place. I don't know either. But I have to tell you, the support means a lot. Because this giant man's scary as hell, and his breathing is growing heavier, sucking all the oxygen from the room, making it hard to breathe.

Meeting Lachlan's eyes, I give him a look like he's lost his mind, and mouth *'what?'* praying he'll be able to read my lips.

"Ye think I haven't seen a pussy before? Ye think I'd care if I saw yers? Ye seen one, ye've seen 'em all, lassie. Dinnae know why ye had tae go puttin' yourself in harm's way just tae shave it off. Women are supposed tae have hair down there."

He's not done. "And if ye remember, I've gotta wee daughter. And seein' yers ain't any different than seein' hers. So quit yer worryin'." He finishes with a long exhale.

Ouch! That stung a little. No different than if he'd seen his daughter's? I realize I'm not much to look at. But come on; that was still harsh. My heart concurs as it begins to ache behind my ribs.

Shoving those terrible feelings to the side, I place him and his notions about women shaving on ignore. And I point, with the shaver still in hand, to the shelf that holds the towels and washcloths. Lachlan swings his head to where I'm aiming and then back to me.

"Ye want a towel?" he queries.

I shake my head.

He tries again. "A wash rag?"

I nod once, and he quickly retrieves one for me.

Mouthing a quick '*thank you*', I lay the shaver on the lip of the tub and lean back to dampen the washcloth in the trickle of water coming from the faucet. I use it to wash off the tips of my fingers before I drape it over the edge of the tub and pull my phone from my dress.

I have three missed texts from him.

What're ya doing in there?
Why aren't you done yet?
What's all that noise?

I disregard those and send my own.

Regardless of your feelings on the matter of shaving, I do need to finish and clean up. And I can't very well do that with you in here. So, if you'd please leave, I'd appreciate it.

I'm trying to be polite. He's not intentionally being a jerk right now, so there's no reason to sass him in return; even if I do kinda want to.

Lachlan slips his cell from his pocket and reads it, then he speaks. "Aye, I'll leave ye be. But when ye're finished, let me know and I'll come back in tae help ya into yer chair."

Fair enough.

Calmly nodding my reply, I mouth, *'okay.'*

Lachlan dismisses himself, shutting the door in his wake, and I get back to work. I could use a little privacy now. I'm all socialized out. See ya on the flip side.

Later.

CHAPTER 9

How much more food are you going to feed me? I'm stuffed already.

Through text, I'm whining at Lachlan as I melodramatically rub my distended stomach, pretending I'm about to explode. Because I feel like I might actually do that. I ate way too much tonight.

Lachlan's sitting beside me on the couch right now. A little too close for comfort, but I'm trying not to notice, or dwell on the fact that he smells ridiculously good. Like soap and spice and garlic.

Sideways glancing at me, he shakes his head in amusement and snorts. "Yer the one who had the second helpin' of cheesecake, and I was only offerin' popcorn," he teases, bumping shoulders with me.

An electric current shocks my system, and my breath falters. He can't be touching me. It's one thing if he's doing it mechanically just to get something done. That, I can sort of withstand. But at this moment he's doing it to be silly. And a silly Lachlan is a whole different side of him that I don't know if I can swallow; it's too much.

Across the room, the TV plays some sort of nighttime movie. One I've never seen before. Not that I've seen many. The sun has slipped below the horizon, leaving a beautiful afterglow as the moon hangs in the star speckled sky. I watch it through the uncovered window. Mother Earth sure puts on an even more peaceful and miraculous show than anything the TV could play. Pirate must agree because he's lying in front of the sliding glass door, his nose pressed against the pane. I grin slightly as I watch him. He's probably waiting for the moths and lightning bugs to appear so he can chase them with his eye. If I was a dog, that's what I'd do.

Not wanting to be rude, I flick my eyes back to my lap and text Lachlan.

Cheesecake is delicious, and you had three helpings of it. More than me, buster.

Snuggling deeper into the couch, my propped up legs slide further down the coffee table as I try to get comfortable. It doesn't work very well, but I make do.

The phone resting on my stomach vibrates.

I didn't have three helpings. I had one.

One, my butt. He's full of it.

See, that's exactly how today's gone. I can never tell whether Lachlan's going to text me a reply, or say it aloud. It definitely keeps me guessing. And I'm not gonna lie; I do look forward to those times when he speaks to me instead. His accent's incredible.

After the bathroom shaving incident earlier today, I'd texted Lachlan and he returned to help me into my wheelchair. Then we set about eating lunch together. He traipsed upstairs to grab some sandwich fix-ins, and we had ourselves a smorgasbord of deli sandwiches with big juicy slices of tomatoes, real mayonnaise, and that delicious sourdough bread that you buy in the bakery section of the supermarket. I was in heaven as we munched our sandwiches and kettle cooked potato chips in companionable silence at the bistro table in the kitchen.

Licking the last bit of mayo off my finger, I'd pushed my plate to the side and took a gulp of lemonade.

"Ye done?" Lachlan asked, pointing to my empty plate.

A soft smile curled at the edge of my lips as I nodded. He snatched it up, took it to the sink, and rinsed it off before slipping it into the compact dishwasher under the counter.

Afterward, I'd wheeled myself to the bathroom, used the facilities, and spent the next hour sponge bathing myself in front of the sink. I cleansed every part, aside from my hair, which I used dry shampoo on. That's a product Bridget showed me yesterday. I'd never heard of the stuff before that. It smelled good and seemed to help. Although, my curls are still wild and crazy if I don't tame them with a bit of water and TLC. I'd also slipped that blue dress on, throwing the yellow one in the hamper; and retied my hair into a low ponytail at the base of my neck.

The rest of my afternoon was spent back outside on the lounger, sipping lemonade next to Lachlan. This time, I remembered to wear panties.

Around dinner, Lachlan vacated his seat as Pirate stayed with me, sprawled out on the patio at my feet. It didn't take long for the smell of spaghetti to begin wafting through a crack in the backdoor, followed by the mouthwatering scent of garlic bread as Lachlan prepared our meal.

Once finished, he'd wandered back outside with a blue dishrag slung over his shoulder, and scooped me off my lounger without permission. Sitting me in my chair, he wheeled me back into the house with one hand oddly cuffed over my shoulder. It made that feeling reappear in the pit of my stomach. Again, I tried to disregard it.

At the bistro table, yet again, we sat and ate in silence. This time over a hearty plate of spaghetti with meat sauce, garlic bread, and a fresh green salad that had more of those juicy tomatoes diced in. It was dressed with a light vinaigrette.

For dessert, we had store-bought cheesecake. As if dinner wasn't already amazing enough, adding thick slices of moist, decadent cheesecake to it tipped the scales to mind-blowing. I had two slices, and Lachlan, as he so eloquently put it, had *one* helping of *three* hardy slices. Not that he wants to admit that. But the man can sure eat. And looking at me, you'd know I enjoy a comforting meal or two. Hey, what can I say? I'm not hard to please.

Bumping shoulders once more, Lachlan steals me from my thoughts. "Ye ever watched this movie before?" He thumb points to the flat screen TV mounted on the wall above a stone-faced fireplace. It's not a real one. The fireplace, that is. It's one of those electric ones with flame and heat settings that you can adjust. It's burning right now, except it's not emanating any warmth. Lachlan switched it on before we sat down.

My eyes focus on the flat screen where some guy is hopping on a motorcycle and a woman is jumping on behind him. They're in some sort of high-speed chase.

Turning to Lachlan, I shake my head.

"What's ye favorite movie?"

I'm not sure if it's out of politeness or genuine interest that he's asking. I decide not to ponder that much and go back to using my phone. It's grown on me today. It gave me the ability to communicate without feeling like a fool. Not having a voice for this long has left me feeling incomplete. You don't realize how much you use it until it's not there, and you're forced to use alternative methods of communication. The phone is a godsend. I'd be carrying around a pad of paper without it.

Never watched this movie, and I don't have a favorite.

You don't have a favorite movie? he clarifies.

Nope.

How's that possible?

I'm not trying to delve into the whys, so I change the subject, moving the spotlight away from me.

What's yours? I type.

Don't have one.

Is he messing with me? He asks mine, and now he doesn't have one. Maybe he was trying to engage in small talk. Or in this case, small text.

Seriously? I probe.

Aye.

Maybe I shouldn't type this, but I do, anyhow. *What do you do besides work at the fire department and sit outside drinking lemonade?*

Today, I've come to the conclusion that Lachlan's favorite drink is lemonade. He sucks it down like an addict. Bet he'd have an IV of it tapped into his vein if he could. He seems to love it that much.

Workout. Spend time with the boys at the clubhouse. Ride. Not home much.

Likes to keep busy. That's admirable. I do, too. Can't help but wonder how Meredith and Bridget fit into that schedule, though. But I'm not gonna ask. It's none of my business.

Instead, I inquire: *Is that what you were doing in the barn this morning?*

Workin' out?

Yes.

Aye. I got a gym membership in town at Thor's, too. Mix it up sometimes.

Thor's? I question.

He's got a wee gym in the middle of Carolina Rose. Street over from the firehouse, two stores down from Whisky's, and across from Casanova's Car Repair.

Interesting...

Sounds like Lachlan knows a lot of people. I mention that much as we lapse into a short texting conversation about nothing much.

It doesn't take long for me to stifle a yawn, and the TV movie to roll the credits. Covering my mouth for the third yawn in a row, I feel a set of warm fingers dust over the bridge of my shoulders and cuff around my bicep on the other side. It startles me enough to gasp and jerk my head to the side to see what the heck Lachlan's up to. I don't get a chance to ponder that thought when he proceeds to tug me toward him in a downward motion.

"Rest yer head, lass," he breathes.

Without putting up any resistance, Lachlan tips my head into his lap and helps me onto my back with both of my ankles resting on the arm of the couch. The heat of his short clad thighs burns the back of my head, searing its memory there.

Unable to spare a glance at him in fear of embarrassment, or possibly something else, my eyes remain closed as I feel him fan my ponytail over his lap. A finger snaps my elastic band in two, unleashing my wild curls. I want to scold him for doing that, but that inclination quickly fades when ten thick fingers begin combing through my locks. I stifle a moan. It feels sooo damn good.

"Ye should keep yer hair down, Mags," Lachlan whispers on a throaty groan.

I shiver at the sound, my nipples turning to sharp pebbles in my dress. In succession, an even deeper groan emanates from his chest. I bet he sees them poking out. I'm not sure if he's disgusted, or being a guy and perhaps enjoying the show. I can't pinpoint which I want him to feel. But after his comments about my vagina being no different than his daughters and that he's married, I'd say he probably finds them an annoying occurrence. Although, if I'm honest with you and myself, I do kind of wish he thought they were pretty or something remotely like that.

I'm being stupid, aren't I? Of course, I am. Why do I even care? That's right; it's because I'm a loser who hasn't had any attentive male affection like this in years. It's my own fault, though. I know that. I try to keep all men at an arm's length, except Lachlan because he's safe. For one, he's married. Secondly, he's just being nice. That's something he does. Thirdly, he's shown zero interest in finding me attractive, aside from telling me I should keep my hair down. And finally, if all those things didn't compute—yet, again, he's married. A wife plundering, bending her over the kitchen counter to have his way with her, kind of married. Or that's what I'm insinuating, anyhow. Seems pretty spot on if ya ask me.

Shuffling below me, Lachlan gets more comfortable as his fingers continue their delicious assault on my hair, forcing this hungering ache in my gut to ease. The tips of his rough fingers move higher, tracing the edge of my forehead. Oh. So. Good.

My brain turns to sated mush as dreamland beckons me. The last thing to register is a quiet rumble in my ear as my head is curled closer to Lachlan's warm abs, brushing the cotton of his t-shirt. Spicy cologne and those marvelous fingers drug me, making the world feel lighter. Soon, my body melts into the soft cushions of the couch, and the world gradually breaks away.

"G'nite," he whispers softly.

Night, night, Lachlan.

CHAPTER 10

Throwing my head back into the cushion of my lounger, I shake in silent laughter—I can't believe he just said that!

Last night, I fell asleep on Lachlan's lap. Nothing happened, I swear. It was entirely innocent. This morning, rays of sun had me waking up, tucked away in my bed, with Pirate curled up on the pillow beside me; his wet nose poking my temple.

Using the bar above my bed, I swung my legs off the mattress and rose to a surprise. There, on my nightstand, sat a single daisy in a water glass, my cell phone, and a note scribbled on a sheet of ripped notebook paper.

Bridget's in bed. I'm at work. Be good. Made ya lunch. It's in the fridge.

My heart went a little wonky at the sight, but I dismissed that immediately. Sliding into my wheelchair, I snatched up my cell phone and got on with my morning rituals.

About an hour ago, I was sitting in the living room, minding my own business when there was a knock on the sliding glass door. I wheeled myself to it, and peeled back the edge of the curtain. Standing on the welcome mat was a pair of scuffed, black leather boots, and inside those boots was a man. It took me a long moment to register who I was looking at through the frontal view of tight jeans, thick leather belt; further up, a crisp white t-shirt was tucked proudly under a leather vest or *cut*, as Bridget had previously explained it to me.

A deep, cumbersome laugh had me tipping my head back to meet the man's eyes. It was Thor, and he was smiling that same megawatt smile; his blond hair now tied back in a low man-bun. A white sack was gripped in his hand. "Ya gonna let me in, beautiful?" He winked flirtatiously through the glass. I went shy immediately, and shrugged my shoulders, nibbling the corner of my lip.

He tried again, more politely this time. "May I please come inside, Magdalene?" His voice was soft and sweet—less playful. I liked it. I liked it a lot.

No one had told me Thor was coming over. But, I guessed it was safe enough to unlock the door and let him in, since he's part of the same motorcycle club as Lachlan. So I did just that; flipped the latch and he let himself inside.

Wheeling myself backward, I allowed him to pass. "I like your dress. It's nice," he complimented before rounding my chair and making himself right at home on the sofa. Tossing the white bag on the coffee table, he then stretched his arms across the back of the couch.

"Pip sleepin'?" he asked, kicking his boot up and resting it on his knee.

Thanks to having spent time with Lachlan, I was a little less uncomfortable with such a larger-than-life biker sitting in the living room, as I sat in my wheelchair, unable to speak. Lachlan with his dark and broody, intense thing is much more intimidating and harder to digest than Thor's light, carefree attitude. I envy Thor in that way. Just like Bridget, he never seems to stop smiling.

"Smoke's workin'?" he probed before I was able to answer the first question.

Curling my fingers into my lap, clutching my phone, I nodded tentatively.

"And Pip's in the bedroom, sleepin'?" he repeated his previous question, his eyes raptly assessing my face.

I contemplated whether or not to be honest, or not reply at all. All the attention he was giving me was making me shy; and, he was giving plenty. His eyes couldn't stop roaming my body, still dressed in the light blue outfit from yesterday. It matched well with the blue of my eyes. I guess I hadn't realized how much it did until his own started glittering with mischief like he wanted to see what was under everything. The sordid thought was plainly written across his naughty face as his lip curled suggestively, and his eyes zoned in on my heaving breasts. Shivering under his gaze, my nipples turned into sharp points, poking out of my cotton dress.

Thor languidly licked his lips. "Pip...sleepin'?" he drawled in a groan, and reached down to adjust something hard in his pants. My stomach dove to the floor in recollection. I knew what he was touching, and I couldn't remember the last time a man had to do that in my presence. It was both disconcerting and a little flattering, too; it made me feel like a teenager again. And mostly, I felt desirable—something I hadn't felt in a very long time.

It was that moment in time, when I couldn't decide if Thor was going to try to throw me down on the couch and ravish me or not, that Bridget chose to make her sleepy appearance, bursting the sweltering bubble Thor had sucked us into. I was beyond grateful for her abrupt entry, and visually sighed with relief, wiping my brow.

Clearly, I was getting too swept away in Thor and the indecent looks he was giving. There was no doubt about it; he found me attractive. And I liked that. I liked that a lot. Not because he's handsome in a surfer-boy, Norse-God kind of way. But because he'd reignited something dormant deep within me. Instead of being self-conscious about my thick curves, they felt womanly and beautiful in his presence.

Listen, I get how crazy that sounds, but that's how it felt.

Bridget shuffled to the kitchen and pulled a bottle of water from the fridge. When she turned around, she screamed, "Oh!" as her hand flew to her chest and her wide eyes flicked back and forth between Thor and me. Stopping, her eyes zeroed in on Thor, who was more engrossed in watching me, paying her no mind.

"Thor, what're you doing here? Dad hadn't mentioned you stopping by while he was at work." There was definitely some tension weaved through her words.

Thor casually leaned his head to the side, smiling at Bridget. "Oh, hey, Pip," he coolly greeted like he hadn't noticed she was standing there in the first place. "I figured I'd keep Magdalene company while he worked a shift."

"Oh, how nice of you." Sarcasm dripped from her every word. I was getting uncomfortable as I began questioning if maybe I shouldn't have let Thor inside, and maybe should have asked permission first.

Bridget's lovely teal eyes frowned at Thor for a fleeting moment before she diverted her gaze to me and smiled genuinely. "Mornin' Magdalene. Sorry I missed ya yesterday. Whisky's was slammed with cupcake orders for a wedding this weekend, and the club's cookout on Sunday. I tried to leave in time to come home and have dinner with you and Dad. But—"

Her words were cut short when Thor interrupted, "You ate alone with Smoke last night?" Swinging his eyes to me, his brow peaked in question.

Unable to communicate with him other than using signals, I did what I've been doing since I woke up in the hospital. I nodded, meekly.

Thor's face blanched before transforming into a scowl. "What'd he make ya?" His snarky change in attitude wasn't lost on me. Since I'd normally refuse to reply to that, I decided to ignore him and stare at my hands instead, pretending he didn't exist. Hoping for it.

What did it matter what Lachlan made me? We had an enjoyable evening. One that didn't include him eyeing my body like a piece of meat. Not that I would have minded. Okay, I would have minded; Lachlan's eyes affect me differently than Thor's. Don't know how or why, but they do.

"Thor?" Bridget's chastising words cut through the air like a knife.

"Huh?" he grumbled.

I couldn't bear glancing up, so I picked at my nails as Bridget laid down the law. "You said you're here to see Magdalene. So why don't you spend time with her, without making her uncomfortable, like you're doin' right now? Let the stuff in your head stop, right here, right now. She doesn't need to get dragged into somethin' she has nothing to do with," she demanded in that sweet, no-nonsense tone.

"All…right," Thor conceded, like a dog who had been scolded and told to go lie down.

And thusly, the rest of my day began. Bridget left us to change out of her pajamas and into a pair of jean shorts and a tank top. Which made me insanely envious, because I'm dying to wear anything other than a dress.

Thor dispersed the giant doughnuts he'd brought us in the white paper bag, and we ate them in the living room before retiring to the patio. Which is where we currently are.

Bridget's seated next to me on her father's lounger, and Thor is sitting in a chair that he's pulled up, closer to me. Not that I need him that close. But it doesn't bother me much either. My heart hasn't leapt once. Maybe I'm not experiencing much change after all. It's kind of relieving, to be honest. I was worried for a while since I've been constantly flustered around Lachlan. With Thor, I feel my sense of normal. It's nice to feel that way. Maybe I'm back to my usual self. Sure, I felt a little excitement when Thor was looking at me like he wanted to eat me for dinner. But, that was my normal excitement; it was the kind I felt with most the men I dated. Level, disconnected, desired, but my heart wasn't in it. I prefer to live my life that way. It's easier, and a lot less painful that way. You don't understand how wonderful it feels to get that back.

Moments ago, all of us just finished busting a gut about this ridiculous story Thor told us about Lachlan at the gym. Essentially, he'd walked into the women's locker room on accident, and finally realized where he was after he'd already undressed and was headed to the showers in some boxers. From the way Thor explained it, Lachlan ran out of there, forgetting all of his clothes in the process. Thor had to be the one to retrieve them and deliver them back to Lachlan in the men's locker room; where he sat in a bathroom stall, waiting for clothes so he could leave. It was pretty funny. Considering the fact that I could never picture big, badass Lachlan running from a women's locker room like that.

Calming her laughter, Bridget asks, "Did he seriously try to outrun Sniper on the treadmill, too?"

Thor grins slyly, and bobs his head in confirmation. "Oh, yeah, that boy did. He was cussin' up a storm, callin' Sniper a bloody cheatin' arsehole."

Thor trying to mimic Lachlan's accent has me silently chuckling to myself. Out of politeness, I cover my mouth with my hand.

Thor continues. "I dunno how he thought he was ever gonna outrun, Sniper. Man's got legs for miles, and he's what? A buck fifty soakin' wet?"

Don't know what Sniper looks like, but I do know Lachlan has to have at least a good hundred pounds on him. If that is, in fact, what Sniper weighs.

Bridget nudges my arm and slides her phone in front of my face. I stare down at the picture on her screen. "That..." she points to a man standing next to her dad in the photo. This man's taller than Lachlan by maybe two inches. He's lean with jet-black, military style hair, flawless coppery-brown skin, coal-black eyes, and sharp cheekbones. He's beautiful, like an authentic Native American. "That's Sniper," she finishes.

Just like Thor said, Sniper did have legs for miles.

"Sniper can run ten miles without running outta breath or breakin' a sweat," Thor enlightens smugly. "Smoke's a terrible runner. All that bulk's gone to his biceps, not his brain. He was like a cow cloppin' on that treadmill," he chortles, thinking he's hilarious.

I don't find his concealed jab humorous in the least bit.

Not able to hide my annoyance, my lips tip into a frown. Calling Lachlan a cow is outright rude, and demeaning. I think he might have insinuated he's fat, too. Not that I have anything against cows; they're beautiful creatures. I drink their milk, and their meat is delicious. But comparing Lachlan to one steams my broccoli, and not in a good way. You're not supposed to talk about your friends like that.

"Oh, hey." Thor's hand shoots out to rub my shoulder. I'm half tempted to shrug it off out of spite. But I don't. "Hey," he whispers, squeezing my shoulder tenderly.

Reluctantly, I tilt my head to meet his eyes.

Thor smiles, timidly. "You went icy all of a sudden. You okay?" He seems genuinely concerned.

Indecisively, I lift my shoulders and drop them in a leaded shrug. The phone in my lap vibrates, and I raise it to read the incoming message. It's Bridget.

Thor calling dad a cow make you mad?

Yes, I reply honestly.

Me, too. Don't let it get you upset. Thor and Dad have a strained friendship. Remind me to tell you about it later. Kay?

Kay. I click send, nodding at my screen in agreement.

Just as I begin to contemplate how Thor and Lachlan's friendship could be strained, and why it became that way, Thor disturbs my thoughts.

"Whatcha got there?" He points to my phone, resting his feet on the edge of my lounger.

Since I can't speak, Bridget graciously explains for me. "Dad was worried about Magdalene being home alone when he was working. He wanted her to feel safe, so he bought it for her," she states proudly, somehow leveling the playing field once more after Thor's impolite remarks.

He seems unaffected by her tone when he nods to the phone in my hand. "It's got daisies on it," he observes, his nose crinkling in deep thought.

I nod, because he's right; it does have daisies on it. Pretty obvious. *Duh.*

"You like daisies?" he tests, like he's digging to find something, though I'm not sure what.

Even if I didn't like daisies, I'd tell him I do, just so he'd stop looking at my phone and the case like it has magical powers. It's just a phone, a nice one.

To put his mind at ease, I deliberately nod my head multiple times, allowing it to sink in.

Daisies have always been my favorite flower; ever since I was a little girl, picking them from my grams's flower garden. By the time I was a teenager, they'd taken on a life of their own, sprouting up all over my grams's yard. I suspect she secretly planted them herself just because she knew how much they made me smile. Guess I'll never know now, will I? But the memory of vases overflowing with daisies will be forever imprinted in my mind.

"You want to put my number in there?" Thor jerks his chin at my cell. He's testing the waters, obviously. I suppose it can't hurt to have his number, too. Another brilliant smile explodes from his mouth as he takes my phone and brushes his fingers across the back of my hand before plugging in his number and returning it to me.

"Text me real quick so I have your number, too?" he proposes.

I know what game he's playing. But he's a decent guy, so I figure 'why the heck not' and shoot him a text —*Hi.*

Fleetingly, I'm rewarded with another one of those pearly white smiles. "You comin' to the club grill-out on Sunday?" Thor asks, his eyes casting downward, thumbs tapping his screen.

I'd heard the grill, party-thingy mentioned in passing, but I wasn't invited so that would be a no. Even if I were, I still wouldn't attend. Meeting an entire lot of bikers and their families in my condition is not something I want to engage in; especially after only knowing Lachlan and Bridget for such a short time. Let's not forget the fact that I'm socially inept, and not even remotely a biker. I don't think I could handle the awkwardness of being on their turf. Is that what they call it? I don't know. Maybe I'm just thinking too much.

Putting my phone to good use, I text my reply to Thor instead of shaking my head.

No, I'm not.

To save face, I'm not going to admit that nobody actually invited me.

Thor replies, *How come? I can swing by in my truck and pick ya up before I head. You can be my plus one. And it'll give ya a chance to see my grandma again. She's gonna be there, too.*

Not to sound rude, because his grandma seems decent and all, but the woman's kinda scary. I'm not sure I want to have a sit down with her, even if she thinks I saved her life. I don't believe I did at all. I did what any decent person would do, and tried to protect a little old lady from getting severely injured. It's commonsense, the way I see it, and I don't need to be thanked for it, or have it paraded around. I'm just happy knowing that she's alive and well.

Just as I start typing my reply to Thor, an incoming text pops up and I dismiss it to continue typing his.

Thanks, but no thanks. I think I'll stay here. Got a big week, next week.

It is sort of true. Next Thursday, I'm due to have my arm casts removed, and arm braces will take their place. This'll allow my wrists mobility and make it possible to start physical therapy the following week. All of those things I'm highly looking forward to. It'll be one step further to getting out of here, and on with my life. No longer stuck in another one horse town—the very thing I'm trying to escape from.

Fishing through my messages, I check the previous one I had received. It's from Lachlan. Does is sound ridiculous that I'm a teensy bit giddy knowing he texted me from work? It does, doesn't it? God, I'm pathetic. And apparently, a mental home-wrecker, too. Well, not exactly. Damn, I don't know. Ignore my cuckoo thoughts and let's read this message together, shall we?

Ya up?

Yes, I reply.

Now, why do I feel so guilty texting him?

Ya sleep good?

Awe, now he's asking how I slept?

Yes.

The guilt's growing substantially heavier. Should I tell him about Thor? Why do I feel like I should tell him? I should, shouldn't I? It's his house.

Lachlan immediately responds. *Pip up?*

Yes. How are you?

Fine. Just got back from a call.

Oh, gosh, I forgot how dangerous his job can be. *Everyone okay?*

Aye. Minor accident. No major injuries. No fire.

I sigh, relieved, as I type then press send. *Glad to hear that nobody is hurt.*

"You just playin' with your phone or you talkin' to somebody?" Thor interjects, tearing me from my Lachlan world of concern.

Boldly, Bridget cuts in, "She's talkin' to *Dad*," she clips, emphasizing her last word. A certain petite redhead is steaming, her feisty attitude out in full force.

I sideways glance at her; she doesn't look happy at all. Her eyes are narrow, mouth tight, body tense. Turning my attention to Thor, he doesn't seem much better. A little less tense, but his face is just about the same.

"Ain't he supposed to be workin' and not textin' you?" Thor reproaches crassly. He's right; Lachlan's supposed to be working. However, I'm not his keeper and he's a grown man who can make his own grown-up decisions.

Lifting my shoulders in suspension, I drop them suddenly in an overstated shrug. I'm trying to make a point here. Thor seems to catch on when his expression turns sour. Making a disgruntled noise in his throat, he thrusts his phone aggressively into his jeans front pocket and shoves off his chair to stand.

Taking a step forward, he stops next to my patio lounger, and I peer up at him as he glances down at me. "I'm gonna head, but I'll be in touch." Leaning over, he presses a chaste kiss to my upturned forehead.

"Later, beautiful." Thor winks at me as he walks away and flashes me a faint disheartened grin. I wave goodbye just as he turns the corner and ambles up the incline. Listening, I catch an engine purr to life and rocks crunch under tire treads as he pulls away.

Um…What just happened? That was…um…awkward?

"What a fricken jerk!" Bridget hollers next to me, making me jump and snap to look at her, eyes sprung wide.

She barks a silly laugh and covers her mouth. "Sorry," she murmurs behind her dainty fingers. "But seriously," she drops her hands to her lap, "he only came here 'cause Dad's at work. Dad would kill him if he knew."

That last statement makes my eyes blast even wider. Now that's not something I expected her to say. More guilt floods my system, and I immediately text her a sincere apology to make things right. I knew this was all my fault.

I'm so so so sorry. I didn't know.

After I click send, my eyes guiltily stare at my lap, and Bridget wraps her petite, polished fingers around my bicep. Hesitantly, I peek her way. There's a soft, sentimental smile curling from the corners of her lips as her eyes search mine.

"Don't tell me you're sorry. There's nothing to apologize for." She gives my bicep a tiny squeeze and lets go, but retains eye contact. "I was textin' Thor while

Dad was messaging you. I didn't tell Dad about Thor bein' here. You can. But he woulda came home, and I'm sure there woulda been a fight."

Using my phone quickly, I punch a text to her.
A fight?!

Humorlessly, Bridget laughs. "Yes," she nods, "and Thor would have lost."

Bridget pauses for a moment, deep in thought, before she continues. "I'm gonna tell you something, but you have to promise not to tell my dad, or anyone that you know. *Especially* not my dad."

I cross my finger over my heart. Bridget nods her understanding of the gesture. It's a girl thing.

"When we first moved here, Dad joined my uncle Sniper's club. They didn't prospect him, which is what most motorcycle clubs do. You know what that means?"

Since I have no idea what that means, I shake my head.

"A prospect is a grunt they take on, and make do stuff to prove himself and his loyalty to the club before he'll be patched in as a full member," Bridget clarifies.

That makes sense.

"My dad didn't do that. Sniper and Dad have been friends since elementary school. Thor joined a couple months before Dad. Except, Thor had to prospect for an entire six months before he patched in."

So that's what made Thor mad? I text.

"Right." She nods, twisting in her chair to face me. I lean back and do the same, so we're face-to-face, before she keeps on. "Dad started going to the club parties by himself at first, 'cause Mom wanted nothing to do with this '*stupid boy stuff*'," she air quotes. "Those were her words, not mine."

I bob my head, letting her know I comprehend.

"But she's also a very jealous person." Bridget's eyes roll with that statement. I grin at the silliness. "From what Whisky's told me, my mom showed up to one of the parties, got drunk, and snuck away to make-out with Thor..."

I gasp with my hand covering my mouth.

"Good thing Whisky caught 'em before my dad did, or Thor woulda been a dead man. Apparently, my aunt smacked my mom around a bit and ordered Thor to leave. She had Casanova drive Mom home before she and Sniper sat my dad down to tell him what happened."

Meredith cheated on Lachlan?! *See! She is a bitch!* I knew it! Poor Lachlan.

Bridget's not finished. "The way Whisky explained it, 'cause Dad would never tell me any of this, was Thor 'apparently'," she air quotes again, "didn't know she was my dad's wife. So he just thought she was some club groupie who wanted a piece. Thor's used to getting pieces, if you know what I mean." She winks, and I shake my head in disbelief. Ridiculous.

"Thor apologized to Dad. And Dad was given a shot to kick the crap outta him, but wouldn't take it. Now, Thor and Dad's friendship has been sorta strained. They're club brothers and they get along, but my dad doesn't really like him, and I know Thor definitely doesn't like Dad."

All because your mother cheated on your dad, and your dad didn't prospect? I ask for clarification.

Bridget reads the message, then lifts her eyes to mine again. "More or less." She shrugs. "I think, but I don't know this for sure, that Thor's jealous of Dad. He's a decorated military veteran. He's ten years older than Thor, but he's Scottish, so his muscles and build are massive. Dunno what Dad's told ya, but Thor owns a gym in town, and it doesn't look good when a man my dad's age has a better body than the younger gym owner. In a bigger city, maybe nobody'd notice or care, but in Carolina Rose, everyone knows everyone, and gossip's worth more than gold."

I know that small town rule quite well. Everyone knows everything. It's sweet in some senses, but privacy robbing in others. I also get what Bridget means about the jealousy; she could be right. Though, I don't really think that Thor could be jealous of Lachlan if he's getting lots of *pieces*, as Bridget explained. Lachlan doesn't seem to be the cheating kind, but I don't know him well enough, I suppose. Thor…he does seem like a smooth operator, and Meredith messing around with him is pretty sick if you ask me. Whether you like your husband or not, you don't make out with some random dude you don't even know. I don't care if you're drunk or not; that's just a lame excuse. And I really have to stop thinking about this before I get even more worked up. My heart rate is rising.

I'm saved by my phone as it vibrates, stealing me from reeling thoughts. Most of them not so nice. Most of them centered about Whisky telling Bridget things about her parents that she probably shouldn't have told her; which kinda ticks me off, too. The other part is me trying not to picture Thor with his pretty blond head smashed under the heel of my boot for being such a jerk. At this point, I'm so stinkin' upset that I'm tempted to delete his number from my phone and never speak to him again, just because I can. Guess I can contemplate that later and check my phone instead.

Good grief, I don't have one message. I've been so caught up with Bridget that I have five—all from Lachlan.

Me, too, is his first text. Which coincides with me telling him that I was happy to hear nobody got injured. The next follow in succession:

You there?

What are you wee lassies gonna do today?

Why am I not gettin' a reply?

Need me to come home? If I don't hear from ya in the next hour, I'm coming home.

The last one was sent a minute ago.

Making haste, I tap out a response to calm his concern.

Not doing much today. Outside on the loungers talking. You don't have to come home.

Bloody hell, don't make me wait that long again. What'd ya both eat for breakfast? You did eat, didn't you?

Doughnuts, I reply.

How'd ya get those? We don't have any in the house.

Slamming my eyes shut, I shake my head and pinch the bridge of my nose. I'm so stupid. I shouldn't have said that, but I can't lie either. What am I doing?! Gah.

Reopening my eyes, I take a gander over at Bridget, who's smiling as happy as can be while playing on her phone. With a deep, resigned sigh, I relinquish control and bite the proverbial bullet before self-loathing and guilt starts to take its toll.

Here goes nothing.

Thor came by today, and he brought Bridget and me some doughnuts.

I tap send, and my thumbnail instantaneously goes to my mouth. I nibble on it, fearful of his reaction. The phone clutched in my hand buzzes with an incoming message. Peeking at it, I swallow thickly.

Thor, you say?

Yes. He dropped by, and without thinking, I let him inside. I'm sorry. I probably should have asked first.

Mags, you don't have to ask permission. It's your home, too. Is he still there?

Mags...Just seeing the name he started calling me makes me...oh...I dunno...but it's a good feeling. A very good one. I'm just going to skip over the *home* part before my stomach starts doing cartwheels and I throw up.

He left already. Didn't stay long.

Did he ask you to the clubhouse on Sunday?

Yes. But I told him no thanks.

Do you wanna go? I was gonna ask, but I didn't want to push. I know you've had a lot to deal with since your accident.

Was he really going to ask me? Or is he just trying to be nice? He doesn't seem like a bull-shitter, but I've been wrong before. Too much thinking. I've got to stop this before I over analyze this too dang much. My grams always said it's a female thing, but I've never had a close female friend in my entire life, so I can't say I know if that's true or not.

I'd rather stay here, if that's okay, I respond.

Sure. If that's what ya wanna do.

It is.

Fuck, we gotta another call. I'll be in touch. Don't forget to eat your sandwich for lunch. Tell Pip I'll text her later. Be safe.

You, too.

Setting my phone in my lap, I stare out into the peaceful yard and send a small prayer to heaven, asking God and my grams to keep Lachlan and his crew safe.

Amen.

CHAPTER 11

Lachlan

Straddlin' the table bench, my arse, cock, and balls rest bare on the cold, damp wood as my kilt drapes over my thighs. Aye, I know I should probably tuck it, but it's bloody hot out here and it feels damn good. My black ridin' boots rest on the grass as I scuff my toe into the turf, diggin' up dirt due tae boredom. Pip and I arrived at the clubs cookout aboot an hour ago. She's been busy helpin' Whisky, my sister, with the food ever since. Pip had asked me yesterday if we could come early, even though I didnae want tae 'cause that meant I had tae leave Mags home by herself. Five times we asked her tae ride with Pip in the Tahoe, and five times, she told us na thank ye. Thought I was gonna stroke the bloody hell out when I rode my *Harley* here today without her in the truck that followed me in. Wanted tae throw her arse over my shoulder and make her come, but I didnae wanna scare her.

Scratchin' my chin with my palm, I growl lowly in my chest. Fuckin' hell! I knew I shoulda forced her tae ride with Pip. Now, I'm not gonna stop wonderin' what she's doin' or how she's doin'. I texted her when we arrived, and she's not replied back.

Yesterday, I got home after my shift at the firehouse and I was lookin' forward tae seein' Pip and Mags. Only

Mags didnae wanna see me. She spent the whole fuckin' day in her room or the bathroom. This mornin', when I went tae the barn tae let off some steam, I threw on my workout playlist, thinkin' it might make her come outside. Na, it didnae work; she ate breakfast with Pip in the kitchen, and I only got tae see her right before I rode out. I dunno what's wrong, but she's been actin' different ever since Thor came tae the house. Her texts have been shorter. Not that she's said much, anyway. I'm lucky tae get anythin' outta her. She won't share aboot herself, or how she's takin' this whole bloody mess. Most lassies wouldn't be so calm and collected as she is. The only time I get a rise outta her is when I'm in her space. I can tell she's either nervous or scared around me. I dunno why, though. And she's always holdin' her wee breath, and her eyes are always gettin' wide. It's cute tae watch.

The sound of boots approachin' has me lookin' over my shoulder tae see who's comin' my way. I chose this table, because it's the furthest from the clubhouse. Dinnae like tae socialize if I dinnae have tae. Club parties aren't my thing, but I come because it makes my sister, Sniper, and Pip happy. Too many bad memories from club parties in the past; now I avoid 'em if I can.

Casanova, the club's VP, raises his hand in silent greetin' and lifts his chin. I raise mine in return. Kickin' his boot up and over the bench, he pops a squat across the table from me, and I turn my body just enough tae make eye contact.

"What's up, bro? Didn't bring the new chick today? Just heard Whisky bitching about it with Pip. We all figured she'd be here," he says, pullin' a pack of *Marlboro*s from his chest pocket, tappin' the end, and slidin' one out before hangin' it from his bottom lip. Lightin' it with the flick of a match, he takes a long drag.

Figured my sister would wanna know if Mags was gonna be here. Wish she'd stop bein' so bloody fuckin' nosy and mind her own damn business. Let me handle this my way.

"Na. She didnae wanna come," I explain. Good thing aboot Cas is he's quick as a fuckin' whip, so it ain't too hard for him tae understand me when I'm talkin'. Nice tae have a brother, other than Sniper, who gets me right away.

Blowin' smoke outta the corner of his mouth, Cas grins as his grey eyes cast behind me, toward the clubhouse that Sniper built out of an old barn, that's connected tae an oversized garage. The barn itself has turned into a man's hangout spot for the brother's tae wrench on cars and fuck on straw bales, which reach the ceilin' at certain times of the year. On the other side, the garage was converted into a dive bar with a pool table, beer posters, and a sweet sound system. Right now, we're at the back of my sister and Sniper's property, behind the clubhouse. Sniper'd bought this shithole country house and land after he was medically discharged from the *Marine Corp* after only three years. A torn rotator cuff and nerve damage durin' a trainin' exercise gone wrong. He changed his tune and fixed this place up. Then, he decided that my sister was gonna warm his bed at night and he started the club. That was aboot twenty years ago.

Cas's grin grows till he's showin' teeth. Fuckin' hell, I know who he's gotta be smilin' at. I don't have tae wait long tae find out. Whisky purposely bumps into my shoulder from behind as she passes by, then hooks both her legs over the bench and takes a seat next tae me.

Restin' her elbows on the tabletop, she sideways glances my way after pleasantly greetin' Casanova. "What're you doin' sittin' out here while all the brothers sit their asses up there, drinkin' and havin' a jolly ol' time?" She nods her head back the way she just came. "Peanut even brought Rosie out on the bike with him today. You're bein' an asshole not socializing with your family," my sister, who's two fuckin' years younger than me, scolds with her fiery Scottish attitude.

Instead of arguin' with her, I grumble my response, and she cuts me a sharp glare, pursing her lips.

I dunno what she expects. I'm not gonna argue with her, 'cause that's what she wants. She likes tae argue. I do not. All these bloody fuckin' lasses and their need to bitch aboot somethin', yell aboot somethin', complain' aboot somethin'. I've lived with it for seventeen years, and I dinnae have the patience in me anymore. I know Whisky means well; she always does. That's why I love my sister, even if she's a stubborn arse. But I've got too much goin' on in my life right now. Addin' her shit ain't gonna help. Definitely not when I'm sittin' back here tae stay away from Thor, the fuckin' bastard who came tae my home tae see Mags without my permission. I'm afraid when I do see him, I'm gonna gut the grimy bastard. Far's I'm concerned, I shoulda done it a long ago.

Briefly shakin' her head in exasperation, Whisky's voice softens, "You're even more of a sullen sourpuss today than usual. What gives?"

I cannae lie tae my sister so I tell her the truth. "Mags didnae wanna come today," I growl. "She's at home, alone. And I know Thor's sittin' up there with Sniper by the grill. I canna be around him today."

I cross my arms over my chest and squeeze tae help take the ache away, even for a fuckin' minute. It's been constant for weeks. The more my adrenaline pumps and my mind thinks, the worse the feelin' becomes. I cannae describe it. But it fucks with my head and I cannae think straight. It's centered in my stomach and spreads into my chest—even my arms and legs get consumed by it if I don't squelch the intensity. Never felt it before in my life. It's like a cavernous, soul-burning heat, that I cannae put a name on.

"What'd Thor do now?" She tilts her head tae the side patiently waitin' for me tae answer.

"Thor dropped by the house the other day tae see Mags while I was workin'."

My lip curls in a snarl just thinkin' aboot those texts from Mags apologizin' for Thor's stupid arse. My first instinct was tae be pissed the fuck off, but I squashed that before I lashed out at the bonnie lass. Spent three hours in the firehouse gym that night workin' out my pent-up rage, and afterward, I jacked-off twice in the locker room shower. Nothin' worked.

Whisky's hand tenderly brushes my cheek, and I recoil, my instincts takin' hold. Before I can control the impulse, I've got her hand tightly clutched in my palm. Across the table, Cas makes a noise like he might do somethin'. But he dinnae, because I lock my emotions down before I hurt someone. My sister taps her freehand on the one I have wrapped around hers, and I let go with a rushed exhale. Peerin' at my hands, I stretch my fingers wide, kickin' myself in the arse for reacting that way. I've gotta get a fuckin' grip. All the brothers are here with their families. Now ain't the time tae act like some barbaric arsehole.

"You got all this anger, Lachlan. It ain't good. And you hidin' back here away from Thor ain't gonna settle anything. You gonna be a man and stand your ground?" Whisky tests.

Sneaky lass.

Snortin' somberly, I scowl at her. Casanova snorts, too, blowin' smoke our way. Except he finds this shit funny. It ain't. I'm tryin' tae keep this rage on lockdown and not get into a fight in front of those children, includin' my Pip. Nobody wants tae see that 'cause I'm dealin' with some unresolved bullshit.

Bloody fuckin' hell, I'm edgy today. My entire body's tight, buzzin' with adrenaline at the pace my manic heart races. Even my balls ache and my shoulders are hunched with tension. Jaw tickin'. Teeth grindin', tryin' tae calm the fuck down.

Closin' my eyes, I take a relaxing breath tae center myself. Reopenin' them, Whisky, with her wild ginger head is starin' right at me. I twist my face, givin' her a funny look, and she busts up laughin'. "Don't give me that, Lachlan. You can't hide your demons from everyone."

The hell I cannae. Done a bloody good job of it for years. Not gonna change that now.

"She's right," Cas puts in, jerkin' a nod tae Whisky, who puffs up her chest in victory. Playfully, I growl at her as Cas keeps on, "I get you don't wanna deal with Thor's childish bullshit. But, the man came to your house uninvited and you're the one back here hidin' out to avoid him. He should be the one avoidin' you, Smoke. Don't get me wrong, I like the man, but after that voting shit went down 'cause you two were about to throw down at Church, he shoulda known to back the fuck off. He's startin' this shit on purpose." He flicks a black strand of his unruly hair off his forehead and stands, stepping away from the table.

Aye, he's right.

"See you two later. I need a beer." Cas tips his imaginary hat tae us before he heads back toward the clubhouse where the music is blarin', and the scent of grilled food is floatin' through the midafternoon air. It smells damn delicious.

Whisky's quick tae follow in Casanova's tracks as she, too, pushes off the table. Stoppin' next tae me, she kisses the top of my head just like our mother used tae. My hand reaches out and wraps around her wee forearm, giving her a squeeze before she moves away. I know she's leavin' tae give me some space. I need it right now; almost as much as I need Mags tae message me back.

Pop Pop* Pop*

The roarin' fire crackles as it burns. Flames lick the timbres in the oversized fire pit. The brilliant orange-white glow softly illuminates faces as they sit around the fire on sawn logs bein' used as stools. I'm sittin' on one, my legs spread, kilt tucked between my thighs. Slantin', I rest my elbows on my knees, and my hands curl into fists. I use them tae prop my chin on. The coarse hair of my goatee grates into my knuckles—a welcomed distraction.

Keepin' my eyes cast frontward, I watch Banjo strummin' his banjo with his long, unkempt beard tucked into the front of his cut. Huckleberry Hound, another one of Corrupt Chaos' brothers is sittin' next tae him, singin' his heart out as he strums on a guitar. Never liked country music before I met the likes of these two. Now, it's startin' tae grow on me with each party they play at. They're damn good.

A wee hand slides over my shoulder from behind, and I dinnae have tae look tae know who it is; I'd know that pineapple scent anywhere—it's Pip.

"You eat enough?" she comments, takin' a seat on the log beside me.

Outta the corner of my eye, I watch her mimic my exact position. It warms my heart, and I smile on the inside. That's my sweet, sweet, lassie. She's made of all the best parts of her mother and me. But she's also a whole lotta Pip; her own unique brand of young vibrancy. I dunno how I lucked out gettin' a daughter like her. She's smart, caring, strong, and stays far away from that bloody teenage female drama. For that, I'm grateful as hell. I dunno how I'd handle her havin' meltdowns over boys, and gossipin' till her tongue fell off. Whisky's big mouth is enough tae deal with. I'm happy my wee bairn didnae get that trait from her aunt.

I jerk a sharp nod. "Aye."

Pip chuckles. "What's enough, Dad?" Like always, she's tryin' tae take care of me.

Earlier, I'd sat on the bench until I finally got a text from Mags tellin' me she was bloody all right. Afterward, I walked up tae join the family, doin' my best tae stay away from Thor, who's spent most of his time talkin' tae Muff, a younger brother who got his road name from lickin' pussy. My club brothers, their wives, or ol' ladies as some of 'em are called, all sat around and bullshitted with me for a bit. Most of 'em gettin' mad wi'it. I didnae, though. I only shared a six-pack of Kilt Lifter with my sister. We Scots got a much higher tolerance for alcohol. Not that my sister's much of a Scot, besides her looks. The lassie dinnae have an accent. At least I dinnae think so, but Pip thinks she does. Maybe a wee bit of one.

While we drank, we ate brats and hamburgers off the grill. My sister bought Sniper a new one for Christmas. He loves the fuckin' thing, and cooks on it anytime he can. I devoured three brats, a cheeseburger, Whisky's potato salad, eight of Rosie's deviled eggs, chips, and on top of all that: a handful of cookies from my sisters' bakery. I'd say I had enough. The food helped me concentrate on somethin' other than my tense shoulders and wanderin' thoughts.

"Enough, is what I ate," I tease my wee daughter, winkin' at her. Pip laughs again, shakin' her head and smilin'.

A round of applause and appreciative whistles cut through the still air as Banjo and Huckleberry Hound take a break.

"That he did. Enough food for five people." Good ol' Peanut drops beside me on another log, clappin' his hands for the brothers. "Looks like it might be time for me to take Rosie home," he notes as a set of bright headlights cast up my sister's long driveway, which can only mean one thing—groupies.

"Aye, looks like it's time for ye tae take her home. And," my head swings tae Pip, "for ye tae go inside, or drive home." I straighten, and lift my chin toward the back of the house.

Headlights shut down, and car doors open and slam shut. The babbling of excited females approach, and the brothers start their catcallin'. I grumble under my breath and turn back tae Pip, waitin' for her tae move. She knows if she comes tae these parties, she's gotta go inside when the women folk start tae show. I know she gets why they're here, but I'm not gonna let my daughter watch these women get mad wi'it, felt up, and fucked. She dinnae need that kinda influence. And I really dinnae need one of the brothers thinkin' she's fair game, too. They'd end with their throat slit from me, and a bullet tae the chest by Sniper. Nobody fucks with our lassies.

Pip kisses my cheek then makes haste, clamberin' up the back steps of my sister's house. I watch her walk in the backdoor, and close it behind her before I turn my attention tae the five women who just arrived and are splittin' off, findin' their prey. Peanut pats my shoulder as he gets off the stump with an aged groan. I lift my hand in goodbye, and he takes off tae gather up his wife, Rosie, who's the best damn cook and sweetest old lassie I've ever met. Peanut's a lucky lad tae have snatched that treasure up in high school.

"Lachlan!" a woman's voice shouts from across the yard. I lift my head tae find who's callin' my name. When I meet her eyes, another low, unhappy grumble rumbles in my chest—it's Carrie, the dispatcher.

Weavin' through the sawn logs, she sways her hips and plays with her hair as she heads my way. I dinnae have it in me tae deal with this fuckin' shit tonight. I wanna go home, but I know Whisky'll have my balls for leavin' early.

Bloody hell.

Carrie, in her short denim skirt and blue belly shirt, stops in front of me. I glance up.

"Hey, sexy," she purrs, layin' her palms on my shoulders.

The next thing I know, I've got a slutty dressed woman who smells like beer straddin' me, and tryin' tae grind her arse in my lap. She ain't my type. What'll it take for the lassie tae get the point?

Grabbin' her hips, I lift her off me and set her on the ground. She wobbles a bit, and I keep hold of her arm tae steady her.

"Come on, Lachlan; you're hot, I'm hot, and I know what's under that…" She bends over and tries tae lift my kilt. Glowerin', I pry it from her wee fingers before pushin' off my knees with my hands tae stand. My movement forces her tae stumble a few feet backward, and before I can reach her, she bumps into a log and trips; fallin' flat on her arse in the grass. A giggle bursts from her lips, and she throws her head back, hysterically laughin'.

"What the fuck, man?" Thor clips, comin' tae her aid and helpin' her off the ground.

I'm an arsehole, I know, but I didnae ask her tae sit in my lap and I'm not fuckin' interested. And most importantly, ye dinnae try tae lift a Scotsman's kilt. My body tenses at the thought.

"Hey! Smoke! I asked you, what…the…fuck?" Thor yells.

I pivot tae glare at him, and tuck my arms over my broad chest. This bastard better check his sissy boy attitude before I kick his fuckin' arse. I have na patience for his bloody shit today.

Thor tucks Carrie tae his side, his hand around her tiny waist. Kissin' her forehead, he makes sure she's good. "It's okay, baby. Smoke's just a jerk. I've got you." He sweet talks tae her, and I roll my eyes. He'll help her all right, all the way tae his bed. Then, he'll never talk tae her again.

Pressin' one more kiss tae her temple, he slices me a sharp glare. "I don't know what your problem is, but treatin' beautiful Carrie and Magdalene like shit ain't gonna get ya anywhere, brother."

I take a step closer, my jaw clenched. He did not just compare fuckin' Carrie tae Mags. Hell na! "Ye best not talk aboot, Mags," I threaten with a deep growl.

Thor slides his hand up tae cup Carrie's average breast over her shirt. On a soft moan, she melts further into him, gratin' her body tae his like a bitch in heat. Aye, definitely not like Mags.

"You worried I might get my hands on Magdalene's big fat tits just like this?" He pinches Carrie's firm nipple through her shirt as his other hand glides over her hip, and slips between her parted thighs. Pushin' her skirt up, he exposes that she's not wearin' anythin' underneath and her pussy's bare. "Afraid I'm gonna..." He glides a finger between her pussy lips, and I tear my eyes away, disgusted. "What? Can't look? 'Cause you're afraid I'm gonna have Magdalene just like this, grinding her sweet pussy on my hand, beggin' me to fuck her with my fat dick?"

Exhalin' a long, rage-fueled breath I crack my neck tae the side, and roll my shoulders loosenin' 'em up. Grindin' my teeth together, my jaw tickin', I squeeze my eyes shut and try tae get this gut twistin' need tae murder Thor outta my mind. I dinnae need tae go tae jail.

Red, bright red blood paints the backs of my lids as my mind slips backward, takin' me away from the present....

The rain was comin' down for hours, and we'd just finished our fifth call at the station. I was drivin' home in the Tahoe after workin' half a shift for one of my fellow firemen. My truck was runnin' low on gas, so I pulled into Miller's tae fill-up. Only, Miller's didnae look like Miller's anymore; the roofed had buckled and the windows were all but gone.

A classic car sat in front of the station, beat tae bloody hell. Without a second thought, I called in tae report possible injuries, slammed into park by the entrance, and shot outta my truck.

It was still pourin' rain when I traipsed up the steps, over shards of broken glass that grated under the heel of my boots as I opened the door. The local radio station still played over those damn speakers, even though the ceilin' had a giant hole through the middle. Most of the windows were shattered, shelves toppled over, food scattered everywhere. The stench of rain and mildew was nauseatin' as it hung in the air.

Then, I heard a soft groan.

Steppin' over the rubble, I called out, "Is anyone in here?"

Another groan replied.

Cuffin' my hands around my lips, I formed a megaphone with my palms. "Hello, is anyone there? I'm a fireman. I'm here tae help ye." I spoke slowly so the person groanin' could understand what I said.

"In the back," a woman rasped. "We're by the back."

Steppin' as lightly as I could, I trudged through the sodden debris, glass, and smashed food, pushin' shelves outta the way as I went tae clear a path.

"Where ye at?"

"We're trapped," the same woman responded.

Carefully, my eyes swept the store, lookin' for a body part, or anythin' tae show me where the lass was. It was dusk, and the rain kept fallin' in fat droplets through the ceiling, soakin' through my t-shirt and jeans. It was chilly, and I might have shivered if my adrenaline wasn't blazin' through me like a wildfire, forcin' me tae breakout in a cold sweat.

"Where's the other lass—woman?" I corrected, steppin' over a fallen beam.

"She's unconscious, lyin' on top of me. Please help us."

It broke my heart tae hear the desperation in her voice. I've seen people on fire, their flesh boilin', scarin' them for life. I've carried dead bodies from burnin' buildings, and pried people from cars. I've seen femurs snapped in two, pokin' out of torn flesh. Brains scattered across the highway. A baby killed from smoke inhalation. Men and women losin' an arm, a leg, a finger. I've suffered nightmares from it. It's haunted my dreams. Some may become numb tae the gore and the anguish, but I've soaked it in and embraced it, bearin' the burden of their pain, of their circumstance. It's one of the hardest damn jobs I could ever have, and the most rewardin'.

A wee hand poked out from under ceilin' tiles and I stopped walkin'. Sirens blared in the distance, mixed with the crackle of the thunder rolling overhead. "I'm gonna help ye," I soothed.

Pickin' up tile after tile, I tossed them tae the side. Another set of hands became visible, covered in dirt and rain. I bent down and touched one. It didnae move. I brushed another. It didnae move. Below those, I touched another, and it twitched. "Are ye Thor's grandma?" I asked, brushin' the wrinkled hand again.

"Smoke?" she sounded relieved.

"Aye."

"The storm, it came and trapped me and this broad under here. She's bleedin', and I can't move."

Shovin' more debris off the trapped lassies, I lightened the load piled on them and bent down, wrappin' my fingers around the unconscious woman's wrist tae check her pulse. It was faint. Releasin' her wrist, it went limp, and I started workin' faster tae free them. Immediately, I stopped when I saw a thick support beam laid crosswise on the woman, runnin' from her head, tae her neck, and down her back, tae her leg.

"A beam fell on her," I explained.

"I know. She tried to push it off us and screamed when she said somethin' stabbed her. That's when she started bleedin' and passed out." Her voice was muffled; even so, I could clearly make out each word.

Shufflin' my feet safely forward, as tae not step on any body parts, I bent down and brushed a wad of the lassie's strawberry blonde hair tae the side, exposin' her neck.

"Are ye hurt?" I kept talkin' tae Thor's grandma calmly, tae keep myself from doin' anythin' rash without assessin' the situation. I needed tae get the beam off the lass, and do it without hurtin' her any further. Yet, I

wasn't sure what kinda damage it had already caused. That's what worried me. There were long rusted nails and splinters of jagged wood pokin' out every which way.

"I'm not. But is it normal for someone to stop breathin' for about fifteen seconds at a time?"

Fuck!

"Twenty-three seconds," she corrected. "Twenty-four, twenty-five."

Bloody fuckin' hell! I didnae have time tae waste. Liftin' the massive beam off the lass, I grunted under strain, and I shoved it tae the side, exhalin' a rush of air. A string of curses flew from my mouth as blood shot like a rocket outta her neck. Quickly, I scooped her limp body off the floor and into my arms. Her warm, slick-blood bathed me, soakin' us both. Her lips were blue and her body boneless. She was dyin'.

Placin' my lips tae hers, I blew hard, fillin' her lungs with air. Yet, I was still unable tae give her CPR as I protectively held her in my arms. Blood seeped slowly through the back of her shirt onto my arm, as the geyser in her neck continued tae pulse. Without a second thought, I licked my blood coated finger tastin' the metallic tang of her blood. Once cleaned, I wiped it on the wet edge of my shirt before I carefully slid it into the soft, warm hole in her neck. She didnae move. I fished through the rushing blood as it tried tae force me out, and pressed on the punctured vein. Pluggin' it, I held steady, feelin' her pulse increase, thumpin' on the pad of my finger. By the grace of God, she inhaled a shallow, ragged breath, her lips regainin' a wee bit of color. Thank fuck! I sagged in immediate relief, watchin' her lungs wheeze air in and out unsteadily.

The sirens roared into the station's lot as I stood there in the middle of the store, holdin' the bonnie lass in my arms, rain pourin' down on us, washin' the blood from her face. I was afraid tae move her in fear of trippin' over debris or losin' the pressure on the wound. Instead of movin', I found myself in awe of her. My eyes traced the delicate lines of her face, down tae her long blonde eyelashes that fanned over the tops of her cheeks. Na longer on the brink of death, she appeared tae be sleepin' peacefully, serenely. A ghost of a smile graced my lips, watchin' a trace of color slowly return tae her pale cheeks. Her soaked body wrapped in my arms felt good—right. I pulled her tighter, her plush curves moldin' against the hardened plains of my chest and abs. Her back nestled into the crook of my arm, while her head cradled in my palm, as my finger held fast.

My firemen brothers and three paramedics filed in, one-by-one. Even though I knew I should've paid attention as they attended tae Thor's grandma, I didnae care. My eyes were on the bonnie lass's breathin', her pulse that steadied against my finger, her full lips, and her wee perky nose. My gut tightened as my heart longed tae see her eyes open. For her tae look at me. Maybe even smile.

John, an older paramedic I've worked with for years, slid beside us and checked her vitals before helpin' guide me through the store tae the ambulance parked outside. I climbed in, laid the lassie on the gurney and ran down with the paramedics what happened as I kept my finger in her neck on the way tae the hospital. They placed a nasal cannula into her nostrils, wiped off a portion of her bloody, dirt covered skin, IV'd her, and checked her vitals numerous times before we sped into the ER dock.

Arrivin' at the hospital, trauma nurses rushed outside. Openin' the back doors, they pulled her gurney safely out, until the legs sprang free. I was zonin', my eyes and finger focused solely on the unconscious beauty, that I barely heard a thing they said.

"Tell me what happened," a nurse asked John as he held the lassie's IV bag over her body and rushed through the ambulance bay doors.

The blast of cool air, and strong scent of disinfectant, was enough tae tug me from my preoccupation tae quickly get us through the O.R. doors. Inside, the nurses cut the lassie's clothes off, and I averted my eyes. I couldn't bear tae watch as cold sweat dripped down my cheeks and I began to shiver from my adrenaline wearin' off.

Once she was draped, and stable enough tae slide her onto the O.R table, I was instructed tae remove my finger. Instruments flew, doctors and nurses worked fast, and I was forced into the waitin' room, where a nurse handed me a set of clean scrubs tae change into and a plastic bag. In the visitors' bathroom, I washed the grime off my skin and changed into the clothes. Splashin' one last handful of water over my face, I dried off with paper towels and tossed them into the trash as I exited the bathroom with my bloodied apparel in the bag.

In the waitin' room, I sat my arse in a chair for hours, waitin' tae hear anythin' aboot the lass's condition. Eventually, I texted Pip tae tell her where I was, and she joined me at the hospital.

Six hours later, while pacin' the halls, drinkin' my fifth cup of joe, a doctor came tae inform us she was in the ICU in a coma. For some reason, the bottom suddenly felt like it had fallen outta my world, and I dropped into the nearest chair. The loss, the worry, the fear, and this deep, intense ache...it was bloody fuckin' instant and all-consumin'. It hurt tae breathe. Tae talk. Tae do anythin' except think aboot my hands coated in her blood, the gentle lines of her face, the color of her hair, and how juicy her bottom lip was.

I can't remember much after that, but sometime later, Pip convinced me tae go home. I was a zombie, but I went anyhow. It was torture, and felt like my insides were bein' ripped from my body when I walked outta those hospital doors and into the early mornin' sunrise.

Three hours of restless sleep, followed by a quick shower, and I was back at the hospital, patiently awaitin' the day I got tae see the lassie's eyes for the very first time.

Thor's disgusted noise tears me from my memories. My memories of the very first moment I met Mags, and how it changed me forever. They always say there's that one person that ye help that never leaves ye, and I thought it was a bloody myth until that day.

Gradually, I open my eyes, and he hasn't moved. Watchin' Thor stand there like he's the fuckin' king of the world while his hands continue their ministrations, my abhorrence triples, and my stomach turns over, as a foul taste bathes my tongue in acrid revulsion. What a sick bastard.

I take a powerful step forward, and his smugness grows, his eyes dancin' with malevolence. I'll show him the difference between a man and a boy. Real men take their lassies tae bed; not parade them around like ripe whores for the pluckin'.

Lost in ecstasy, Carrie's eyes roll back in her skull as her body undulates against Thor's. Her lips part, panting for air, and she moans.

"That's it, baby." Thor edges her near completion.

My booted feet, on their own volition, take me one step closer. "Ye can do what ye want tae whoever else, but ye will stay away from Mags," I demand.

The corner of Thor's lip tips into a sly smile. "We'll see, Smoke." He's bloody amused. "I know she digs me. And one of these days, I'll prove to her what kinda man I am. Imagine all the dirty fuckin' things I can show her sweet little body as it's spread under me, screamin'—"

A streak of red-hot lightnin' surges through me, stealin' all logic. One second I'm glarin', and the next I'm forcefully yankin' Carrie's half-naked body behind me. A roar tears from my lips, and I lurch forward, my forehead slammin' into Thor's. The crack is deafenin', rattlin' in my skull. The pain is nonexistent.

Thor yelps, staggerin' backward, holdin' his forehead. His face is beet red.

Unable tae stop, I advance on him. Shock, then fear flashes in his eyes. I dinnae care. The world around me fades into oblivion as molten rage fuels my every muscle. My thighs tighten and abs ripple in contraction.

Grabbin' the back of Thor's neck, I squeeze until he submits and tries tae slap it away.

Na, na, na, wee lad.

Next, my boot connects with the back of his knee, forcin' him tae the ground. He stumbles, catchin' himself with his hands, but I quickly jerk him back onto his knees.

Curlin' my other hand around his throat, I release the back of his neck and meet his eyes. They're wide with shock. "Ye dinnae talk yer childish bullshit tae me. And ye certainly dinnae threaten my fuckin' family."

Reachin' tae my side, I unsheathe my Clan MacAlister dagger and bring it tae his throat. He swallows hard as I press the tip tae his flesh until it draws blood. Tears well in his eyes and the fresh scent of piss stings my nose, but he doesn't move. "Men dinnae talk; they *do*. And ye fuck with my lassie, my face will be the last bloody thing ye ever see. We clear?" I growl lowly.

Thor barely nods, which is good enough for me. I release him with a mighty shove and sheathe my dagger. He topples tae the ground, clutchin' his neck, watchin' me with fear in his eyes. Aye, he best be scared. Next time, I'll cut his wee balls off. I'm done with childish arseholes; and I'm even more fuckin' tired of sittin' here at this party, where I dinnae even wanna be.

Turnin' on my heel, I stride across the yard over tae my bike, and kick my leg over to straddle it. Turnin' the key, I tuck my kilt between my legs tae keep the air off my balls, and I fire the engine. Flickin' on my headlights, I heel up my kickstand, rev the engine a couple times, and tear outta my sister's driveway, kickin' up rocks as I speed tae the main road.

Fuck that bloody bastard. I need tae get home, and I need tae see Mags, I miss her already.

CHAPTER 12

Mags

My blood runs red; within it lies agony, defeat, guilt, humiliation, and this soul gripping torment that I know all too well. It rises from time to time when my self-pity rears its big ugly head.

Everywhere hurts. Everything seems to crumble around me. Why did I do this? Why did I allow myself to come here? I knew it was wrong. I felt it. Nobody truly cares that much for someone they don't even know. There's always a shoe to be dropped. And I'm lying in it now; writhing in pain on the white tiled floor in the kitchen. Paralized and unable to move, call for help, or do anything but wallow; falling deeper into sadness and this black despair I've come accustom to.

Crying and bleeding, I lie here in wait. I don't know how long it's been, but it's dark outside now. The light over the sink is on, allowing me to see. Pirate hasn't left my side as I shiver from the cold tile. He vibrates, too, scared. His tongue pokes out from time to time, lapping the cut on my head; keeping the blood from trickling down my face. The rest has dried under my cheek, on my fingers, forearms, and in my hair.

Seconds, minutes, perhaps hours ago, the bleeding subsided from the gash on my forehead and busted lip.

The intense pain in my gut and ribs could mean something else entirely, but I can barely move to find out. Why didn't I fight harder?

The taunting sound of motorcycle pipes roaring outside brings me the faintest hope. I've imagined them for hours. Though, once again, they could be another hallucination. They've all been that way before.

Pirate curls closer, his head tucking into the crook of my sore neck. I wish I could tell him it'll all be okay, so he'll stop shaking. Even if I don't believe that myself; I don't know what to think anymore. When does life grant you some sort of reprieve from all of the world's crap? When do I catch my break? Can you tell me? God, I'd really love to know.

The sound of boots stomping outside draws my attention. The door glides open, and the relief is so immediate that I begin to weep. Tears spill over, and my bottom lip trembles, muting the constant sting. A light is clicked on and a sharp gasp expels. Then, a growl so dark and grizzly it makes my insides quiver. Boots pound across the tile as they run to me.

"What the bloody fuck?" Lachlan explodes, and I flinch at the intensity of his words echoing off the walls.

Stepping over my prone body, he kneels at my front. I can barely see him through my teeming tears as I suck in a shuddering breath. I hear him move, and something slap the floor before a piece of soft cloth dabs the tears from my cheeks and eyes. It smells just like him, mixed with the smoky scent of bonfire, and wind. It's perfect. Inhaling deeper, there's a hint of women's perfume lingering in the cloth that makes my insides recoil. I try to turn away.

Is that her perfume? Did she go to him after she did this to me? Did she pretend nothing happened? Did he—

I choke another sob.

How could she do that? How?! His shirt...it smells like a woman. *Like her.*

Hours ago, I was downstairs in the bathroom. Once I exited, I found Meredith in my bedroom rifling through my belongings on the dresser. We were both caught off guard, gasping, as our eyes met. She was not at all like I pictured in my mind. She was tall, at least five foot ten, and slender, like a runway model. And she had long, straight, jet-black hair that was smooth as it draped down her slender back. Her shrewd eyes staring at me were crystal blue. She was gorgeous. Which served as a double punch to the gut; knowing she's not only the one who warms Lachlan's bed at night, but was the same disrespectful woman tearing through my stuff.

Taking a long look at me seated in my wheelchair, she stuck her nose up, repulsion written across her face. "What the hell is your fat ass doing here? Aren't you supposed to be with Lachlan at the club thing?" she curled her lip at me.

Taking a clicking step forward on her jade green stilettos, she closed the gap between us. There was no denying that she looked glamorous, like she'd just returned from the red carpet in her jade green, strapless dress that hugged her body as if it was made for it. Diamonds sparkled from everywhere—her wrists, ears, and fingers. The thick, diamond-encrusted choker that hugged her slim neck made me jealous. Even though I was disgusted with myself for feeling that way, I felt it nonetheless.

I kept my face impassive at her insult, since I couldn't sling them back. But I could retain my composure and pretend her words didn't offend me. Although they did; and they cut deep.

"Are you gonna answer me, bitch?" She cocked her hip out.

I had plenty that I wanted to impart, but couldn't. It killed me to keep my cool, but what other choice did I have?

She wasn't finished. "Lachlan didn't want his flavor of the month to go?"

Flavor of the...what? Did Lachlan do this often? We didn't do anything together that was inappropriate, but had he engaged in that before?

"You're fatter than the last one." Meredith fake laughed, grinning like the devil. "Though, I gotta say your hair's much prettier. The last bitch had a shorter somethin' or other." She flicked her hand out like it was of no consequence to her.

Unable to listen to another word about Lachlan's referred cheating exploits, I wheeled myself backward to get away from her. Meredith moved forward and grabbed the handles of my wheelchair, stopping me. Then she got in my face, bathing it in her rancid breath. I tried not to gag.

"You tell Lachlan that you want to leave here and never see him again, or I'll sic Whisky on you and you'll be dead by the end of the week," she sneered.

I may have not been sure about Lachlan's past, but I wasn't scared of her poorly executed threat. Whisky wouldn't touch me. To get the point across that the bitchy Barbie failed to frighten me, I straightened my back and held my head high, treating her like she did me—trash. This futile effort was awarded with a stinging slap across my face. Tears sprung to my eyes, and I bit my cheek. Blood bathed my mouth as she bent over, cackling with pride.

Reacting on impulse, I swung on her, connecting with her face with the casted heel of my hand. Curses were slung as she palmed her blazing cheek. It was my time to laugh, even if I couldn't speak. I opened my mouth and shook with mock laughter, holding my belly for effect. Served her right for touching me.

The silent laughter died on my lips when she stood up straight and advanced on me, eyes wild. Seizing my chair, she forced me toward the kitchen, pushing it fast as if she was going to wheel me out the door. Struggling, I put my feet down to stop her, but it didn't work. I ended up catapulting myself from my chair, and the chair kept going as she shoved it from behind. I flew forward, barely able to use my hands to brace my fall. The impact was severe, my arms collapsed under me and my forehead ricocheted off the tile. I blacked out for a moment, and my lip burst open as my forehead trickled with warm blood.

When I came to, Meredith was on me, yanking my hair, hands slapping me, feet kicking me in the gut, ribs, and back. Crazed with fury, she screamed in repetition, "You stupid fat bitch! You stupid, stupid fat bitch! Why'd you have to come here, huh?!"

My attempt to fight back was minuscule when I could barely move. I went on the offensive, putting my hands up to shield myself from her never-ending blows. I don't know how long it lasted—minutes, hours, I couldn't guess. Eventually, her breathing became labored as she wore herself out, and the screaming died on her lips. My eyes matted with tears, as my own body struggled to breathe, while she continually knocked me around with haphazard strikes.

Wrenching my head back by my hair, I suffered in silent pain as she knelt over me, her breath raggedly wafting over my face. "You leave here, you stupid fat bitch, or I'll kill you myself." She spat on my forehead and eyes, smacked my cheek for good measure, and then released me.

Swiftly, her heels clicked away as she ambled up the stairs to the main floor, slamming the door in her wake. I sighed with relief, heavily consumed by agony, as I prayed to God for unconsciousness to take me. It never did. For hours, Pirate lay curled next to my head, whining in my stead, siphoning some of my grief into himself, sharing in my heartache. For the first time in my life, I had someone there to go through it with me. Not through it *for* me, but to somehow understand enough, to care enough, to feel the pain alongside me, even for a little while.

Thick fingers comb through my matted hair, peeling it off my face. "What happened tae ye?" Lachlan whispers tenderly.

Arching my sore back, I groan. I want to tell him about his wife. I want to ask him if that's her perfume on his shirt. I want to say so much, but can't.

His thumbs massage my cheeks with care, and slide up to roll over my brows. "My leannan, who did this tae ye? Did ye fall? Look at me." He is being so sweet and gentle; it tugs at my heartstrings and I swallow hard. Taking a deep breath, I twist my eyes to look at him. His face is softly immersed with concern, his broad chest bare, and he's still wearing his red and green kilt. He wets his bottom lip with the sweep of his tongue. "Aye, there's my lassie." His finger runs along my jaw to my chin and back up to trace around my ear, and stops when he meets Pirate's lazy head. "Time for ye tae leave her be, lad. I've got her now. Ye've done a fine job." He pats Pirates head; I feel it through my neck.

Pirate lifts himself and licks my hair before backing away. Lachlan stretches out beside me. Turning onto his side, facing me with his massive arm tucked under his head, his face slides closer so I can smell the faint scent of beer on his breath. It's magnificent.

"I dinnae wanna lift ye until I know if ye broke anythin'. Can ye blink twice for Ay—yes, and blink once for na?" He scoots a bit closer. Close enough that I can feel the heat emanating from his body. Still shivering from cold, I welcome it.

Rubbing his rough palm along my arm to my hip, he awaits my reply.

I blink twice.

"Aye. Thank ye, Mags," he says before continuing, "Did ye fall?"

Twice, I blink again.

"Was it an accident?"

I blink twice. Of course it wasn't. Meredith wanted to hurt me on purpose. At the same time, I'm the one who did this to myself by putting my feet down, which was an accident. Could be either.

"Do ye think ye broke anything?"

I blink once.

Why is he being so patient with me? He's worried, I can see that, but it's like he knows I need him to be calm and strong for me. I don't want to break down and lose more of myself to circumstance.

His soothing hand running along my body warms me, ceasing the shivering.

"Do ye want me tae call the ambulance?"

I blink once. I don't want to go anywhere.

He frowns. "Do ye want me tae take ye tae the hospital myself?"

I blink once.

Lachlan grumbles under his breath. "Mags, ye got me worried. Ye need tae be seen. I'm takin' ye one way or another. Aye?"

I just want to forget this happened. I don't want to go anywhere. I want to go to bed and sleep away the pain and embarrassment. Is that too much to ask?

I blink once.

His grumble turns into a rumbling growl, and he moves so close that his body is molded to mine, my side to his front. He lifts my arm and lays my palm on his prickly cheek. My heart palpitates, and my throat runs dry. What's he doing? Lachlan doesn't stop there. He dips his head, his cheek coming to lie on the bare floor, eyes level with mine, noses almost meeting. "Ye dinnae have tae tell me what happened right now. But..." His hot hand lays over mine that's resting on his cheek. I think I'm dreaming. This can't actually be happening. I can almost taste him from here. His scent is intoxicating.

"But," he repeats, "I need tae have ye checked out. I dinnae care if ye want it or not. I need it for myself. Can ye do that for me?"

For him? God, why does he have to play that card? I know it's bull-crap, he's full of it, and he's just trying to work around my stubbornness. But the way his soft voice is speaking makes my insides turn to mush. I'd lick his teeth if he asked me.

I need to get a grip.

Sighing with defeat, I blink twice and he leans in to press a tiny kiss on my nose. I feel it travel all the way to my toes, sprouting goosebumps along the way.

"Thank ye." He brushes a faint kiss upon my forehead before he rolls onto his back and gets up.

Scooping me off the floor with ease, my body protests, but I bite my tongue to keep from showing real pain. I don't want him to call an ambulance or think I'm that hurt. My wheelchair's resting nearby like it hadn't just been used to try and almost kill me. He sets me in it, before walking over to his vest lying on the floor. He extracts his phone from the inside pocket. Dialing, he exits the kitchen and goes to the bathroom.

Moments later, he returns with a first aid kit and washcloth. "Ye're almost home?" he asks to whom I assume is Bridget on the other line. Either that or Meredith. I tense at the thought, acid boiling in my gut. I hope I never have to see her again.

Finishing the call, he sets his phone on the kitchen counter before striding over and kneeling at my feet. Looking up at me, he runs his palms over my exposed thighs. The touch shoots straight to places it shouldn't. "I didnae tell Pip what happened, but she's gonna go with me tae take ye tae the hospital when she gets here. She's aboot five minutes away. Will ye allow me tae clean ye up before she sees ye?"

I blink twice. Of course I'd let him do that, even if I hate the idea of his hands touching me because of how they make me feel. But, I don't want Bridget to see me like this. I know it's not a pretty sight. My lip is swollen and my eyes have to be red from crying.

Lachlan works fast, cleansing my face, the cut on my lip, and my forehead gash. Then, he wipes the rest of the dried blood off my neck and hair. Trying to wipe the blood off my casts doesn't seem to work. They're stained, so he gives up.

Opening a *Band-Aid* out of the kit, he carefully places it on my forehead. "Ye're gonna need a few stitches. Dinnae wanna scare Pip."

I nod my agreement. She's going to be broken-up enough whenever she finds out that her mother did this to me. Lessening the blow seems like the best choice. Lachlan seems oblivious, too. Though, he's not seen under my clothes, to which I'm grateful for. I'm sure there are plenty of bruises to tell a much more graphic tale of how Meredith MacAlister unleashed an entire can of hatred on a woman who couldn't defend herself. I can't imagine what anyone will think. Maybe I shouldn't tell them? Do you think the doctor will be able to tell the difference? I could protect Bridget and Lachlan from having to deal with the aftermath of Meredith's treachery. It's the least I could do, considering the circumstances. None of *this* would have happened if I hadn't come here in the first place.

A lance of guilt punctures my heart. *See,* I knew this was my fault.

The sound of tires crunch down the incline outside as Lachlan finishes his last swipe on my neck and throws the contents of the first aid kit and towel down the hall. "Time tae go." He pats the top of my pounding head, and grabs the handles of my wheelchair. He wheels me to the door just as Bridget is coming onto the patio, seeing us through the glass.

The outside porch light illuminates her stricken features. "What the?" she comments, her mouth falling open. Maybe I look worse than I thought. Breaking out of her momentary daze, she glides open the door and backs away, allowing her dad to wheel me to the SUV. No words are exchanged. The sounds of crickets chirping fill the pregnant silence.

Unlatching the door, Lachlan yanks it wide before lifting me and gently sitting me on the passenger side bucket seat. Leaning into the cab, he softly pecks my cheek before shutting the door. I'm stunned by his sweetness and cup my cheek where his lips seared my flesh. Did I just imagine that?

Through the window, I watch Lachlan saunter back into the house while talking to Bridget. Moments later, he returns wearing a fresh shirt and his vest, and in his hand, he clutches my cell phone.

A shaky Bridget climbs into the backseat with me as Lachlan slides behind the wheel and starts the engine. More silence hangs in the air as we pull away from the house and head to the hospital.

On the drive, I make up my mind. I'm not telling anyone what happened. Bridget can't stop fidgeting in her chair, playing with her hands. And Lachlan's lowly growling under his breath, filling the air with palpable tension. This isn't their fault; this is mine, and I'm gonna suffer in silence. Thank you for keeping my secret.

CHAPTER 13

"No! No! Brian, wake up! Wake up, Brian!" I scream bloody murder, shaking his lifeless shoulders. His blond head lulls to the side, eyes closed, chest still. "Brian!" I wail a sob. "Brian!" Curling into a ball, I lie my head on his toned chest as tears fall from my eyes. My fist clutches into his white t-shirt. "Brian," I whimper, praying to hear any sign of life rattling in his cold body.

I can't breathe!

Clawing at my throat for air, I wake up with a start. Eyes flying open, I force a deep inhale as tears mat my eyes and I wipe them away. Lurching my head over the side of the bed, my insides twist. With a choked gag, I purge the contents of my stomach all over the hospital floor.

Uh! I hate that.

Leaning back into the mattress, I press the nurse call button. I can't believe I dreamed about Brian again. It's been years since I had to relive that nightmare. The first two years after it happened, I dreamt of it nightly. A trashcan sat next to my bed for me to puke into as it never failed to happen. Afterward, I would brush my teeth, wipe my eyes, rinse the trashcan out, and fall back to sleep for a few more hours. Men were not allowed to stay over because of that; not that I wanted them to, anyhow.

Finally, I broke down and saw a doctor. They put me on a low dose of anti-depressants, which helped some. They curbed the sadness, and the puking turned into a weekly occurrence more than a nightly. Five years after his death, I was officially off the anti-depressants and sleeping easy. I could finally share my bed with a man if I wanted; though I rarely did. The idea of sharing my space with a person I could never feel anything but lust for was out of the question. Love—now that's something they speak about in fairytales. I thought I had it once—well, I *know* I did. But that was so long ago, I forget what it even feels like.

Combing my fingers through my disastrous hair, I sigh heavily at the fact that I'm stuck here again; under twenty-four-hour observation to make sure I didn't suffer further injury. My brain is fine, and all I have is bruised ribs and a sore back; there is no internal bleeding. They glued my busted lip closed and put in eight stitches on my upper forehead, partially hidden in my hairline. My casts on my forearms weren't salvageable so a doctor cut them off a few days early and put me in braces instead. My leg is fine, though they figured I'd have a bruised hip for a few weeks. I guessed as much.

After the doctor had asked me a series of questions about what had happened, most of which I refused to answer—unless it was the absurd ones where he asked if Lachlan had abused me. I set that one straight. Then, I fell asleep. Good painkillers and too much crying will do that to ya.

A soft knock raps at the door and the nurse enters. Banishing an ashamed sigh, I point to the floor.

Smiling sadly, she asks, "Are you okay? I'll get that cleaned up...But is there anything I can get you? Are you comfortable?" Using a device clipped to her scrubs, she calls for someone to clean up the mess.

I nod to answer her question, and the phone that she brought me hours ago vibrates for the umpteen time on the table next to my bed. My body was x-rayed, CAT scanned, and my blood drawn all in the ER before they moved me to a room. In the ER, I requested that Lachlan and anyone else please be kept out. I wasn't sure what my body looked like, and I didn't want him seeing it. To be honest, seeing him just makes the guilt worse. It's easier this way, because, like I'd predicted, my bruising is pretty significant. New ones are sprouting up every time I look, or the ones I already have seem to grow. They're ugly and dark, and not anything I want anyone but the doctors and nurses to see.

Lachlan doesn't deserve to be burdened with this, too. I can handle it on my own. No sense in making things worse for them. In two weeks, my leg cast will be removed and I can leave. Somehow, I will do it. I can't bear to put anyone through more of my problems.

Lachlan

I'm pacin' the waitin' room, my hands fisted at my sides as my jaw grinds, tryin' not tae go on a bloody rampage. It's been fuckin' hours since I've seen her. The nurses said I wasn't allowed in the ER room with her. They said that they needed space. They're full of bloody shit, is what they are. Somethin's not right, I tell ye. I can feel it. My heart won't stop poundin' outta my fuckin' chest. I'm sweatin' like a damn pig.

Tae make matters worse, everybody's here. My entire family. Pip called Whisky, and her stubborn arse called everyone else. Now, the waitin' room is full of a bunch of sobberin'-up bikers and their lady folk.

The first time I was told I wasn't allowed tae see Mags, Sniper had tae take my dagger from me before I used it on the nurse. I'm tryin' not tae make a scene; that's the last thing Mags needs right now. If she'd answer my fuckin' texts, or let me bloody fuckin' see her, then I'd be okay. I could actually breathe.

Argh! Why won't she see me?

I knew when I walked into the house tonight that somethin' wasn't right; I could sense it. Just like I could sense it before I left my sister's. Aye, I was right. As she laid there, motionless, on the floor and tearin' my bloody heart out with her silent tears. My instinct was tae ask her what happened, tae pry it from her and take the burden away. But her wee body tremblin' on the floor, and Pirate's frightened eyes, told me not tae push. It killed me not tae. So I wiped away her tears and laid down beside her tae give her comfort. When what I really wanted tae do was— na, I dinnae need tae think aboot that right now. It's not the time.

Pip comes up behind me and cuffs her hand over my shoulder. "Whisky just talked to a nurse she's friends with. She said that Magdalene just woke up. Maybe you should try to text her again." She rubs my shoulder once and lets go, leavin' me tae pace.

"What's the update?" Thor intrudes, talkin' tae Pip.

I spin on my boot heel tae face him. Aye, the bloody bastard showed up, too. Whisky said she and Sniper'd keep the fucker away from me, and that I should let him stay tae support Mags since they're friends. I dinnae care what they are. He needs tae go home. She dinnae want him here. If she did, she'd have told him. And I dinnae care if she wants me here or not; I'm not givin' her a choice. She's mine tae care for, whether any of these bastards agree or not. I'd like tae see 'em try tae come between me and my leannan.

"All the nurse said was that she just woke up," Pip explains tae the waitin' room, not lookin' at Thor.

Aye, that's my lass. She dinnae like the bastard either.

"Are you sure that's all? Did they say what happened?" Thor's diggin'. I get it, he cares. I just dinnae care that he cares.

"No. Nobody knows what happened, and the doctor won't tell us either," Pip clarifies, calmly standin' in the middle of the room.

"Neither of you asked her?" He won't shut the bloody hell up, as he runs a hand through his *pretty* blond hair, sittin' on a chair next tae Muff.

"Dad said she didn't want to explain, and she can't talk yet."

Thor's eyes lift tae me, and he glares, jaw tickin'. "You're tellin' me that you brought her here and nobody knew what happened?"

Tuckin' my arms across my chest, I stiffly nod once. "Aye."

"That's a load of bullshit, brother! You talk like you wanna take care of her, and you can't find out how the hell this happened?!"

See, this may piss me off, but at the same time, it's showin' me what I already knew; Thor needs tae grow the bloody hell up. Do I think Mags just fell outta her chair? Fuck na, I dinnae. Is that gonna change what happened tae her? Na. Is pushin' her tae talk gonna change anythin'? Na, except make her close down. She's not an open person. She has demons. It goes beyond any of her words and into her eyes. They're not the eyes of a woman her age who's lived a happy life. They're the eyes of a lass who's seen things and been through things that still haunt her. Those kinda lassies ye dinnae push. Like a flower, ye let them open on their own time. Wee lads like Thor could never understand that, because he's never been through a bloody thing in his life. He served in the Army reserves and got out. Didnae do shit. Thor has never held a dyin' baby in his arms, or watched a woman burn tae death in a car, screamin' for ye tae help her. He dunno what demons are like cause he's clueless aboot life and he's bloody fuckin' stupid.

"Are you gonna fuckin' answer me?!" Thor demands.

Liftin' my hand tae scratch my chin, I shake my head at him in pity. Pity for bein' such an arsehole, and he dinnae even know it. "Ye think forcin' a lassie who's bleedin' and cryin' on a cold tile floor, scared outta her bloody fuckin' mind, is when I should be interrogatin' her?" I speak slowly, lettin' it sink in.

Thor rears back like my words slapped him, and some of the women folk gasp. Aye, it wasn't a pretty thing tae see; even more so when ye care aboot the person.

A nurse pokes her head into the waitin' room. "Could you please stop yelling in here? You're disturbing the patients," she snaps.

I turn tae her. "Can ye please ask Magdalene Murdock if she'll permit Lachlan MacAlister tae see her?"

"Can, what? Who?"

Bloody hell, why cannae people understand me? "Can ye—"

Pip cuts me off. "My dad wants to know if he can see Magdalene Murdock. He wants you to ask her if she'll let him in her room."

The nurse switches her eyes between Pip and I, then she sweeps the room. Her eyes widen. "She...um...Magdalene...she doesn't want to...be..."

I take a step in her direction, and she retreats a step backward, givin' me a wide berth. Her eyes lift tae mine. "Sir...please..."

"Ask my lassie tae see me," I demand, takin' another step forward.

The nurse visibly gulps. "I can't...she doesn't...um..."

"Ye ask her."

Fearfully, she bobs her head as her face turns white as a ghost.

I nod. "Thank ye."

"Um..." She doesn't finish her sentence when she whips around and darts down the hall.

If she knows what's good for her, she'll ask Mags. If not, looks like the nurse and I will be havin' some words.

Mags

An abrupt knock pounds on my door before it swings wide and a nurse scurries in like she's running from someone or something. If I had to guess, I know what. The yelling a few minutes ago gave it away.

She stops at the end of my bed, smiling nervously. "Um...Magdalene, I was asked to see if you would permit a Mr. Lachlan MacAlister into your room. He...um...he...really wants to speak with you. The...um...room...I mean...the waiting room is filled with men wearing...um...lots of leather...and they have lots of tattoos. They were yelling. I...um...told them to be quiet." Her voice drops to a whisper, and her eyes widen to saucers. "You don't think they'll hurt me for telling them that, do you?" Her breathing is erratic, and her face is as white as a sheet; she's dead serious. It's kind of funny, but then again, it's not. I know how scary Lachlan is without trying; imagine him when he is trying. I'd probably pee myself.

To lighten the burden on her, I shake my head. Her face falls.

"You won't see him?!"

Crap! That's not what I meant. I don't really want to see him, but I feel terrible. She's obviously in a bind. He's scared her, too. That seems to be a common occurrence with him and his thighs-for-arms.

I wave her forward, grab my phone from the stand, and type out a message for her to read.

They aren't going to hurt you. They're not like that. And I don't want to see him. But if he's not going to leave, and is causing trouble, send him in. I'll handle it.

Reading my message, she blows a relieved breath. "Thank you. He seems really concerned. Maybe if he comes in here, he can make the others leave, so my job won't consist of patients complaining about the noise."

I nod, my lips tight, and she thanks me again as she leaves. Less than a minute later, heavy footfalls echo near my room and there's a loud rap on the door just before Lachlan enters. He doesn't say hello as he wades into my room and makes himself right at home on the edge of my bed. His eyes go directly to my arms, which are no longer casted. He lifts his chin, gesturing to them. "They took 'em off?"

I bob my head.

"Are ye okay?"

Keeping my face blank, I lift my right shoulder in a tiny shrug.

His expression tells me he's not convinced. "Are ye ready tae tell me what actually happened?"

Lachlan

Mags shakes her head as her face casts down, checkin' the invisible dirt under her nails. I asked a simple question; one that isn't so simple, as she obviously dinnae wanna talk tae me aboot it.

I reach out tae rest my hand on her uncasted leg, over the white hospital blanket, causin' her body to tremor under my fingers. Leisurely, I brush them up and down her calf. She squirms more as wee puffs of air burst from her swollen lips. My cock twitches on its own accord. *Bloody hell.* Why does this always happen when I touch her? I cannae control it.

My fingers travel tae her knee, and a shudder rolls through her. My cock jerks again, chubbin'. "I need ye tae tell me what happened tae ye," I whisper slowly.

Mags shakes her head again. Her fingers better be clean with how much she's pickin' at 'em.

I dunno what possesses me, but I scoot further up the bed and my hand travels along her thigh. Body stiffenin' under my palm, she stops breathin'.

"Breathe," I mutter, and she does, gulpin' for air.

Twistin' in the bed, I rest my knee on the edge tae face her. Tappin' my finger under her chin, I try raisin' it up for her tae look at me. She refuses tae make eye contact, so I gently trap her chin between my fingers and coax her. Meetin' my eyes, her cheeks blush somethin' fierce, making my balls draw up—achin' at the sight. Nervously, she nibbles the corner of her lip, and I spring tae rock-hard, my tip droolin' with pre-come, rollin' down my shaft. Briefly closin' my eyes, I wince at the feelin' as my stomach turns over in self-disgust. With the sweep of my tongue, I wet my dry lip. Mags watches me with fascination. *Bloody hell, what's she lookin' at?*

"No woman wants a man that makes that kinda mess. Look what you did to the sheet. You'll have to wash them." Meredith's words ring through, and I shove 'em away.

With little effort, I focus solely on Mags. "Tell me what happened." My words break her outta wherever world she was livin' in, and she shakes her head. My fingers drop from her chin and adjust my cock. She doesn't notice.

Reachin' between her thighs, she crushes back into the mattress as I lift her phone off the sheet, handin' it tae her. She accepts it with fumblin' fingers.

I nod tae the phone. "Tell me, please."

Mags starts to tap on her phone, and my inner pocket vibrates. I retract my cell.

I don't want to tell you.

Leavin' one hand on her thigh, I respond with my free hand. I'd rather cut my arm off then remove it from her. I can feel her pulse thumpin' erratically under my palm. Her skin is hot tae the touch, which means she's alive and breathin'; and that's all that fuckin' matters.

Why? I ask.

It's not good.

Please.

She sighs before another texts comes through. A text that breaks my heart, and sends a bolt of rage through my system.

It was Meredith.

Mags

All the air is sucked out of the room, and my world detonates as Lachlan explodes off the bed with a roar that forces me to cover my ears. Striding two giant steps, his fist meets the bathroom door. A crack echoes and he unleashes again. Chaos erupts as he loses control, rage fueling every blow. If the door were a person, they'd be dead by now. Blood sprouts to his knuckles, running down the wood. My heart leaps into my throat and my body aches to reach him, to make him stop.

"That bloody fuckin' bitch!" His back arches, and both of his arms fly wide, curve, and then arc as they both ram against the door simultaneously.

Tears silently tumble down my cheeks. See, I told you I shouldn't have told him. It's all my fault! Curling my arms around my middle, I dip my head and cry. Cry for hurting him. Cry for allowing her to do this to me. Cry, because everything's my fault. Gram's died, because I never made her go to the doctor. Brian died, because I didn't check on him. My mother stole everything, because I didn't help Grams create a will. My body's broken, because I couldn't accept Johnathan for who he was and marry him. My car's ruined, because I stopped to get gas when I should have driven through. I'm sitting here now, because I took advantage of a man and his daughter who have the two biggest hearts on the planet. *See?* It's all my fault.

A nurse creeps in; fear flashing in her eyes. I wave her out, and she retracts slowly, looking between Lachlan and me. I shoo her again. She needs to leave him be. He's having a damn moment; nobody else needs to see him lose control. Finally, she backs out and shuts the door quietly.

Taking a shaky breath, I calm myself enough to pick up my phone and text him.

Lachlan, please stop.

It does no good. He doesn't check it. His fists turn raw, pummeling the door. His breathing becomes labored, and his muscles that ripple with each strike, slow. Resting both fists on the door, he leans forward, relaxing his forehead against the wood. A maddened cry tears from his throat, swirls around the small room, and lunges into my soul, finding a home there. My heart devours the pain, adopting it as its own. I welcome it. I deserve it.

Rolling his shoulder to the door, he turns and his back sags against the support. He runs his hands through his short hair; his face's red and matted with sweat. His broad chest rises and falls from exertion as a flash of sadness and pain slide across his features, leaving just as quick as they came.

Expelling a low growl, he shakes his head, pushes off the door, and strides to my bed.

Possessively cupping my face, he tilts my head back. His glowing teal eyes meet mine, stealing the air from my lungs.

"I'm sorry."

His mouth swoops down and crashes to mine with desperate need, forcing me to freeze. Warm lips slant over mine, and his tongue lashes out seeking entrance. Growling, he demands more, his lips working mine even though I'm not kissing him back. My legs tremble and my nipples spring to sharp points, aching at the delicious sensation. His intoxicating scent drugs me, and I'm lost in his touch. His mouth. His hungry growls. The air that pumps from his lungs and out through his nose, that's bathing my cheeks. A tooth nips my bottom lip, and I wince, breaking from the trance.

What the hell is he doing?!

Placing my hands to his pecs I shove him away. He takes a staggering step back and thoughtfully brushes his lips with his bloodied fingers—dazed. Then he looks at me, and his face falls as all of the color drains from his cheeks. "Fuck, I'm sorry. I couldn't. I'm..." he retreats three more steps. His back smashes to the bathroom door, and he slides down it until his butt rests on the floor. Trembling, he rakes his hands through his hair and down his cheeks to his goatee. "I'm so fuckin' sorry, I shouldn't..." his knees come up and he pushes his kilt between his thighs. I catch a glimpse of hidden flesh but not enough.

Why is he...oh... my... did... he just tried to kiss me! What is wrong with him?! Why would he do that?

Tumbling my fingers in my lap, I mull over my thoughts and lancing guilt. I haven't kissed anyone else but Brian. Does this constitute as that? Did I betray him? Oh my god. Did I?

"Mags, look at me." He's practically begging in that rough Scottish accent.

I don't look up. How can I? How can I face him? I touched lips with another man. *A man I wanted to kiss back.* My stomach dips. *A man who's married.* It revolts. *Whose wife put me in the hospital.* It aches. What was I thinking? What's wrong with me?

The phone in my lap vibrates.

I'm sorry. I shouldn't have kissed you. It was wrong

If it was so wrong, then why did I like it so much? My tongue sweeps my bottom lip. I can still taste him. My thighs tremble. God, I'm the worst kind of home wrecker. I'm going to hell.

Turning my head away, I throw my phone to the side ignoring the message that just came in. Pushing the button on my bed, it lowers, and I close my eyes. Lachlan tries to speak to me. I think he says something about being sorry again and something about it never happening again. And, maybe even something more heart-wrenching like him wishing he would have never done it in the first place. I wish he wouldn't have too, and that he would just go away. I wish that his scent wouldn't steal my breath, that his hands wouldn't make me tremble or that his deep, gravelly voice didn't make me feel funny. I wish he wasn't so kind and caring. I wish I couldn't see the depths of his soul in his eyes. A soul that has lived many lives, seen tragedy, and holds back from life.

What I wish for even more is the ability to ignore the ache I feel when he finally stands, fleetingly touches my leg, and leaves me alone. Alone, as I should be, because that's what I deserve.

Two weeks— only two more weeks and I can run far, far away from the man with the beautiful eyes, who has a daughter with the brightest smile. Can't I just sleep the time away? Can't the pain just recede a little? Can't lov...

CHAPTER 14

"Pirate, do you...think I'll be...okay?" I whisper hoarsely to my best mate, who as of right now, is lying on the pillow next to me in bed.

Nudging his wet nose to my cheek is his reply. I pat his head in thanks and run my fingers down to his tail before I scratch my way back up. He crawls closer, closing his eyes.

"That's a...good...bo-y," I croak, disjointedly.

A tiny knock raps at my bedroom door. Flopping my head to the side, Pirate, the attention hog, crawls partway onto my chest. I shake my head at him with a smile, and rub his ears as Bridget enters, wearing shorts and a hot pink, smiley faced shirt that matches her cheery disposition.

"Are you ready?" She claps, bouncing on her heals, a smile lighting her face. I nod my reply. "Okay!" She claps again. "I'll wait for you in the living room." Bridget excitedly thumb points in that direction, but doesn't wait for my response when she exits, leaving the door open.

Internally, I grumble at the prospect of getting up. Yeah, yeah, yeah, I know I need to stop being lazy and embrace that I'm getting out of the house today. It's only been a few days since Meredith assaulted me. When I was released Monday evening from the hospital, Bridget made sure I arrived back here safely. By then, Lachlan had already changed all the locks, and I had my very own house key hooked on a daisy key ring that he'd laid on my nightstand.

I know, I know, I'm sure you're dying to find out what happened since that life altering, one-sided kiss. Life altering for me; not you, of course. Or maybe for you, too. Crap, I dunno. I'm not sure what I can tell you at this point. I haven't seen Lachlan.

Have I woken up to the same loud, upbeat rock music? Yes. Every single dang day. But I've stayed locked in my room with Pirate. Have I noticed how Lachlan's scent lingers in the basement everywhere I go? Yes; it's taunting me with its rich uniqueness that only he can smell like. It's manly. Though, not in a bad, stinky, gross-man way

For hours, I've tried to ignore his absence, his smell, *his everything*. It's hard to do when all I can *do* is think about it. You know when something happens and you should just forget it ever happened and move on? That's what the logical part of me is saying. But some other part of me that I didn't even know existed until recently is eating at my mind, replaying all of those little moments over and over and over, on a tormenting repeat. It sucks, but not as much as the radio silence from his end. His lack of texts, or anything really, doesn't help A: My mind or B: My nonexistent self-esteem. It amplifies my '*I'm a loser card'* tenfold.

Eh…I'm done thinking about that for now before I start to dwell again. There's not much else to do.

Patting Pirate's head, I whisper, "Can I tell…you a secret?"

He licks my chin in reply, and I giggle quietly.

"I'm nervous," I mutter, and it's terrifying to admit that. But I'm scared to go to Whisky's with Bridget.

Yesterday, after I'd spent the majority of the day in the bedroom, Bridget suggested we take a trip to town today so she can show me around. I know she's trying to mend whatever's broken in me, because that's the kind of person she is. Even though, nothing can fix me. I just don't have the heart to tell her *that*; and I definitely don't possess the willingness to tell her that my voice started coming back the morning before I left the hospital.

I'd had another Brian dream and threw up again. The crazy thing was: in the midst of heaving, I might have slipped out a few less than stellar vernaculars in the heat of the moment and actually vocalized it. It felt incredible for about half a second until my stomach purged bile and Jell-O into the wastebasket beside the bed. Now, I've been cautiously playing with words ever since. They come out choppy sometimes, like a bad case of laryngitis, but I'll take that over not talking at all.

With a final pat on Pirate's head, I roll him off me and sit up using the bar Lachlan installed. Grabbing my wheelchair arm, I hoist myself into my seat and head to the living room.

Bridget stands from the couch, her denim purse slung over her shoulder. "Now, you ready?" She sounds way too chipper as she gestures to the door with the sweep of her hand, but I nod anyhow and follow her to the door. She slides it open, steps outside, and waits for me to exit before shutting and locking it.

Together, we head to the SUV, in companionable silence. I get in first, this time in the front, 'cause I'm daring like that, even with my leg like it is. Bridget takes my chair to store in the back before she slips behind the wheel. My anxiety revs its engine when the Tahoe is put into gear and we start up the incline. Bridget flips on the music as my fingers dig into the door handle and I take a deep breath.

Fields of green line the road on either side until the *Welcome to Carolina Rose* sign greets us on the town's border. My hands have now begun to clam up, and I do believe there is sweat dripping down the sides of my cheeks. I can't tell for sure, because my skin's on fire.

I can't believe we're doing this!

"There's the post office." Bridget points to the left at an old brick building that has a giant stamp in the massive front window. Further along the main street, she points to the only bank, then the outdated supermarket that I know has to have some of the best baked goods and homemade goodies. All the small towns do. We also pass a one-stop, florist-monument shop that has gravestones lining the sidewalk leading to the store. Remind me never to buy flowers from there. There's a deli with a green awning, a *Subway* franchise shop, and a bunch of cutesy mom and pop stores. All the basics you'll come across in a small town, including a hardware store, a locally owned shoe store, and a feed store for the farmers. Bridget leaves *Thor's gym* out of her town guide, although the bright red letters on the gym's window that says *Thor's Gym* is pretty much a dead giveaway.

We circle around to the second most popular road in town, which is where the firehouse and tiny police station are located. Catching a fleeting glimpse of Lachlan's *Harley* as we pass, my eyes become more focused on the open and empty, firehouse bays. They must be out on a call.

Making another turn back to where we came from, Bridget parks in front of her aunt's shop. *Whisky's Corrupt Confections* is cutely scrolled in the large front window under the pink and white ruffled awnings. It looks like one of those adorable bakeries you dreamed about when you were a kid.

Turning the Tahoe off, Bridget turns to me. "It's all right." She reaches across the console to touch my hand that I didn't realize was shaking. Glancing down, I watch our hands and force myself to stop overreacting. I'm sure Lachlan's sister is less scary than him. If I can live through a day with him, I can surely survive a few hours with her.

I nod to Bridget and give her hand a reassuring squeeze. Lifting my eyes, I flash her a tiny smile, and she beams back. "I'm going to get your chair out of the back. Whisky will be on her best behavior, but I have to warn you: she's *very friendly."* Bridget emphasizes those last words. I'm still reeling about what they mean as she hops out of the SUV, making quick work of delivering my wheelchair to my door.

Bridget slams my door shut and walks beside me as I roll myself to the front of Whisky's shop. I stop and cast my eyes inside the glass front door, taking in the black and white tile flooring blend with the wire framed bistro tables with hot pink cushions. From here, the hairs on the back of my neck stand at attention, and I swallow hard.

Bridget secures the door and a bell jingles cheerily when it's opened wide.

Here goes nothing.

Crossing the threshold, a knot forms in my throat as the cold, sugary air blasts me in the face. Proverbially pulling up my big girl panties, I wage on and move deeper into the bakery.

"I'm—" A short, thick, curvy redhead stops talking when she turns the corner from the back room and makes instant eye contact with me. Struck dumbly, I stop moving and Bridget runs into my chair from behind, expelling a pained *Oaf.* Whisky, the woman with the same eyes as Lachlan, bursts out laughing while scrubbing her face with her hands and shaking her head. I'm not sure what to think, so I try not to think at all.

"I'll be damned!" she shouts, calming her laughter and smiling so big I can see where Bridget gets it from.

"Hey, Whisky." Bridget slips out from behind me and rubs her stomach before looking down at me. "Your chair tried to impale me."

I shrug and mouth *sorry;* then scold myself for not voicing it aloud.

My eyes move from Bridget back to her aunt, who's looking at me in a strange way that I can't put my finger on. She moves around the counter to the front and sits at the nearest table. Not saying a word, she pushes the chair directly across from her out from under the table. Reaching across, she drags it to the side, and pats the top of the table with her hand, her eyes still on me.

"You're lucky she's not ordering you to sit there," Bridget explains, clearly in awe of this action. I take that as a good sign and wheel myself to the empty spot across from the redhead.

"Pip, you're on. Get an apron, then bring us some lemonade and shortbread cookies," Whisky instructs.

"No problem, boss." Bridget heads to complete the task, claiming an apron off a hook on the back wall. It must be a uniform of sorts, because Whisky is also wearing one that's pink, black, and white with little skulls over it.

Whisky leans back in her chair, crossing her arms loosely over her ample chest, and smirks at me. "I wondered what you might look like." Her eyes give me the once over, then a twice over, and by the third time, her lip curls into a big Cheshire grin, her eyes dazzling the same way Lachlan's do. Just thinking about his eyes makes my stomach go wonky. "But I gotta tell ya, I wouldn't have believed Pip if I hadn't seen ya with my own two eyes."

I'm not sure what she means, so I lean forward and decide it's now or never that I speak, because if I don't, I'll be typing for the rest of the afternoon. Like my grams always used to say, *'There's nothing better than the present'*.

"Wh-wh-y?" I fumble, and her eyes spring wide.

Bridget gasps and something clatters to the ground. I turn my head to catch Bridget scrambling to pick up the mess she made on the floor; behind the glass front display case that's full of colorful pastries that would make any person's mouth water.

"You can talk again?" Whisky sounds more surprised than anything else.

"Why didn't you tell me?!" Bridget clamors spiritedly.

Righting her mess, she carries us a plate of cookies, a pitcher of lemonade with fresh lemon slices floating, and two glasses. She pours our drinks and sets the cookies in the middle of the table. Whisky taps the top of the pitcher, so Bridget sets it to rest beside the cookies.

My eyes switch between both ladies. "I...can...ta-lk a...lit-t-le," I make out with some effort before I grab my glass and down a gulp of fresh lemony goodness.

Standing at the edge of the table, Bridget runs her finger over the lip, giving me her undivided attention. "When'd you get it back?"

I set my glass down and swipe the back of my hand over my mouth. "I...um...hosp-it-al."

"This week?" Bridget asks.

I nod in reply; this talking thing is already starting to mess with my throat.

"Does it hurt?"

I shake my head.

Bridget blows out a relieved breath, and reaches over to pat me on the shoulder. "Dad's gonna be thrilled you can talk now." She's practically jumping out of her skin with excitement.

That's what I was afraid of. I don't want to speak to Lachlan.

Dipping my head and staring into my lap, I pick at the nonexistence lint on my navy dress and mutter, "K."

Whisky clears her throat. "Pip, can you do the prep and clean up the frosting mess I made in the kitchen?"

"Sure." I can hear that same happy smile in her voice.

Swiftly, her footfalls move away and I dare to glance up. When I do, Whisky's eyes are on me, assessing again. For what? I dunno. They're calculating, similar to Lachlan's, just less daunting.

She flicks an errant curl out of her eyes and tucks it into the side of her hair. "Pip told me you were a hot, curvy, big breasted blonde. I wasn't sure if I believed her or not, since my brother doesn't seem to take a shine to anyone. If he did, I assumed he did it because he was being a good citizen and you'd be some old woman with missing teeth and wrinkles."

Um...I'm not sure what this is supposed to mean. And I'm pretty sure I've never been called *hot* in my entire life. I know I have large headlights, that's what happens when you're not skinny. The fat has to settle somewhere—boobs and butt it is.

She's far from done. "Gonna be frank here, sister. My brother's kind of an asshole. Don't get me wrong, he's nice to me, and a great dad to Pip, but people don't get to know him and the kinda man he really is, because he don't let 'em. I was shocked when he let ya move in. And lookin' at ya now, I'm even more shocked."

I open my mouth to ask her why, but she keeps going, cutting off my train of thought.

"Lach doesn't like people, 'cause women always want something from him. He's stupid and thinks they dig his accent. They dig what they're lookin' at. He doesn't know he's hot, and that all the ladies in this damn town wanna jump his bones. But, he's not only clueless; he's also married to that wench."

That affirmation has me leaning closer to the table and resting my elbows on the top to listen to her story. If it includes said wench, I'd love to hear more.

I've come to the conclusion there have only been two people in my life I've hated, aside from hating myself. Those people being my mother, and now Meredith. I came to that conclusion when I first saw myself in a mirror the day after I left the hospital. It was after I had lifted myself out of the wheelchair to stand for a minute in front of the sink to wash. That's when my eyes finally took in the damage she'd inflicted on my body. It was appalling. Dark purple bruises were everywhere. My lip was even black and blue. My head wasn't so bad after the stitches, but I still got them from her. That's when I decided that she was added to the hate list. A list I don't take lightly.

That's why Mark, a tall bear-of-a-man that I dated many years ago, didn't get added to that list, because he wasn't evil enough. I only upgraded him to strongly dislike after I ran away from him. He'd tried to force me to have anal sex, which ended in a fight and him calling me a tease. *"Nobody has an ass like that and not like to get fucked in it!"* he'd screamed. I didn't argue with him; I just left, and the next day I packed my bags, dropped my keys at the landlords, picked up my security deposit, and fled town. I stopped fifty miles later to dump my cell and pick up a new one. Three months after that, I had another steady boyfriend and a crappy job at some rink-a-dink lube place. As in oil changes. Not the sexual kinda lube. Get your head outta the gutter.

After that, I came to the conclusion men aren't worth the fight when you don't love them. If it had been Brian, I would've stayed and I would have fought through the hurtful words. But Mark wasn't Brian. No one could ever be Brian; no one could ever compare. Men barely ever look past the nose on their face to see that the woman they're sleeping with doesn't love them, is unhappy, or that she's picturing another man when she has sex with them.

The first time I called Brian's name out in the middle of sex, the guy was so drunk he didn't even care. After the twentieth time, I tried to stop thinking about him when I had another man inside me. It sometimes worked. Other times, I bit the pillow when I came so I didn't moan his name when my climax hit. It's sick, I know, but I never said I was a saint, or mentally all there. I'm also not ignorant of the fact that pining after a man who died ten years ago is unhealthy. I just can't help it. It's impossible not to long for him.

We were together for seven years, and those were the best years of my life. We made love under the stars, and he picked me flowers every Sunday. We fed each other just so we could make a mess of each other's faces, we kissed, we hugged, we cuddled after having sex, and he whispered sweet nothings to me like I was the only person on the planet he was made to be with. I fell helplessly in love with him. We were together almost two years before I ever lost my virginity to him, and even then, he said he was grateful for my gift. Which is silly if you think about it; but he thought I deserved to be worshiped, and I loved him unconditionally. I've never looked at another boy or man the way I did him, and I've never felt the things I did with him with anyone else. I had been pretty sure that part of me had died until recently. For the past ten years, I wasn't even sure I had a heart, much less one that could feel. Now, I'm slowly learning that I can, and it's a scary feeling.

A hand touches my elbow, and I blink. "There ya are." Whisky smiles. "Ya left me for a minute."

I open my mouth to apologize, and she waves me off like she knew what I was going to say.

"Meredith hit a nerve?" she asks.

My face twists, and she grins wider. "I...don't...like her."

"Nobody does." Whisky shakes her head. "Nobody in this town can stand Meredith. I've tolerated her for years, but she's a piece of work. Should be. She was married twice before Lachlan, and only married him because he made her."

What?!

Cocking my head to the side, I whisper, "What?"

"Have you heard any of these stories?"

I'm not sure what stories she's referring to, so I shake my head.

"Ooooo, sister, you are in for a treat." She takes a sip of her lemonade before leaning back and tapping her chin like she's deep in thought. "I was hoping nobody had filled your head with lies, yet. People in this town are good at switchin' the truth."

I nod, understanding that perfectly. It's a small town thing. Gossip is huge. And the juicier, the better. That's why truths turn into lies with the snap of your fingers.

"Before you find out about Meredith, I'll tell ya about Lach," Whisky offers.

I take a sip of lemonade to wet my tongue. "Okay."

"Lach's my older brother, and our parents were late in life parents. Mom was in her forties when she had us, and my dad was fifty. My dad was from Scotland, and my mom from Ohio. Long story short, 'cause I don't wanna bore ya…My mom studied abroad in Scotland, and my dad was her teacher. They had a love affair that turned into a marriage. My mom then moved to Scotland to be with my dad. A few years later, my mom's parents were sick, so they moved back here for her to take care of them. Dad got a job at the local university teaching a culture studies course, and my mom became an elementary school teacher."

Teachers as parents, and now a son who's a fireman and a daughter who owns a bakery. They raised good kids and should be proud.

I nod so she knows I'm paying attention.

She continues. "Then Lach and I came along. In elementary school, he kept having problems with the other kids, always getting into fights. My dad decided it would be best to send him to live with our uncle, his brother, Craig, in Scotland. Lach lived there until his junior year of high school, and moved back to finish out school here. I only saw him in the summer for a day or two. My mom missed him, but my dad said he was a Scottish lad, and Scottish lads needed to live in Scotland."

"That…explains…his…ac-cent," I state.

"Aye, it does." She copies his accent and winks at me.

I grin, stifling a chuckle.

"After graduation, he joined the *US Navy* and was stationed in San Diego…This was when Meredith came into the picture," she warns before going on.

"From what he said, they met before he was due to be stationed in Virginia. The guys had thrown him a farewell party the weekend before he was leaving, and that's when he met her. They shared a hot weekend. Two weeks after he arrived in Virginia, he was put on an extended deployment, and when he got back, he had papers for child support waiting on him. Found out Pip was a few months old. When he went back to San Diego to meet her for the first time, he talked Meredith into moving to Virginia with him. But the *Navy* wouldn't grant him on base housing without being married, so he married her in Vegas on their drive across country."

Shock. That's all I can seem to feel at this point. It's a good thing Whisky's not done talking, because my mouth has run dry and my mind is whirling with so many thoughts. Lachlan married Meredith because she had Bridget? I can't believe he'd do that. But then again, I could because he's that type of a person. A genuinely nice one if you can get past that scary exterior and jagged tone.

"Meredith started partying as soon as they moved to base. Got a DUI. Lachlan had to find babysitters for Pip when he worked, because he couldn't trust his drunk wife with their daughter. He put her in rehab three times. The booze was an issue, and so was emptying their account to buy outlandish shit; and she was also fucking random men whenever she could. Lachlan tried to keep their family together and to get her help. He wore condoms when she wanted to have sex with him, because he was afraid of the STDs she might have. He took her to the doctors and paid all her bills. Her ass never worked. She just drank and fucked her way through life." Whisky shakes her head in disgust, and I follow that same motion. I can't believe this. Can you? What a terrible person.

She keeps on. "Lach was fine until our parents died and he lost it, went on his own binge, and blamed her for everything. That's when she went and got knocked up by some random dude and got an abortion to spite Lachlan. He fell deeper into his hole. She blamed him for her dead baby, even though she's never taken care of Pip a day in her life. She's an awful mother."

Yes, she is. I can't believe Bridget is such an amazing girl in spite of her mother being so horrible. It's Lachlan's and Whisky's doing that she turned out to be such a beautiful, smart, young woman. Now, I hold a whole new respect for Lachlan than I did before. He's not a good dad; he's the best there could ever be. Considering I never had one, I should know.

"They moved back to San Diego when he was re-stationed. Then, as soon as Lachlan's twenty was up, he got out and moved here. He wanted Pip to know her family. Decided to join the club, and moved into our parents' old place."

I voice the first thing that pops into my head, "If...she...was...so...bad—"

"Why did she move here with him and he not divorce her?" Whisky finishes for me, and I nod. "Fuck if I know. I guess he felt like he owed it to Pip to keep her mother around. Not sure why, though. The woman never went to a school play, took her shopping, or even painted the girl's nails. If it wasn't Lachlan doing those things, it was me, and since I don't have any daughters, I was happy to do it. She's a great girl."

"Yes...she...is," I agree.

"You know Dad's going to be mad if he finds out you just told Mags all that," Bridget pipes up.

Crap! I forgot she was here. She shouldn't be hearing all this about her mother.

Whisky cocks her head to the side, looking at Bridget. "You think I care? Do you think he woulda told Magdalene that he can't stand the woman who beat the bloody shit outta her?"

Bridget lifts one shoulder and drops it, deflated. "Probably not."

"Do you think Magdalene should know that the woman who was kicking her and beating her on the floor, is a piece of shit? You think your dad would tell her that? You think he'd tell her that he doesn't sleep in bed with her? Or that he has to pick her off the bathroom floor after a binger? Or maybe he should tell her that he's been married to a fucking cunt for the past seventeen years and never cheated on her once."

Until he kissed me in the hospital, I tack on for her. And according to Meredith, he cheats all the time. At first, I might have considered it; not anymore. I trust Whisky. Not sure why, but she's a straight shooter and I respect that.

I watch as Bridget's face shuts down, her eyes become watery, and her bottom lip trembles. "Dad won't tell anyone that stuff. He won't even tell me."

"Exactly!" Whisky jerks her chin, throwing her hands up. "He doesn't want his daughter to know this shit. How do you think he's gonna go tellin' a woman who's sleepin' under his roof? A woman he obviously likes."

He what?!

Swiping at her eyes, Bridget smiles through her sadness. "He does like her," she mutters.

I open my mouth yet again to ask what in the world they mean, but Whisky beats me to it when she cuts her eyes to me. "Now, I'm a woman, I know that look. It's one of disbelief."

She's right. It is.

My mouth falls open.

"I'm sure you're telling yourself all sorts of shit, denying that he could like you. That he's married, and he's this and that. My brother doesn't like anybody. *But,* he likes you."

I didn't know it was possible, but my mouth falls open further.

What the hell?

"Let's just cut to the chase. His wife's a bitch. After what she did to you, I know he won't be tolerating her shit anymore. First time he's ever changed those locks. And you didn't see how angry he was in that waiting room."

"He saved…my…life…That's…wh-y." It has to be why. Has to be.

Whisky shakes her head, and behind the counter, Bridget bursts into a fit of laughter. Apparently, what I said is funny.

"He's saved a lotta people. Never had one at his house before. And, seeing as though you're young, and not covered in wrinkles and missing teeth, I'm sure he's noticed how good looking you are," Whisky states.

I am not!

She won't let up. "I don't know your story. I'm not gonna pry. But I'm here if you need someone to talk to." She nods her head to the side, toward Bridget. "Pip's young, but she's smart and a fine listener. She's been through a lot. Dealt with having a piece of shit mother. She's good people…" She pauses for a beat and rubs her chin. "And I'm not gonna jerk your chain. My brother carries his own set of baggage. He's clueless about women. And he's harder on himself than anyone I know. But he's a good man. And if you like him, too, tell him. He's too thickheaded to figure it out on his own."

What? Huh? Tell…

My thoughts are cut short when the bell chimes and all of our heads swing to the front door. Whisky jumps out of her chair and runs full throttle to the front of the bakery, throws her arms around the customer's neck, tugs him down to her level, and smashes her lips to his with a moan that he swallows. His tan, lean hands cup her thick bottom, and he lifts her. Whisky's legs wrap around his waist, and he stumbles until his back collides with the door, jingling the bells on impact.

I know it's impolite to watch, but I can't stop myself. They're going at it like hot and heavy teenagers in the front of her bakery. Whisky's mewling to his mouth, and he's grinding himself to her front. Their breathing is so heavy it's starting to fog the windows.

A hand taps my shoulder, and I sideways glance at Bridget, whose face is a mixture between grossed-out and sentimental. She bends at the waist and rests her elbows on the tabletop. Unable to help myself, I swap my eyes between her and the hot and heavy session that people would pay good money to see. Despicably, wetness dampens my panties.

"They do this almost every day," Bridget whispers, amused. "Sometimes they stop after a while, and sometimes Sniper takes her to the back. I'll put a closed sign on the door if they do, and we'll go over to Cas's across the street. Trust me; you don't want to hear them when they start having sex."

A bang against the door rattles the bell once again as Sniper turns the tables, and now has Whisky's back pressed to the door. One of his hands is folded between their bodies, and Whisky has started to moan louder, her body rocking to his.

I've never seen anything like this!

Sniper's lips trail down her neck, and Whisky screams in pleasure when he sinks his teeth in. Her back arches against the door and her hands claw at his shoulders, legs tightening around his trim waist. I can now make out that she's wearing a skirt and he's doing something up it—something naughty.

"Looks like they're gonna start right here," Bridget briefly mumbles, and then I'm in motion. My chair's being wheeled backward, even though my eyes haven't left the show. Back, back, back, Bridge wheels me until I'm pulled through the large kitchen and away from the sight that has left me panting.

She moves us out the backdoor, up the alley, and around to the front sidewalk. Down the wheelchair ramp we go as she rolls me past the curb and across the street, to the auto body shop within eyeshot of Whisky's. Close enough to see that Whisky's now bent over a nearby table with her skirt pooled around her waist, and her husband is busy doing his duty. I still can't believe I just witnessed that! I didn't know people in the real word, outside of porn, actually engaged in that sort of lewd behavior.

Lordy!

Bridget stops outside the open garage bay, and a man with dark, unruly hair and an unlit cigarette hanging from his lip saunters out. His intense eyes sweep from Bridget to me, and stop to linger. My already pounding heart thumps harder, and I find myself squirming under his gaze. A grin curls at the edge of his full lips before he extends a dirty hand to me that he doesn't bother to clean.

"I'm Cas," he grumbles, and I accept the hand for a brief shake.

"I'm…Mag-da-lene," I greet as I pull back to wipe my damp palm on my dress. Not that I care about the grease and grime. I welcome it.

Cas nods to my hand. "Sorry about that."

"I…you didn't…make…me…dirt-y."

Coolly, he bobs his head in reply, pulls a lighter from his pocket, and fires up his cig. Cas takes a long drag before he speaks again. "Prez bangin' his old lady?" His eyes are on me, but he has to be speaking to Bridget, doesn't he?

Bridget answers, anyhow. "They are going at it in the front of the shop. Last time they got caught doing that—"

"Health Inspector Dip Shit caused a problem," Cas finishes, flicking ash to the ground and stomping on it with his boot heel.

"Yeah; a very big deal. She had to sanitize the entire place. It's not like they're making a huge mess, and everyone who comes in knows this about them anyhow."

He chuckles. "You'd think town's folk would like the show."

Bridget nods. "Exactly."

Sensually, Cas forms a ring of smoke with his lips, and I watch it float into the air. He catches me staring and winks.

Geeze, he's smooth.

"You doin' all right after that lousy bitch fucked with ya?" he grinds out, blowing the next puff of air out of his nose.

I shrug, and find that imaginary lint on my dress to pick at again.

"You really that shy?"

My eyes snap up to meet his, and Bridget momentarily giggles before pulling a phone from her pocket. Her face falls as she examines the screen. "I'll be right back," she remarks, scurrying down the short driveway and up the sidewalk.

"I'll keep an eye on her," Cas notes to her back, and then turns around to saunter unsteadily back into the shop bay. "Come on in." He waves me forward, and I follow, stopping at the entrance where a white *Ford* pickup is parked with its hood up.

Cas leans his hip against the truck and snuffs out his cigarette between his fingers before tucking the butt into his front jeans pocket. "The car I towed back to Smoke's...it yours?"

"Yes."

He crosses his thick arms over his messy, white t-shirt clad chest. "You paid a lot of money to have that much custom work done. How much it set ya back? Thirty K? Forty?"

Not even close.

"Car was...free. Labor...free. Parts, a...couple...thous-and," I stammer both from my throat issue and because I'm really freaking nervous around him. It's like his eyes can't stop evaluating me, trying to find something hidden. Although, he seems polite enough.

"You're fuckin' with me, right?" He laughs unamused, his eyes narrowing suspiciously.

I shake my head. "No."

Smoothly, he combs a hand through his wild, *Herbal Essence* commercial-worthy hair. "Who in the hell gives that kinda car to a woman for nothin'? You forget I saw the interior? That's fuckin' premium—you're not a hooker, are ya?"

The fact that he thinks I could even remotely be a hooker has me busting a gut. Me, a hooker? Ha! Covering my mouth, I double over and unleash a storm of laughter until tears wet my eyes and my stomach starts to ache.

"Ye gotta be bloody shittin' me!"

Humor dies on my lips at those potent words, which shoot straight to my soul. Daringly, I glance to watch Lachlan stomp his way up the driveway with a sour faced Bridget on his tail. He stops right in front of me and kneels down. His massive hands cuff the tops of my thighs. My breath falters, and those strange sensations in my stomach are back. They have me close to puking.

Clutching my hands on my wheels, I try to back away. Working with all my strength to move is a feeble attempt once his hands clamp tighter over my thighs, keeping me in place. Uneasily, I gulp with fear, my legs trembling under his attention.

"I'm sorry, Mags," Bridget whispers from somewhere. I can't see her, or even look at her when all I can do is stare at Lachlan and those teal eyes. His chest is rising and falling as he looks straight at me. The muscles in his shoulders contract under his tight t-shirt.

My stomach dips.

He's got to stop getting so close to me. I can already smell him, and I don't want to smell him. I want him to go away. Far, far, far away. Scotland would be a good place for him to go right about now. Although, I would be lying if I didn't say that one part of my anatomy is loving this sort of attention. I decide to forget about that part, and try to gain some sort of ground, before I sink deeper into all that is Lachlan.

"Ye shoulda told me ye were talkin'," he scolds, and I try to ignore the pang of guilt that he makes me feel. It smarts.

His eyes move to spot Casanova, who hasn't moved. However, Bridget has now slid up beside him, and he's got his arm loosely thrown over her shoulder. Both of them are leaning against the *Ford*. "Why ye over here with Cas?"

"We were at Whisky's," Bridget answers, pointing to her apron.

"Sniper and her are over there fuckin'," Cas finishes.

The sound Lachlan's throat emanates as his hands stiffen on my thighs makes me feel genuine terror. "She was meetin' with Mags and started in with Sniper?" he seethes.

Bridget nods, her face paling.

"She run her wee mouth?"

Bridget nods again as Cas pulls her in close. Tucking her head to his chest, she lays her palm flat on his stomach, snuggling deeper.

"I'm gonna bloody murder her," Lachlan whispers under his breath before his eyes slip back to me. "What'd she tell ye?" he demands roughly, sliding his hands further up my thighs.

Dear God, he's got to stop touching me!

I close my eyes and force my brain to stop feeling anything. It has to stop. This feeling thing is too much, and he's too close. My heart is pounding so hard, and my hands are wet. Why does he always do this to me? Can't he see I don't like it? That he freaks me out?

Lachlan frees one hand, and squeezes himself between my legs. My outer thighs smash against the inside arms of the chair, and my dress draws up. His hands glide up to clutch my waist.

This can't be happening. I think I'm dying!

"Mags, what'd the bloody wench tell ye?"

Nope, I'm not answering him and throwing Whisky under the bus like that. He's making me uncomfortable, and I might not be able to get away, but I can choose not to talk. Maybe, just maybe, that'll give him the hint that I don't like him getting so close. Not much good that'll do me. He doesn't seem to have any sort of problem pushing his weight around, or doing whatever the hell he wants.

Remaining frozen, I glue my eyes shut.

"Lassie?" he prods. "Mags?"

I keep him on ignore, and the fingers locked around my waist start to caress in tiny circles.

Holy crap!

Seconds, minutes, hours, I don't know how long, slips by as he continues to caress my sides. Nobody talks. The sounds of cars passing and my heavy breathing is all I can hear, as the only thing I feel is the searing warmth of his touch. Shamefully, I relish in it.

The serene moment is cut off when the sounds of footsteps fast approach, and the hands at my sides freeze mid-circle. "Ye finally done fuckin'?" Lachlan growls, and the footsteps halt.

"Look who's talkin', asshole. At least Sniper did it in the bakery. You're out here feelin' your woman up in broad daylight," Whisky's voice slices through the air, ringing in my ears.

I can't believe she said that! I'm *not* his woman.

Chuckles erupt all around from everyone except me and Lachlan.

The hands at my waist don't even flinch when he responds. "Ye can talk all the shit ye want, sister. But I tell ye, I will find out what ye told Mags aboot me."

Peeping through tiny eye slits, I catch a glimpse of Sniper's arm curling tighter around his wife's shoulders.

"What'd ya tell her?" Sniper demands, jerking Whisky closer.

She twists out of Sniper's hold and pushes out a hip for her hand to rest on. "I didn't tell her anything she didn't deserve to know," Whisky defends haughtily, glaring at both men.

Lachlan grumbles a curse, and Sniper shakes his head, a low sound rumbling in his throat.

Whisky's about to get in deep trouble. I can see it happening, and feel the masculine energy filling the air between Lachlan and Sniper who are livid with her.

"I'm not...a...hook-er!" I yell to take some of the tension out of the air. And it works, when all eyes swing to me in surprise. Cas's cheek twitches—I can tell he's trying not to laugh—and Bridget can't seem to decide whether I've lost my marbles or not.

Lachlan's hands drop back to the tops of my thighs as he regards me tenderly. "Um...Lassie, nobody said ye were a hooker."

I sweep my eyes to Cas, and back to Lachlan. "We...he...asked about my car...wondered...how it...got...so nice...and asked...if...I...was a...hook-er," I explain, my body trembling. From what? I dunno. I just know I'm shaking and I can't stop it. Adrenaline? Fear? I can't be sure.

Lachlan's neck twists to the side, eyeing Casanova. "Ye asked her if she was a hooker?" He raises a brow.

Cas pecks the top of Bridget's head that is still tucked against him before producing a one armed shrug. "She's got a sweet ride that would cost any normal person at least forty g's to fix. Can you explain how she got that car? Why she's here? Why we know nothin' about her? Except that she got trapped at the gas station where you saved her, and, according to her ID, she's clean? I dunno, brother; it just seems fishy, is all."

My shaking stops and my temper takes over.

The nerve!

"I'm...not a... hook-er... and I'm not... anything else...you...might...thinkin'!" I hold my head up high, scowling at Cas for thinking ill of me. My hands grip my wheels. "I am...from...Kansas. I left...was going to...New York...when...the storm came...and I got...hurt." I take a break to catch my breath and let my throat rest, but I never take my eyes off Cas. Nobody else speaks. At least they're respectful enough to give me the floor.

Swallowing hard, I start again. "My car...I did...myself. I...work-ed at...shops before. Learned...young. The car was a...gift. *Okay?*"

Cas's intense eyes light up. "You did that car?" He sounds skeptical.

I nod. "Over...ten years...ago."

Sure, it needed a lot of updating since, like a back panel to be replaced. Matching paint was a pain, but it turned out okay. The engine I've kept rumbling like she ought to, only because I'm obsessive about how she runs. The slightest jerk, click, or weird noise and I'm spending hours under the hood, making sure nothing's wrong. I even had the undercarriage repainted three times to keep rust from eating at her. Viola deserves to live a long and joyous life; that way, I can live vicariously through her. She gets more action than I do, anyhow. People love her.

"Wait…" Cas holds up his palm and Bridget moves back to standing beside him; his arm doesn't leave her shoulder. "You're tellin' me you fixed that fuckin' car up yourself?"

Is he really that dense? Didn't I just say that? Hello!

"Uh…yeah." I throw down with attitude.

Cas's hand moves up to scratch his chin. "Do you wanna job?"

I squish my nose at him like he's nutso. Didn't he just ask me if I was a hooker and basically say I'm not trustworthy because he knows nothing about me? Now, he's offering me a position at his garage? Seriously?! Am I dreaming? This has to be a lucid dream, and any minute I'm going to wake up.

I stare at Cas, wondering what his play is, and I keep staring like this until Lachlan squeezes my thighs to yank me out of whatever staring contest I'm having with myself. Shaking my head, I bring my eyes back to Lachlan, whose face is soft and strangely sweet; and not at all scary, even though it's scruffy from not shaving. Now, I know I'm definitely not awake. He's never this complacent. Like, *ever*. My eyes take another gander over to Sniper and Whisky, who are both staring at me with that same sweet, pliable expression. What in the world just happened here? Did I miss something?

I move back to Cas. "Did you…just…offer…me a…job…after ask-ing…if I was…a…hooker? Like…a real…job, not a…hooker…one?" I need clarity, because I can't be sure if he's baiting me or what. This doesn't make any sense.

Cas chuckles, and Lachlan's hands slide up my thighs. I shiver from head to toe as my eyes flip back to him and those big hands that make my thighs look tiny.

Then, he speaks. "He's offerin' ye a job, lassie, for the shop. Do ye bloody want it?"

Do I want a job? What? No...I don't want anything! Okay, that's a fat lie. I want to be able to walk and talk normal again. I want Lachlan to stop rubbing his hands up and down my thighs like he's doing right now. And I really want that to stop, because he's making something between my legs get more excited. I hate this. I shouldn't have come to town, when I should have stayed in bed and wallowed with Pirate the one-eyed dog for the rest of the day. Blah! Why did I have to learn how much more charming and amazing Lachlan can be from his sister? And by doing so, cementing that attraction in my mind. One that I don't want. So no, I don't want a job. I want to walk and talk and move to flippin' Nova Scotia. Is that too much to ask? *Geeze.*

Shaking my head to answer his question, Lachlan's eyes continue to stare into mine, looking for something. I stare back, only because he's staring into mine and those eyes of his are killer gorgeous. And, since I know I'm dreaming, I can stare all I want.

"Then how do you expect to fix your car?" Cas rudely steals my attention.

I continue gazing into those teal eyes and dreamily mutter, "I...don't...know. I do know... that...I'm living...in...the...*Twilight Zone*...and...this...has...to be...a...flippin' dream."

Bridget's giggle vibrates in my ear, but barely registers when I keep on falling deeper into those eyes as those warm hands, that do funny things to my belly, move up to cup my waist again. The massaging resumes with tiny circles at my sides. "Ye know I'll get yer car fixed for ye," Lachlan offers on a throaty whisper.

"Your...hands...are...warm on...my...skin," I reply dumbly.

Lachlan sweeps his tongue across his bottom lip, and I squirm at the sight, my eyes growing heavy, my insides burning hotter.

"Uh oh," a voice says with laughter.

"I think we need to leave them," another teases.

"I think Smoke needs to adjust himself," a man notes.

The words bounce off me, and Lachlan leans closer. I lean in too. Our faces become inches apart, where I can study all of him. Lachlan has full lips, and a scar that's tucked into his eyebrow. He's magnificent, in a rough, manly, kinda way.

Someone loudly clears their throat, and I jerk to, my back slamming into the wheelchair. Lachlan slips out from between my legs, shaking his own head while standing up. I catch him touch downstairs, but only for a second before I look around and realize what just happened.

Crappy-crap-crap!

Cas is silently laughing next to Bridget, who is also laughing with her hand covering her mouth.

I blush.

Instead of making me feel like even more of a fool, Cas returns to our previous subject, allowing me to save face. "About that job..."

Now that I know this is real, and I do need a car to leave as well as money to travel with, I nod my agreement. Whisky claps to my right, and Bridget joins in, bouncing on her heels and breaking away from Cas to go to her aunt and uncle, who are locked in a side embrace. Lachlan's now down the driveway, pacing quickly, his hands threaded on the top of his head, face tipped, staring at the concrete.

Cas saunters unsteadily over to him, and Sniper breaks from Whisky to join them before Whisky and Bridget come to crowd around me.

"Cas must like you if he's offering you a job," Bridget states.

Lifting my shoulders, I drop them heavily in a shrug. The guy's known me for...what? Twenty minutes? And now he's given me a job and Bridget thinks he likes me. This town is weird. Before this, it sometimes took me months to find a job. Nobody wants to hire a chick. And more importantly, a chick that nobody knows. I've been through this routine a billion times before. Okay, not a billion, but more than a handful. I know the drill. I'm mysterious and quiet, and nobody wants to trust a woman who's mysterious and quiet. *Whatever.*

Whisky lays her hand on my shoulder. "This is a good thing for you. Cas runs a tight ship. When your doc okays it, it'll be a good place for ya to be. Gain your footing. Fix that car. Sort shit out. And maybe take the load off Cas."

I cock my head to the side. "A load off Cas?"

Not sure why, but Whisky looks to Bridget and back to me. Then she glances over her shoulder to the men at the end of the drive, who are submerged in some sort of heated conversation that has forced Lachlan to stop pacing and engage with them. His hands are now crossed over his chest. It doesn't look good from here.

"Cas," Whisky tosses her head in their direction, "only has Sniper, and occasionally a couple of the brothers to help out here. He needs to take a load off. He works too much and needs to have time for himself to relax. Between the club, his daughter, and this place, it's too much. His leg needs the break."

"His...leg?" I ask.

Whisky taps her foot on the cement. "Yeah, his leg. Didn't ya notice?"

Not sure what she means, so I shake my head.

Bridget, who is standing beside me, makes a clucking noise and blows out a sigh. "Whisky thinks it's obvious," she groans. "It's not. I keep telling her it's not."

"What's not?" I look between the two of them.

Whisky ganders at the men one final time before she starts. "Cas lost his leg in the *Marines*. Was in when 9/11 went down and was sent on two deployments. On his second, his truck exploded and he was the only one to survive. Lost part of his leg and got PTSD. Doin' better now after he joined the club. And he opened the shop a few years back. But he works too hard and needs to enjoy life a helluva lot more."

I wondered why Casanova walked differently. Although, I wouldn't have guessed that.

My mouth opens to reply when the heavy stomping of boots tears everyone's attention away. It's Lachlan. With a huff, he rejoins the group by maneuvering around his sister to stand behind my chair. Without a word, he flicks my brakes loose and grabs hold of my handles, propelling me forward. I try to stop him by replacing the brakes, but think better of it, because the last time that happened, I ended up flying out of a chair and getting beat up. Not that I think Lachlan would beat me up or anything. However, I think my body has experienced enough damage to last me a lifetime.

"What…are…you…doin'?" I ask, which is ignored. And down the slope of the garage we roll, like he's on a mission, stopping only to check for cars. He continues until we are behind the SUV, where he stops.

Parking me at the back, he rounds the side and opens the passenger door. "Lachlan, what…are…you…doing?" I question as he strides back to me, hooks his arms under my legs, and lifts me from my chair with no effort. My arm curls around his neck on instinct, and my face moves close to his. He steps onto the curb, and tucks me closer to his chest. A warmth seeps into me, calming my pounding heart.

He steps closer to the door. "I'm takin' ye home."

Slipping me into the seat without my help, he then shuts me inside. Moments later, he has placed my wheelchair in the back and is climbing behind the driver seat. The back passenger side door opens and Bridget silently slips inside.

A knuckle knocks on the outside of Lachlan's driver window, followed by his sister's face.

He rolls it down. "Can I help ye?"

"Don't you gotta work?" she teases.

Lachlan shrugs and runs a steady hand through his short hair; the noise that he emits under his breath is enough for me to know he's getting impatient. "I already called someone in."

Curling her hands over the lip of the open window, Whisky scowls, throwing out her attitude in spades. "When'd you do that?"

"When I bloody found out my daughter had Mags in town without me knowin' aboot it," Lachlan growls back, his accent getting heavier with each word.

"Who told you?"

Lachlan blows out an agitated breath. "Ain't none of yer bloody fuckin' business, Whisky. I'm taken the lass home, and I'll get my ride in the mornin'."

"You're leavin'—" Whisky starts, only to be silenced when Lachlan heatedly cuts her off. "It's my fuckin' business, Whisky," he grunts. "Not askin' for yer nosy input. Ye've already done enough by openin' yer big bloody trap. Now back away from the fuckin' door so I can take Mags home."

Sniper approaches and peels his wife's hands off the window frame with some effort. "But—" she argues, trying to regain control, and failing considerably.

"But nothin'," Sniper states, curling her back to his chest, arms locked around her breasts to keep her from getting away. Lachlan turns the ignition over and revs the engine.

Whisky's face falls, frowning sadly. "I wanted to give her some cupcakes," she mutters.

With a curse under his breath, Lachlan turns off the engine and throws the keys on the dash. His eyes cut to his sister. "Go get the cupcakes," he bites off, then adds softer. "And some cookies, too."

Whisky tears herself from her husband and hustles into the shop. Minutes later, she's back and handing us a bag full of goodies through the driver side window. "I threw in two of the Sacred Sister cupcakes. They're the favorite 'round here. When ya get a chance, I'll tell ya a story about them. They're the pink and black ones," Whisky explains to me, ignoring Lachlan, who is giving her a dirty look of both love and mild irritation. He takes it and reaches back to hand it to Bridget, who sets the teal, skull printed bag in her lap.

Lachlan doesn't speak, but nods to them when he reaches for the keys and turns the Tahoe back on.

"It was...nice...to...meet...you."

I wave as Lachlan rolls up his window, and Whisky waves back. Sniper does another nod thingy to us as we idle, and Lachlan keeps his eyes centered forward, not saying goodbye as his jaw ticks and hands tightly clutch the wheel. I want to ask what bug crawled up his butt and died, but then I think better of it, because I really don't need him mad at me. This is the first official time I've actually been around him for any length of time since *The Kiss*. Not sure if he holds any resentment or not. However, I'm not going to test him to find out. The tension is already surging off him in waves.

Staring out of the passenger-side window, I watch the world fly by. With no music and only Lachlan's loud breathing to take up space, which seems to be fogging the windows, I decide that the silence is too much to bear. "Whisky...seems nice," I note to whoever is listening.

When no reply is returned, I continue. "She has...a...nice...shop."

Still, nothing; not even from Bridget, who is mighty quiet in the back. She must be in trouble. Not sure why. Although, if I had to venture a guess, I'd say Lachlan wasn't too keen on her taking me into town without his permission. Not that I think he has a right to be mad at her. I'm an adult and I can go wherever I darn well please. Granted, I can't drive myself; not yet, anyhow.

Call me crazy, I guess, but I keep going. "You...didn't...have to...take...off...work." I mean it to be friendly, and not at all judgmental or pushy. Nevertheless, the growl and heated huff that Lachlan blows out in reply scares the pee right out of me, and suddenly, I need to get home to use the restroom. My hands start to tremble, and I tuck them between my thighs before I position myself as far away from Lachlan as possible.

"Bloody fuckin' shit," he curses under his breath. "Fuck."

Out of the corner of my eye, I catch his hand hit the wheel, and I decide that I won't talk for the rest of the ride home. It can't come quick enough. I've got to pee, and what I need more is to get far, far away from him for so many reasons I don't have the energy to name right now.

CHAPTER 15

Lachlan

Why cannae I bloody sleep?

She's talkin' now—the wee voice in my head reminds.

Aye, for fuckin' days she's been talkin', and not once has anyone told me. *That* makes my blood boil.

Mags sounds different than I thought she would. Sweeter, and softer with more fire. More bloody fuckin' strength. More—everythin'.

Reachin' between my legs, I palm my hard cock over my sweats. See, just thinkin' aboot her gets me this way. What in the hell's wrong with me? And, tae think…I almost kissed her again today. Cannae forget that. What was I thinkin'?

"Nobody wants to kiss a tongue that big," Meredith's voice haunts.

Aye, I know they dinnae. I just cannae help myself. Sometimes, all of that milky white skin, freckles, and now sweet voice, flips a fuckin' switch in my damn brain. I've never experienced anythin' like it. It's like I'm me, but I'm not. Somethin' takes over. Somethin' that I cannae control.

I've spent plenty of time around lassies in the service. And plenty more since I've joined the club. Lots of 'em who try tae throw their skimpily outfitted bodies at me. For what? I dinnae know. None of it makes sense, just like my own actions as of late, dinnae know either.

"You gotta get a grip, brother," Cas scolded me today as I paced outside his shop.

I stopped and crossed my arms over my chest. "If Thor hadn't seen them and texted me, I wouldn't have known Pip had brought her tae town. What the fuck was she thinkin?"

Cas shook his head. Apparently, he thought I was bein' an arsehole. I probably was. I am one most of the time. "That Magdalene needs a break," he replied. "And seein' as though your ass was workin', she was being nice and takin' care of the chick," he paused, then added, "your chick."

Closin' my eyes, I slip my hand under the waistband of my sweats. I hate boxers, so I ain't wearin' any.

Your chick. That sounds damn right.

Wrappin' my hand around my cock, I tuck my other behind me head. It flattens against the arm of the couch, cradlin' my head.

Using my thumb, I swirl my pre-come over my cockhead and use the rest to lube my shaft. Slowly, I jack up and down my length, usin' my nail tae scrap the head. The wee bite of pain makes my balls ache, drawin' up tighter. I thrust my hips, fuckin' my tight fist. My breathin' hastens, and my heart knocks at my ribs as I let my mind shift tae somethin' I shouldn't be thinkin' aboot—*Mags*, and the day she passed out on my lap.

Mags smiled shyly at me, her head restin' on my legs while my fingers combed through her long hair. Back flat on the couch with legs over the armrest, the cotton of her dress stretched snugly over her body, moldin' over her taut nipples. My eyes tried tae pay attention tae anythin' else, but I couldn't seem tae stop starin' at them. I tried not tae get hard.

Relaxed, her eyes fluttered shut. I inhaled deeply, smellin' her fruity scent drift through my nose and into my brain, where it settled, carvin' a tunnel to live in forever.

At the thought, my cock swells, throbbin' in my hand. Groanin', I lick my bottom lip and thrust harder into my fist.

Fuck, those nipples. That perfect mouth. Her soft, silky hair runnin' through my fingers. I tried not tae tremble with pleasure. It was hard not tae.

Almost tae sleep, she half-sighed, half-groaned, floatin' deeper, closer tae dreamland. The noise made my stomach coil and balls ache, needin' a desperate release.

Bloody hell, she's perfect.

I fuck myself even faster, my hand roughly jackin' my foreskin. More pre-come rolls down my shaft. My arse tightens as I jerk my hips, plowin' into my fake fuckhole. My nail scraps my crown sharply, and my back arches off the couch. I growl as the pain ignites an addictive sizzle in my balls.

Aye. She's gonna make me come.

Zeroin' in on those nipples tauntin' me through her dress, my mouth waters, wantin' tae suck them, nibble on them, and run my tongue around their wee peaks.

Twistin' my hand on my cock, I squeeze and all the blood thumps powerfully against my palm.

Oh, fuck!

Diggin' my heels into the couch, my hips thrust one last time before I erupt. Come jets in hot spurts as I groan in satisfaction, coatin' the inside of my sweats.

With a rushed exhale, I sink back into the couch and yank my hand from my pants.

What the shit fuck is wrong with me?!

Openin' my eyes, I take one look at my hand, and the guilt I hoped wouldn't come wins over. My stomach revolts at the sight. Quickly, I stumble off the couch and run tae the bathroom, throwin' myself in front of the toilet. I barely make it in time for my stomach tae purge into the porcelain. Heave after heave surges through me until I'm left empty and pathetic.

Finished and exasperated, I fall back on the tile, nab some toilet paper, and wipe my mouth before I toss it into the toilet. Tuggin' my knees tae my chest, I scrub my palms unsteadily over my damp head. The guilt burrows deeper.

How did I expect anythin' else tae happen? I cannae come thinkin' aboot her like that. Why'd I do it? *Fuck!*

"No woman wants a man who has a dick like that. You wonder why I sleep around, Lachlan? You wonder why I want Barry and Thor? I want them, because you disgust me. Your cock is ugly. It's deformed. No one wants to see that," Meredith's words ring through.

I know she's right. I know it's deformed and ugly. I know nobody would want it. But I cannae help what I look like. I cannae help I was born that way. I... *Fuck it.* With a tired groan, I push off the floor, stagger back tae the couch, and fall into it. The guilt shadows me every step of the way.

On my side, I cup my cock over my pants and squeeze 'til I wince. "Ye stupid fuckin' thing. If ye'd stop gettin' hard then I wouldn't have this bloody fuckin' problem." Smackin' it once, I leave it be and try tae get comfortable. Sleep is gonna be difficult tonight.

Stupid bloody cock!

Mags

"This is bullshit!" a woman screams, and is followed by a succession of frenzied pounding on the downstairs door. "Open this fucking door, you stupid, fat bitch!"

In bed, Pirate scoots closer, his nose nuzzling my cheek, and I reach up to pet him. "I know, I know. It's all right." I attempt to sound soothing and sweet, but what I really feel is a mixture of fear and anger. I can't believe Meredith is here, and it's three in the flippin' morning. What kind of woman shows up to yell at me at three in the morning? Think about it...seriously. That is ridiculous.

My bedroom door opens, and I watch a sleepy-eyed Bridget in cartoon pajamas lazily stroll in. She doesn't wait for me to say anything when she plops on the end of my bed and draws her knees to her chest, curling her arms around them.

"Why is she here?" she whispers miserably.

I'm tempted to shrug, but know she wouldn't be able to see me, so I don't. "I dunno, but let your...dad handle...it."

Heavy footsteps from upstairs have both of us tipping our heads to glance at the ceiling.

"He doesn't want to deal with her."

"Does anybody?" I scoot up in bed, and Pirate follows. Tucking him into my lap, I rest my back against the headboard, my legs still covered in the blankets.

More pounding ensues. "You stupid bitch! You had me locked out of my house! Open this goddamn door!"

Bridget sniffles, and my heart gives out. Why does this woman keep wrecking her child? Can she really be stupid enough *not* to think about her being here? I mean, that's common sense. Which, apparently, isn't all that common...but still.

My phone vibrates on my nightstand. It's Lachlan.

I'm gettin' dressed. Don't touch that fucking door. I will handle this. Please make sure Pip's okay.

I reply, *She's in the bedroom with me.*

Just as I hit send, a loud noise squeals in the back and boots start to descend the stairs. And then it happens—a crash. A heart-stopping, glass shattering, wheels screeching—crash. The house violently shakes, and both of us jump out of our skin.

Oh, crap!

"Ye've gotta be fuckin' kiddin' me!" Lachlan roars.

Heart in my throat, I push Pirate to the side and slide into my wheelchair. Bridget unfolds from the bed and we both look at each other. Something major just happened.

Meredith's screaming, and Lachlan's yelling as we make our way out the door.

My eyes bug out of my head at the sight. Meredith's car is sitting in the living room, still running. The couch is in shambles; the glass door completely shattered. It's a wreck.

Meredith begins to climb out of her car window.

"Shut yer fuckin' car off," Lachlan demands. Luckily, not putting up a fight, she slips back in and shuts down the engine before climbing back out. I expel a relieved breath. At least we won't die from exhaust fumes.

"What the hell are you doing here?!" She wobbles once she's standing, unsteadily pointing to Lachlan. With a phone to his ear, he approaches her and she tilts her head back to look up at him. Her face falls, frowning dejectedly.

"I took Mags home," he snips, answering her question even though she doesn't deserve a dang answer. "Yer not allowed here."

"It's my fucking house, too."

"Not anymore," he bites off, restraining his fury.

With his back to us, his bare shoulders bunch in coiled tension as Meredith weaves on high heels and cuts her eyes to me. "You!" She tries to dive my way.

Thankfully, Lachlan hooks an arm around her waist and propels her backward. She doesn't seem to like his tactic when she starts punching his arm and shrieking for him to let her go. With a phone still to his ear, he ignores her completely, unfazed by her violence and breakdown.

I don't know what comes over me, but I reach out a hand and grab Bridget's. I give her a squeeze, but don't let go. She seems content with that as we silently watch her father move around the car and kick out the remaining tempered glass from the broken door. Then, he maneuvers both of them outside, away from us.

Sirens blare in the distance.

"This place is going to be swarming with cops," Bridget mutters. I'm not sure if she's talking to herself or me. Then again, we're both in a bit of shock at this point. This place is a disaster. Ruined. Such a shame. Idiot woman.

The sirens grow nearer before Lachlan reappears through the door, and his eyes instantly lock on us. "She's tied up outside," he explains, stomping through glass and debris to get to us.

Bridget drops my hand when her dad curls his arms around her in a giant hug. I melt, watching him embrace his daughter. She begins to sob into his chest, and he locks her closer. Her hand fishes out and snags mine again, causing me to smile through my own watery eyes, squeezing her tighter to give my support.

Lachlan's hand smooths down her back. "It's okay, sweetheart," he soothes. "Shhh, shhh; it's gonna be all right."

Bridget hiccups a sob, and the tears I'd hoped would stay away, teem down my own cheeks. This is so unfair. My heart breaks for what she has to be feeling. Life really does suck sometimes.

Sirens cut-off, and we hear the sound of tires approach from outside. Lachlan breaks from Bridget, and she sags, exhausted. His eyes float to me. "They're gonna need tae talk tae ye."

I nod, then tug on Bridget's hand, tilting my head up to look at her. She swipes a tear from her reddened eyes. "It's…going…to…be…okay." I try to sound convincing, although I know it falls a bit short. Her attempt to smile at me falls a bit short, too. Guess that's as good as it's going to get right now.

She sighs. "Thanks."

A police officer wades through the opening, joining us inside. "We've got her untied and in the back of the cruiser, but I'm gonna need y'all to give me a statement."

Lachlan turns and nods. I nod too, and the officer dismisses himself without another word. The noise of men talking with a hysterical woman outside filters through the gash in the side of the house. I try not to pay attention; it's impossible not to, though.

Lachlan pats his daughter's shoulder, giving it a gentle squeeze. "Whisky's on her way. Ye're gonna go with her tonight."

"Okay," Bridget mutters in reply.

"Go pack a bag, sweetheart. Daddy snuggles."

Daddy snuggles? Huh?

"Love you too," she says, then bends down, pressing a kiss to my forehead. "Thanks, Mags." She releases my hand and shuffles back to her bedroom to pack her bag.

She kissed me on the forehead! Oh…my…geee. I feel all squishy inside. Dabbing my eyes with my fingers, I attempt to keep my emotions in check. *I'm not going to cry anymore.*

Lachlan snorts his amusement. "She likes ye," he comments, and moves closer; into my dang bubble. The bubble I want him out of.

I like her, too, a lot. But that doesn't mean I like him the same way. Five feet is the perfect distance for us. Now he's too close, again!

He kneels at my feet, his hands touching my thighs. Why does he always touch my legs?! Why doesn't he put on a shirt? Or wear a paper bag over his head so I don't have to see that ridiculously attractive face? It's even better looking up close. *Geeze.*

Placing my hands on my wheels, he shakes his head, apparently knowing what I'm up to, so I stop. "I gotta carry ye outside. Yer chair won't fit through."

Sighing heavily, I resign myself to the fact that he's correct. So I nod and fold my hands into my lap. He makes his move, scoops me up, and carries me like a doll through the house and out of the broken door. Outside, only one chair remains that isn't damaged. He carefully sets me in it and I thank him.

"Welcome," he grumbles, moving away.

Three cop cars are out here, and Lachlan wades over to talk to a group of officers. A woman's scream tears my eyes from them.

The back window to one of the cars is rolled down and Meredith sticks her head out. "You stupid, fat bitch! You stole my home from me!" she screeches.

"Meredith, stop," a youthful cop scolds, resting his back against the passenger side door of the cruiser, ankles crossed.

"Fuck you!" she spits at him.

Shaking his head, and grumbling under his breath, the man moves his attention to me. "Ma'am, just ignore her."

"I...will." I give him a tight lipped smile through the dark.

Meredith is relentless. "You can fucking talk! The fatty can talk! Lachlan! Your fatty can talk!"

Like a prowling animal in the pride, Lachlan moves away from the officers and closer to the car. He stops two feet away from where her head is poking out of the window. Tipping her head to look at him, she grins, and he growls fiercely. Her eyes widen at the sound and the grin is wiped off her nasty, beautiful face. My insides tremble in a good way at the display. It serves her right.

Lachlan's grizzly noises simmer to a heated breath that rumbles in his chest before he speaks. "Firstly:

Mags is not fuckin' fat," he snarls. "Secondly: ye will stop talkin' tae her, or aboot her. We clear?"

"I will do whatever I want," she barks.

"The bloody fuck, ye will." Lachlan crosses his arms tightly over his chest. From this angle, I can see the side of him, his pecs popping over his forearms, his biceps flexing. The noise in his chest deepens, expanding with his heaving muscles. When she doesn't respond, he continues. "I'm done with yer arse. Already filed for divorce on Tuesday."

"You did not." She sounds surprised. Almost sad, yet, still surprised.

"Aye, I bloody well did. Hell, I cannae believe I didnae do it sooner."

A cop approaches me from the side. I have to force myself to stop listening to Lachlan and give him my undivided attention. They continue their bickering match back and forth as the cop—a very handsome grey haired police officer—kneels by my feet, but doesn't touch me like Lachlan does.

I swipe the sweat off my brow, grateful for the distance.

"Ma'am, I need to get your statement," he explains with a southern drawl. For the next ten minutes, I run down everything that Meredith did to me. I don't leave anything out. It serves her right for hurting her daughter, me, and Lachlan. She's a sick piece of work.

By the time I'm finished, most of the officers have retreated back to their cars, and the one that has Meredith inside pulls away. An all-consuming sense of relief washes over me as the car rolls up the hill and out of sight.

The cop finishes my statement just as Whisky, riding in a pickup truck, descends the incline.

"If you need anything, give me a call." Smoothly, the cop flicks his wrist down, a business card secured between his two fingers. I slip it out and fiddle with it. "My cell number is on the back," he explains, strolling back to his cruiser. I wave goodbye, saying thank you. Lachlan two finger waves, grumbling something I can't catch under his breath before sliding closer to me, leg brushing the side of my chair. Too far into my bubble, but at least he isn't touching me.

Whisky climbs out of the passenger seat of the truck, and Sniper gets out of the driver's. They meet us on the patio. Lachlan doesn't waste a second, leading right into the explanation of what happened.

Bridget wades outside through the mess, a suitcase in her hand and her purse over her shoulder. Whisky takes her bags and puts them in the back of the truck before rejoining us.

"How are you?" she asks, and I shrug.

I guess I'm okay. Nothing really bad happened, for once. Which is an enormous relief. Although the house is in shambles, and that really sucks. But nobody was hurt, Meredith is being carted off in a police car, and justice has been served. Plus, if what Lachlan said is true, he filed for divorce and she won't be comin' 'round here no more, no more, no more, no more. I could almost do a little jig. But I won't. Now's not the time.

Once they finish chatting, Sniper convinces Lachlan that the brothers of their club will help fix the house. Bridget gives her dad a final hug before leaning down to hug me. "See ya soon." My arms wrap around her tightly, and I pat her back as I inhale her scent, locking it away in my memory bank.

I never knew I'd love to hug someone so much as I do right now.

Afterward, all three climb back into Sniper and Whisky's truck, Bridget between them in the cab. Lachlan and I both wave to them as they leave. Once the sound of the trucks loud muffler dies in the distance, we are suddenly submerged into an uncomfortable silence.

A hand lands on my shoulder, and I flinch, caught off guard. "Ye sleep upstairs tonight," Lachlan orders, not giving me any chance to object.

Since it's early and I'm still tired, I give in with a nod. Sleeping upstairs, the same floor as Lachlan...this isn't going to bode well for me. I'll probably be clinically insane by the weeks end.

Dang it.

"Lachlan, I am...not...sleeping...in...her...bed," I'd argued twenty minutes ago when Lachlan tried to convince me to sleep in his soon-to-be ex-wife's bedroom. Not sure what in the world he was thinking, but sleeping in that wench's bed would never happen. Obviously, he refuses to sleep in there, too. Whisky had been right; he's been sleeping on a brown leather couch in the dang living room. I don't know how he can even fit on the thing, let alone sleep comfortably. Guess he's been doing it for years; by the unfortunate shape of the couch, it shows.

Succeeding my stubborn refusal, Lachlan decided to throw Meredith's mattress out of the front door, and carried up the one I've been sleeping on in the basement. Now, I might not be thrilled about staying in her room, but from the looks of it, he's already packed away most of her stuff in the boxes that are now currently lining the walls in the bedroom. There are no personal touches left. Kind of like the rest of the house.

Truth be told, I've been curious for some time about how the upstairs might look. The basement and its cool, beach feel was a far cry from the upstairs. Lachlan's area of the house is a shell, devoid of most things; like a sad bachelor pad. And considering a woman has lived here, it surprises me.

There are two bedrooms, a living room, and an open kitchen-dining room blending as one. The other bedroom is a junk room and office, from what he says; I wasn't shown, so I'm not sure what it looks like. The living room, though, is bland. It has a boring, old coffee table, an old TV on an even older stand, and a couple pictures of Bridget hanging on its stark-white walls. There's no rugs or knickknacks—nothing. The kitchen's the about same; it's sad.

Don't even get me started on the bathroom. I peeked, and it's way outdated. Definitely modeled in the 1970s. It has this geometric, puke-green and orange tile covering all of the walls. It's hideous and in serious need of a renovation. The toilet has a wooden toilet seat, for cryin' out loud; if that's not old, I don't know what is.

Slipping out of the bedroom, Lachlan walks around the couch and drops into it with a weighted sigh. His eyes set on me after he throws his arm wide, stretching it over the heavily worn back. "Bed is made." He tips his chin to where I'm seated, in my wheelchair, on the opposite side of the room. To say this is uncomfortable would be putting it mildly. The insane asylum is already beckoning me. I don't think I can do this. Downstairs was already enough to handle; the upstairs is hell.

Picking at the rubber on the ends of my chair handles, I keep my eyes glued to the wall above Lachlan's head.

Why did I agree to this?

"Did ye hear me?" He sounds friendly enough at this juncture. The question is: if I tell him that I'd rather sleep outside in the barn than inside here, would that ruin the levity? I'm willing to bet it would.

Instead of speaking, I nod. It's my perfect scapegoat. A dang good one.

"Are ye gonna go tae bed?"

I shrug at his question.

Lachlan's voice drops to a low mutter. "Are ye not talkin' tae me?"

Crap! Fine...

"I don't...um...want...to...sleep up...here," I stumble, not because I can't talk, but talking to him when we're alone, when it's pitch-black outside, it's disconcerting. My stomach won't stop doing nervous somersaults.

"Because of my ex?"

My eyes drop to his. He's already calling her his ex? That's...umm...different than I expected.

Lifting my right shoulder, I drop it in a lazy shrug. "I...this...this...is your home." I gesture to the nearly barren room.

"It's yers, too," he comments, propping his bare feet on the coffee table and crossing his ankles. Even his feet are sexy. Big, long, and perfect. *Dagnabbit!*

With difficulty, I try to ignore the squishy feeling his words ignite in the pit of my stomach. If I don't, who knows what might happen.

Turning my head away, I quit looking at his feet before I start staring like an idiot. "And your wife's, too," I reply stupidly.

Lachlan growls under his breath at my words, sending a row of goosebumps to sprout across my body, as I shiver. I hate that I like when he sounds like that. All manly, and grizzly, and *yum*. And to think: not too long ago, I thought those sounds were scary. Funny how things change.

"I filed for divorce," he states, and my shivering intensifies.

He takes notice. "Are ye cold?"

Shaking my head in response, I rub my hands up and down my arms, trying to make it stop, but it doesn't work.

Kicking his feet off the table with a thud, Lachlan stands, crosses the room, and sweeps me from my chair without my frickin' permission. I bark out a startled cry as he tucks me close to his bare chest. I'm pretty sure my lungs forget to breathe when he tips me into his torso so that my body is melted to his, causing me to go ridged in his arms and for my brain to freeze.

Oh. My. God. His. Chest!

Carrying me into the bedroom, he gently deposits me on the freshly made bed. As soon as my body hits the mattress, I scurry as far away from him as possible. Then my voice finally unfreezes. "Why...did you...do that?! Your...naked chest...touched...me!" I shrill, wagging my finger at him.

Eyes wide, mouth gaping, chest heaving, I try to inhale enough oxygen as my body trembles uncontrollably.

I think I'm going to faint!

Smirking—yes, freaking smirking—Lachlan leans against the white bedroom wall with his arms tucked over his broad, tattooed chest. I've never seen him smirk, or smile, or anything. It's sexy. Ridiculously sexy and lopsided. *Lord help me.*

"Aye, my naked chest touched ye. And my hand was close tae yer arse, too."

Did he just make a joke? I think he did.

Knitting my brows together, I frown. "Did you...just...make a...joke?"

The smirk that I didn't know even existed, until now, grows. The damn thing grows! Something between my legs takes notice and likes it; likes it a lot. This isn't good.

"Aye, I did." He sounds like he's making fun of me.

"You made...a joke," I reiterate, because I'm lame and apparently want to make myself sound even dumber than usual.

Way to go, Magdalene.

He nods this time, and those gorgeous teal eyes of his light up with humor. Then, out of my periphery, I swear I catch something enormous twitch in his sweats. This cannot be happening!

Keeping my eyes tipped, so I don't look at something that may or may not be moving in his pants, I fumble with my hands in my lap to distract myself, and blurt the first thing that comes to mind.

"Why...didn't...you...leave her...sooner?"

This is none of my business; I know I shouldn't have asked. However, I'm still curious to know. Ever since Whisky explained that stuff, my curiosity has been eating at me.

Parting my lips to apologize, because I know it's not my place, Lachlan beats me to it as his smirk drifts away. "I'm sorry she hurt ye. And I'm sorry I didnae make ye come with me tae the party that night."

Ummm...that wasn't his choice to make.

"I didn't want...to...go." It's true; I didn't, and he needs to understand that.

Lachlan's body twists back and forth like he's uncomfortable with the subject. "Aye, I know." He stops twisting. "But, I woulda bloody well preferred ye bein' there. And if ye'd come, then she wouldn't have hurt ye." His tone turns sour. "I know I shoulda left her arse years ago."

I'm not going to argue with his last statement, because he's right. He should have. She doesn't deserve to breathe in the same room as him or Bridget, let alone living under the same roof. Not that I deserve that either, but I'm nothing like Meredith, I can tell you that much.

Lachlan

Why in the bloody fuckin' hell am I standin' here, actin' like her sittin' on that bed, in that pretty little nightdress, isn't all I can think aboot?

Did I crack a joke? What was I supposed tae say? Na? That her talkin' aboot my chest makes me just as uncomfortable as it does her? Then I had tae fake a smirk, which turned into a real one after that expression of wonderment crossed her bonnie face. Why cannae I act like a normal fuckin' lad in her presence?

My cock jumps.

Aye, that's bloody well why. I like her too much. Even after pukin' in the bathroom after jackin' off, I still cannae keep from gettin' hard. I'm at half-mast now, lookin' at her look at me, with those big green-blue eyes, tryin' not tae stare at my chest. When she falters, my cock happily takes notice. Not sure why, but I like her eyes on me. And I sure as bloody hell love havin' my eyes on her. That creamy nightdress she's wearin' barely covers her luscious tits that are now heavin' out of the top. Na wonder the officer takin' her statement couldn't take his eyes off her, and went and gave her his number. I'm gonna find that card and throw the damn thing in the trash.

Pokin' my tongue out, I sweep my bottom lip as Mags shifts on the mattress, yankin' up the covers tae meet her waist. Leanin', her shoulders rest against the wall where a headboard should be. Pirate chooses then to enter the room, and jumps on the bed. Tuggin' him closer, she sets him in her lap and scratches him as he nuzzles closer. *Lucky bastard.*

Yawnin', she tips her head toward the ceilin'. The long, slender skin of her neck has me samplin' my bottom lip again as I wonder what her skin tastes like right there—below her ear. *Bet it's sweet.* That thought has me springin' rock-solid. Pre-come drips off the head of my shaft, dampenin' the cotton of my bloody sweats, as my ravenous guilt rears its ugly head once more. I think it's time tae leave.

Pushin' off the wall, I turn tae the door and stop when she calls tae my back. "Lachlan, I'm sorry…you…have to…divorce her."

Spinnin' back around, I scowl at her for the misplaced sympathy. I dinnae need it from her. Not when I shoulda divorced her years ago. That's my own damn fault.

"I was pregnant, Lachlan!" On her tippy toes, Meredith screamed in my face. *"And it's all your fault!"*

I hadn't asked her tae fuck around, and had bloody well tried tae be a lovin', dotin' husband. I must admit I didnae know the first thing aboot the job. I'd never had a serious relationship before her. And with her, I kinda fell into it, because I love my daughter. Meredith fuckin' another man wasn't my fault, but it didnae keep the guilt from eatin' away at my soul.

She'd cheated on me, because of me. If I coulda provided what she had needed, I would have. It never stopped me from tryin' tae make up for all my downfalls, and the bloody fuckin' things I lack. I know I'm not perfect. I know my cock's ugly, and a turnoff. I dinnae even like touchin' it myself.

Hell, I'd only fucked two lassies before I'd ever been with Meredith. My focus back then had been on joinin' the military and workin' hard at that, the lassies never caught my eye. Not sure why, but I've always been uncomfortable around 'em. I cannae talk tae them, and they cannae understand me. Takin' my clothes off in front of the lassies could never work either. That's why admirin' Mags is the most I'm ever gonna do. She cannae see what's in my pants. Na one but Meredith has. All the other lassies I fucked once, at night, where they couldn't see it. Tae this day, I'm relieved that they hadn't gotten the chance tae be appalled by it.

Mags tone softens. "Did ya...hear me?"

Bloody hell. My nuts draw up as the ache tae release unfurls in my groin. If she doesn't stop soundin' so damn cute, I'm gonna have tae fuck my fist in the bathroom. Then I'll purge myself of guilt into the toilet. I'm such a goddamn mess.

Mags

Lachlan returns to leaning against the wall, arms across his chest—his go-to stance.

Right now, it's impossible to overlook the erection he's sporting. It's huge! I try not to stare, and find my efforts paying off while I keep my hand busy petting Pirate. But, can you see that thing, and stare at it for me? I mean...umm...yeah...it's huge. Or, at least, I think it is. Could be that I haven't had sex in a while. That greedy part of my anatomy is seriously begging for some attention. Not that I'm going to get any action, or want any attention. Pretty sure I'd faint or die, or a combination of the two if he even tried to come near me with that thing.

Did you look? Are we on the same page? It's huge, right?

Not that I'm surprised by that or anything. His feet, his arms, and the rest of him are gigantic, so why shouldn't Little Lachlan be proportionate?

Shitty-crap-crap-shit! I can't believe we're sitting here having this conversation, and I'm even confiding in you about that. Pretty sure I've never discussed a man's woody with another human being in my entire life. Confessing to flowers and vegetables? Probably, since I do love to garden and they can't talk back. Female to female, interaction, though? That's never been my thing.

"I heard ye." Lachlan recaptures my attention. It's better than focusing on you-know-what. "What I dinnae understand is why ye keep focusin' on Meredith."

That's easy. "'Cause you're...a...good person...and she's not."

Not liking my reply, Lachlan grumbles in his throat and his nostrils flare. "I'm not a good person," he argues.

Now that's where he's dead wrong. I could give him 101 reasons why he's a good person, but I don't think he'd let any of that sink into his thick skull. And here I thought I was the stubborn one.

Time to go in for the kill. "You're...good. She's not. Why'd you...marry...her, you...know, anyhow?" I can't get Whisky in trouble if he admits it to me himself.

Shaking his head in obvious exasperation, Lachlan's accent thickens. "Pip was born when I was on deployment. Came home and found out. Decided, even if I dinnae love the lassie, that I loved my bairn enough tae suck it up and take care of what's bloody well mine. Dinnae regret a fuckin' thing doin' that. Got me a daughter, and that's more than I coulda hoped for...." He tilts his head to the side, his face expressionless and tone sharp. "Now does that answer yer nosy question?"

My *nosy* question? Geeze, he's acting like an ass.

Fine. Two can play at this game.

"Nosy question? That...is a question...I think I'm entitled...to ask." I throw out my sass, take a deep breath, and hope to God that his reaction doesn't cause me to pee my pants. To aid in distraction, I return to petting Pirate, even though my heart is about to pound its way out of my chest. I can't believe I actually threw sass at him. Since when do I have sass? *Son of a biscuit eater!*

Lachlan curses under his breath. "Why in the bloody fuckin' hell do ye think ye deserve tae know a damn thing?"

Uh-oh, I've awakened the scary Scot.

Guess, if you can't beat 'em, join 'em. My nose bunches, wrinkling between my eyes. "I think...I...deserve...to...know...because I barely...know...you. *And,* I live...under...the...same...freakin'...roof."

Not of like mind, Lachlan overzealously twists his thickly corded neck along with his obstinate head, back and forth. "Ye dinnae have tae know me tae live under the same roof, *lassie*."

Seriously?!

"Yes! I do. I've never lived...with...a...man...*ever*."

If that's not reason enough, I don't know what is. I never lived with a dad, or with Brian. This is the most I've ever slept under the same roof with a man in my entire existence. Now, can you see why being here makes me feel weird? And the only person I have ever lived with was my grams. I can't help that I'm mostly a loner; it's how my cards have been dealt.

"What?" Lachlan stops shaking his head and cocks it to the side, his eyes rounding as he takes me in. Not sure what he expects to see. "Ye have two rings on yer hand." He nods to my left hand where a small engagement ring and wedding ring encircle my finger. "Aren't ye married? Divorced?"

Ha, I will not answer that question. He wants to bark at me about being nosy, now look who's the nosy one. Like my grams always used to say, *"What's good for the goose, is good for the gander."* Well, this goose isn't allowed to know jack, so he's not gonna know jack either.

Strengthening my spine to appear tough, I reply as levelly as possible. "I will...not...tell you...*any-thing.*" Then I swallow thickly to keep from throwing up. My hands start to tremble, so I tuck them under Pirate to hide the evidence.

Growing scary quiet, the palpable tension floating in the air turns dense.

Arms still folded, Lachlan scratches his chin in contemplation. The *scritch-scratch* bellows in my ears. "Fine," he eventually huffs. "How aboot we cut a deal?" His brow quirks in question, those intense teal eyes strangely soft. I've never seen anything so sexy in my entire life, other than maybe his smirk—a smirk that would make any woman weak at the knees. I'm just glad I was sitting down when he first laid that bad-boy on me.

"Go on." I nod while continuing to hide my shaking hands.

"How aboot I won't be an arsehole tae ye, and let ye ask me a couple questions. *If,* ye answer mine, too."

Sounds fair enough.

"Fine." I shrug noncommittally, as my insides jump up and down in tactile triumph. On the outside, though, I remain poker-faced. Don't want to show all my cards at once.

Firmly, his head inclines. "Rings?"

"Grams's wedding ring...and my...old...engagement ring." That's simple enough.

"Old—" He starts on another question, no doubt about my rings, but the stern shake of my head and the *tsking* under my breath makes him stop.

To provide him some reprieve, I go with something lighter. "Why...the...nickname, Pip?"

That heart-stopping grin returns, curling at the corner of his lip. My insides somersault, delighted by the gift.

"She's a ginger," he states the obvious. "Not many ginger stories, so Whisky got her hooked on Pippi Longstocking. We ended up readin' all the adventures tae her."

By *we*, I assume he's talking about Whisky and himself, not Meredith.

Pausing for a beat, he then tacks on. "Now, tell me aboot that old engagement ring."

Sighing, I slip down the wall, wanting to disappear into the mattress. I've never told anyone about my rings. Not that they haven't asked; I just refused to disclose. Nevertheless, I've made a deal, and as painful as talking about Brian is, I know asking Lachlan to talk about Meredith can't be much easier. At least I know I'm not alone in some sort of the torment.

Here goes nothing. It's like ripping off a *Band-Aid*, right?

Looking away from Lachlan, my eyes fixate on the wall. I don't think I can watch him when I voice this. God, my heart already hurts. I don't want to do this.

Digging my nails into my palms, I take a deep cleansing breath as tears that I wish wouldn't come—well, in my eyes.

Why is this so hard?

"Mags?" Lachlan's voice is soft, sweet, and so painful to hear that it forces a hiccupped cry to tear from my throat. Tears run, slipping down my cheeks as my bottom lip waivers, and my pulse rushes through my ears.

I can't do this. I just can't. I can't tell him about Brian. I can't share something I've never shared. That's too much, too soon. I barely know the man. Kind or not, Lachlan and I can't speak about—another hiccupped tremor racks my system.

The bed dips, and I keep my eyes on the wall as my vision blurs. The weight in my lap lifts and the warmth is replaced by a massive furnace of heat, curling around my shoulders, dragging me closer. I close my eyes. Thick bands of steel lift me and set me crossways on hard planks, pulling another tumbled cry from my lips. I raise my fists to my eyes to wipe away the salt before my head sags in emotional exhaustion, dropping to my chest. A strong heat presses to my cheek, coaxing it to rest on the best smelling, soft, smooth granite that I've ever felt. Then a charming thud methodically resonates in my ear, and I curl closer, clinging to the force of comfort.

Fighting to breathe through my anguish, five thick prongs soothingly glide through my hair.

Brian. How…can I talk about him? He died. He was my everything. He was it. The one. The man who sang stupid songs to me, and made love to me. Brian made me feel so much more than I could have ever thought possible. How can I talk about him? Why does Lachlan want to know?

Moving my fist to my chest, I rub over the painful shredding behind my ribs. It's tearing me apart inside.

Why me?

Twisting my head toward the heat, my nose buries into a patch of soft and fuzzy perfection. The rich scent of man intensifies, flooding my senses. And the prongs in my hair gently glide down my back, stopping just above my butt. They flatten there, anchoring me in place, before injecting a sense of peace and serenity into my veins. Instantly, my body relaxes, mind clears, and the tears run dry as the vice surrounding my heart slackens.

Oh, sweet relief, I can finally breathe again.

"Yer, gonna be all right," Lachlan whispers, and I snuggle deeper, clinging to the person I know I should be running from, but can't.

Prying open my eyes, I come face-to-face with the knowledge that my nose is pressed into the soft patch of rusty hair between his pecs.

That funny feeling in my gut sprouts once more.

Not daring to glance up at his face, I do the only thing I want to do, and give in to this strange temptation. I run my nose through his hair, smelling him, enjoying him, relishing in his heat, and all the things I didn't even know I crave. It settles a warmth deep within, and excites an untamed wetness to dampen between my thighs.

Up and down I rub my nose, as he grumbles in his chest, his arms tensing, turning to stone around me.

I don't stop until he groans thickly as if he's in real pain. "Ye gotta stop doin' that, Mags."

"Why?" I whisper daintily, running my nose in circles, gliding further into his meaty, tattooed pec.

When I expect to feel a sense of dread and need to run, I don't. The heat ignites hotter, deep-down, fueling my nonexistent courage.

I strike gold and circle his small, firm nipple.

Growling lowly, like a gravelly purr in his throat, the hand on my back presses harder, fingers gently digging into my flesh. His breathing grows heavy, chest noisily pumping for air.

Dormant flames of desire lick my spine, and I grow bolder. My tongue lashes out, striking his nipple, and I'm rewarded with a short, grizzly moan before his fingers slip through my hair and tighten on my scalp. Then he yanks my head back, stealing me away, unable to taste his succulent flesh.

My eyes are met with teal ones laden with desire. I swallow thickly, and he laps at his bottom lip, his eyes still locked on mine.

I squirm at the sight, my brain catching up with my actions.

I can't believe I'm touching him! I licked his nipple! I...Me...Magdalene...I did that! How is that possible? Holy hot damn.

"Mags," he drawls. The sound of my name coming from his lips in that husky tone makes me melt like ice-cream on a hot summer's day.

"Uh?" I squirm again, unintentionally grinding my butt into his thighs.

The erection that I've desperately been trying to forget is there, twitches against the outside of my leg.

Lordy, I can't do that again, I think as the wanton clenching in my core objects to my decision.

"Mags, ye cannae be touchin' me with yer tongue." He gives me a stony look. "And I dinnae want ye tae be bloody cryin'."

Fine. Consider me well scolded.

Now please excuse me while I crawl in a hole and flippin' die!

Shaking my head to make him release my hair is a futile effort, because he won't let go. Next, I reach on top of my head to pry his fingers off. Still, he doesn't release me. The man is too damn strong.

"Let go," I snap in frustration this time. Still, he doesn't budge.

"Lachlan!" I whine, going for desperate. Still, nothing. It's like I'm talking to a wall.

Relenting, I expel a defeated '*humph*' and my body deflates. In silent retort, his fingers slacken, but don't let go.

"Now, tell me aboot the ring," he commands gently.

Stubbornly, I glower and shake my head. Not gonna happen.

"Mags, a deal's a deal." He blows out a breath. "I can see it's not easy. But ye're gonna tell me anyhow."

"Nope."

"Ye got two choices," he grumbles. "Tell me, and I'll let ye go back tae sleep. Or dinnae tell me, and I keep ye up, holdin' yer hair." His fingers tighten on my scalp for a moment, displaying his dominant upper hand.

I don't know what possesses me, but one second I'm giving him a dirty look, the next I'm smacking his chest, hard. It stings my palm, spiking pain up my arm.

Struck with shock, I look at my hand and to the red mark I've left on his pec. Guilt tramples forward, carting my instincts with it. Like my grams always used to do, my lips crash down on the damage and I try to kiss it away.

What was I thinking? Who hits someone? *Meredith does.* Uh...I'm such a bitch!

Guilty tears spring forth and tumble down my cheeks, as I continue to kiss the violence away. What is wrong with me tonight? I'm such a horrible person. I licked his nipple without permission, then I hit him. I'm so messed up. A nutcase.

The hand on my head grips my hair, yanking me off his pec, now damp from my lips. "Ye didnae hurt me," he states.

My bottom lip trembles, meeting his eyes. "I...hit...you."

Lachlan shrugs, unaffected. "So what. I dinnae care. Now, be a good Lassie and out with the fuckin' story."

Well, if he insists.

Lachlan

If she doesn't start talkin' aboot this bloody fuckin' story soon, I'm gonna have her on her back with my cock buried in her pussy. Not that I want that, but my body's whistlin' a whole other tune at this point. Those lips kissin' her wee slap had me close tae comin'. Now, I'm so bloody wound and my adrenaline's poundin' through me so fuckin' hard, that I dunno if I can keep a grip on this ache much longer.

What was I thinkin' tryin' tae console her in the first place? She stuck her nose in my chest hair and licked my fuckin' nipple, for Christ sake. I cannae believe it. Let's not forget I can now see down her silky dress that feels like butter glidin' over my skin.

Inhalin' a lungful of her scent, I feel my control slip a fraction further as my ravenous cock throbs painfully in my sweats. With considerable strength, I force myself not tae thrust against her leg. The friction makes my fuckin' blood roar, and all thoughts move tae one carnal need; tae release inside somethin' wet and warm.

"I…really…don't want to…tell you." She sighs, tearin' me from my horny fuckin' thoughts. Shame forms into a boulder, knottin' in my gut.

"But I will," she finishes, and a sweet relief washes over me. A distraction is exactly what I damn well need. And I truly do wanna hear all she has tae say. I love her voice. If only my cock would shut the bloody hell up sometimes, and give me a chance tae think straight and pay attention tae the important shit.

My focus settles on her face as she opens her perfect mouth tae speak.

Thank fuck.

Mags

"His name…was…Brian," I start, and Lachlan exhales like he's content to be where he is, like he's comfortable. "He asked….me to marry…him…after I graduated…high school."

"That's young," he mumbles, not trying to deter me.

"Yes," I agree with a nod, because he's right; it was young. Too young for most people. Just not Brian and I.

I continue. "He was a few...years older. A farm...boy. We fell in love. Planned to be married...after he...finished college." I sigh with sadness. We had great plans to buy a farm, get married, have three kids, and grow a giant vegetable garden that I'd tend. So many beautiful plans ruined by the dark cloud that looms over my life, turning everything good to shit.

"What happened?" Lachlan asks, his hand tightening on my back as if he's scared of what my reaction might be.

I get that. I did just cry like a fool. Somehow, though, I feel better after that cry. I don't cry much, or never did before my near-death accident. But I've come to the conclusion that crying is cathartic, even if it makes me feel like a weak woman.

"He died." I let it all hang out there for a moment before I explain the rest, because I know if I don't, he'll ask anyhow.

The body below me goes ridged.

"It was planting season. Brian...ran...his...father's farming equipment. I...was supposed to bring...him...dinner. And I ran...late, helping...my grams. Something...must have happened...that he got...out of the cab...and...ran over...by a...tire. By the time...I got there... he was ice cold. Called the...ambulance, anyhow. They took...him...away. His father...then had him...cremated. Even though...Brian wanted...buried. Never...got the...ashes. His father...kept them all."

I leave out the gory details, even though Lachlan could probably handle them. But I don't think he needs to know about his organs being crushed, and rigor mortis had set in by the time the ambulance had finally showed up. Or that the cop that also came had to peel me off his dead body, because I refused to let him go. It's also best I don't tell him about being sedated by heavy medications for the entire month after Brian's death just so I'd stop puking and crying day after day. At that time, nobody knew that only a few months later my grams would also be dead, too, and I'd be left in an even deeper pit of despair that I've had to live with since.

Lachlan squeezes me in a hug, pressing my face to his chest. "I'm sorry for yer loss." His arms loosen around me, and the one in my hair disengages, moving to curl around my side. I raise my head to meet his gaze.

Somehow, I feel like a massive weight has been lifted, making me feel lighter.

"How long ago did he die?" he asks.

"Ten years."

Answering his question leads to another and then another. Soon, I feel like I've shed my skin and I'm opening up like I've never opened up before by telling him things that I've never spoken aloud to anyone. From Brian and I, and our car rebuilding, to my love for gardens, and obsession with my garlic bulbs. Which he reassured me he found under his ex's car downstairs, somehow untouched. Divine intervention strikes again, and for that, I'm immensely grateful. By the time I've exhausted all of my stories about Brian, and a tiny bit about grams, the light of dawn begins to shine through the bedroom window.

Covering my mouth with my palm, I yawn behind it, and Lachlan leans in, resting his forehead on mine. "My leannan, I think it's aboot time for ye tae lay yer wee head down tae rest."

The urge to argue arises, because I don't want to sleep. If I sleep, I'm afraid this entire night will have been a dream, never to have happened. I don't want that. I want to remember sitting on Lachlan's lap for hours, talking and sharing my life, while he listens contently, chiming in when necessary. The truth is, he's not confided in me much, and Whisky has filled in most of the holes. But I hope one day he'll feel comfortable enough to let his guard down, and maybe I'll be the one to hold his hand through it. Then again, maybe not.

Lachlan lifts his forehead from mine, rubbing his hand up and down my back. "Ye need some sleep."

Innocently shaking my head, I burrow deeper into his chest, snuggling my face between his pecs, while my arm curls around his thick torso, holding on. "I don't...want to," I whine like a teenage school girl, swirling my nose in the most amazing chest hair. I've never loved chest hair before this. Brian didn't have any. Now, it's like chocolate to me—addicting. I don't want it to go.

An amused rumble battles in his chest, and those arms lock tightly around me, keeping me just as close as I want to be. Taking pleasure in his tenderness, I expel a satisfied sigh at the comfort in this moment. There's nothing like it in all the world. I just had to get over my closeness and insecurity issues and pretend that I'm beautiful, worthy, and not completely scared out of my mind to be here. With those falsities in place, I can indulge and bask in the airy lightness, and accept the sense of satisfaction that has budded and tunneled roots, deep into my soul.

"I gotta workout, and ye gotta sleep." He tries again to coax me from my Lachlan bubble. I don't think it's going to work.

Stubbornly, I shake my head this time and lightheartedly argue. "You... need... sleep... too." He hasn't slept any, either.

In reply, I'm gifted an untamed growl from his chest that vibrates through me. If it were any other day, I'd probably be terrified. Now, it awakens other parts of me to take notice. And to distract those parts, I inhale sharply to focus on his scent, which does nothing to ease the hunger igniting below. If anything, it makes it worse. Next, to offer further distraction, I shift enough so I'm able to lay my hand on his stomach. Hair tickles my palm, as does the heat of a warm, feral man, who is now growling louder, deeper; so fiercely that it's making him breathe harder, and by doing so, I, too, begin to pant.

God, listen to that noise.

I shudder.

Distracted by him, I don't realize where my hand travels. Heading north, it glides between the hard rippling plains of his abs to the base of his pecs, where I am forced to stop when my fingers meet my own chin resting there. I jerk away in surprise, staring at my palm in astonishment. I can't believe how bold I've suddenly become.

Lachlan doesn't let me go far, for too long, when he yanks me back to his chest. My arms instinctually hug his torso, head tucked back in its rightful place.

Lips graze the top of my hair, and my body shivers again, my southern parts throbbing. "I'll stay until ye go tae sleep. Then I'll go tae the barn."

"Okay," I whisper before pressing a tiny kiss between his pecs. Not sure if he feels it or not. And secretly, I hope he doesn't so that I can treasure the memory for myself. "Thank you…Lachlan." My eyes grow heavy, body turning into emotionally sated mush.

"Goodnight, Mags," is the last thing I hear before the sandman takes me away, to sweet dreams of a warm Scottish man and his perfect body melded to mine.

Bliss.

Lachlan

Punchin' the heavy bag hangin' from the rafter in my barn, I try tae focus on my need for exertion as the throbbin' music of Rob Zombie fuels my adrenaline. Not that I need his help. I could run twenty miles nonstop in this fuckin' state.

Mags slept on my chest? *On. My. Chest.* Lips, on my bloody fuckin' chest! Didnae take her long tae pass out. I knew she was tired by the way her body kept saggin' against mine. Not that I minded, but fuck, all that soft, warm plushness rubbin' all over me—I'm half surprised I didnae black out from bein' so wound up. My cock even stayed hard through her tragic stories. That's fucked, I know. I just cannae help it.

Hell, her fiancée died in a farmin' accident. What was I supposed tae say aboot that? Then, she decided tae tell me all that other shit, aboot them, aboot her life back then, aboot fixin' up her car, and all that other important stuff that made me jealous as bloody fuckin' hell. I cannae believe I want tae kill an already dead lad for proposin' tae her durin' sex in the back of her car. I dinnae want tae think aboot her havin' sex with anybody, in any place, even the back of her car. Just aboot saw red at that juncture, until she shook in my arms, aboot tae cry again. I cannae stand watchin' her cry. It rips my own damn heart out.

Dinnae take this the wrong way, I'm happy she told me. But, when a woman ye seem tae care aboot is tellin' ye aboot the lad she's still in love with, it's a slow agonizin' death. Thought I knew what pain was until I got tae hear how great and perfect the lad was. And I'm not gonna deny that he was. From her stories, he seemed like a perfect fit for her. Which tells me, even more than I already know, that I'm the last lad she could ever want. Cannae blame her. Meredith thought I was shit; makes sense that Mags would feel somethin' similar.

Throwin' my bare fist into the bag, it swings wide and I plow it with a one-two twist, and pitch a roundhouse kick. Movin' back tae stance, I bounce off the balls of my feet, shakin' my arms out at my sides. I'm gonna need a good three hours out here today tae work some of this aggression out. If not, I might as well never set foot around Mags again, or I'm liable tae bite her bonnie little head off. That, or somethin' worse—like try tae fuck her.

One thing I now know for bloody sure, is I need tae keep my distance from her. It's for her own good.

CHAPTER 16

6 Weeks Later

Mags

I can't flippin' believe it! I just can't! Today is my first day on the new job. Yes, that means at Cas's shop. I'm nervous, and a little excited, too. It'll be nice to have some time away from the house. Lord knows, I'm in desperate need of it.

Standing in front of the dresser, I stuff my legs into my overalls and click the metal tabs together at my shoulders. My matching white tank top, bra, and panties are concealed underneath, along with my leg brace. I can't decide if this itches more, or if the cast was worse. I'm just happy to be on the mend and able to walk again. It's only been a couple weeks, but my freedom has never felt so sweet, and I don't think I'll ever miss that wheelchair for as long as I live.

Finishing with socks and my worn work boots, I slip out of the bedroom and into the bath to finish my hair and makeup. While I do that, why don't I fill you in on my boring life for the past six weeks? Sound good? You nodding? Yippy skippy...I thought so.

Other than my voice turning back to normal, and my cast coming off, there's not much else to explain. The basement took two weeks to fix with the help of

Lachlan's club brothers. Who knew there were an entire slew of heavily tatted bikers to lend a hand? Not me.

During those two grueling weeks, where hammers and saws worked at all hours of the day, I stayed in my room, as far away from them as possible. I'm not comfortable around Lachlan part of the time, and adding half-dressed men, some of which are quite attractive, made me not want to risk embarrassing myself—or worse, Lachlan. So yeah, it's fixed now, and Bridget's back to living downstairs while I remain upstairs. I like it better up here, anyhow. It gives Bridget more privacy, and me a covered front porch or the raised back deck to lounge on while I indulge in fictional fantasies.

Hum…what else can I tell you? Bridget's back to school and still working part-time for Whisky. Not that you really need to know that. Lachlan's continues to work two days a week, and any time he's not working, he's working out, or gone. He hasn't spent much time here, other than to catch a few winks and grab a bite to eat now and again.

To be helpful and pass some time, I've made it my duty to have sandwiches and lemonade stocked in the fridge for whenever he does drop in to munch. He must like it, because the food's always gone.

A couple of days ago, I whipped up a batch of brownies, which I'm sure aren't even close to as delicious as something Whisky can bake, but I was craving chocolate. Not much good that did me. By the time I'd made them, took a shower, and had a nap, I woke up and found most of the pan empty on the stove and no Lachlan anywhere to be found.

Unfortunately, or fortunately, depending on how you look at it, there's not much I can say on that front…Lachlan-wise, that is. Our conversations now resemble those of a traveling roommate, or neighbor; always basic and straight to the point. We haven't shared anything of importance since the night Meredith was carted off by the cops. Sometimes I wonder if that night ever happened at all. It seems like more of a fantasy that I concocted in a state of emotional exhaustion, not one based in reality. Yes, I've been tempted to ask why he doesn't speak with me anymore. But every time I see him, he looks worn-out and irritated. And I don't want to poke at the bull, because I'm sure I'll get the horns. Instead, I keep it light and pretend I don't care. Even though, I do. I care so much it hurts.

Hey, now don't you frown, too. One of us has to try to stay upbeat. I'm leaving that to you. Okay?

On a less of a Debbie Downer note, on nights I know Bridget's going to be home, I make us supper that we eat on her little table in the basement. It's really nice, and highly informative, since she's always spilling girly gossip; sometimes more than I care to hear, but like it anyhow. However, most days and nights, I read. I've also taken to walking around outside with Pirate, and through the woods surrounding Lachlan's property to try and regain strength. Other than that, life's been boring, and for once, anticlimactic. Except for the two days a week I travel into Carolina Rose for therapy. That is one experience that is an utter waste of my time and not something I need bother you with right now. So I won't. Instead, I'll finish coating my eyelashes in mascara, and dab on the lip-gloss that Bridget gave me.

"Ye aboot ready?" Lachlan startles me and I jerk to, dropping the lip stuff into the sink. On instinct, my hand clutches at my chest, where my heart pounds, as I use my free hand to snatch up the rolling lip-gloss before I swing to face him.

"You scared me," I breathe, flustered.

He shrugs, standing in the doorway, arms hanging casually from the frame. The blue *Harley* shirt he's wearing today leaves nothing to the imagination. Not that any of his shirts afford me that reprieve. Guess when you have a body like that, you should show it off. Some women probably love it. I don't, not anymore. It tends to make the attraction I feel more potent. When really, I need it to be watered-down. Watered-down is ideal. Ideal, is a pipedream. *Damn it.*

Lachlan eyes me from head to toe, stopping on my face. "Ye're not wearin' that today," he comments, non-threateningly.

I'm not?

Stuffing my hands into my pockets, I cock my head to the side. "This is my work outfit. I'm wearing it."

"Ye need to put more clothes on." His eyes rake my form again, landing back on my face. Those intense eyes bore into mine.

He can't be serious? More clothes? I'm in jean overalls and a tank top. The only thing more concealing is a freakin' parka. And I'm not doing that; it's too hot out. Plus, it's not his call. I can wear whatever I want. He never seemed to have this problem when I wore all those dresses. Now I'm back to normal clothes, clothes that I feel comfortable in, and make me feel like *me*. I'm not changing. He can eat dirt for all I care. Okay, I do care. I don't want him to eat dirt. Ignore that.

"I'm not changing. There is nothing wrong with this." I stick my hip out, going for defiant attitude, and failing just a little at it. I'm not one for drama, and he's slowly opening that can of worms.

"Yer tits are aboot tae pop out." He motions to my chest, which most certainly isn't going to pop out anytime soon. I have a bra on, a full coverage one, and the tank top touches my throat. It's not low cut. Someone is off his rocker today, and to prove my point, I untuck one hand from my pocket and tug on the collar of my tank.

"This isn't going to move from my neck." I pluck at the collar once more, shaking my head in exasperation, my tone suggesting the same. "It doesn't accidently drift down as the day goes on. I don't know what imaginary clothes you think I'm wearing, but this is standard shop clothes. Clothes that are plenty appropriate for the workplace."

"Do ye know car magazines and porn show all of the lassies in overalls and white shirts? Ye're wearing overalls and a white shirt. Ye need tae change." He's resolute, and too flippin' tense about my clothes.

I don't even want to know what magazines and porn he's been watching or reading. Most of them don't have women covered. Most of the time, they're in skimpy clothes, with their fake headlights flashing like shiny beacons for the men to feast their dirty eyes on. None of them dress like this. So instead of making a big scene and fighting with him, I travel the high road. *Sarcasm.*

Clasping my hands in front of me like a shy school girl, I try my best to act the part and keep my voice timid. "Why, Daddy, I'm sorry I look like a tramp. I shall go change into a velour pantsuit and parka." I curtsy, bowing my head, and keep it bowed until he responds. I don't have to wait long for a rushed growl and the word *'fuck'* to ricochet off the walls in the bathroom.

I glance up, still playing my part of the shy girl. I know it's craptastic to act this way, but it's fun, and he's got to learn a lesson one way or another. I'm not sure what his deal is today. I just know that it has nothing to do with my clothes. Then again, I'm not going to pry either. This is the most he's interacted with me in almost a week. The last thing I want to do is make him angry when he already looks broody and irritated most of the time.

Taking a bountiful step forward, where I'm merely a foot away from him, I tilt my head back to meet his gaze. "Shall I pass, sir?"

Not budging, he curses under his heavily accented tongue. Then drops his arms from the frame, standing tall and towering over me while his chest expands with each laden breath. "Go get yer coat, and I'll meet ye out by the bike." He slowly steps to the side, giving me just enough room to pass.

Out by the, what?

I'd spoken to Bridget just yesterday about driving the SUV to work, and that Whisky would pick her up from school. I'm not riding any bike. Especially not Lachlan's.

Frozen, feet glued to the ugly tiled floor, I expel a long bated breath that I didn't realize I was harboring. Unable to look directly at Lachlan, I stare straight ahead, out of the bathroom door, and reply as strongly as I'm able, "I'm not riding on your motorcycle."

He doesn't give me a chance to formulate a rebuttal before he shoots back. "Aye, ye are. Pip has the Tahoe, and ye need a ride tae work. I'm goin' into town, and I'll drop ye on my way. Then I'll pick ye up when ye get off."

Snapping to face him, I glower. "Why would Pi—Bridget have the Tahoe? She told me yesterday that she would catch a ride with some friends in the morning, and Whisky would get her from school. We planned this," I heatedly explain, which seems to be lost on him when my tone doesn't penetrate his Macho Man exterior.

Another haphazard shrug is what he offers me. "I unplanned it."

What?!

The kicker to this is he doesn't even sound the least bit remorseful. What is wrong with him? This is a load of bull-honky!

"You *unplanned* it? Unplanned, *my* plans?!" I shrill, then drop my tone to one that comes from a deep place; a place where I care for Lachlan. "What's going on with you today? Are you okay?" Months ago, I would've been too nervous to address him. Now, I'm not the least bit afraid.

"Aye, I unplanned them with Pip this mornin'. I'll meet ye by the bike." Lachlan dips his head, and doesn't wait for my subsequent argument before he saunters away.

I watch him go with tight lips and the itch to unleash, arguing the unfairness of it all. However, I keep it bottled up where it belongs. This isn't my house. I might feel at home here, which is strange enough in itself, but it's his domain. I'm only a visitor passing through.

Stomping like an errant child to gather my things, I then clomp my way out the front door, slamming it in my wake. The adult temper tantrum does nothing to squash my irritation as I grumble my way over to the motorcycle that Lachlan is suavely straddling in the drive.

When I moved in here, I'd made a deal with myself that I wouldn't spend more than three seconds staring at him on his motorcycle, in fear that my ovaries might explode. I'm at twelve seconds now, and any moment, they're bound to detonate like a stick of dynamite.

Some men own *Harley*'s because they wanna be badass. Then there're men like Lachlan, who put the *badass* in *Harley*. Black and sleek, with lots of chrome, his motorcycle nestles itself between his legs like it was made for him, like they're one. The engine loudly idles, and the rumbling of his tailpipe turns my legs to Jell-O.

I wobble forth, resting my hand on the black, leather bitch-seat to stable myself.

God, I really wish I didn't love motorcycles and cars so damn much. They're a serious weakness.

Watching Cas tow Viola from the barn last week to his shop had me in tears of both remorse and happiness. Her history and getting the chance to fix her was all emotionally coinciding.

Now, as I watch Lachlan on his motorcycle, wearing his Corrupt Chaos vest, a pair of shades, and a black helmet covered in stickers, I'm getting a much different feeling than remorse or happiness. It's a lot different.

I'm screwed. Way, way, way screwed.

Lachlan drapes a matching black helmet off his finger and gestures to it with the incline of his head. "Yers."

Slipping it on, I tighten the chin strap before my first attempt of swinging my leg over the bike. I fail miserably and die a little on the inside at the sheer embarrassment. Redness showers my cheeks as Lachlan watches with keen eyes but doesn't say anything. Apparently, he's letting me go at it alone. With my outburst in the house, I can't blame him.

Defeated, I slump my shoulders and kick the gravel, berating myself for even trying to get on the back of his bike. I wish my leg worked like she used to. It's still too stiff.

"Here!" Lachlan yells over the roar of the pipes, and I lift my head.

Scooting forward, he leaves enough open space at the back of his seat for me to straddle. It's lower than the bitch-seat, and easier for me to hike my leg over. Taking his offer without argument, I place my hand on his shoulder, feeling the smooth leather under my palm, and kick over. This time it works, only my body is suddenly plastered to Lachlan. Boobs to back, thighs cradling his butt. Touching. Too much touching.

Like I've been scalded, I shoot to the rear of the bike and Lachlan slips back into place.

Unfazed by our closeness, his hand coolly taps the pegs for me to place my feet, and I comply.

"When I lean, ye lean a wee bit, but mostly stay straight," he instructs, unemotionally.

Now wanting to sound like a complete amateur, I respond confidently. "This ain't my first rodeo." And it's not; it's my third. Truth be told, I don't trust most men with motorcycles. They're unskilled, and adding a person on the back is an extra liability. I don't want to be the liability. Too many variables. Too much trust. Too much of everything that you have to willingly place in the operator's hands. Lachlan has skilled hands, and he rides his motorcycle more than he drives a car. This, is why I trust him, and some other reasons that I don't wish to discuss right now.

"Right." He thumps his helmet, pats the outside of my leg, and then we're off, rolling through the tree-lined path, away from Lachlan's and toward the main road. Gravel kicks up under us, spitting out of the back tires.

A mixture of nervousness and excitement crashes through me as I swallow hard and cup my hands on Lachlan's sides to use as support for the upcoming turn. God, I hope I don't screw this up and further humiliate myself.

A furnace consumes my hand on his side and yanks me till my arms are curled around his torso, my boobs smashed to his back. I don't like this one bit.

The turn has us leaning before we hit open road, then eyes move to roaming his helmet. It's the only distraction there is at this point. Thinking about where my arms are will only do stuff to my insides that I'd rather leave dormant.

Sticker reading it is...

Too Loud? Too Bad.

You don't need a dick to ride a motorcycle, but it helps to have balls.

My inner child is a mean little fucker.

Then I hit the one that makes me giggle aloud.

Up Yer Kilt.

That sounds like something the brooding and exceedingly stubborn Lachlan would say. I don't know how I know that; I just do. It suits him. The fact that it's directly in the back of his helmet, and not overlapped by other stickers, tells me he loves it too.

I continue to focus on reading the stickers on the way into town. Halfway there, I might have attempted to sneak a peek of the countryside and the beauty it offers. Mainly, though, I ignore all the sensations trying to capture me. The vibrating between my legs, and the hard body I'm plastered to, mixed with the smell of leather and his scent...not to mention the outdoors wafting in my face. I try my best to disregard it all and focus on something else, like stickers and my new job. A job I know I'm going to love maybe even more than any job I've had before. If only I could stick around long enough to really appreciate it. Fat chance that'll happen, though. Once Viola's fixed, I'm gone. New York is still screaming my name.

Lachlan rolls to a smooth stop in front of Cas's, puts his feet down, and Sniper strolls out of the bay, wiping his dirty hands with an even dirtier shop rag.

This is home. Home sweet home.

I disengage from Lachlan and don't wait another second to clumsily dismount the bike. My hands are seriously craving to wrap themselves around a wrench, something—anything. A firm hand on my shoulder halts my need to sprint inside and see my Viola. I've missed her.

Lachlan spins me around, before releasing me and setting his hand on his long, thick, ridiculously sexy, jean-clad thigh. Sniper halts at my side.

"What's wrong with yer leg?" Lachlan flicks his eyes to my bad one.

I shrug dismissively. "It's nothing."

I'm lying, lying, and lying some more. Not that I want to lie. I just don't see another way out of this. Another Dr. Jerk-head had suggested a specific physical therapist to aid in recovery. I don't know the area well, so I relented and took his advice—big mistake. Melanie

Drexel has become the bane of my existence. Two hours a week I have to spend with her, and that grates on my nerves so severely that I find myself snappy and ran ragged by the time I leave. And, no, it's not because she's working me over hard. She's working on my last flippin' nerve, that's what. The woman's immature, flighty, and doesn't know how to do her job. If, in fact, she actually graduated with the degree she's supposed to have obtained, which I highly doubt.

The first time I'd been in her office that she shares with four others, I thought I was in the wrong place. Pink walls and a bubbly receptionist greeted me, before I sat in the posh waiting room for almost an hour for her highness to finally see me.

How can anyone take a platinum blonde Barbie doll, with brown roots, fake boobs, and bubblegum pink lipstick seriously is beyond me. Especially when her voice matches her looks. It's like "air-head" should be tattooed across her botoxed forehead. Now, I'm not one to stereotype or discriminate, but I've been paying this woman to do a job. A job she's incapable of.

I spend most of my time working myself over as she flirts with the men. It doesn't matter what male—old, fat, hot, young, they're all fair game. They all chew her up like the bubblegum on her lips, and adore her so much that they undoubtedly fake ailments to get the unencumbered attention. Can't tell you how many times I've witnessed her paying them gushing compliments about their biceps, rugged good looks, or sweet personality. *Yuck;* make me gag.

Earlier this week, I'd stretched for ten minutes and spent the remainder of the time in the bathroom texting Bridget, who knows Melanie's the bane of my existence and sympathizes with me. In a nutshell, I dread physical therapy because of her. The end.

Lachlan grumbles something unintelligible under his breath, and Casanova joins us at the end of the drive. He's covered in grease.

"Ready for your first day?" Cas bumps my shoulder.

I gift him with a bright, closed mouth smile. "Yes, Boss."

"How's the leg?" he adds.

Bobbing my head in reply, I slap the side of my pant leg. "Pretty good. Yours?" My gaze drops to his leg, the fake one, then returns to his face.

Swiping his hair off his forehead, he pushes it back. "You know about it, huh?" He taps the side of his leg, and I nod. "Wasn't sure if you'd got the memo about it yet. Livin' in a small town, and you knowin' Whisky, figured ya already knew. Nice to see ya don't beat around the bush. I like that." He bumps shoulders with me again, which warms me from the inside out, feelin' accepted already.

"Now," he winks, "how about you get your sexy ass to work?"

Lachlan doesn't seem to like Cas's forwardness when he crudely curses at him, as his intense eyes convey something that I can't interpret. So, I try to ignore Lachlan's flare-up altogether. But, Cas seems to pick up on the unspoken words when he mutters, "Rightttt," in an amused manner before turning his attention back to me.

"Viola's got her own dock in the back. Why don't ya go check that beaut out, and I'll give ya a tour in ten?"

Fair enough.

Removing my helmet, I set it on the back of Lachlan's bike and wave to him as I all but skip into my new job. It's a decent size garage, and it's not too hard for me to find Viola. She's all-by-her-lonesome in the back with a huge toolbox setup right next to her. I run my fingers over her sleek hood, and stop when my eyes catch a name engraved on the black toolbox.

My mouth gapes in astonishment. *Mag's tools*. Oh. My. God. It says Mag's tools, and I'm Mags!

Running my finger over the nameplate, I'm unable to suppress the girly squeal that rushes out. I have my own toolbox! I've never had my own before. This…oh…god…this is too damn sweet.

Tears dampen my eyes, and my bottom lip quivers as I suck in a sharp breath.

They got me my very own toolbox…

They really do accept me.

A couple of tiny tears drip down my cheeks and I rub them away. Now's not the time to go all estrogeny. I'm a woman in a man's world, and it's time to show them what I'm made of.

Wish me luck.

Ekkk.

Lachlan

Mags doesn't even say bye tae me except for a fuckin' wave. I tip my head tae her when all I wanna do is kiss her, hug her, and tell her tae have an amazin' first day at work. Not gonna happen.

My eyes narrow on Cas as Sniper snorts his enjoyment. "You called his woman sexy."

"I did. And she's not actually his chick yet. Who knows what—" Cas tries tae finish, but I'm off my bike and in his face before he can say another bloody fuckin' word that'll make me take my dagger out and stab him in the gut.

"Enough," I bite off, nose-tae-nose, my hands fistin' and unfistin' at my sides, ready tae kick his arse. "There are gonna be some ground rules if Mags is gonna be workin' here." I dinnae give a shit if he likes it or not, he's gonna listen and he's gonna listen good. Club VP or not, she's mine, and he bloody well understands that he cannae be tryin' tae fuck her. I call dibs.

Cas takes a step back, and I let him. Then he pulls the cigarette from behind his ear and lights it, takin' a long drag with the corner of his lip tipped in amusement. A loud squeal tears my attention from him tae the garage bay. I take a step forward. I know that was Mags, and I need tae be sure she's all right.

Sniper pats my chest, haltin' me. "She musta found her toolbox. Let her enjoy it."

"Her toolbox?" I cross my arms over my chest. A toolbox? They'd better not have.

Cas blows a ring. "Yeah, a fuckin' toolbox. She needed her own, since we don't share. We talked," he gestures tae Sniper, "and knew she didn't have the money to afford her own. Rallied some favors and got her, her own box."

I should be grateful, and be over the damn moon that my brothers like her enough tae buy her a toolbox. I should be slappin' them on the backs, and thankin' them for doin' this. There's a lotta shit I should be doin' or feelin' at this point, but happy and grateful ain't one of 'em. I'm pissed and guilty as hell for not thinkin' aboot her needin' this first. I shoulda been the one tae buy her the tools. We shoulda bought 'em together. Not my brothers. *Fuck!*

Sniper's hand on my shoulder rips me from the deep abyss that my guilt resides in. "Take your hand off your hip." He jerks my shoulder, and I drop my hand from my dagger that I didnae know I was grippin'.

"Rules?" Cas prompts, not the least bit concerned that I'm ready tae do some damage. Glad he knows me well enough tae know that I wouldn't kick his arse unless I had tae. Really hopin' I dinnae have tae.

Right. Rules.

Time tae pull my head outta my arse.

"Na tryin' tae fuck her, and na more buyin' her shit. If ye think she needs somethin' ye tell me. I'll take care of it."

Cas rolls the tip of his finished cigarette between his fingers, snuffin' it out, then tucks the butt into his front pocket. "I get what you want, Smoke. Problem with that is: you know the rules."

Rules, my arse. He better not be talkin' aboot what I think he's talkin' aboot.

"She ain't your old lady, brother." Sniper sympathetically claps me on the shoulder, givin' it a squeeze. "Club takes care of ours. She's one of ours. But she ain't yours." He nods tae Cas. "If he wants to go there, there's nothin' stopping him. I respect you. And I love you, brother. But you know the rules. Only way to change that is if you want Mags to be your property."

What kind of fuckin' question is that? *Shit.*

"Aye." I throw my hands up, growlin'. "She's mine."

Mags might not know it, but that bonnie lass is mine. Cannae touch her, or fuck her, but I sure as hell can make sure na other bloody arsehole gets tae touch her either. Not that Cas is an arsehole; he's a good lad, and a damn fine brother. Problem with that is: he didnae get the name Casanova for nothin'—he's smooth with the lassies and fucks anythin' with two legs, a decent rack, and a pussy. Mags has way more tae offer than that. Doesn't surprise me he'd wanna piece. Still, his arse ain't touchin' it. Nobody's touchin' a piece of her but me, and I'm not even gonna do that.

When I look tae Cas, he's got a shit-eatin' grin on his face. "I was hoping that'd get you to step up to the fuckin' plate and take what you want."

Fucker was testin' me. Shoulda known.

Sniper punches my shoulder. "Welcome to the world of dick whipping."

Dick whipping? I chuckle under my breath. Only Sniper would come up with that shit.

Smirkin', I raise an amused brow at him. "Dick whippin'?"

"Hell yeah…It's when you bang your old lady so good, that she'll do anything for you, anytime you want. It's like pussy whipped, except we're the ones who're…In. Fucking. Charge."

Shakin' my head, still smirkin', I punch his shoulder, nod tae Cas, then turn back tae my bike and swing my leg over. I fire her up, and when I do, I'm hit with the memory of havin' Mags wrapped around me, tits tae pussy, heat on heat.

My cock stirs.

"Be good tae her. I'll be back at four tae pick her up!" I yell tae Cas and Sniper, who've already made it halfway back up the drive. Cas raises his hand in acknowledgement, and I take off, hittin' the open road tae let off some steam.

Told Mags I had shit tae do today, when I actually have jackshit planned. If she'd known I'd argued with Pip this mornin' aboot her takin' the Tahoe, she'd have dropped more attitude on me than she already did. Dinnae blame her. I was bein' an arse. What the hell was I supposed tae do? Not tell her that she looked like every man's wet dream in that bloody fuckin' outfit? Did she listen? Na! She got me hard. Rip-roarin'-ready-tae-lose-my-shit, *hard*.

Who the hell am I kiddin'? As of late, I've spent more time with my hand on my cock, and pukin' afterward, that I can barely think straight. Thought the distance would work. Thought stayin' busy, and workin' out would take this sick cravin' away. Na, it makes it worse.

Headin' into my house, I can smell her. I look in my damn fridge, and she's made me food and lemonade. I take a piss, and her stuff's on the counter and her towel's hangin' on the rack. I cannae tell ye the last time I've ever seen a towel hangin' from a rack, or havin' a bathroom that doesn't stink like vomit and alcohol because of Meredith. When I do laundry, her wee panties are always there, mockin' me. I try tae sleep on the couch and find myself unable to. So, I become a bloody creeper and stand in the doorway of her bedroom, watchin' her sleep. Which makes me rock-hard, and my mind so damn crazed that I'm back tae jackin' in the bathroom and purgin' in the toilet. The guilt keeps barrin' down, sinkin' me lower, makin' it harder tae breathe and do anythin' but think aboot her in my house, in my bed, under me, or in my arms. And when I finally do sleep, I'm dreamin' these vivid as hell dreams, aboot her blood on my hands. Aboot her dying. Aboot her fuckin' me. Aboot her movin' away. Aboot all sorts of jacked up shit, that leave me once again horny or near tears. I dinnae cry, but that doesn't mean I dinnae get that unrelentin' ache in my chest or tension in my gut. The tears may not fall, but those bloody feelings are there, and they're real.

If I didnae know any better, I'd say this feels like a helluva psychotic break. It's not, though. I felt more at ease than I have in weeks, havin' her on the back of my bike with me today. Which reminds me, I gotta drop by the flower shop tae get Pip some apology flowers. Our argument was pretty heated this mornin', and I gotta make it up tae her.

"I told Magdalene I would ride with Josie to school, and I already told Whisky to pick me up," Pip explained, finishin' up her makeup in the bathroom.

"I'm takin' Mags tae her first day, and it'd be a lot easier if ye'd take the Tahoe," I said, standin' in the doorway, watchin' her watch me through the mirror.

Poppin' her wee hip out, she met my eyes in the mirror, holdin' her lip shit close tae her mouth. "I promised her, Dad," she argued before smearin' it on.

"Then, un-promise her," I contended, knownin' damn well the truck was mine, but I didnae wanna force my upper hand if I didnae have tae.

She shook her head. "You, of all people, know I can't do that. I don't want to let her down. We're friends, and I love her. I want her to trust me. If I do that, she'll think I'm not her friend, and I've been working really hard trying to get to know her."

Hell, I knew she was right. I just didnae have the heart tae back down. Takin' her tae work was more important.

"She's yer friend and she'll understand. I'm takin' her tae work myself. Let me take her tae work, Pip," *I spoke softly, selfishly playin' with my daughter's big heart.*

Droppin' her lip shit into some container, she turned around, shakin' her head. "You like her, I know. But, you aren't around. She and I are here. We have dinner together...Did you know she made me meatloaf and garlic mashed potatoes the other night?"

I didnae, so I shook my head as the guilt climbed up my throat and settled there.

She kept on. "I don't even like meatloaf, but I loved hers. It was the best tasting thing I've ever had. And those potatoes were fresh and delicious. If you'd have been here, you would've known how good the meatloaf was, and how much I talk to her. She listens to me. Really listens, Dad. And she asked me a favor, this one time, to leave the Tahoe here so she can go to work, and I bail on her?" *She was tappin' her foot now, the stubbornness winnin' out over her sweetness. She is my daughter, after all.*

I swallowed the guilt down tae deal with later, when I could process how much I was hurtin' my daughter for my own self-satisfaction. Then, I tried a different approach. "Do ye want her tae drive tae her job alone, on the first day? Dinnae ye think she's gonna be nervous?"

Pip shrugged. "Yeah, but—"

Cuttin' her off, I continued, "I wanna take her on her first day, Pip. That's what I need tae do. Tae see *she's all right, and movin' forward. I wasn't there when she started goin' tae the physical therapist, ye were."* I nodded tae her, watchin' the pleased acknowledgement spring a wee smile from her lips. *"I wanna do this, and she won't let me if ye leave the Tahoe here."* I tried tae reason with her, and won out. She conceded with a sigh, before comin' over tae hug me.

Told ye, I've got the greatest daughter.

Now, before I pick up a ridiculously big bouquet of flowers for Pip, I gotta make one more stop.

Parkin' in front of Mags's therapist's office, I swing off my bike and head inside. I need some answers, and this lassie better give 'em tae me. Mags's leg isn't better, and there better be a damn good explanation as tae why. I'm aboot tae find out.

CHAPTER 17
KANSAS '42

Mags

This has been the best work day ever! After Cas had finished speaking with Lachlan, he showed me around as Sniper went back to working on an old Nova. The operations here are modern and efficient. Something you definitely wouldn't expect, seeing the beat-up exterior of the place.

Once we were done with the shop floor, he gave me a tour of their small waiting room, which I found manly, yet, homey. Then I was introduced to Rosie, a friendly, elderly woman, with curly gray hair, who runs the books for Cas, and mans the phones for him in the office three days a week. They're open six. My guess is she likes to keep busy, and he's doing her a favor. Seems like a thing he does a lot. Taking her in, and now me. I'm curious to see what else he's got tucked under his softhearted sleeve.

It being a slow day, I changed two oils and a corroded battery before Cas gave me the green light to work on Viola. I've spent most of the late morning and early afternoon cleaning glass fragments from her interior, and popping some of the easier dents out.

Now, I'm almost done taking my break.

Ten minutes ago, Bridget had dropped by with a Scared Sister cupcake and an ice cold bottle of water for me, which she used to administer an unnecessary apology. I'm not angry with her in the least.

I'm not sure how Whisky came up with that recipe, but it's the best tasting cupcake I've ever had. The frosting is sweet and light, the cake dense, with a chocolate chip cookie base. It's heaven in a little baking cup. Ever since the first one Whisky gave me, I've been special requesting that Bridget bring me some home each week. And if she doesn't stop, I'm gonna get fat. Although, getting fat while eating these delectable Sacred Sister cupcakes might be manageable. It'd be worth it, as I'm sure I'd die happy with high cholesterol and boobs that sag to my toes. Still, mighty worth it.

Throwing my Whisky's Corrupt Confections napkin in the trash barrel, I dust my hands on my overalls and leave Viola to check on the progress in the front.

I hear Cas and Sniper bickering about something as I approach. They're both draped over the hood of the Nova.

"No; that costs too damn much. It's smarter to do it the way I said," Cas chastises his club president. When he notices I'm looming, he stands and Sniper follows suit. They both yank the rags from their back pockets, wiping their hands off.

"I'll see you boys later. I'm heading out for the day," Rosie calls from behind me.

Sniper raises his hand, tipping two fingers to the side. "Okay, Rosie, have a good one, and say hey to Peanut for us."

"Will do, dear," she replies, before disappearing down the front drive with her patchwork purse slung over her frail shoulder.

My attention reverts to the two men standing in front of me. Both lean, tattooed, muscular, and by any woman's standards, so handsome you'd need to throw a bucket of ice in your panties to cool down. That's where the buck stops on their similar looks, though. Cas has dark, messy hair, a stubbly jaw, and caring eyes. The tattoos on his forearms are flames that lick up his skin with screaming skulls of the underworld trying to tear through. They're pretty sick. Sick, as in good, not bad. Sniper's Native American skin is also inked, but not as heavily, as say, Lachlan's or Cas's. But his complexion…I imagine most people would pay good money for—it's gorgeous.

Shaking my head, I clear my thoughts to stop myself from staring at my boss and coworker.

"What're you two having troubles with? Can I help?" With the sweep of my hand, I motion to the opened hood.

"Sure," Cas comments, as a pissed off Sniper stomps away, cursing under his breath.

Uh-oh. Perhaps I shouldn't have butted in.

Cas slaps the corner panel, drawing my attention, and nods to the engine. "He's not mad at you; he's pissed at me, and about to go take it out on Whisky's cunt. Now, check this engine and tell me what you think we should do about it."

Taking three steps to the car, I lean over and take a quick gander. Without question, this needs a major overhaul. It's rusted, hoses are dry rotted, and I'd be willing to bet that the oil is seeping into the engine. And there's probably a coolant leak, too. I can't even imagine what else we'll find.

I open my mouth to express my sincerest regret that his engine is a piece of shit and needs to be replaced. But when I do, Cas stops me by saying, "Keep in mind, the owner doesn't want to spend over a thousand on her."

Tilting my head, I sideways glance at Cas, who's tucked under the hood of the car with me. I tap the coolant tank. "I bet that has a leak, and that's the least of our worries…A thousand bucks ain't gonna cut it. And dropping the engine is going to be the only way to make sure it's rebuilt properly."

He snorts. I'm not sure if it's an amused one, mocking one, or something else I can't pinpoint. "Would you rebuild what's here?" He signals to the engine. "Or would you find one in better shape first, and rebuild what's needed?"

Is he seriously asking me this question? A man, in a shop, is asking his new employee, who's a female, this very question. I can't believe it!

I stand back, knowing my eyes are wide with wonder. Cas takes notice when he stands, too, and bumps his shoulder with mine. "What? Cat got your tongue?"

Stuck with shock, I swallow hard before clearing my emotionally clogged throat. "Um…I've worked at many shops and nobody's asked my opinion on an engine rebuild for a classic car like this one."

Stupid, weak female tears pick the corners of my eyes and I blink them away before they fall, making me look like a damn wuss.

"Seein' as though I hired you, and you probably have a helluva lot more experience than Sniper, I expect you to know your shit. And by knowing your shit, I'm gonna ask you what you think of this unfortunate hunk of junk." He yanks a smoke from behind his ear, points it to the engine, and then puts it to his mouth, lighting it with a match he snatches from his front pocket.

On a sighed exhale, smoke billows from his lips. "So?" he prompts.

Here goes nothing.

"If you rebuild what's here, it's gonna cost a lot more money, because of the unknowns and labor. But, it would be more authentic to the car, keeping it as the original." I shift to face him, cuffing my hand over the lip of the car. "To be honest, it looks like this car's sat in a leaky old barn with the hood up for about a decade or two. The bird shit, smell of mildew, dust, and poor condition of the engine, are pretty much all the evidence I need."

Cas nods like he's listening, as he continues to smoke.

I keep talking. "A grand isn't enough money. Might as well sell it to someone who would put the dough into making her beautiful again." My palm smooths over the lip, loving the feel, getting off on the feel. My lady parts tighten. "I would replace the engine with another if you could get it for a steal. *Then* I'd rebuild it. This way there are way fewer variables. And it's obvious the owner doesn't care about originality, because they only wanna drop a grand into her. Which is a shame, because ten to fifteen grand, if done right, could make her beautiful...*If* her undercarriage hasn't already been eaten alive by rust." I shrug. "That's my thoughts, anyhow."

The sly grin that Cas produces makes my mouth go dry and feel slightly uncomfortable. I'm not sure if that's a good expression or a bad one.

Cas snuffs out his cigarette. "I knew I hired you for a reason..." He sounds pleased with himself. "You're tellin' me the same shit I just schooled Sniper on. He's only been workin' for me about two years. Good with bikes, decent with basic car shit, and sucks at rebuilds. You and I are gonna take the lead on all of 'em. Including Viola."

"Okay," I squeak out, unable to say anything more in fear of breaking into a fit of tears.

I can't believe I not only got a job, but now I have one where I can focus on the things I excel in—like rebuilding engines and body work. Not simple oil changes, which I've been stuck doing for years. Not that I mind. It is money, after all. However, this is something much more. Something I've dreamed of doing since Brian and I restored Viola and his old 1957 *Ford* F100, which I'm sure his dad sold for over a hundred grand after he died. I can't believe I'm even thinking about that horrible man. Not after he cremated the man I loved. Not after he'd kept everything, including Brian's F100. Not after he'd dismissed that I ever existed.

"I don't care, Magdalene! I'm his father, and you were just some girl he liked!" he yelled, standing on the front stoop of his farm house as I stood in the gravel drive.

"I'm his fiancée!" I screamed, tears teeming down my cheeks, as I threw my hand in the air and pointed to the tiny ring on my finger. *"His fiancée!"*

"Fiancée don't mean wife, little missy," he sassed unapologetically, like the knockdown drunk he was.

"And I'm his father. I know what's best. My son will have his place on the mantel text to my Papa, Mama, and Sheldon, my old coon dog...And that's final!"

It was final. I'd attended his wake, where an open casket sat in the front of the room with Brian's beautiful body resting inside. A body that looked like him, but didn't. The suit he was wearing had been new. Brian never wore suits. He loved his *Wranglers* and white t-shirts. It was rare to see him in anything else.

On the way there, Grams had to stop every five miles to let me throw-up alongside the road. Then, when we'd arrived, I couldn't stay long. The flowers were all wrong; he didn't love roses. The music was all wrong; he loved country, not rock. It was too hard, and hurt too much. I'd cried so much that my eyes were almost swollen shut. And his father ignored me, didn't care who I was, or that I'd been the love of his son's life. Until death parted us.

Grams had nearly punched the old, drunken farmer in the face when he'd refused to let me stand with him in the receiving line. But everyone knew who I was. I still received condolences and hugs from the visitors. They knew I was his, and he was mine.

Then that was it. No more Brian. No more happiness. No more car rebuilds, or men who appreciated me for my brain. That is...until now. Now, I have a boss who values my opinion, who bought me a toolbox full of normal tools. Not ones for women. Not ones to make me feel lesser. Ones to make me feel accepted like I've never felt before.

Cas shoots me a wink. I'm pretty sure he's aware of the emotional rollercoaster I'm riding right now. "Why don't ya get your sexy ass back to work?" He winks again, smirking at me, which causes me to grin, too, and heat to trample my cheeks.

Still grinning, I shyly wave and turn to leave, but halt midstride when a friendly male voice booms, "Casanova and the pretty Miss Magdalene; just the folks I came to see!"

Spinning on my boot heel, I stop and freeze when a colossal man, bigger than Lachlan in girth but shorter in height, stops at the entrance of the bay. He's wearing a white button down, rolled up his swole, tatted forearms, a pair of black dress slacks that look painted onto his massive thighs, and at his base, he's sporting expensive dress shoes. My gaze lifts to meet his eyes, and find those hazel beauties trained on me. He smiles in my direction, all teeth, straight and movie star white. I gulp, stuffing my hands into my back pockets, trying to curb the unease that's creeping up my spine.

Cas is the first to burst my haze when he fist bumps with the silver-haired goliath. "What's up, Bonez? What brings you by today?"

Bonez, or whatever his real name is, stops staring back at me and shoves his own hands into his front pockets. I watch them slip in next to a massive bulge. A bulge that's so frickin' difficult to ignore, that I don't. I gape. Then I turn red before I finally stop being an idiot and lift my eyes to Cas, who's grinning hugely at me right now.

Crap. I've been made.

This is the time I should crawl into the corner, chew my nails, and die. Only this Bonez fella apparently doesn't want that, because he unhurriedly advances on me. It's like he's preparing me to be near him, by affording me the chance to scurry away and hide if I need to.

Using this time to sort my pathetic self out, I give my brain a short scolding about keeping my eyes to myself and away from men's privates. And, I also take a moment to tack on a lesson to stop being surprised if most of the men I come in contact with are stupidly hot. Some of which might come with arms the size of King Kong's—like Lachlan's do. Or some of them might have bulges that look like a grapefruit has been smuggled in their pants. I blame it on the water. The water here is laced with something; something that makes all these men too attractive. You really need to visit Carolina Rose sometime and see for yourself.

By the time I complete my internal dialogue—which doesn't make me crazy, okay?—Bonez is a mere foot away, extending his hand to me in greeting.

Zoning in on his moving lips, I come to when I hear him repeat my name three times.

Get your head out of the clouds, Magdalene.

I do the quick shake, expel a nervous *"hey"*, and shove my hands back into my pockets where they're most comfortable.

"Guess you're probably wondering why I'm here?" Bonez swaps glances between Cas and me.

"I'm guessin' Smoke sent you," Cas comments and slams the hood of the Nova closed, before running a hand through his hair to remove it from his forehead as he leans against the Nova. "That why?"

Bonez doesn't answer him, and looks to me instead. "Smoke dropped by, said your leg isn't gettin' the physical therapy it needs...That right?"

Lachlan went to Bonez? Why would he do that? I didn't tell him about the bane of my existence. And there's no way he could know, unless Bridget told him. I don't think she'd do that.

"I would like it to be better," I reply.

Bonez extracts a card from his slacks and extends it to me. I accept it. "I'm a chiropractor who specializes in rehabilitation and massage therapy," he explains. "And since I already gave Smoke hell for not bringin' you to me in the first place, I'd like to take you on as a patient. Get that leg, and your arms, back to the way they were, or close to it."

I cock my head to the side, assessing him. "Do you know much about numb spots?"

"Some. You having trouble with that scar on your back?"

How did he know?

"Yes," I mumble, nodding. "It feels strange. I think it's nerve damage."

"Might be, but we won't know unless you let me work with ya two days a week. Cas might even let ya come in during work hours, so you don't have to drive into town more than ya have to."

That actually sounds pretty darn perfect. New doctor. No more bane of my existence. And since insurance from the gas station is covering all my medical expenses, aside from the Meredith one, I don't have to be able to afford it. It's already covered.

Both of us swing our heads to Casanova for his input. "Fuck, yeah, you can go there. Just as long as your sexy ass is back here afterward."

With a firm shake, I accept Bonez's gracious offer and set up a verbal appointment with him for tomorrow, then I get back to working on Viola.

Soon, it's four o'clock and before I know it, Lachlan is here on the nose.

With a wave, I say my goodbyes to Sniper and Cas before following Lachlan down to his *Harley*. Slipping the helmet on that he silently hands me, I slide onto the bike like I had earlier, and soon we're off, headed home.

What an incredible day.

"So, how was school today? Did Marcy interrupt you in Spanish again?" I ask Bridget before taking another bite of my grilled cheese and dipping it into my tomato soup.

Bridget wipes her mouth with her napkin, and Lachlan grumbles. "Some lassies causin' problems?" he probes, lifting his glass of lemonade.

This is the very first time we've eaten upstairs together. And since the night Lachlan made me spaghetti, he and I haven't eaten *any* meal together, let alone the three of us. So when Lachlan said he was staying home for supper, I offered to prepare it. I used an entire loaf of bread to make grilled cheese, and Lachlan's already eaten six of them. Although, he won't dip his sandwich in the tomato soup; he prefers to sip it with a spoon.

Holding up her finger, Bridget makes an '*Mmmm*' sound while polishing off her lemonade. Lachlan refills her glass with the pitcher before setting it back down next to a large bouquet of white daisies. I didn't buy them. Lachlan did. He didn't say they were for me, but they were on the table when we got home, so I'm assuming they are. It's a sweet gesture that makes me a little squishy on the inside, as I've missed my daisies a lot.

Bridget sighs heavily. "*Dad*," she stresses. "Marcy and I haven't liked each other since the beginning of high school. This year, I have Spanish with her. It's no big deal. She's just a preppy girl who likes to push her weight around. I can handle it."

Lachlan's not convinced when he grumbles again. "If she gives ye any more trouble, ye tell me. I'll handle it. Aye?"

Shaking her head, Bridget snorts sarcastically. "How are you gonna do that? Threaten a seventeen-year-old girl? Beat her up? Run her over with your motorcycle?" Her tone turns sweet. "Thanks for caring, Dad, but Mags and I have already got this one covered." She winks at me with a genuine smile, and I want to shrivel up and disappear by the look of sheer annoyance Lachlan veers in my direction.

What? All that I suggested was that she have Whisky or Sniper drop into her Spanish class to drive the *Corrupt Chaos* point home. I didn't want to involve Lachlan. He's too scary. Sniper or Whisky can instill just enough fear that'll make the bully notice. If that doesn't work, I've considered kicking the girl's butt myself. Those Marcy stories are hard enough for me to let go of. If she doesn't stop, I'm not sure what I'll do. It won't be pretty, I can tell you that much.

A staring match commences between the two of us, and suddenly, I'm not hungry anymore. I push my plate to the side and lean back in the chair, refusing to cower to Lachlan.

"Well, I'm done," Bridget dismisses herself and puts her plate in the dishwasher. "Thanks, Mags." She opens the basement door, and I wave goodnight to her. Lachlan exchanges his unique form of I love you, before we're propelled into a sea of silence.

Lachlan tears a piece of another sandwich off with his teeth like a savage, his eyes never wavering. He swallows harshly, and the Adam's apple in his throat bobs. Following by example, I, too, swallow hard. The tension thickening between us is so dense that I could reach out and touch it.

The question is: should I stay here and take the tongue lashing he's preparing to unleash, or do I leave? Should I have sought permission from him before offering my opinions and solutions to Bridget? Did I overstep? *Gah*! If only I knew. If only he'd tell me. If only he'd set some ground rules, and try being present and not distant. Perhaps he could tell me when my time here has been worn out? Or, maybe tell me how he feels for once?

Is that why he's giving me those crude eyes? Growling lowly in his throat, his body hunches over the edge of the table, elbows on the top, and body coils tightly. Should I offer to leave? Should I be the one to make that choice?

Darn it. If only he'd say something—anything.

The silence, mixed with his heavy breathing, becomes deafening. So deafening that I can't take another second of it. "Do you want me to leave?" I blurt, trying hard not to flinch at the thought of leaving Bridget. Of leaving the place I consider home. It makes my heart ache just thinking about it, especially after the amazing day I had today. New York doesn't sound so appealing anymore.

I don't want to go.

Lachlan snarls in reply, his lip cruelly curling over his teeth. With force, he shucks his plate across the table, and I jump as it clatters to the floor. "Dinnae ye ever fuckin' ask me that again," he whispers harshly, as his chest rises and falls so severely that I can see it pumping in and out like the piston of a car.

What did I do?

My eyes drop to pick the imaginary lint off my jeans that I changed into after work. I don't know what that means, or what I'm supposed to say? *Don't you ever fuckin' ask me that again*...Does that mean I should go? Or does that mean he doesn't want me to? Uh, so many damn things I can't understand, and too many mixed signals.

A chair scrapes across the old tiled floor. I hear the plate being picked up and placed into the dishwasher before a set of firm hands land on my both of my shoulders. I jerk, too, nearly screaming, but my heart lodges in my throat, muting me.

"Calm down, Mags." Lachlan starts to rub, massaging his giant fingers into my shoulders. Carefully, he kneads them, and I melt into a puddle of sated mush on the floor.

Closing my eyes in bliss, his fingers caress the back of my neck as pleasure fueled goosebumps crash like a tidal wave down my body. "I'm sorry aboot the plate. I know I'm an arsehole," he apologizes sincerely, softly, and so heavily accented that I'm pretty sure I just had a mini orgasm. If only every day could feel this way with him.

"It's okay," I concede breathily.

"Pip loves ye. And she trusts ye." His fingers move to my scalp, and my body relaxes further, turning me into an overcooked noodle. "I just need ye tae keep me informed. I dinnae want her not tae speak tae me, but I know ye're a female, and she needs another female tae have her back."

"I always have her back," I confirm.

"I know that."

He does?

"You do?"

"Aye, I do" He changes the subject. "How was yer first day at the shop?"

Did he really just ask that? Did you hear it, too, or was that a figment of my imagination? That sounded awfully domesticated for a man who's been continually withdrawn since I met him.

In response, I want to scream *it was flippin' awesome* before I kiss him hard. Instead, I go the smooth, evasive route. "It was fine. They were fine."

Wait?! What?! Did I just say I wanted to kiss Lachlan? Holy crapola, I did.

His fingers comb through my loose hair, and I sigh. I'd taken a shower when we got home and let my hair air dry. Now, I'm so glad that I did or I wouldn't have his fingers sifting through it. If he keeps this up, he might put me to sleep.

"Just fine? Did Cas treat ye all right? Ye didnae get mistreated, did ye?" He sounds genuinely thoughtful, and the squishiness triples.

The tips of his fingers tickle down my neck. "He…" I shiver head to toe. "He was fine, Lachlan. I promise. They were all very nice, and helpful. I think I'm gonna like working there."

"Are ye plannin' tae leave after ye get Viola fixed?" he puts me on the spot.

"Do you want me to leave after I get Viola fixed?"

I turn the tables on him, to gauge something about him—anything. I can never get a steady grip on anything he does or says. It's all too vague and wishy-washy. One minute, he's sweet and caring; the next, he's growling, broody, and pee'd off. It's whiplash at its finest. Whiplash I'm happy to endure if it leaves me with his hands in my hair, talking like a normal person with me. This is kind of nice.

Lachlan

Do you want me to leave after I get Viola fixed?

Smart lassie. Mags is changin' my question, just like that. If she could see what touchin' her is doin' tae my cock, then she'd already know her bloody answer, now wouldn't she?

My fingers comb down tae the bottom of her long hair, untanglin' the soft curls.

"Lachlan?" she mutters.

"Aye?" I reply, even though I know she's waitin' tae hear my response.

"Do you want me to leave after I get Viola fixed?" she repeats with a wee tinge of attitude. The attitude I didnae know she had, or if I even liked it when she first threw it at me. Now, I dream aboot that attitude. I dig that shit.

Time tae set the truth free. I dinnae wanna admit it, but I dinnae wanna hurt her feelings by bein' an arsehole either. "I dinnae want ye tae leave. This is yer home. Ye belong here. Pirate, the bloody bastard, likes ye better than me now." I chuckle under my breath. It's true. The wee bastard loves the shit outta Mags. I'm the consolation prize when she's not around. I bet he's sleepin' in her bed right this second. "And Pip would be sad tae see ye go," I tack on for the hell of it.

Sighin' deeply, her head drops back and I cradle it in my palms. Openin' her sleepy eyes, she looks up at me. "I love my new job. And, thank you for this house, and for all of your help…And, for the flowers." She points tae the daisies that I bought for her today. I'd only planned on pickin' flowers up for Pip, but couldn't bear tae leave Mags out. She's the first lassie I've bought flowers for, other than Pip, in a long time.

She's not done. "Bonez came by today and I have an appointment with him tomorrow."

"Good."

After I'd left her piss-poor physical therapist's office, I went straight tae Bonez. He cut a client loose so we could have a sit-down. Loungin' on the couch in his office, I laid it all out for him and told him aboot the flirtatious lassie who Mags was seein'. Bonez already knew her, and didnae looked surprised. We got a plan mapped out and my rules laid down, just like I did with Cas. Bonez may not be as much of a horny bastard as Cas, but he still needed a talkin' tae. Got our shit square. Now my leannan has a lad tae fix her leg. Just like she should have had in the first bloody place. If I had taken my head out of my arse long enough tae help her, instead of avoidin' the lassie, she woulda recovered faster.

"Lachlan, are you okay?" She gazes up at me, dreamily.

Damn it. I was starin' at her with my head tipped down and my mouth open. I close it. "Aye. Sorry aboot that."

"Were you thinking?"

Bloody hell, I hate when she sounds so sweet. It makes my heart beat faster and slower all at the same damn time. I tell ye, it's the wildest feelin' in the world.

Keepin' one hand under her head, I use my finger tae trace the smooth line of her jaw up past her ear, and back down again. I lick my bottom lip, as the pad of my finger shoots pleasure straight tae my cock. Pre-come soaks through my jeans, givin' me a wet spot.

"Lachlan," she breathes huskily, and I know this is doin' somethin' for her, too. Her chest is risin' and fallin' quickly, her hands clutchin' the front of her t-shirt just under her tits.

Fuck, I should stop, but cannae.

My finger passes over her jaw, and her eyes flutter closed as she exhales a shudderin' breath. "*God*," she groans, "that feels good. Soooo good."

My balls draw up, achin'.

I cannae last much longer. I've gotta stop and run tae the barn tae relieve this pressure. My cock bucks against my zipper, agreein' with me.

I cannae tell ye a time in my entire life that I've had this uncontrollable urge tae cuddle, fuck, kiss, touch, and blow inside a particular blonde lassie, with big round tits, flawless skin, and soft curves in all the right places.

This urge is so bloody strong that I'm startin' tae feel like somethin's wrong with me.

How have I never felt this bloody way before?

When I was a young lad, I focused on school and never dated. Even in Scotland, where I felt more like myself, I still dinnae date. I'm too shy for that, and I dinnae trust anybody. My uncle was a fair lad; we got along well enough, and he took me in when my father didnae want me. I was "too much trouble, and gettin' in tae too many fights," he'd said.

Fights that all started back when I was a wee lad in primary school, and the boys used tae tease me aboot my fiery ginger hair. And if it wasn't that, it was how big I was, or that my cock looked funny tae them. When I came back tae America for high school, my hair had grown darker and I was even bigger than before. Only, this time, none of the bastards fucked with me. I played American football, then joined the *Navy*. That's when my *Navy* brothers started tae flock tae me, wantin' tae be my best pal. The accent drew in the lassies, and they reaped the benefits of screwin' those lasses, since I had na desire tae fuck my way through life. But I did get a ton of free beer outta bein' the Scottish wingman. It was a win-win; they fucked and I drank.

Then along came Pip, changin' the game. Changin' everything, makin' life better and worth livin'. But with her came her mother.

I *was* coastin' along in a dead marriage that died pretty much as soon as it happened. A marriage I've hated bein' in for years, but didnae have the balls tae end, *until now*.

Obviously, Meredith would never leave me. Why would she? I was her meal ticket. Bought all of her clothes, and took care of her messes. I slept on the couch, even though I knew when she stumbled through that front door at three in the mornin', she'd reek of spirits and been freshly fucked. Then I'd hold her head back in the mornin' as she threw up from her hangover. Afterward, I'd workout tae release all this fuckin' aggression I've got bottled inside.

Never told anyone this before, and I'll never tell Mags. It's not somethin' I'm proud of.

Four years into my marriage, if ye can call it that, Meredith and I were fuckin' once a month or less. I never initiated it. She did. The one time in the four years of our marriage that I forgot tae wear a condom, I ended up with The Clap. Na matter how many times I've taken antibiotics since, I'll never forget the day the symptoms started. It was the same day my doctor assumed I had cheated on my wife, and gave me hell aboot it. In the military, they dinnae take the shit lightly. I had tae attend marriage counselin' with her, and we both took a round of antibiotics tae cure it.

I'll never fail tae recall the fury on that doctor's face when he thought I'd screwed around on her, as he lectured me on the responsibilities of a husband. Those words stuck with me and were repeated over and over in my head whenever I was gonna leave her. Whenever she came home pregnant or had the crabs (twice), I lived by that mantra the military doctor had instilled. Then, five years ago, I stopped carin' altogether, and also stopped takin' her tae the doctors after I found out they had diagnosed her with genital warts. Couldn't take the pain anymore. Enough had been enough.

Guess it wasn't enough though, 'cause she stayed and I tolerated her bullshit. I endured her tantrums when she'd be bloody pissed that I didnae give her enough money tae buy booze, or whatever the bloody hell else she wanted. I tolerated the slaps across the face, when she was so angry she couldn't contain her rage. Rage at me for knockin' her up. Rage for not givin' her enough money. Rage for her car breakin' down. Rage for bein' the lousy husband with the ugly cock.

Rage…Rage….Fuckin' rage.

"Lachlan." Mags's concerned voice tears me from my memories, and into the present. Shakin' my deluded head tae clear it, I gaze down at her, my finger hoverin' just above her lips, my cock now flaccid. "Tell me what you were just thinking about. You were staring off into space, but it wasn't a good kind of space. Your face is all mean and scary looking. Did I do something wrong?"

Bloody hell.

She does every damn thing *right*. It's not her that's the problem. It's me.

Fuck!

Mags

Something's wrong. I can feel it. Lachlan's demeanor isn't the usual sullen. It's a different kind of sullen; a broken one. His finger paused at my chin minutes ago. When those eyes clouded over, his finger skimmed the skin below my lips, lifted, and has been hanging there motionless for what feels like forever. I wanted to give him a chance to break through whatever fog he'd leapt into, but when he didn't reemerge and those lines between his eyes sunk deeper, I knew I had to impose.

Scooting me back in my chair, Lachlan grabs my hands and pulls me to stand. I stumble forward, my palms connecting with his rock-hard chest. He growls something under his breath, and his hands trap my hips. Gently digging his fingers in, he pushes me back and my palms fall away. Coldness seeps into me.

It's obvious he doesn't want me to touch him, and wants to keep his distance. And here for a moment, when he was touching me, I thought maybe he wanted more, wanted to keep going and make me feel good. But it was all a fantasy. One I've conjured up. I know it. I know I did this to myself. He was merely trying to make up for being a jerk. I should have realized that from the get-go.

Shame ignites in my gut, and I frown.

Lachlan taps my chin with his finger, lifting it to meet his gaze. "Ye never did anythin' wrong…I'm fucked up in the head." He knocks the side of his skull with his fist, and I flinch at the harsh sound. "Ye're a good, wholesome, pure woman. A lassie who's been through too fuckin' much. I hate that ye're always havin' tae deal with me bein' a bastard tae ye. Ye dinnae deserve that shit."

I love that he's opening up, I really do, but I can't help but feel that he's deflecting on purpose. He hasn't answered my question, and I want to know.

"What were you thinking about earlier?"

Screw it.

I set one palm back on his chest, which I have to say might be my favorite part of his entire body, aside from his handsome face. Taking a step forward, my front meets his and he goes ramrod straight. The fingers at my waist plunge deeper, and the sharp bite sends shockwaves to my lady parts. Like a match strike, my clit ignites into a dull throb and I suppress a moan.

A hard thickness presses to my belly, and I feel it twitch, pumping fuller, turning to velvet steel. Roughly, he clears his throat. "Mags, ye need tae leave me be. I dinnae wanna talk aboot it." His sharp edge is gone, replaced by a vulnerability.

Glancing into his eyes, all I can see is his raw pain, raw need, and something else that I can't put my finger on. He tries to retreat and create distance, only I follow him all the way to the wall, where I mold myself to him. My breasts press to his abs, my legs brush his, and my hands now lie flat on his pecs that are pumping with the speed of his reckless breathing. The heart pounding under my palm mimics mine.

"Talk to me," I beg softly, unable to take his distance any more.

I hate that he's been gone. And what I hate even more is that he treats me like I don't matter to him, which is a damn lie. As much as I try to deny it, I must, or he wouldn't have taken me to work this morning. He wouldn't care enough to get angry around me. He wouldn't have done a lot of things he's done. Maybe it's a fantasy I've created about him, and I'm the lunatic. I told you I was going to need to be admitted to the loony bin after I lived upstairs with him. But this feels real. The static between us can't be imaginary; it flows around us every time we're near one another. It's an uncontrollable magnetism.

I've tried to negate my attraction, I've tried to deny anything that I've felt, I've tried to keep my own detachment, and it's impossible. He drives me mad. Flippin' mad! One minute, he can't stop touching me, which fills this void deep-down, while giving my self-confidence a jolt, like a car battery that needs juice to run. The next minute, he bolts, leaving me wrecked and confused.

At first, I couldn't want him because he was married, and because of my love for Brian. Now he's getting a divorce. For all I know, it's already been finalized. The only thing that's come of Meredith since that night was the letter I got in the mail, containing the restraining order. I haven't been told anything else. Not that I've cared. If she's gone and I don't have to see her face again, or hear her call me fat one more time, then that's just fine and dandy with me.

As for Brian, I know he would kick my butt if I continued to live my life pining for him. I knew that ten years ago, and I know that even more so now.

"We're gonna be together until death do us part, babes. I love you." Brian expressed that to me a million times. It was the way he said I love you. I always replied, *"Death ain't got nothin' on us, and I love you way more."* We had loved each other, deeply, and it was death that parted us. Until the night that I revealed everything to Lachlan, I hadn't known the amount of pain I'd been harboring all of those years. A weight had lifted and the sky had parted, allowing the brilliant blue to shine down on me. Ever since then, I've been walking around lighter, and with a bit more optimism in my life. Something I can honestly say I never thought could happen. *Ever.*

Am I still insecure? Scared out of my mind? Hurt about losing Brian and then Grams? Hell yes, I am. Do I want to let that rule my life? No, not any more. I'm not a victim. I'm a survivor. A survivor who now has a job where she's respected, who has a roof over her head, and a haunted man she cares about, that might just feel the same way. I've also got Bridget, who adds insurmountable joy to my otherwise boring life. I don't know how I've gotten this lucky, and I'm not sure how or when life went from pain and sucking, to this. To me cooking dinners, making sandwiches, and feeling like I'm a part of something real. Something that I need. Something that I love. Something that I'd die fighting for.

Ignoring my plea, I touch Lachlan like I've never touched him before. Raising one hand from his chest, I cup his scruffy jaw in my palm. It scratches me in the most delicious way. Pained, teal eyes, hooded and dull, stare back me as he remains still.

"Six weeks ago, I cried in your arms after your wife decided to break into this house." My thumb gently brushes over his goatee. "You listened to me pour my heart out to you, about someone I'd never talked about with anyone but my grams before."

I pause to let my calm words penetrate. His reaction is...naught. "Since that day you've pulled away more than before...Not that we were ever close." I shrug. "But you were around more, we texted, we tried to be friends...I thought we were friends." With sincerity, I pour all of my emotions into his eyes.

"I cannae be yer friend, my leannan," Lachlan mutters quietly through gritted teeth.

"What does that even mean? My...however you pronounce it."

"Leannan," he repeats slowly. "It means I cannae be yer friend, and I cannae have ye touchin' me like this." His face lurches away from my palm, and it falls to his chest. "I cannae give whatever it is ye think ye want." He shakes his head. "Not ever."

Just like that, I think I died a little. The small flicker of hope fades into the black recesses of my heart.

"Your friendship? You can't be my friend? You can't talk to me and tell me what's going on with you? Why you're so distant? Why you're always so hot and cold? I'd prefer warm, Lachlan. Warm is good. Warm is steady and safe. But, *nooo,* you have to give me burning hot. Hot to the point I think I might actually combust when you touch me. Then two milliseconds later, you're stalking away as if you could care less, as if I don't even matter." I'm panting for breath by the end of my rant, and my blood pressure rises to volcanic.

I can't believe he doesn't even want to be my friend! That's all I'm asking. I'm not asking him to kiss me, or hold me, or god-for-freakin'-bid, love me. Not sure if I want that either. But I do want him to touch me, and I do want his hands to do more than grip my hips. I want them to embrace me. Is that too much to ask?

"Ye matter." He confirms as the fingers on my hips dig deeper, cementing his statement.

My clit nearly bursts in reaction. Holding back a moan, I bite my lip and shove my face between his pecs. The scent of him surrounds me, drugging me, and I rub my nose in my favorite spot; the spot that has soft, red hair underneath.

Lachlan grunts disapprovingly, and before I'm able to inhale his magnificent scent once more, he's shoving me away.

My back collides with my chair, and a sharp pain follows.

"I'm so sorry. I cannae do this." With the shake of his head and a grimace, Lachlan sprints from the kitchen. I hear the door slam shut, signaling his departure, and wait to hear his *Harley* roar to life; only it doesn't. The music in the barn begins to thump louder than ever before, rattling the windows and the scarce pictures mounted on the walls.

Something's wrong with him. I don't know how I know it; I just do. And if he doesn't want to tell me, then I'm going to find out myself, even if I have to tie him up and torture it out of him. Not that that's what I wanna do. I wouldn't know the first thing about tying up a giant with thighs-for-arms. But I have to try. I may not be cured, and yes, I have my moments, but Lachlan's helped me. Now it's my turn to help him. It's for his own good.

Approaching the barn, the waves of music blast me in the face, making it difficult to catch a full breath. I skirt the edge, my booted feet crunching in the grass as I try to conceal myself in the shadows. The moon and stars are hidden behind dense cloud cover, turning the darkness nearly black.

Arriving at the corner of the open barn door, I peek around the edge and quickly pull back, gluing my body to the wall.

Oh. My. Jiminy Christmas!

My heart thunders in my chest.

I do it again, peeking.

Oh. My. Pancakes and gravy!

And one more time to make sure I'm seeing things straight.

My mouth hangs open and my eyes widen, as I linger in the doorway a little longer than I should. I can't believe what I'm seeing!

A knot lodges in my throat, and I turn away with the vivid memory of him burned into the back of my eyelids. I sag against the barn side, resting my hands on my knees as my head drops to my chest, and I expel an emotionally ragged breath.

Lachlan's pants were pooled around his booted ankles, his body leaning forward as his left hand gripped a thick, square post to hold himself up. Head hanging low, with his shoulders hunched, Lachlan pumped himself in his fist; fast and hard and without remorse. Through his hasty jerks, I was unable to get a look at his shaft, but watched as the clear pre-come continuously leaked from his tip, dropping to the floor.

I'm not sure if I should feel sorry for him, or turned on. It didn't look like he was enjoying himself at all.

My heart cracks a fraction, acid boiling in my gut.

"Come on, ye fucker; just get it over with," he growls dolefully between song breaks.

Two minutes later, and the sound of something horrid resonates from inside. He's...he can't be, can he?

Glancing around the corner, I watch him with his hand still gripping his cock, as he kneels weakly over a metal bucket, puking violently into it. Pulling back, he wipes his mouth with a towel on the floor, and then the next round of vicious purging begins.

I don't know when, or how, or what comes over me...One second, I'm outside staring at the heart-shattering show; and the next, I'm kneeling next to him on the dirt floor with my hand caressing his back.

"It's okay," I soothe.

"Go. Away!" he roars before diving for the bucket again, his body curling smaller as if he's trying to shrink and disappear.

Running my hand along his spine, paying attention not to touch his bare butt, he stops puking and lurches away from me, falling onto his side, body tucked into the fetal position, pants around his ankles. "Get out of here, now!" he shouts, his eyes rimmed in red, body shaking, hands tightly cupping his package.

"Now! Out! Now! Get out! Now!" His head starts twisting back and forth in agony. "Now! Out! Get out!"

Tears mat my eyes and my heart breaks a little more.

To keep from outright bawling, I get up and shut off the music before I return to him, sitting on the floor a couple few feet away.

His bottom lip quivers as silent tears start to tumble down his cheeks. I want to go to him. I want to curl my body around his and tell him everything's going to be okay. That whatever demons he's trying to ward off, I'll help him with—that we can battle them together.

"Get the... fuck...out!" he shouts, choking on a sob. "You cannae...see! You cannae...see!"

Slowly, on my hands and knees, I crawl toward him.

Horrified, he scurries further away, dragging his half-naked body across the dirt floor.
"Out...Please...Go!"

Ignoring his devastating, painful pleas that are ripping my heart to shreds, and the tears that run down my face, turning my vision of him blurry... I forget the dirt on my hands and the cry that I swallow to focus on one thing—*Him*. The broken man on the floor. The strong man who took care of me when I almost died. The man who brought me back to life. The man whose body is shaking so violently that his teeth are chattering in an eighty-degree barn. Death, sadness, remorse, pain, anguish, hatred...I can feel it all through his wounded gaze.

Again, he cries out another gut-wrenching plea, and again, I stay put, keeping my distance, but holding my ground.

"Talk to me." I reach out my hand to him, hoping he'll take it. Praying he will.

Glancing at my hand and back to my face, he shakes his grim head and rolls to his side just as another round of heaves rack his massive frame. Over and over, he tries to expel, yet, only a little, if nothing, comes hurling out. More full body quaking ensues as he struggles to catch his breath.

Minutes pass and he begins to level out. Staying put, I give him my silent support as I sit on the dirty floor, a yard or two from him, knees to my chest and my arms hugging them. He may not want me here, but I've seen the worst and I'm not leaving. Not until he tells me something—anything.

"I...I...think I'm done. Can...ye please turn around so I can get dressed?" He sighs, exhausted.

I don't speak as I stand and turn around, providing him the privacy he needs. Feet move, clothes shuffle and a zipper is secured, then there's walking.

Water running steals my attention, and I turn without permission. Lachlan's rinsing his bucket under a spigot and tossing the contents into a tall, overgrown bush outside. I take this time to examine him, and watch him as he slouches back to the spigot to refill the bucket and rinse it again. He's worn and ragged, just like he has been for over a month.

Is this what he has to live with? Is this what he endures every single day? Is this what stomps out all the light in his eyes, leaving him part man, part death? I can't be sure, but my gut says I'm spot on. Something has clawed its way into Lachlan and sunk its teeth in, refusing to let go…And here I thought I lived with pain and guilt.

The strong man we've all come to know is even stronger than we thought. He's a survivor, too. He's just like me. *No*…he's stronger. He's braver, and a hero. A true-to-life hero, who risks his life on a weekly basis to save other people. People like me. And for years he had to come home to a house with a wife like Meredith, where nobody cooked for him, or cleaned for him—Bridget told me as much. No wonder he's so distant; he hasn't had any other choice. He's tried to stay alive and get by, not to actually live.

How could I have not seen this sooner?

Why was I so selfishly stuck on myself?

Ugh, I feel awful.

I should have tried to save him, too. Saving the savior. Saving the man who has probably been drowning longer than I have. The darkness that swallowed me whole has swallowed him, too. Only, I'm rising to the surface as he sinks deeper into the murky abyss.

I feel his eyes searing me before I glance up and catch them pinning me in place. Opening my mouth to talk, I'm silenced when he shakes his head sharply, running a shaky hand over his cropped hair. "Ye were never supposed tae see that," he exhales. "Ye should have bloody well left...I told ye tae leave."

"You were in pain. I'm not leaving if you're in pain."

"This is where I come tae take care of things." His hand gestures to the weight bench and punching bag in the corner that's next to a wooden workbench littered with tools.

I raise a challenging brow. "To *jack-off* and *puke*, is what you mean?"

Wincing at my harsh words, he then nods. "Aye. That, too."

To ask my next question, I mimic his stance as we both tuck our arms across our chests, and I reach down deep to pull courage from a place that I didn't know existed. "Are you going to explain to me what just happened over there?" Confidently, I point to the spot where everything came undone. A spot I will never forget for the rest of my life. My nightmares will be haunted with those memories for years to come.

"Na, I'm not. It's none of yer business." He's stanch.

"So you're just going to keep shutting me out? You don't want to be my friend. You don't want to tell me what makes you feel pain instead of pleasure when your hand's touching down there." I nod his crotch, and he groans. It's not a happy, pleasurable groan; it's one of fatigue and irritation. He's tired of me digging. I can feel the waves of malice wafting off him as we speak, trying to throw his protective shield up.

Well, as my grams always used to say with a knowing wink and a grin, *"Magdalene, you're as stubborn as a mule. Always gotta have it your way"*. Time to conjure that old part of me and stick to those guns. Make my grams proud, while I prove to Lachlan, once and for all, that he has someone who can bear the brunt of his pain. I've weathered my own storms, and I sure as hell can take on his, too. Let's do this damn thing.

Subconsciously, I crack my knuckles to prepare myself for the battle of a lifetime. It took me six months to break down Brian enough for him to tell me that his old man was a deadbeat drunk. I might be comparing apples to oranges. Nevertheless, Brian still needed someone to lean on, and I was that person. Just as I was Jake's person, a man I dated way back when. He was going through a divorce and the wife got custody of his kids. I was the sounding board, and in the end, a doormat that took a slap to the face. A week later, I was gone and I've never seen that man again. Now, I'm going to be Lachlan's person.

Leaning against the far wall, Lachlan tilts his head to the side and grins. It's not one that's sweet or makes my stomach turn somersaults. It's demonic and frigid. It's all wrong.

Chills slide glacially down my spine, as my toes tingle, curling in my boots.

"Ye know what, lassie?" Derision drips from his lips like rich, golden honey, and then his grin broadens, flashing a sliver of teeth. "I liked ye much better when ye couldn't talk."

He can't mean that. Can he?

Puffing up his chest, he goads me with his eyes and stance, wanting to see if I'll retaliate. If I'll fight.

I could run and let the part of me that wants to cry myself to sleep do just that. Or, I can stick it out and battle him. However, that small part of me that I have to hold on tight to; it knows that this will end up a slaughterhouse by the time we're finished. Me, being the stuck pig writhing on the floor in a pile of my entrails, as the butcher stands above me in victory. I'm not saying we'd kill each other. But I am saying that if things were to come to a head, it wouldn't be pretty. I'd end up broken all over again. I don't know if I have it in me to endure another blow. Not now, and certainly not from him.

So that leaves me with one final option—to walk. To treat him like he's been treating me, by distancing myself and not speaking to him. Maybe he needs to be treated like a child and taught a lesson for talking to me like I'm nothing, like I'm lesser than him—pond scum. If I'd done something to warrant his contempt then I'd apologize. But I've done nothing of the sort. All I've done is care, and that's not a crime in my book. Is it in yours?

Ignoring the tightness in my chest, and my sour stomach, I pretend his words have no effect on me. Holding my head up high, my back straight, I drop my hands loosely at my sides to appear as if I don't care, even if it's killing me inside.

"Fine, Lachlan." I take a step toward the door, my eyes still on his, my expression neutral. "If you don't like me now that I can talk, then I won't be talking to you. It will save us both a lot of grief, now that I'm aware of your problems with my speech. So please excuse me as I head to bed, and I hope you have a fantastic evening." *You beautiful, broken lughead,* I tack on in silence as I leisurely stride out of the barn door and up the incline. Once I reach the porch, I feel my resistance dissolve and those tears that I prayed would stay away, don't.

The first tear falls when my hand grips the door handle and turns. The next when I close the door behind me. I swipe them away with the back of my hand, and inhale a deep breath to keep from dashing to my bedroom and slamming the door shut. I don't know where Lachlan is, and I can't let my guard down just yet. Five more steps and my legs feel like lead weights. Only five more to the bedroom door, and it feels like I'm drowning from the pressure that's painfully squeezing my chest.

I make my way into my bedroom and gently shut the door behind me. Pirate perks his lazy head off my pillow with his own doggy smile. Normally, that would make everything else in the world feel a little bit brighter. Unfortunately, right now, nothing can fix this. Nothing but a lot of time, patience, and perseverance. I know I can do this. I know I can prove that I'm strong and caring, and that Mags won't be someone's punching bag. Maybe he'll miss me. Maybe he'll learn the lesson I hope is the right one. Or, maybe I further damage an already damaged man. Maybe, he won't care that I'm speaking to him or not, and actually take joy in the silence.

Frickity-flippin'-fudge toads, I don't freaking know. I don't know anything. Why can't life be simple?

Shaking my head, I strip my clothes off and lay them in a pile on the floor. Not even bothering to don pajamas, I finish tossing my bra into the pile and slip under the covers next to Pirate, wearing my panties. Pirate crawls closer, shoving his nose in my neck, and that's what undoes me. I wrap my arm around him, bury my face in his fur, and sob. Sob, until his fur sticks to my face. Sob, until I'm so emotionally tattered that I pass out with the light still on.

As grams always used to say, *"Tomorrow's another day for a fresh start."*

Goodnight.

CHAPTER 18

"How are you feeling?" Bonez offers me his hand and gently tugs me from his chiropractic table onto my feet.

Shaking out my arms and legs, I twist my head a few times, and then release a marvelous sigh of total body relaxation. I feel lighter than air, and it couldn't have come at a better time. "I feel…I feel *muuucchhh* better. Thank you." I grin slightly.

Bonez smiles, delighted at my reaction, and flashes me all of those perfect teeth; even his eyes light up. He must take real pleasure from helping his patients, and that's a welcomed bonus. "I'm happy to hear that. When you came in, I wasn't sure if we could work all that tension out. Damn happy we could. How's the leg?" With the flick of his chin, he indicates to it, and I lift, bending at the knee. It feels a hundred times better already; a lot less stiffness and pain.

I set it back on the floor. "It's a lot better."

Together, we walk in silence to the front door of his business. I stop to turn around. Then, suddenly, I'm plastered to his front. I bark out a startled laugh, and his hands shoot to my waist, holding me steady. "Whoa there." He smiles down at me as I tilt my head back to see his face. It's such a handsome face, too. Hard and beautiful, but soft and friendly around his eyes. I'm not sure how old he is, but if I had to guess, it'd say around Lachlan's age.

"Maggie, are you all right?" He yanks me from my dazed stare.

Dagnabbit! I promise I can't help it. I'm halfway between deliciously relaxed and asleep. Spending two and a half hours here with Bonez did that. Those magical hands of his did that.

Shaking my head to clear it, I break from his arms and take a step back, and he lets me. "Yeah, I'm sorry. I'm kind of tired, because your hands are sort of amazing." It just kind of slips out before I can swallow my stupid word vomit, and he grins huge at the compliment, while I turn beet red. Why can't I act normal? *Uh!*

"Why don't I take you down to Muzzie's?" Bonez opens the front door, spins me around, and places his hand on my lower back as he propels me forward. "I'll be back, Rita. Cancel my next two appointments!" he yells to his receptionist, and then we're off. I don't argue, because I'm not sure what we're doing, or why he's strolling with me down the sidewalk with his hand touching me in a place that's making me feel weird.

At the corner, we stop and Bonez pulls out a plastic chair in front of a quaint little shop with green and white striped awnings. "Here. We'll drink outside." He sweeps his hand to the seat, and I plop down, still unable to process what in the heck just happened. Did he just ask me for coffee? Is that what Muzzie's is?

Bonez takes the seat opposite me just as a petite waitress, with a pile of black hair tied on top of her head, exits the shop. She stops at our table, and her smile dazzles when she addresses him. "Hey, Bonez. The usual?" I swear she sways in his direction like there's some magnetic pull. Sadly, he seems none the wiser.

"Sure." He nods before cutting his gaze to me, his tone softening. "What would you like, babe?"

Whoa! He just called me *babe*! I'm not sure if I'm going to throw up or blush. The heating of my cheeks radiates like fire. Bonez seems pleased with my reaction, when his eyes stay glued to my face, ignoring our waitress, who doesn't like her attention stolen. I can tell. She's staring daggers at me right now, probably wishing for my untimely death.

"I'll..." Nervously tumbling my hands in my lap, I clear my throat and glance up to the waitress. "I'll have a lemonade."

"We don't do lemonade. If you want lemonade, go to Whisky's, where you belong," the waitress snaps, and Bonez comes off his seat, literally. Stepping into her space, she backs up, visibly gulping.

"Tina, Terri, Tonya, whatever the fuck your name is," he flicks his hand out like he doesn't care, "I know we had a good time six months ago. I know I fucked ya *real* good...Made ya come...But that's all it was. That's all it was ever gonna be. I told you that shit then, when you came home with me. And I'm telling ya the same shit now."

Attentively, she nods her understanding, her bottom lip stuck between her front teeth, biting hard.

He's not finished. "I get that chicks don't like to see a man they've fucked sitting with an even hotter *lady*. But you don't fuckin' talk to my family like that. Do you need to write that shit down?"

She shakes her head.

I can't believe this is happening... He called me *hot,* and told her I'm his family.

My blush intensifies.

"Good," he clips. "Now, get me my coffee and Maggie whatever the fuck she wants. If you don't do lemonade then make some, or you go to Whisky's and bring it back. We're having drinks here, and you're gonna serve us with a little respect. Ya got me?"

The waitress doesn't reply before she races back inside. Bonez retakes his seat, all of that anger displaced. Poof—gone, floating in thin air. "Sorry about that," he apologizes.

"It's okay. She was kinda rude. I've just never had someone...um...."

"Someone, what?" he prompts, casually leaning back in his chair.

"Stand up for me like that." It's true, nobody has.

Apparently, he finds this funny when he starts to laugh, his body actually vibrating with humor.

"You live with Smoke," he snickers, calming from the hilarity of whatever it is I said. I'm not sure how *that* has anything to do with this. I go to ask, but stop when he carries on. "Smoke's an asshole to everyone."

He doesn't seem bothered by this, and I agree with him one hundred percent. He was definitely a jerk to me last night. Good thing Bridget woke me up this morning as soon as he'd gone to the barn to workout, or do, you know...other horrific things. Anyhow, she'd told me to drive her to school so I could keep the SUV. She didn't want her dad to find out and make her drive it instead, and I didn't want him to do that either, because I wouldn't have come to my physical therapy today if that meant Lachlan would have to bring me. I'd rather eat nails then do that.

So I'd gotten dressed, went downstairs with her, and we'd snuck out of the back just in time for me to catch him staring in the review mirror as we drove away. Lachlan didn't look pleased, which pleased me to no end. *Check*—one point for Magdalene.

"Yeah, he's one of those," I agree, leaning back in my own chair, even though I'm too tense after the waitress's foul attitude.

And here I was, rather enjoying the relaxation high following an hour of workout and stretches with Bonez. Afterward, I'd gotten a one hour massage—my first one ever. I was naked, yet, covered with a sheet. Thought I might die of sheer embarrassment, although, surprisingly enough, spending two minutes with his thick fingers kneading my neck and I was putty in his hands. I didn't care one bit. He left me to dress when he'd finished, and then I'd gotten my chiropractic adjustment in the main part of his offices.

Bonez stops laughing, but is still smiling when he says, "Not to you, he's not."

I gasp aloud that he could even believe that. Sure, he's a butt munch to me, too. "He is too," I debate, childishly. "He was rude to me last night. He said some very mean stuff." I'm not going to go into details, because I can't share Lachlan's secrets. They're not mine to tell.

The waitress makes quick work of delivering my lemonade in a tall glass, and his coffee in a white ceramic mug. Once she dashes back inside without saying a word, I take a sip of my lemonade. It's *okay*.

"Is that good?" He nods to my drink.

"It's fine. Thank you and yours?"

Holding the mug to his mouth, he blows on the top. Steam billows from the cup, before he takes a sip from the edge. I watch in fascination, awaiting his response. Hoping that his coffee is better than my lemonade.

In our friendly silence, a strange sensation unexpectedly washes over me and I shake it off. *Weird.*

"It'll do." Bonez shrugs with indifference. "As for Smoke...I'm sorry he was an asshole to ya yesterday...But I gotta tell ya, he's sweet on you. If he was a dick, it's because he's a guy, and guys do that sometimes. Especially guys like him and me, who've been takin' care of themselves far longer than most."

"What does that actually mean?" I know I might sound stupid for asking. Nevertheless, I have no clue what he's getting at.

I take another sip of lemonade, and Bonez fixes his white collared dress shirt by refolding the sleeves up his forearms, exposing all of those colorful tattoos. "Listen, I suppose you've been through the same. Lived like us."

I still don't get it.

"When you first arrived, Sniper put a call out to some contacts," he adds, providing little clarity.

"A call for what?"

"We needed some Intel, and my brother's a tech nerd," Bonez explains, and I don't know why that strikes me as funny, but it does. I try to throttle a giggle, only I'm not completely successful when a fraction bubbles out. "You think it's funny?" From his grin, I can tell he's amused with me.

"I think it's funny you have a tech nerd for a brother," I clarify, although I'm not sure why I do.

"He's not *that* kind of tech nerd. He's also a biker, part of a club up north. A bigger club that we support. His name's Gunz."

"You're Bonez, and he's Gunz?" I can't hide my joy from this knowledge. That's kinda cute. Weird, but cute.

"Yep." He proudly jerks a nod. "And we've both got gray hair, 'cept he's bald. And his legal name's Erik, while mine's Eli."

"Lots of similarities there," I note.

"Oh, you don't know the half of it," he winks mischievously, grinning.

I'm not even going to ask what that's supposed to mean. I'm sure I don't want to know what *the half of it* means. If I'd wager a guess, I'd say it starts with a *k* and ends with an *inky*.

He continues. "As I was sayin', we asked for some Intel and he gave it. You ain't got much of a paper trail. No dad on record, and you weren't raised by your mama. Says you're from Kansas. Your grandma adopted ya. But after she died, the trail went cold. Guessin' you've been takin' care of yourself just as long as Smoke and I have been takin' care of ourselves. I joined the military, and my brother joined a club. Parents been dead since forever. And Smoke ain't much different. Had a daddy who shipped him off, a mama who was too naive to fight it. And, like me, he joined up to make some sense of his life."

He pauses to take another sip of his coffee, and I follow suit. "Except Smoke got burned when he married a whore just so he could keep that little ray of sunshine in his life. And it probably doesn't help that most people can't understand a fuckin' thing he says half the time. So…like I said…Smoke's gonna be an asshole. He's only ever had himself, and now Whisky and the club to rely on. As I'm sure ya can relate, seein' as though you don't have any family, or anybody else 'cept us lookin' out for ya," he pauses a beat before adding, "you've been doin' it all on your own, am I right?"

How does he know so much? How could he be any more spot on? He's not only a hand wizard; he's smart as a whip, too. No one can get anything past this one. I'm not sure if that's endearing or freaky—maybe a little of both.

Playing with my nails, I bob my head in reply. "Yeah, I've been alone for ten years. Since, like you said, my grams passed. I know what he's been dealing with, but it doesn't make it right for him to treat me that way. Or any man for that matter. And, to be honest...if I had a place to go and I knew that it wouldn't break Bridget's heart, I probably would have left last night." *And if I didn't care for the Scot as much as I do.*

"Is that why your eyes were swollen when you came in?"

"Yes," I blurt honestly. "I cried last night after I decided I'm not speaking to him for a while. Not that he'll care, anyhow," I tack on, because that's how I feel. It's got me worried sick that maybe he'll just throw me away like yesterday's trash. I hate feeling vulnerable like that; I haven't felt this way in years.

Bonez finishes off his coffee, while flicking his eyes to the road behind me, then back to my face. "Don't look now." He speaks behind his cup, although I can see a huge smile crinkling at the edges of his eyes as his shoulders bounce in light, understated chuckles. "But the man you think doesn't care if you talk to him, has been sitting over at Whisky's, staring this way since we sat down. And I'm willin' to bet he's been over there a helluva lot longer than that." Setting his empty mug on the table, he raises his strong chin in the same direction his eyes move.

"Lachlan's over there?" I can't withhold my disbelief. Would he be spying? Or is he just over at Whisky's helping out? I'm not going to look to find out. Don't want him thinking I care that much. Or do I? *Geeze*, I'm so confused.

"Yes, Smoke's over there, and he's coming outside right now."

I feel his eyes on me before I hear his boots stomping their way over. The hairs on the back of my neck stand at attention. Each heel scrape on the asphalt has my heart fluttering to the beat. I swallow hard.

Lachlan steps up next to me, so close that I can feel the heat emanating off his body, and his manly scent intoxicating my senses. My mouth waters in recognition. God, it's been less than a day and I already miss him. This is going to kill me.

"Smoke." Bonez is the first to speak, as he extends his arm across the table, offering his fist to Lachlan.

"Bonez." He bumps his fist in return, his voice husky and raw. It melts over me like a rich chocolate.

A hand touches the back of my chair. "Mags," he says. I'm not sure if it's in greeting, or if he's wanting my attention. Either way, I ignore it and keep my eyes focused on Bonez.

"Mags," Lachlan repeats, stronger this time. I feel it deep, so deep that my lady parts take notice as they answer his call, awakening in my panties. *Damn.*

By the grace of God, Bonez comes to my rescue. "I was just talking to Maggie, here, about the club party next weekend. Asked her if she'd like to accompany me.

She said she'd be delighted to…Didn't ya, Maggie?" His expressive eyes are alight with mischief.

As much as I want to scowl or huff, or tell him he's being unreasonable for putting me in this spot, I know I can't show my aversion because an angry Scot is standing right beside me, growling under his breath, grating his jaw.

"Didnae Sniper fill ye in?" Lachlan rumbles, speaking to Bonez.

"Fill me in about what?" I think Bonez knows what Lachlan's referring to, because he's grinning like a madman. This man is definitely up to no good, which he knows and apparently likes, too.

Lachlan's leg moves and glues itself to the side of my chair. It bumps my elbow, and I tuck my arms into my lap so I'm not touching him.

Fiddling with my hands, I use them as a distraction to try and ignore the sensation of his penetrating eyes drilling into me, or that minor touch scalding my skin. I hate that he has this effect on me.

"Ownership, brother. Ownership," Lachlan bites off, jerking my chair backward. The scraping feet make a horrid noise, as my chair vibrates, being moved further away from the table.

I've had enough.

Grateful to have my legs back in action, I stand and swiftly sit in the chair closest to Bonez. He scoots closer to me, throwing his arm across the back of my seat. I still refuse to look at Lachlan, but feel the air shift into something not good, not good at all.

"Ye better stop touchin' her chair, brother," Lachlan warns.

"If Maggie wants me to stop touching her chair, I think she's old enough to tell me herself. Right Maggie?" Bonez interjects calmly, patting my shoulder in reassurance.

I hear boots shuffle closer, followed by a soft click.

Continuing to stare into my lap, I cuff my hands over my knees, before I dare to glance up. Tipping my head to the side, I look at Bonez, not Lachlan. Faintly, I grin at him, "You're right, Bonez. If I don't want something, or don't wanna do something, I'll let ya know." Wow, I sound much stronger than I feel. *Check*—two points for Mags.

Bonez winks at me, as if he's communicating that was the right answer, and his hand moves to squeeze my shoulder, cementing my assumption.

"Mags, ye are not goin' tae the party with Bonez." Lachlan fixates his argument on me, and it falls on deaf ears. I don't want to hear it. He can't have control over everything. I'm not a possession; I'm a flippin' person, and he needs to realize that. I've been on my own for far too long. Taken care of myself for far too long. I don't have it in me to let a man dictate my life. Life's too short to be someone's slave. Not that that's what Lachlan expects.

Drilling my eyes into Bonez's neck, where a black tattoo peeks out from under his collar, I stay preoccupied and politely accept his offer. "I'd love to go to the party with you, *Bonez*." I emphasize to get my point across, and I think it's driven home when Lachlan repeatedly curses under his breath. The word *'bloody'* attached to every other word.

Bonez doesn't respond to me, but his head tilts to the side, just as I hear Lachlan fiddling with something. "Put that fuckin' thing away, Smoke. It'll end with you in a place you don't wanna be. This ain't worth it, man," Bonez reasons evenly.

Lachlan doesn't seem to give a crap when he seethes, "I told ye...*ownership*. Ye're fuckin' with what's mine."

I sure hope they're not talking about me. *His*? I'm not anyone's. If anything, I'd prefer to be an equal.

"*Riiight,*" Bonez drawls, "and bringing that thing out is gonna change what's happening right now?" He's rapidly losing his patience. "*No,* it's not. Maybe you should be more focused on righting some shit you did wrong, instead of threatening me with your fuckin' dagger. I'm not Thor. I'm not gonna piss myself. And I sure as fuck ain't gonna pussy foot around the fact I got my brother standin' here challenging me with that damn thing. Put it the fuck away, and go back to Whisky's where you can keep starin' at her, 'cause she obviously don't wanna talk to you."

Yep, they're talking about me, and I hate that I have to listen to this. Moreover, I can't believe Lachlan has his dagger out. How did I not even notice he carries a dagger? He did something to Thor, too? Made him piss himself? I can see how he could do that by just looking at someone. He's scary as hell when he wants to be. But to yield a weapon, right here, right now, in the early afternoon? That's stupid and crazy. What if a cop comes by? And what if Bonez wasn't so understanding? Lachlan's not thinking clearly, and part of me wants to reason with him and tell him to go, because it's for his own good. While the weaker part of me wants to wrap him in a hug and tell him it's going to okay, and I'm not mad at him anymore. Even though that's partially a lie.

I'm not actually mad. I'm hurt, and sitting here with him so close is fucking with my senses. Oh. My. Whoa. Buddy. I just dropped an F-bomb. Crappy crackers, I really need to calm the heck down. My brain's moving too fast, and my senses are too riled up.

I inhale a deep cleansing breath.

"Fuck off," Lachlan bellows. "This ain't none of yer business."

"Yes it is. We're all family. You made sure of that. Now, I'm taking care of family by taking her out for some shitty lemonade. Now put it away." Bonez's eyes flick to what I assume is said dagger.

Something moves, and a snap is clicked into place. I release my breath.

"Smart move," Bonez notes, keeping his cool. He's the master of Coolville. I'm impressed.

"Now, do the right thing and walk away before you make Maggie more uncomfortable," Bonez suggests amicably.

More uncomfortable? There's such a thing? *Riiight*...Pretty sure this would be hard to beat. I'm squirming in my skin over here. I don't like confrontation, and I especially don't like it when it's about me and includes Sir Moody Pants.

"If ye touch—" Lachlan starts.

And is quickly cut off when Bonez abruptly declares, "It's not like that. You have nothing to worry about."

"I better not," Lachlan rumbles lowly, before his tone turns sweet. "Mags, I'll see ye at home for supper."

I nod in reply, but don't face him. I can't; my resolve will fade too fast, and that can't happen—not yet.

"Later," Bonez calls to Lachlan, and I hear a grumble in response. Boots stomp away, and when I finally hear the faint ding of Whisky's bell floating through the air, I'm able to breathe easier. Releasing another breath I didn't know I was holding, I slip into my previous seat.

When I meet Bonez's eyes once again, he's grinning tenderly at me. "You did well. I thought you were about to come out of your seat a couple times."

"Am I that transparent?" I reach out to take a sip of my now watered-down, lemonade. It tastes even worse than it did before, if that's even possible.

I purse a sour face, swallowing the contents in my mouth, and Bonez chuckles. "That bad?"

My nose wrinkles at the awful aftertaste lingering in my mouth. "It's disgusting."

"I won't bring ya here again. Wanted to take ya to Whisky's, but with Smoke bein' there, I figured this was second best," Bonez explains.

"Again?" I ask as my mouth involuntarily falls open with doubt. He plans to do this more often?

"Since I'm gonna be seeing you twice a week, and we're gonna be doing them on your work days, I figured we could grab a bite to eat. We both gotta eat, and you're good company...Killin' two birds with one stone."

I blurt the first things that comes to mind. "You don't think that might give the wrong impression?"

Bonez shrugs with a calculating smile. "Seein' as though you're pissed at Smoke and you almost gave in, this might help with whatever devious chick plan ya got going on in that pretty little head of yours."

He can't mean that. "You want to help me teach him a lesson?"

"More or less." He shrugs again. "We both get to eat, and I like the company. You're funny. Plus, it'll be good for me to have a lady friend who I have no intention of fucking."

Wow, he doesn't beat around the bush, does he?

Regrettably, I can't help it when my face falls a little at his *'no intention of fucking'*, comment. My chin meets my chest and I stare into my lap. That stung. Can't deny that. No girl wants to hear that come from a man's mouth, especially an attractive man's. It's a hard blow. You and I both know it.

"Get that fucking frown off your face, Maggie," he scolds lightheartedly, slapping the table top. I jump a little and lift my head to meet his gaze, still sulking. "You're extremely fuckable, so don't be getting this *'I don't wanna fuck you because you're not sexy'* into your head. I prefer a woman with something to hold on to. And I loovvee big tits and a juicy ass. You're *bangin'*," his hands move to his chest, cupping imaginary breasts, "in *all* ways." He winks. "But, you're not mine to fuck. A claim has been rendered, and I'm respectful enough not to step over that brotherly line. Even if I wouldn't mind trying to screw a *lady* who's much sweeter than I'm used to."

His no holds barred compliment has my entire body blushing something fierce. I can't control it. Even my ears burn hot, and I bite my lip, trying to swallow his brashness like a hard shot of liquor. It burns all the way down, and once it settles in my gut, it warms me from the inside out. Nobody has ever been that forward to me. Not about finding me…um…you know…pretty…or whatever. It feels amazing, but kind of embarrassing, too. I still like it, though, and it'd feel a whole lot better if it came from the one person I wish felt the same way.

"Thank you," I mutter shyly, rubbing my palms on my jeans to wipe away the clamminess.

"No, thank you...for your company. I'm looking forward to doing this again next week." He winks and gets up from his chair to pull out mine. Offering me his hand to help me to my feet, I accept it. Although, I'm caught off-guard when a warm bear hug wraps around me, and a soft kiss is pressed to the top of my head, making my mind swim with contentment. Pulling away, he winks once more. "See ya next week." He walks up the sidewalk, headed back to work, and I wave a farewell

. "Next week!" I call to his back.

What a flippin' day, and now I've got to hit the grocery so I have something to cook for dinner. Guess, I'll be setting the table for three. *Uh*....

CHAPTER 19

Hugging Bonez, I lift onto my tiptoes and press a kiss to his stubbly cheek. "Thanks for lunch," I mutter, stepping back.

"Always a pleasure, babe." Bonez offers me a two finger wave as he watches me walk up the driveway back to my job. "See ya Saturday!" he hollers to my retreating form.

"See ya there," I return, entering the bay and heading straight to Viola, who I've been working like crazy on.

She's not perfect yet, and she'll still need a fresh coat of paint. Overall, though, she's drivable and I plan on taking her out for the first time on Saturday when I meet Bonez at the club party. A party I'm a nervous wreck about.

Today marks one week since my first appointment with Bonez. It was my third, and from the sounds of it, I only have four weeks to go. Granted, I'm not too thrilled about his newest suggestion…he wants me to start working out. He recommended I get a membership at Thor's, and since I'm family, it should only cost me twenty bucks a month. I don't like the idea of Thor's, and I really hate the idea of working out. It's not that I'm opposed to the working out itself, just the part about having my body moving in front of people. More specifically, my headlights jiggling, as other parts jiggle, too. It's gross to think about. All of *this*, shouldn't be doing all of *that*. It's…um…not sexy. It's grotesque and embarrassing. And the last thing I want to do is make someone sick in the midst of all my feminine jiggling. *Yuck.*

Let's just leave that on the back burner for now. Talk about it later…*much later.* K?

Sliding into the passenger seat of Viola, Sniper approaches the open door and rests his forearm on the door frame and car, boxing me in. He crouches down, taking a looksee inside. "The seats are almost done," he observes.

I bend forward, my head between my legs, chair all the way back, as I work on fixing the carpet. I replaced it all. It needed it. "She's almost done. Just waiting on Cas's buddy to drop by next week to pick her up to take her to get repainted." I sigh, defeated. "I'd be nice if Cas had a paint room so I could do it myself."

"You're such a control freak," he teases.

Sniper's not wrong. I am a control freak, especially with Viola; she's like a daughter to me.

"Yeah, I am. But so is Cas. He's the one who picked out the best carpet and talked the guy down to three percent above cost." I'll never forget that day. It was last week, when we'd been working on Viola. He didn't even seek approval when he blurted his decision, "This carpet has gotta go." And that was that. New carpet arrived yesterday. We installed most of it this morning and now I'm just finishing up, checking seams and whatnot.

"He's a tightwad." Sniper chuckles.

"Fuck yeah I'm a tightwad, asshole. If I wasn't, this place woulda been dead years ago." Cas makes his grand entrance and pushes Sniper out of the way to steal the same position, his strong arms boxing me in.

I glance up from the floor. "She's about done." My finger points to the last edge.

"She's lookin' good. So how was lunch with B today?" Cas is digging for information. He's been doing it for days. Ever since I informed him I wasn't speaking to Lachlan and refused to give him a reason why. It's none of his business. That's why. If Lachlan wants him to know, he'll tell him. I'm not about to stupidly run off and tattle on him to his club president and VP.

Speaking of Lachlan: last week when he said he'd be home for dinner, he was. Just as he's been home every night except the nights he's working. On those nights, I pack his bucket with leftovers. I know that makes me a weak idiot, because I said I wasn't going to fix him any more food, but I feel guilty if I don't. Don't judge me.

However, over this past week of supper, Lachlan's been different, way different. Bridget seems to have taken notice, too, because he's moved from six-word sentences to full on paragraphs.

On Sunday I'd taken a bite of lasagna, as I listened to Bridget prattle on, in another one of her tangents. "I don't understand why Whisky doesn't hire someone else. I'm bad at frosting, and I can never get the recipes right. She wants me to know them by heart, like she does, but I can't store the measurements up here." She softly knocked on the side of her head, reminding me so much of her father. *"It's like she wants me to work there forever. But I'm going to college so I can get a job working with kids. I don't want to be a baker,"* she whined.

Lachlan shook his head, took a drink of his lemonade, draining the glass, and when he set it down, he started his own lecture. "Whisky loves ye, Pip. She only wants what's best for ye. If she wants ye tae remember her recipes, it's because she loves ye; not because she expects ye tae work there forever."

"But—" Bridget began, and was cut off when Lachlan waved his hand for her to be quiet.

Then he continued, "I know ye're young and she's bossy, but Whisky's the only lassie who's cared enough aboot ye tae do what's right." His eyes drifted to me. "Now ye've got Mags, too."

"I know I do, but—"

"Na buts," he cut her off again. "Ye'll work there until ye graduate, and then ye'll go tae university. But ye should learn her recipes before ye do. It's a family thing. It's not aboot work. Aye?"

"Yes, Dad." She slumped down into her chair with her arms tucked across her chest, unhappy that she'd been scolded.

I, on the other hand, was kind of turned on by his parenting skills, and thrilled to see him assert himself. I hadn't seen that many times before. As much as Bridget appears to be mature, fun, and outgoing, she's still a teenager who needs guidance. The more I've gotten to know her, the more I've noticed and tried to help. But there's something special about the bond a father and daughter share that no one can sever. Not that I'd want to, anyhow.

The entire week has been the same nightly routine. I cook dinner, we eat together at the table upstairs, and Bridget spills her girly teenage guts to us both. Lachlan gives his input as I remain quiet and let them hash it out.

It's not always a reprimand; most of the time it's more of a father-daughter battle of wits, to see who backs down first. Normally, it's Bridget, but it's all in good fun. Honestly, I get my own sort of silent pleasure in listening to them talk. Its makes for sweet dreams at night.

And, yes, just in case you've been wondering, I've stuck to my guns. I haven't spoken to Lachlan. I've nodded and shaken my head, but that's it. Nothing verbal. It's been torture, yet, effective. I can tell it's frustrating him.

Last night, after Bridget had settled her plate in the dishwasher and went downstairs, Lachlan had turned his attention to me. *"Are ye really going tae the party with Bonez?"*

I was surprised he hadn't brought it up sooner.

In response, I nodded my head, and he growled, slamming his fist to the table. "Ye're not goin'," *he ordered as I sat there and stared, biting my tongue to the point of almost drawing blood. I wanted to tell him to kiss off. I didn't, though. I let it slide off me, even if it was hard.*

Standing up from the table, I dismissed myself by setting my own plate in the dishwasher before I left the kitchen to retire to my bedroom. Evidently, Lachlan had plenty more to say when he followed me like a dog, still angry and domineering.

"Did ye hear me?"

Sure did.

"Ye're not gonna be his date."

Sure I am.

"I dinnae bloody like ye ignorin' me."

I didn't like it either.

"If ye wanna go, I'll take ye, but ye're ridin' on the back of my bike."

No, I'm not. I'm taking Viola.

I entered my bedroom and gently shut the door in his face. This didn't deter him from speaking his mind. He was on a roll.

"What're ye wearin' tae the party?"

Whatever the hell I want.

Walking over to the bed, I slipped in next to Pirate, who snuggled up close. Leisurely, I pet his head as Lachlan continued outside my door.

"Yer pot roast was damn good," he complimented.

That made my stomach somersault, and my cheeks heat in a way that felt so good. I was kind of giddy.

"I know ye're still pissed at me."

I'd never been anything of the sort with him. I was hurt. The end.

"I didnae mean what I said aboot yer voice." He sounded like he was in pain. A thump hit the door that had to have been his head, as his voice lowered to a raw whisper. "I miss ye, my leannan."

It broke my heart to listen to the words flutter from his lips. Words that I had been needing to hear for a week—dying to hear. What hurt even more was my determination to keep my distance for my own sanity. I couldn't let him hurt me anymore by shutting me out. The line between teaching lessons and my own self-preservation had already started to muddle. I was getting in way too deep. Feelings were morphing into much more than I've been willing to acknowledge.

He'd left after that, and I cried myself to sleep. This morning, I came to work early to try and shake off this feeling of guilt that's gnawing at my insides for not responding to his plea last night. I've been kicking myself in the butt ever since. Even though Bonez reassured me that it will all work out in due time. He's been my constant sounding board through this week of hell. We've been texting regularly, and are really turning this patient-doctor thing into a real friendship. One that I value and trust.

Speaking of the devil...

My phone vibrates.

It's Bonez.

He's over at Whisky's again staring at the shop. Maybe you should drop by.

I reply. *And do what while I'm there? Be a stalker?*

"Is that Smoke?" Cas snoops, breaking away from the car door.

"No; it's Bonez. Why?" I know why, but I'm still asking.

Cas shrugs before he moves over to my tool box, haplessly fiddling with my wrenches for no reason. "Just curious," he mutters.

Just curious, my patootie. He's trying to look out for Lachlan. I know that. They're tight. I just wish he'd cut me a little slack. He's been asking me questions every day. It's a little much.

"Hey Cas?" I exit Viola, shutting her the door.

"Yeah?" He leaves my wrenches alone, turns around, and pulls the cigarette from behind his ear, before placing it to his lips and lighting up.

"Is it okay with you if I drop by Whisky's? I gotta ask her what I should bring on Saturday." That's the best excuse I could come up with on such short notice. True, I could just text her to find out, but then I wouldn't be heeding Bonez's gentle persuasion. Plus, I have another question I need to ask her, anyhow.

"Sure." He grins victoriously, exhaling a puff of smoke. "Whatever ya want." He has to know Lachlan is over there, and is probably hoping that I'll change my mind about Saturday. Not going to happen.

With a quick wave and a thank you, I make my way over to Whisky's. Her bell rings as I enter, even though it barely registers, thanks to those teal eyes scorching me as I stroll through the door.

Whisky lifts her head from behind the sugary display, and flashes me a wide smile. "Hey there, sister," she greets happily.

Raising my hand, I return a "Hey," as I make my way to the back counter. Whisky's standing behind it, fumbling with some trays.

"What can I do ya for?" she asks, setting the trays on the counter with a loud bang. "Want some more cupcakes?" she teases, wagging her eyebrows, knowing darn well that as of Sunday I've asked Bridget *not* to bring me any more of those addictive cupcakes.

I can already start to feel my clothes shrink, or perhaps that's my imagination. Either way, I've stopped devouring those heavenly treats, and made a pact with myself to indulge only once a week. So far, I've not succumb to temptation. It's been difficult, especially when I add the stressors of Lachlan to the mix.

Setting my hand casually on the counter, I take a deep breath and do my best to keep calm and collected, even if my palms are now beginning to sweat and my heart's rapidly beating. Its Lachlan's attention; he's doing this. I can feel him, smell him, and almost taste him. It's distracting.

Clearing my throat, I reply, "No, thanks. No cupcakes…but…I was hoping you could fill me in on what I need to bring to the club's get together this weekend? Should I make a dish? Bring drinks? Cups? Plates? Whatever you need, I'm more than happy to bring. I'd really like to help." It all starts to tumble out way too fast that by the time I'm finished, I'm in desperate need of oxygen.

I inhale deeply, and Whisky's smile explodes into Las Vegas itself, lighting the whole damn place. "Be still my fucking heart, you beautiful, big titted bitch! Where in the hell have you been all my life?" She dramatically throws her head back, covering her heart with her hand—swooning. "Woo hoo! I think I mighta just died and gone to heaven!"

Unable to control it, thanks to her theatrical display, I start to laugh, a full body one. I grab my stomach as tears wet my eyes.

Oh my, she's hilarious!

Bridget walks in from the back, catching me in the throes of laughing my butt off, and her aunt still swooning, mumbling on and on about where'd I'd been all her life.

"What in the heck's going on here?" she asks, amused, her own smile blinding me.

Whisky is the first to stop her dramatics as I try to calm down long enough to catch my breath, and wipe the tears from my eyes with the back of my hand.

"Mags asked what she could bring to the club party," Whisky explains, enthusiastically.

"Oooohhhh." Bridget giggles. "That makes complete sense about the whole *'all my life'* craziness." She air quotes before she turns her attention to me with a dab of teal frosting painted on her nose. "Whisky's been saying for years that the boys need to find themselves good women so she's not stuck cooking for the all parties by herself."

"Hey!" Whisky intervenes, cupping her hand on her hip in a playful manner, before pushing it out. "Rosie and you help, too," she argues, mock affronted.

"Right." Bridget rolls her eyes. "We help *some*, but we don't do the shopping, or the cleanup, or any of...*that*." She flicks out her hand. "It's a good thing Sniper's not completely lazy, because he does help you. But get real, Whisky, we only do a dish or two; you do the rest."

"The brother's pay for the stuff," Whisky notes.

"True, but you still cook it, and clean it up. That's a lot harder."

"True." Whisky nods in agreement, then both of their eyes swing to me, and both of them alight with glee.

"Can you make your meatloaf into smaller sizes?" Bridget queries at the same time Whisky asks, "What are you good at cooking?"

They both laugh at each other's disruptions, lay hands on one another's shoulders like close girlfriends do, and give each other a squeeze before letting their arms drop.

"You don't like meatloaf," Whisky reminds her.

Wish I'd known sooner that she doesn't like it, because I wouldn't have made her mine. Maybe I should have asked.

"I like hers," Bridget throws out with a bit of attitude. "It's really good."

Never mind. Guess that was a good decision on my part then. She likes *my* meatloaf, even though she doesn't like meatloaf. How awesome is that?!

My insides go a little squishy at the thought.

We carry on like this for some time, talking about what I could bring. In the end, they leave it up to me, but give me a wide variety of choices to think about. Lachlan's eyes never stop burning through our entire girl chat, and he doesn't interject either. It's strange knowing someone's in the same room with you, listening to your conversation, yet, they remain eerily quiet.

Whisky goes to help a customer that comes in as Bridget walks around the counter, grabs my hand, and pulls me in through the back, coming to stand in a bakery kitchen with a huge mess of teal icing dotting the counters, and a glob on the floor. I guess when Bridget said she wasn't very good with frosting, she wasn't lying. It's a disaster.

"I didn't want to have this talk with Dad out front staring at you like he's thirsty and hasn't had a drop to drink in a century," Bridget remarks with a lopsided grin. "But I want you to know that I know that you're going with Bonez to the party."

Uh-oh, I was afraid of this. I didn't want to hurt her feelings, which is why I haven't brought it up yet. I figured I'd wait until Saturday to let it slip. I guess someone already beat me to it. It was probably Whisky and her big mouth.

Kindly, she taps my cheek. "Stop frowning; it's not a good look on you."

I try not to frown, but it doesn't work. Apparently, I'm a pro at it. "I'm sorry I didn't tell you about Bonez. I didn't want to hurt your feelings. I know you think there's something going on between your dad and me."

"There *is* something going on," she corrects.

"If there is, it's going nowhere fast."

"Not true, because Whisky told me Dad's been sitting here every time you work just to watch the shop and make sure you're all right. He also leaves when you go to lunch with Bonez and follows you there. So he's obviously got some stuff going on up here." She taps her noggin. "I don't know what…And I'm guessing my dad won't share with me, anyhow."

"Probably not," I agree. "And don't feel bad, because he won't share with me either," I tack on, after crossing my arms over my chest.

"Give him time," Bridget reassures, showing wisdom way beyond her years. I know she's right. It's just hard to swallow.

"I'm trying."

"What you need is a killer outfit to go with your *trying*." She bounces her red eyebrows, and I chuckle, shaking my head at her silliness.

Oh yeah…duh…the other question…

"That's what I forgot to ask Whisky…What should I wear on Saturday?"

"Sister," Whisky cuts in, joining us in the back and stopping right next to me, bumping my shoulder on purpose. "If you wait until we close, Pip and I will take you to get sexed up for this Saturday. My brother and all of the boys won't know what hit 'em." She snaps her fingers with flare, before sweeping a mess of red curls off her forehead. "You're gonna knock those motherfuckers dead!"

Bridget giggles at her aunt's over the top antics, and I join right along.

Guess I'm going to get *sexed* up. Gah!

"Sure. I'll see you after work," I concede with an anxious grin, as Bridget squeals, clapping her hands with excitement.

Boy, oh boy, am I in for a treat. I just hope I don't end up looking like an oversexed harlot.

Wish me luck. I'm going to need it.

CHAPTER 20

Nature's Finest

Stopping outside of Whisky's rural farm house, I roll up next to a row of shiny motorcycles—a very long row of them. *Maybe I shouldn't have come?* My thoughts race as I audibly gulp.

The scent of mini meatloaves clogging the air reminds me that I need to pull up my big girl panties and get the hell out of Viola.

Shutting off the engine, I reach back and grab my sheer black thigh-highs and white heels off the passenger seat. They're the finishing touches to my *biker chick* outfit. The very outfit that Whisky, Bridget, and I took two hours to agree on because just about everything had been a "no" in my book. Most of it was too trashy. Which Whisky assured me, men like. I don't, and neither did Bridget, so we bought a mid-thigh faded jean skirt, a white slouched neck tank top, and a fitted black leather jacket. To accessorize, I got these heels and thigh-highs because Whisky refused to let me leave the store without them. We purchased my dainty necklace and earring set that I picked out, too.

Last night, Bridget sat me down in Lachlan's hideous bathroom and we talked about my makeup options. I know nothing about the art of makeup so she showed me a few tricks of the trade which I've used to enhance my features tonight—whatever the heck that means. Bridget's the one who used that mumbo jumbo.

She rattled on something about the swish of a brush to enhance my sharp cheekbones, and a dab of this, here, or a smidge of that, there. I have no clue what any of it means; I just know she wrote the instructions down after we'd gone through it and I'd reapplied it just now before I left. It turned out okay...*I think.*

Opening the car door, I swing my legs out and tear open the package of thigh-highs with my teeth before I slowly glide them up my smooth, brace-free thighs.

Running my hands over the silkiness, I admire the new look. Wow, they really do make me feel sexy, and a bit naughty, too. Not that I'll admit that to anyone, except you.

Once they've been secured without any wrinkles, I lay my white heels onto the gravel and slip my feet into them. Using the door handle to pull my body to stand, I wobble just a bit before my bearings get straightened out. I smooth my hands down my curls to make sure they've not frizzed on the way over. Not sure why it matters, but something deep inside says it does, so I'm going with it.

A voracious catcall catches my attention, and I look around to see who they're whistling at. When I see no one else is around except me standing here, I fidget, as the strong urge to slip back into the car and leave overwhelms me.

"Don't do it!" Bonez hollers across the yard, eating up the distance with his long strides until he meets me toe-to-toe and grabs hold of both my hands. They're shaking. Tipping my head back, I meet his friendly gaze. "You're scared. It's okay to be, but I promise these fuckers are really nice fuckers," he reassures with a smile.

Eyes darting around, I attempt to look around him to get a better view of the yard and all of those in it. More specifically, I want to see Lachlan; it is an indescribable need. I haven't seen him since last night, and my junkie fix needs tended to. Maybe then, my nerves will calm.

"Hey, hot stuff." Whisky arrives, slipping past Bonez to my side and hooking her arm around my waist in support. "You look beautiful." Her voice is tender and genuine, which helps a minuscule amount.

"Those meatloaves, pasta salad, and mini quiches are in the back," I explain to her as I appreciatively take in her fanciful biker chick form.

She's wearing a similar jean skirt as mine, except the bottom of hers is frayed. She's also donning a black, scoop neck, rhinestone encrusted skull shirt that shows a lot of cleavage. Way more than mine does, even though I'm sure we're about the same size in busts. Her feet are stuffed into a pair of black wedges, and her makeup is way smokier. This is also the first time I've seen her with her hair down. It's a thick, gorgeous mane of red, curly beauty, just like Bridget's. I'm instantly jealous. She's striking and sexy without looking like a trashy street walker.

"Sounds good," she replies about the food. "I'll have the boys come and get it."

"You look hot," I blurt, and immediately regret it when her eyes widen and my cheeks catch fire. Me and my big mouth.

"You think I look hot?"

"Very hot," I mumble, and turn my attention to Bonez, who I just realized still has a hold of my hands. I tug them away and wipe the dampness on my skirt. "She looks hot, doesn't she, Bonez?" I bait, trying to shove some of the heat off myself.

Sorry, Bonez.

"She's always hot, as are you," Bonez answers coolly, inclining his head to me, then offering his arm to escort me like a gentlemen.

Whisky pats my butt and whispers in my ear, "Go make him eat his Scottish heart out. You got this, sister."

Duly noted.

I nod in understanding, pat her side in return, then hook my arm through Bonez's as I realize that he, too, looks different tonight. For one: he's wearing a black t-shirt; not a dress shirt. Two: he's clad in his patch-covered leather vest. I thought he looked mighty handsome in his work clothes, but I think I like him better this way. It suits him, and it's sexier. And apparently, he likes to wear his shirts tight like Lachlan does, leaving nothing to the imagination. Talk about hunky muscles galore. If my heart hadn't already been spoken for, I might be tempted. Fiddle Sticks! Did I just say that?! *Get a grip, Mags.*

"You ready to meet the family?"

Bonez leisurely walks me through the gravel and up to the grass where the party's in a full midday swing. I shrug uncertainly, my voice caught in my throat from the overwhelming sight in front of us. There's an average farm house to the right and an old barn attached to a garage straight ahead. I've never seen anything like it before. There's a fire pit roaring to the left, surrounded by tons of sawn off logs that are being used as stools. Scattered among all of this real-estate are men, lots of men of all shapes and sizes. All of them wearing some variance of leather, bandanas, jeans, and some of them have beards that hang over their chests. Most of them have lots of tattoos, and I'm pretty sure black is their only color of choice. Wait...I think I see a man in a gray t-shirt. Okay, so maybe gray's safe, too.

Bonez escorts me toward the house, where the food is being set up on long rectangular tables. That's when I first feel the prick of warmth spread through me as the backdoor of the house is slammed shut, and a set of boots stomp down the stairs. Coming face-to-face with Lachlan, his eyes bore into me just a few feet away, wearing a panty dropping kilt. Jesus, that's a sight to behold. My mouth waters involuntarily as I take in his massive hotness. Tight black shirt, black vest, black riding boots with the edge of white crew socks poking out, and more and more of those sexy tattoos that make love to my eyes. When I finally focus on his face that's hard, unshaven, and stupidly attractive, I catch his eyes roaming me up, down, and back again, not even trying to hide it. He stops and lingers on my face before running through the same motions. His gaze feels like a thousand little fingers ghosting over my skin, sending shivers of raw pleasure straight through me. I smother a needy moan as my legs wobble.

Gaze drifting upward, he stops on my eyes and the corner of his lip tips slightly. I almost miss it before it's gone. Those same teal eyes darken as they leave me and shift to my right. Observing my arm tucked into the crook of Bonez's elbow, a disgusted expression morphs his handsome features and his nostrils flare. With hands clenched at his sides, his forearms turn to inked steel. I take a step forward to go to him, to make it all better, but Bonez stops me by cuffing his paw over my arm. Lachlan takes notice and rumbles a low growl, igniting a standoff between my escort and himself, the man who makes my heart yearn.

Sniper quietly approaches, as does Cas and a few other onlookers. Bonez is stock-still beside me, and I glance up to see his face clamp down, his expression nil. Seconds slip by at a sluggish pace as if they'll last forever. The testosterone congested tension sifts through the air, making it hard and painful to breathe. I want to claw at my throat.

A body bumps me from behind, knocking me forward. Bonez saves me from falling as Whisky stumbles into the mix, landing smack dab in the middle of it all. "Ooopps." She pretend gasps, covering her mouth. "I'm sooo sorry. For a second, I thought we were at an old Western Showdown." Throwing her hands up, she twirls in the center, dissolving the stare-off.

Lachlan's and Bonez's eyes lock on her, and she grins, knowing that she'd accomplished what she had intended. "How about you fuckers stop acting like a bunch of gun slinging baboons and drink some beer and eat some damn food!" she yells, glaring at her brother, before sauntering over to Sniper, where she hooks her arm around his tanned neck and yanks him down to meet her lips. His big hands claim her ass possessively, and suddenly, we're all privy to a hot and heavy porn show as Whisky mewls to his mouth and he devours her lips in a sloppy wet kiss.

Bridget comes out of nowhere and takes my arm in hers. "Let's get this set up." She tugs me forward, away from the hot show and the two men who are about to rip each other's heads off.

"You look pretty, by the way," she compliments as we come to a stop on the backside of the house where my food has magically appeared.

"You do, too." I pat her arm, admiring her clothes. The color of her shirt makes her stunning eyes pop.

A gangly looking man-boy moves in beside us, throwing his thin arm across my shoulders. "Hey there, hot stuff." He licks his lips suggestively, staring straight at my headlights. He reeks of beer, and I try not to gag.

Bridget doesn't take too kindly to this and shoves him away from me with a hefty push. He stumbles to the side, laughing, as his beer bottle lands on the ground, pouring into the grass. Staggering, he snatches it back up and takes a pull, draining the rest. "Mags, this is Muff; our resident vagina licker." She points to the drunken man-boy who desperately needs a haircut. "Muff, this is Mags; Smoke's old lady."

Righting himself, Muff straightens his back, and slurs, "Well, why didn't ya say so?"

"I just did," she snaps, glaring at him.

Smoke's old lady? Those words knock around in my head as an unexpected heat filters through me with sweet satisfaction. Quickly, I thrust that feeling away; it doesn't belong here.

"Right." He tips his imaginary hat to us, bowing. "No disrespect intended, my lady. I'll be going now." He thumb points back the way he came, snatching up a handful of my mini meatloaves before scurrying off.

"That's Muff," she explains once he's out of earshot.

"I gathered that."

"He's a harmless flirt."

"I gathered that, too, seeing as though you just shoved the poor boy and he nearly fell on his butt."

She giggles, smiling at the recollection, and goes about setting up the rest of the table. I join in, putting myself to work. "He's not the brightest, but he's not the one you have to worry about," she notes.

Tearing the wrapper off some paper plates, I tilt my head, raising a brow at her in question. "Who *do* I need to worry about?"

Grabbing my forearm, she hauls me to her side and turns me so we face the yard. One by one, she points to each member, telling me their name, which I'll never remember. And she explains if they're someone I have to *watch out* for, because men in biker clubs aren't to be trifled with. Not that I thought they were a bunch of sweet, cuddly bears, but the way she describes them leaves me a whole lot more leery of this place. Not that it's all bad or anything. Still, some of these men are...how you say? One card short of a deck...if you catch my drift.

Standing next to Rosie, who I've gotten to know a bit more since I started working at Cas's, is her husband, Peanut. "He's probably the nicest man here," Bridget explains as Whisky walks over and joins us, her mouth bright red, hair a mess, wearing a smile on her face the size of the moon.

Righting her skirt, she then smooths her hand over her hair. "Woo," she fans herself with her free hand, "Sniper's the *Energizer* bunny tonight."

"He's the *Energizer* bunny every night," Bridget deadpans next to me, both of us people watching.

Or more specifically, biker watching. It's not that exciting to partake in at this juncture. They're all eating, talking, or drinking, as *Guns N Roses* booms through a set of tall speakers in front of the barn-garage thingy.

"Is my brother?" Whisky playfully bumps her shoulder with mine, and a bad taste in my mouth rises. I don't want to talk about this with her, or anyone.

"Ewy!" Bridget fake gags. "That's your brother and my dad! We can't talk about that with her."

"I'm still a woman. I'm not asking to compare dick size. I'm asking if he's taking care of his manly duties," Whisky defends herself, throwing out her feisty attitude.

Bridget continues to fake gag.

Oh, please. They've got to stop talking about this. "Listen," I snip, "not that this is anyone's business, but we haven't done anything in that department. So I can't tell you. And if it gets to that...I still won't tell you if he is or not. I'm not that type of woman."

"We're all that type," Whisky contends.

"I'm not," I argue right back, slinging my own brand of attitude at her. "I've never had any female friends before. So I've never had anyone to discuss sex with. I'm not comfortable talking about it."

"Well, seeing as though I'm your family, I hope you know what's going to happen here tonight." Whisky's voice turns genuinely concerned.

I shrug. "I sorta do."

"Groupies are going to show up, and those men," she sweeps her hand, indicating the lot of them, "are going to fuck the groupies, or at least play with them. And they'll do it in front of you, without a second thought. So, if you don't think you can handle that, you'll need to go inside with Bridget when they show up, because it doesn't take but a minute for them to strip their clothes off and get down to business." She's not being bitchy; she's just informing me because I think she cares.

Last week, Bonez had warned me that this was going to happen when I came here. He went into a little more graphic detail than Whisky is, but it's still the same information. Naked women, sex, leather, bikes, booze, music, and food. I've got the memo.

"I know," I state more confidently than I am.

"Good." Whisky slaps me on the back. "Now let's get you a shot."

A shot. That sounds perfect.

A shot will dull the senses, and curb this crippling unease that's rolling around inside.

I wish I fit in here.

Lachlan

Standin' outside of the garage, leanin' against the side with my arms crossed over my chest, I watch in silence as Mags recklessly shoots another shot down the hatchet. Pain flashes across her face as the liquor stings her throat, endin' with the burn in her gut. I've seen it a thousand bloody times tonight. Whisky's detained her the majority of the evenin', playin' mother hen tae my lassie, while feedin' her alcohol like it's water. I guess it's better than the alternative—her spendin' time with Bonez, who's been watchin' her like a hawk the whole night, too.

Aye, I only know that because I've been doin' the same fuckin' thing. I cannae help that I have tae keep an eye on my lassie. She's been fuckin' claimed, and I'll be damned if anyone else tries tae make a pass at her. She can stay bloody pissed at me all she wants. We'll work that shit out eventually. I just dinnae need someone gettin' any bright ideas. This week has been torture enough. And dealin' with her lookin' like that, at a place like this, I know it's bound tae stir up some trouble. Not that I'm opposed tae trouble. I could really use a reason tae kick somebody's arse. Mags won't talk tae me, and she has my life twisted in all sorts of ways. The wee outlet would come as a great relief.

Now, I know I bloody well fucked up in the barn. I was scared outta my mind that she saw me like that. And from the looks of it, she saw the whole lot of it. That fucked with my head. I couldn't stand the thought of her seein' me like that. Do ye think I like tae puke after I come? Men are supposed tae enjoy it. I dinnae. I cannae. My head's broken, and somethin' up there hasn't been right for years.

Afterward, I might have said somethin' that was meant tae hurt her. But I didnae mean the damn thing I said. What was I supposed tae do? Tell her aboot my problem? Na fuckin' way. And then what? Have her pity me? Leave me? Think I'm a disgustin' bastard? Which she probably already thinks after seein' me do that; after she'd felt my hard cock brushin' against her in the house.

"Don't you think I deserve a man who can please me, Lachlan? A man who isn't deformed? Whose dick doesn't look like some alien parasite?"

Rubbin' my temple, I blink tae wash the thoughts of Meredith away, and shove them tae the deepest recesses of my mind where I hope they'll stay. That na good lass is outta my life. The divorce is final. Good riddance tae her. Now, all I've got tae worry aboot is her seein' Pip, if she ever decides tae. Thankfully, Pip will be eighteen soon enough and this underage parental visitation horseshit will be done with. Not that Meredith gives a bloody fuck if she sees her daughter or not.

Two sets of headlights flash in the night, headed our way. There ain't nothin' else out here besides Whisky and Sniper's place, which means the underdressed club lassies are here. I can hardly control my enthusiasm. *Not.*

Huckleberry and Banjo cut their music off, and my brothers make their way tae the gravel—tae pick out their nightly pussy.

Mags doesn't seem tae notice as she continues standin' next tae Whisky, her eyes occasionally cuttin' my way, even though I can tell she thinks she's spyin'. There ain't nothin' aboot the way her eyes shift tae me, linger, heat, and then dart away that's inconspicuous in the least fuckin' bit. But I'll just let her keep on thinkin' whatever she wants tae think. As long as my bonnie lass is in that I-need-tae-blow-my-load outfit keeps checkin' me out, and not Bonez. My cock agrees, 'cause it's been rock-solid under my kilt all night. And when she's sneakin' her innocent and sexy-as-fuck little peeks, I get that much harder. That's all I need tae know for everythin' tae stay right in my world. Even if my stubborn beauty won't talk tae me because I was an arsehole. Which, I might point out, is not my standard cheery disposition. Didnae ye know? I'm all sweet, friendly, and shit. Haha, that's funny just sayin' it.

I think it's aboot time tae grab me another beer.

Mags

"Here. Take this one, too."

Whisky hands me another shot. Of what? I haven't the slightest clue. She's been feeding me alcohol all night as she keeps me preoccupied. Personally, I think she's rather enjoying the female companionship. She doesn't seem to have any other girlfriends other than her niece, Bridget. I welcome the interaction and take the shot. It burns like a motherfucker going down, causing me to fan my mouth.

Woo, wee, my mouth and my mind are in a tizzy tonight. I'm feelin' a little too damn good at the moment. Fire in my belly, wetness between my thighs, and nipples that are begging for some attention. Alcohol lowers my inhibitions big time. Although, my brain always seems to function properly, even if my body and fuzzy mind like to revert to the basic carnal need to fuck and be fucked. Oh. My. God. See…I have a potty mouth! I think it needs to be rinsed out with soap. Or something even more tempting—like a certain Scottish man's you-know-what. Mmmm, yes, that sounds much more pleasing. I wonder what it tastes like, looks like, and feels like. Darn it, I'm turning into a horny, foul-mouthed slut tonight. It's time to cut myself off.

Ten minutes ago, scantily clad women arrived and have been making their street walker rounds to get attention. Over by the fire pit there are two men, the ones who were playing music earlier, who are now sharing a woman. One's got his hand up her skirt, doing something to make her moan, as the other man with a long beard massages her naked breasts. Oh, well, now he's sucking on one. I turn my gaze back to Whisky, who is completely unfazed by the lewd displays. I'm not a prude by any stretch of the imagination, but you have to be very open-minded for this to not affect you. Or turn you on. It smells like bonfire, leather, alcohol, and sex. It's a potent combination that's readily fueling my neglected libido.

"How in the...*world*...do you get used to this?"

I gesture to another man getting his dick sucked by a blonde on her knees in the grass. Sniper and Cas are standing next to him, talking as if the woman isn't even down there going to town on his pole. He fists her hair, pumping into her mouth as she reaches between her legs to play with herself. *Wowza.*

A little tingle between my legs makes me shiver while goosebumps prick my skin.

Whisky shrugs. "I've lived this life for so many years. It's not a big deal to me."

"Did it bother you at first?"

My question is rewarded with a barking laugh and a friendly slap on the back. "No, Mags. I used to suck Sniper's dick in the high school bathrooms. And he ate my pussy any chance he could get."

Umm...okay...I guess she was already into public displays way back then.

She keeps on. "We didn't date back then. We dated other people, actually. But that never stopped me from meeting him in the boy's locker room and jacking him off while he acted like he was in the bathroom stall taking a shit and talkin' to my brother."

"You gave him a hand job when Lachlan was there?" I could never be that ballsy.

"Hell yes, I did. I couldn't get enough of that dick. We stopped things when he graduated and joined the military. Then, when he got discharged, he went and got all depressed, and used me as his fuck hole." Her tone softens. "I let him. Then after a while, I got sick of being a fuck toy and decided I needed something real. I broke it off, and he didn't like that too much so he proposed to me."

"Just like that?"

How in the world do you go from being someone's sex toy to engaged? That's wild.

"Just like that." She nods. "We've been together ever since. Bought a house and started the club...Then got hooked up with another club Bonez's brother, is the Sergeant of Arms of..."

"His brother Gunz?" I interrupt.

"Yeah." Whisky gives me a strange look like she's shocked I know that name. "He told you about Gunz?"

"Yeah, why?"

Whisky waves me off. "Oh, no reason. I'm just surprised is all. He doesn't usually talk club stuff with anybody, especially not a female."

"We've become good friends," I state levelly, not wanting her to think I'm defending our friendship. I don't need to defend anything. I'm going to be his friend regardless. He's a very nice man, and he respects me. The end.

"I suppose you have." She sideways glances at me and tips the corner of her lip as she perks a brow. "That's all there is...*right*?"

Great, first Lachlan, Cas, and now Whisky, too.

"There is nothing going on there," I drone.

"Okay, just checking." She smiles and bumps her shoulder with mine, the interrogation immediately forgotten. "So, yeah, the club's called the Sacred Sinners. You'll probably get a chance to meet them all next year sometime when we go and party with them."

We...what?

"What?"

"The Sacred Sinners, we party with them," she repeats like I didn't hear her.

I heard her loud and clear, even if the heat of someone's gaze is burning into me again, and the sound of some woman climaxing is diddling with my equilibrium. Maybe it's the alcohol doing the diddling. I can't be sure.

"No," I blurt. "This whole *we* business."

"You're family; it only makes sense that you'd attend parties with us."

"Parties like this?"

I nod to the same woman who just finished sucking that one man's dick, and has now crawled over to suck Cas's. He's smacking her in the face with it right now. If there's one thing in this world that I don't ever want to see, it's my boss's light saber. That's plain wrong. I can't be working with him and thinking about what his penis looks like. There isn't enough therapy in the world to scrub those memories from my brain.

I turn so my back is facing that scene. That way I'm not even tempted to look. I keep my gaze on Whisky, who's now barefoot right along with me. We took our heels off about an hour ago. Blisters are not your friend.

Whisky grins, noticing my back is now to the chrome sucking scene. "Don't want to see Cas get blown?" she teases, waggling her brows, her eyes dancing mischievously.

"Nope. I'd rather not see my boss's dick in all its glory. Unfortunately, pouring bleach into my eyes won't cure that image. I'd rather save myself the therapy bills," I deadpan, and she laughs.

"You are pretty fucking forward when you've got a bit of alcohol in ya," she notes with a genuine smile, and I blush, kicking myself in the ass for being so bold. "It's cool, though. I like it," she adds, and my nerves simmer.

"About this party thing..." I prompt to move away from the Cas conversation.

She flicks a stray hair out of her face. "Sacred Sinners have parties, and we're invited to some. That's where the Sacred Sister cupcakes were first brought to life. A club sister named Bink loved my cupcakes and suggested I use her cookie... " Her eyes drift to the side, breaking her train of thought, and my stomach grumbles at the memory of those delicious cupcakes.

I snap my fingers to steal her attention back.

Shaking her head to clear it, she meets my eyes. "Um...Mags." She points her finger and lifts her chin toward the garage where I last saw Lachlan standing and drinking beer.

I turn to see what she's looking at, and my heart drops out of my chest. There's some fake blonde bimbo in a micro miniskirt and a tube top, standing in front of Lachlan and talking to him as her sleazy little finger runs up and down his chest. Oh hell no! I pick my heart off the grass, dust it off, and shock it with some electricity before my temper flares to volcanic proportions. That's my fucking chest to touch! Not hers!

"I'll be right back," I growl to Whisky, and stalk across the lawn like a woman on a mission. Lachlan notices me coming right away but doesn't show any emotion.

The bitch has the audacity to take a step closer to him, her tits grazing his stomach. Those tits better get off those abs before I rip them off and feed them to Pirate!

I don't even think when I wrap my hand around her stick forearm and rip it away from him.

"Off!" I snap, shoving her backward.

"What the hell?!" She slaps my bicep with her free hand, triggering me to grab it, too, and keep walking her backward until she's a good fifteen feet from him. "Get off me, you crazy bitch!" she yells, trying to shake her arms free of my hold. Unable to control myself, she winces as I dig my nails into her flesh to make my point known.

Glaring into her eyes, even though she's about five inches taller than me in heels, I curl my lip in disgust. "You do not touch him. Do you fucking understand me, cunt?!" Oh. My. God. I'm going to hell. Fuck it! Liquid courage to the rescue. "Do you?!" I growl menacingly as the urge to shove her to the ground and stomp on her head rattles through my skull. Air pistons in and out of my fire breathing lungs as my body shakes with unspent adrenaline.

"He's not yours, and Meredith is now gone." She dips her bimbo-head, snarling in my face.

"The hell he isn't mine! You will not touch him again, or I will break both of those bony-ass legs of yours. Are we of understanding?" Forcefully, I shove her backward, while keeping my hands wrapped around her forearms. She screams, stumbling, before I yank her back upright and release her from my clutches, her skin bruising instantly under my claw marks. "Fair warning, bitch. You and all of your little friends need to keep their hands," I wave my finger to her, and all of the onlookers that my ridiculous overreaction has drawn, "and whatever the hell else, far away from Lachlan, or you'll have to deal with me!" I thumb point to my chest.

I don't have a damn clue where all of this bold sassiness suddenly came from, but I'm summoning my inner Whisky to get through it, or else I think I might crumble to the ground and bawl like a child. Why am I acting like I'm possessed?

"Are you going to let her talk to me like that, Smoke?" The blonde bimbo glances over my shoulder to him. My palm itches at my side, needing to slap her across the face.

Calm the fuck down, Mags.

If only I could.

Lachlan

I'm. So. Fuckin'. Hard. Right. Now. That I barely register Carrie talkin' tae me.

"Smoke," Carrie whines as Mags stands in front of her, blockin' her way tae me. Mags's arms are crossed tightly over her sexy tits.

My cock jumps, rubbin' pre-come inside my kilt. I groan at the feelin' and lean my shoulder against the garage, foldin' my arms across my chest tae keep from explodin'. My eyes drop to Mags's fine arse in that skirt, and I taste my bottom lip.

Carrie was flirtin' with me and I'd overlooked her advances; she does nothin' for me. Then all hell broke loose when Mags saw her touch me. I almost interjected tae stop her from blowin' up, but my balls needed me tae grab 'em before they blew themselves. I've never been so turned on in my entire bloody life.

I lift my chin tae Bonez tae let him know I've got this handled. He was on his way over tae break up the fight when Sniper grabbed him and held him back. Bonez lifts his chin in return, relief washin' over his features.

My gaze shifts tae my sister, who's frozen in shock. Pretty sure the whole damn yard is feelin' the same way. I've never heard my lassie cuss, and I sure as hell haven't seen her close tae kickin' a woman's arse. Not that I'd mind as long as she doesn't get hurt.

"Isn't Meredith out of the picture? Doesn't that make you single?" Carrie's losin' her patience, 'cause I haven't replied tae her. She takes a step forward, and Mags puts her palm up, pushin' it between Carrie's tits.

"Now that's close enough. I've already warned you once. Don't make me follow through," Mags warns with conviction, and I groan once more at the fierce sound of her voice standin' up for me. Nobody has ever done that. Meredith was never threatened by another lass in our entire marriage. At least not until the end when Mags moved in, then Meredith became jealous. Cannae blame her. There's a helluva lot tae be jealous of. Mags is perfect.

"Aye, the divorce is final," I answer, and Mags whips around, her hair flyin' and eyes as round as saucers.

"It's done?" she pants, her tits risin' and fallin' with each heavy breath.

Out of the corner of my eye, I catch Thor, the slimy bastard, unlatch his mouth from some lassie's tit long enough tae catch what's goin' on. A light bulb must click in his head, because he stands and starts tae walk his way over, the other lassie a distant memory.

"Magdalene," he calls out, and I react, not givin' a fuck.

Saunterin' up tae Mags, her eyes widen further when my abs brush her breasts, our bodies touchin'. Thor calls her name again, and she ignores him as I bend down, grab two glorious handfuls of her arse, and lift her so she's forced tae wrap her legs around my waist. She expels a tiny, surprised squeal and locks her hands around my neck. My cock lurches when her pussy settles on him, her ankles hookin' over the top of my arse.

With a possessive growl, my head dips and I nuzzle my nose tae her neck. She moans loudly, tightenin' her legs around my waist, grindin' her pussy over my throbbin' cock. I inhale, runnin' my nose up and down, gettin' drunk on her scent. My tongue lashes out, tastin' what I've been achin' tae touch for far too long. She thrusts her hips on contact, and I grab her arse harder, usin' it tae lessen the ache in my balls. Even if I cannae fuck her, I'll savor her this way.

Glidin' my tongue down tae her collarbone, she whimpers, "Oh, god," spurrin' me on.

I'm gonna have my mouth on her all bloody night.

Mags

Oh. My…Mmm…Yes…I'm going to come. It's about to happen. It's been so damn long.

Using my legs to ride up and down his dick, my clit gets the friction it needs to crash over into beautiful oblivion. I couldn't care less if people are watching when all I can feel are his hands digging into my ass. His scent that makes me dizzy, and his tongue as he kisses and sucks my neck fervently causes me to become blissfully lost in all that is him.

Releasing a hungry groan, his teeth nibble just below my ear, and that's all it takes. I squeeze tighter, my body tensing, and suddenly, my world comes apart, shattering in white-hot ecstasy. Closing my eyes, I scream a moan and throw my head back, digging my fingers into the back of his neck as I ride the wave of sated perfection. My body shudders and he grinds his dick harder against me, rolling my climax into a long, full body experience. My toes curl on reflex as a shorter wave peaks and fizzles out.

Breathing in sharp, staccato breaths, Lachlan's body freezes. His hands grip my bottom so hard it'll bruise, as he thrusts his hips one more time. A low husky growl purrs from his lips, and his body begins to tremble.

Did he just…

Abruptly, I'm set on my wobbly legs and Lachlan dashes behind the garage. The sounds of him purging his guts into the grass breaks my heart and levels me out.

Sweeping the sweat from my forehead with my hand, I right my skirt and hair as I try to pretend that everyone didn't just watch me experience the best orgasm in my entire flippin' life.

Scared but determined, I walk around the back of the garage.

What if he says something even worse than he did before?

Sitting on the ground with his back against the wall, knees to his chest, Lachlan peeks at me, his face sweaty and red. Extending his legs outward, he pats his lap. "Come." He waves me forward, and I comply, sitting on his iron thighs, but not cuddling close. He doesn't seem to like this and he curls his arms around my shoulders, tugging me so my butt touches his crotch, my side to his front.

Lachlan presses a tiny kiss to my damp forehead. "I'm sorry aboot that."

About what? I'm not. I just came for the first time in a long damn time. Apparently, he liked it enough, too, if he came.

"I'm not," I mutter, staring at my lap, the moon barely illuminating my skin. It's dark out here.

"I dunno what tae do around ye," he whispers, coaxing my head to lay on his shoulder. I settle closer, drawing my legs into his lap, my body molding to his. His arms hold me, and I sigh in sated contentment, snuggling into his warmth.

"I don't know what to do around you either. You're always mad." I don't know why it slips out. I can't control the word vomit. When it starts, it's hard to stop.

"I'm not mad. I'm confused."

My heart skips a beat at those words. *Not mad, but confused*. I can deal with confused. I can help him with confused.

"Is that why you throw up after you...you know?" I have to know why he does this. It's killing me.

He sets his lips on my forehead, and the smell of mint drifts to my nose, mingling with his addictive scent. I stifle a pleasured groan. "I dunno why. It's been happenin' for years. I cannae come without that happenin' afterward."

Why does it feel like he's not telling me the whole story?

"Why did you just...you know...out there?" Gosh, what kind of person am I? I can't even say the words. *Come.* How difficult is that?

"I got a cock, Mags. It dinnae take much for ye tae get me hard. And with ye comin' while grindin' on me, there's na bloody way I could've stopped it."

My belly flutters, and I rub my cheek on his upper chest. He *couldn't have stopped it.* That's probably the sexiest thing any man has ever said to me.

I know I shouldn't be thinking about Brian at a time like this, but it's inevitable when I can't forget all of those times Brian and I dry humped like horny teenagers. Brian never came, and I only did sometimes. Tonight, I couldn't have stopped it either. There's too much sexual tension, too much want, too much need, and way too much chemistry for me not to combust. Why is this different than before? I don't understand.

"Ye know, I didnae tell ye how bon—beautiful ye look tonight." His finger traces lines on my legs. It both tickles and feels good over my thigh-highs.

"No, you didn't," I agree, and all of that weird fluttery feeling grows wilder, like a flock of seagulls dancing the tango in my belly.

"Well, ye do. Ye always look nice." That finger roams higher, tracing the line of my skirt that's barely concealing my white panties underneath. "Ye're skin is soft," he whispers to himself. "And it smells good." His nose presses to my hair, inhaling audibly. "Just like yer hair. It always smells like strawberries or coconut." He groans and my lady parts rekindle their flame, craving more affection.

Turning into him, I lay my palm flat on his pec before tracing my own lazy lines over the muscle, in the deep valley between that's dusted with hair, then to the other mountain of his pec. His breathing accelerates as a rising thickness prods the outside of my thigh. Gliding my finger higher, I trace his corded neck up to his jaw and through his scratchy goatee. "This is sexy," I accidently mutter, and his body stiffens below me, holding his breath.

Captivated, I decide to keep going. Down the other side of his neck, I trace until I dip into the hollow. He gulps, exhaling a shuddering breath. Moving lower, back to where I've been before, my nail catches a hard nipple through his shirt, and the thickness touching my thigh lurches. I do it again, and I'm rewarded with the same reaction.

Lachlan slaps his hand on top of mine, flattening my palm to his chest. "Ye have tae stop doin' that," he whispers, pained.

"You like it, though." I know he does—he has an erection—and I like it, too, because it turns me on when I get to touch him.

His hand cuffs around mine, intimately holding it, his pulse beating against my palm. "I know I like it...but I cannae have ye doin' that." His words render no conviction, so I use my nose to nuzzle him instead.

Inside the hollow of his neck, I trace the tip of my nose in a circle before pressing a tiny kiss there. A groan vibrates in his chest, and I kiss him again, slipping the tip of my tongue out to taste him. It's heaven.

"Mags," he breathes heavily, "ye have tae stop."

"Why?" I whisper, and sample his neck once more, running my tongue in soft circles.

Suddenly, fingers are tangled in my mess of hair, tugging my head and body upright, so I'm unable to touch any more of him. I protest with a small whine.

"I said na." He tilts my head until I meet his penetrating gaze. "Ye're makin' me..."

"Hard," I interrupt quietly.

His tongue sweeps his bottom lip, and he growls. "Aye."

"And you don't like that."

"Aye." He licks his bottom lip again, his eyes never leaving mine as they darken and his lids drop to half-mast.

"Why don't you like that?" I squirm, worried what his reply might be.

His erection nudges my leg another time, as his eyes leave mine and his chin drops to his chest, where he expels a long sigh. Fingers untangle from my hair, falling away. "I cannae like it, Mags."

"What do you mean you *can't*?"

He scrubs the top of his head, exhausting another sigh. "I just cannae."

"Does it feel good?"

"Aye," he whispers, so softly that I barely hear him.

"Do I make you feel good?"

"All the time." I can feel the pain laced through his hushed words.

As much as I shouldn't take pleasure in his confession, I do. A finality of something, something huge, settles upon me. I feel stronger. It's hard to explain. But it feels right. Good and right. Like it's all going to be okay. That I'm going to be okay. And with my help, Lachlan will be, too.

"Smile even if it hurts. It could always be worse." My grams's words ring through, echoing in my mind as if she'd just spoken them yesterday. *"I might be dying, but you're alive and you'll continue to live on. And through you, my joy for life will live on, too. Don't let that go. Hold on tight, and fight. I know you'll make me proud."* I've lived the last ten years not living up to that promise to make her proud. Maybe now I can.

Brushing Lachlan's hand off his head, it drops to the wayside and I lift his chin with my finger, forcing him to meet my eyes. He frowns with a pouty bottom lip. "When you're around, you make me feel good, too." I pause to let those words sink in. They're difficult for me to admit, and my stomach's cramping as I speak them, but he deserves to know, even if his eyes and his face tell me he thinks I'm lying.

When his eyes dart away, I jostle his chin for him to return his gaze, and he does. Then I continue with what I need to say. Nervously, my hands begin to tremble. "I love listening to you speak with Bridget...I love the way you walk and talk, and dress. Even if your clothes are so tight, I can see every part of you underneath, which *kills* me..." He tries to look away and I jerk his chin once more. "No, you need to hear this..." His eyes blink their understanding, even though he remains devoid of emotion, except for the one thing revealing his unease— the rapid rise and fall of his chest as he breathes deeply. "You're supposed to take joy out of life, Lachlan." I lean in to gently kiss his cheek, and linger there for a moment, savoring his warmth under my lips as his cheek twitches. Then I return to meet his gaze, which is now clouded over. He's shutting down. I sense it as his shoulders unexpectedly slump forward. Powering on, with my nerves gnawing me, my voice wavers in conviction. "You're supposed to grab on to the things that make you feel good, and enjoy what you have. Not hide from it. And not try to push it away. Is that why you can't be my friend?"

For so long, I was tied-up in my own mind that I didn't see that maybe he doesn't want to be my friend because he's attracted to me. Because he's scared. Or hurt. Or something else that he hasn't told me, or anyone else. I can deny all day long that he doesn't feel something, even though I know he does. His hardness that's holding strong as it brushes against me is enough evidence to know the attraction is mutual…that there's more here. And if that wasn't enough proof, the intense feelings swimming in my heart would be enough to tip the scales tenfold…*no*…a hundred fold.

Twisting his head so I release his chin, Lachlan tips his head back, resting against the garage, his eyes cast on the sparkling sky above. "I've spent years…" He speaks low and slow, gaining momentum. "…years dealin' with Meredith, dealin' with my own fucked up head issues… I…I dunno know much else, Mags." He shrugs. "I spent years in the *Navy*. Saw things. Lived with them. And durin' part of that time, I had Meredith tae deal with, too I dinnae talk aboot the issues I had with her. Although I'm bloody well sure ye know some of it, since my sister has a big fuckin' mouth."

"I know some," I whisper, not wishing to deter him.

"I figured ye did. Whisky's been houndin' my arse since I saved ye. Said I needed tae see what was right in front of me. Tae stop worryin' aboot Meredith and all the bloody bullshit she put me through. Focus on the now, and not what I've been dealin' with for seventeen years."

That's such a long time.

"What have you been dealing with?" I hesitate to ask, but dangle the bait out there in hopes he'll bite. Praying that he will.

Scrubbing a hand over his face, he shakes his head, emitting a tired groan. "I cannae talk aboot it."

Disappointment lances my hope. "Please," I beg.

"Awe, Mags, dinnae talk like that," he groans.

"I want to know more, and you already know so much about me. And it's not like you have anything else you want to do." I wiggle my butt on his erection, and he growls, frustrated.

"Stop," he grinds out. "Dinnae do that again."

I do it again, and his head comes up so fast as his hands seize my waist that I jump at how quick his reflexes are. "Na more." His fingers dig into my hips, which isn't good. Isn't good at all. He might as well be pushing the volume-up button on my sexual desires.

I grasp his hands over my hips. "You can't do that if you don't want me to get excited."

His hands fly off me faster than Aladdin on his magic carpet, and I grumble a complaint, hating the loss of his touch.

Both of his palms scrub his cheeks as he shakes his head, growling, cursing, grumbling, and huffing heatedly under his breath. "Why do ye do this tae me?" he laments miserably to himself.

Uh! I don't want him to feel this way. I'm just making things worse. I should have continued to relish in his touch, instead of pressing. Why do I have to go and be a big ol' pain in the behind? Fine. Since I've already ruined everything, I might as well finish what I started...I've stuck my foot it in, anyhow. I'm an idiot.

"Because I care about you. Because I want to be your friend—"

"I cannae be your friend," he interrupts.

I throw my hands up in exasperation. "So you say, but won't explain why. Or tell me what's so bad about me. Or why it's such a problem that your dick is always hard around me. Unless your dick is hard all the time, and I'm just the unsuspecting female that gets its attention tonight. Do all women make you hard? Or is it just the slutty, fat ones? Or maybe it's because I'm drunk? Or broken? Or have a dead boyfriend, who I thought I loved more than life itself. And then I went and got trampled on by some big pole, making some big broody, thighs-for-arms pain in my patootie save my life. The man with eyes I now dream about. A man I didn't want to be attracted to. A flippin' man who I tried not to be attracted to, or want to see naked, or dream about what my tongue might feel like running along those stupidly hot abs. Or, oh my god, wonder what maybe his dick looked like under those seriously hot kilts he wears that I find myself wet thinking about. I don't get it! I don't get anything! My life was fine! My life was great, and normal, and sad, and lonely, just how I liked it! Then you!"

Running full speed ahead, I pant for breath and poke him in the chest, hard. "You! You had to come and ruin everything! You brought your daughter into my life. And lemonade. That's now made me obsessed with *it* and *you*! Which is really flippitty frickin' unhealthy! I hate it. I hate feeling like this. I hate not knowing what's wrong with me. Or why I feel weird around you. And I hate sitting here every day worried about what happened in the barn, and if you're okay. And why you do that. And what I can do to maybe help and fix it. I want to help you." I poke his chest again.

"As your friend, even if you don't want to be mine, I want to help you. I want to be there like you were for me. I would be dead...*dead*...D.E.A.D if you hadn't save my life, if you hadn't cared enough to do all these wonderful, beautiful, and amazing things for me. I want to repay something, any—"

Lachlan seizes my finger that's stabbing his chest. "Ye make everythin' better by just breathin'," he interrupts, meeting my eyes.

Of course, he has to go off and say something like that! Oh my....

With a deep inhale, I can't freaking help it, I burst into a fit of crazy hormonal girl tears, and he wraps his arms around me. I stuff my nose to his chest and take a shuddering breath, my tears soaking through his shirt.

"Calm down, my leannan," Lachlan soothes, rubbing his hand up and down my back.

I can't believe I said all of those things. I can't believe I let him know how I feel. Why didn't I just shut up? Why didn't I just put a cork in it and stop when I knew I should have? But, no, I had to go off and ruin everything by flaunting my feelings. Did I seriously tell him I wonder what his dick looks like under his kilt? Please say no. Please say I didn't just crucify myself with that blubbering notation.

I hiccup a mortified cry, clutching his vest.

You make everything better by just breathing? Who says stuff like that? I go off on a tangent, and that is his reply. *That.* That sweet...Uh...I'm crying even more now.

Lachlan rocks me, cradling me to his chest, as I bawl for what feels like a million years. Tears of anguish and embarrassment flow, and slowly begin to dissipate as I'm run ragged and sleep calls my name.

"I think we need tae go home." He runs his fingers through my hair and down my back. "Ye need tae sleep."

I nod, rubbing my nose to his pec. "O—okay," I blubber.

Curling his arms under my legs, Lachlan uses the wall and his boots to gain traction and lift us both. I hook my arm around his neck, nuzzling my nose to his shoulder, my swollen eyes shielded. I don't argue when he carries me through the yard where the music is still blaring and the sounds of moans and men doing naughty things bellow in my ears. Lachlan says bye to Whisky, and I raise a hand in farewell without lifting my face to let anyone see how horrible I must look. Mascara is trailing down my cheeks, I know that for sure.

"We're gonna take my bike, and Whisky'll get yer car home in the mornin'," Lachlan explains, and all I do is nod to his shoulder.

Gravel grinds under his boots as we make our way over to his bike and he sets me on it. I spread my own legs to straddle the seat, not caring if my panties show or not, or that I don't have any shoes on.

Silently, Lachlan sets my helmet on my head and straps it under my chin, before doing the same to himself, mounting the bike and turning it over. "Put yer legs and arms around me." He taps his thick side. "It's safer."

I comply without protest. Scooting forward, my arms wrap around his middle and my legs around his waist, my feet settling right by his crotch. He taps my foot, yelling over the rumble of his bike. "Ye ready?"

I nod to his back and tug on his vest to let him know I'm good to go. And we take off.

By the time we arrive home, I'm practically lulled to sleep. When Lachlan turns off the bike and sets the kickstand, I have to blink rapidly to wake myself enough to get into the house.

"Na ye dinnae. Ye almost fell asleep on me." He lifts me from the motorcycle like I weigh nothing, and carries me to the front door, which he unlocks with one steady hand before carrying me into my bedroom and setting me on the bed.

Pushing me so my back hits the mattress, Lachlan curls his fingers over the tops of my thigh-highs and rolls them down, plucking them off one-by-one before tossing them on the floor.

"What are you doing?" I rasp.

"Ye need tae get undressed, and ye're tired so I'm doin' it," he explains like it's the most normal thing in the world. As if I'm not already partially undressed in front of him. He unbuttons my jean skirt, and it, too, joins the thigh-highs on the floor, leaving me in a pair of panties.

He groans, running a finger over my waistband, and I slap my hand over his, forcing him to stop. "These need to stay on or you're going to see me naked."

"Aye," he whispers, shoving my hand away and hooking two fingers into my waistband and tugging my panties down. I lift my hips to help, even though he doesn't seem to need it.

Coolness prickles my naked pussy, and I cup it with my hands. My heart slams against my chest, and I keep my eyes closed, afraid of what his reaction to me might be. I don't look like Meredith undressed. My body isn't thin. I'm far from perfect, and my stomach isn't completely flat. I'm not a supermodel, and he looks like a Highland warrior with all those deep grooves and plains of muscles that most men only dream of having.

Fingers peel my hands off my lady parts, even though I try to hold on. "Lachlan," I breathe, "It's almost bare down there."

"Aye."

"And you said—"

"I dinnae care what I said, Mags. I wanna see ye. Please."

Oh my…that deep, sexy voice. It's my undoing. I let my arms fall to the sides as they begin to quiver in succession with my pussy out on display.

I peek at him through heavy eyelids to find him standing next to the bed, staring at my pussy, rubbing his own erection over his kilt. He brushes a knuckle over my mound and my back arches off the bed, my fingers clutching at the sheets. *Oh god.*

He jerks his knuckle back. "Ye okay, my leannan? Did I hurt ye?"

"No, if you want to touch me, you can. But I want to touch you, too." I declaw one hand from the sheets and extend my palm, gesturing to his bulge.

He retreats a step, and I frown. "I cannae let ye do that."

"You don't want me to touch you?" I can't hide the disappointment in my voice; it hurts that he doesn't want my hands on him.

"I do. Just not there." He strokes himself, and I bite my lip at the sight.

"Then lay down beside me, so I can touch you and you can touch me." I pat the mattress.

"Na. I think it's time ye get some sleep." He walks toward the door, and I shoot up in bed.

Screw it. I pull my shirt over my head, unclasp my bra, and toss everything to the floor. Lachlan freezes to watch me with desire-laden eyes.

"Fine." I lay back on the bed and spread my legs, as I summon a boatload of false confidence to do what I do next. With a sharp inhale, I place my fingers between my pussy lips, spreading them apart for him, and I pinch my nipple. Pleasure courses through me, and I moan under my breath at the delicious sensation.

"Stop," Lachlan rasps.

"No. You started something, and I am gonna finish it. You can go now." I shoo him with my hand before returning it to my budded nipple.

"The bloody hell ye are." Lachlan stalks to the side of the bed and painfully yanks my hand from my pussy. I yelp, but he doesn't seem to notice when he runs his own finger down my dripping slit and I cry out in delirious ecstasy.

He brings his finger to his mouth, licking it clean, and I just about come from watching him. Jesus, that's the sexiest thing I've ever seen a man do in my entire life.

"Mmmm," he groans, "ye're so fuckin' wet."

Lachlan

Shit, what in the hell am I supposed tae do now?

Look at my leannan on that bed, writhin', excited, wantin' me tae touch her. Why does she even care if I do? How could she have said all those bloody things tae me tonight? Fuck, she poured her heart out and I just sat there tryin' not tae freak the hell out. Can she really mean everythin' she rambled on aboot? My thobbin' cock hopes she does, 'cause he wants her almost as much as the rest of me does.

Hair fanned on the pillow, her tits hard, her body soft and perfect, all sprawled out for me tae touch and do whatever the bloody hell I want, but I cannae do anythin'. I dunno how.

I touched her pussy and licked her juices off my finger. Damn, that almost made me lose it. But that's the only thing I can remember from watchin' my brothers fuck all those lassies these past years. I dinnae have the first clue on how tae please her. I've went down on one lassie, one time, in my whole damn life. Never once was it Meredith. She wanted me tae fuck her tae get off and then she was done. Didnae matter if I'd nutted or not.

Ah hell, she's not gonna want me if she knows I dunno the first thing aboot makin' her feel good.

Squeezin' my eyes shut, I grumble and rub the pain that's stabbin' me right in the heart.

Bloody hell! What the fuck am I gonna do?

Mags

Why is he standing there grunting under his breath as he rubs his chest over and over? Doesn't he see me here waiting, wanting, and needing him to touch me, to show me that he actually wants me? Since Brian, I've never been this exposed to any man, except him. I'm trying here. My confidence is failing and I'm about to cover myself before humiliation sets in.

Damn it, why won't he look at me? Did I taste bad?

Curling onto my side and tucking my hand under my pillow, I reclose my eyes so I don't have to watch him leave. I know that's what he's going to do. I pushed too much, and should have expected this. Shame unfurls in my gut.

"Mags." Lachlan touches my leg, sending a shot of pain and pleasure through me. I don't think I can do this anymore. A woman can only show she's interested so many times, and be shot down so many times before she just can't take it anymore. I'm almost to my breaking point.

"Just go," I whisper, slapping his hand away and stuffing my face in the pillow so he doesn't see the tears that are threatening to fall.

"I wanna make ye feel good." He sighs heavily. "I just dunno how."

I fist the pillow.

Why does he have to sound so broken and insecure? I thought I was that person. Gah, I'm not good at this kind of stuff. I'm trying so hard, and failing at it even harder.

"Mags," he pleads, touching my leg again and trying to turn me over onto my back in a gentle manner. I let him.

"I'm not good at this, Lachlan," I admit painfully. "I throw myself at you, and you don't want me. Am I way off base about you being attracted to me?" I narrow my eyes on his stout thickness.

He sits on the edge of the bed, running his hands through his short hair, an expression of complete loss marking his stupidly handsome features. He releases a long breath, his shoulders slumping in defeat. My heart cracks a little more, splintering more hope along with it. "I cannae let ye see my cock, Mags...because it's not right."

"It can't be that bad," I return without thinking, and lean up on my elbows to see him better. And to be honest, I couldn't care less even if it was.

"It is." He shakes his head, cursing under his breath. "There's somethin' wrong with it. Meredith used tae..."

"Used to what?"

"Talk aboot it," he finishes, pain flashing across his face, before dropping his head low, hands cradling his forehead.

That stupid bitch.

"You do know I'm not her, right?" I snap with a little too much resentment.

"I know ye're not her. Ye're so much better than she could ever be."

That mushy feeling returns. How can he be scary and gentle, at the same time he's broken and strong, and sweet yet cruel? I don't understand it. He's a walking contradiction.

"Has any other woman said bad things about it?"

"I've only ever been with two other lassies, and they never saw it."

"And Meredith talked badly about it?" I confirm, as the thought of him being with only three women bounces around in my mind, screwing with me.

I've been with at least eleven men. Maybe more. I can't remember all of their names. I don't even care to. And here I'm sitting with a man at least ten years my senior who's spent the past seventeen years with a horrid woman who's said nasty things about his manhood. What kind of wife does that shit? Here I thought that night she was talking crap to him, it was out of spite. No, she obviously gets off on making him feel like lesser of a man. When he's more of a man than most.

He bobs his head in his hands. "Aye."

Taking a deep breath, I just let it flow. "I'm not going to lie and say I don't want to see it, even if there is something wrong with him. Frankly, Lachlan, I don't give a damn if you have two heads and one nut that looks like Frankenstein...*But*, I'll respect that about you and not push you to let me see or touch it, if that's what you're afraid of."

"Thank ye," he mumbles.

This has totally killed my sex drive. Thinking about Meredith could do that to anyone.

"Why don't you go put on your sweats or some shorts and come to bed?" I pat the spot beside me. "I'm tired. I've been a complete wreck tonight, and you're going through something in your head that needs to rest."

Lachlan stands, his eyes cast on the side of the bed that I just patted, before they swap to me, landing straight on my hard nipples. "Ye have tae put a shirt on." His eyes rake lower, heating, and he nibbles his bottom lip. A shiver crashes through me. "And ye gotta put some panties back on."

"If you sleep next to me, I'll wear a flippin' parka. Now go get dressed." I shoo him with a tiny smile, and he grins back, sadly, before exiting my room.

Quickly, I make work of picking up the mess on the floor and slipping on a t-shirt and another pair of panties. Then crawl back into bed just as he saunters in wearing his black track shorts and nothing else. I'm unable to control it when my mouth starts to water and my eyes glue to his chest, and the hair that I've been intimately acquainted with. My eyes slowly roam down his body to his V, and I try not to moan. I still can't believe he's going to sleep in bed with me!

"Ye have tae stop lookin' at me like that, my leannan, or I'm not gonna get any sleep." He groans, readjusting his shorts.

Mmmmm...

Lachlan climbs into bed next to me, and I lie on my side, facing him. He does the same after flicking off the light so we're submerged into near darkness with nothing but the moon's soft glow casting shadows around the room.

Sweetly, he reaches over and takes my hand into his, and I swear I feel my heart expand bigger than I've ever felt before. Stuffing my face into my pillow, I smile hugely, then turn back to him as he scoots closer, grabbing my leg and hooking it over his muscled hip. Another shiver rocks through me, and my pussy clenches.

"Are ye cold?" He pulls the blanket up over us both, and I shake my head.

"I'm not cold...I'm..."

"Nervous," he finishes for me.

And I whisper, "Yes."

"I am, too." He leans in to kiss my fingers that are folded in his, and my stomach bottoms out. He's being so friggin' sweet.

Lachlan shuffles the closest we can get, and his dick pokes my stomach. I chuckle, and he curses as he tries to push it down. "I'm sorry aboot that."

"You can tuck it in your waistband." I've dated many men who do this when they're hard; it keeps it from poking out.

"I cannae do that." He nuzzles our hands.

Anxiously, I gulp, before stammering, "Why...why not?"

"Cause ye'll be able tae see it then," he notes as if it's the most normal thing to say, while I'm over here screaming in my head, '*It's that big?!*'

"Goodnight, my leannan. Sweet dreams." He tenderly kisses my fingers.

"Good...goodnight, Lachlan."

Thank you, Lord, for bringing this beautifully broken man into my life, but please grant me the patience and control not to do something naughty in my sleep. Amen.

CHAPTER 21

"Lachlan, no more oatmeal. This tastes like a dung beetle's butt." I take a drink of my morning lemonade, leering at the congealed oatmeal that Lachlan promised me is good for my health and a great energy booster before a workout. I call it a load of bull honky.

He chuckles, and that warms me as it rinses the bad taste out of my mouth. "How do ye know what a dung beetle's arse tastes like, my leannan?" He grins challengingly from across the table, crossing those massive arms over his chest while he leans back in his chair. His eyes are alight with humor. I love that look on him. It's a look I'd like to keep there forever.

I shrug. "I dunno, but if I had to guess... *That*," I point to my bowl, "is what it might taste like."

He takes a sip of his morning coffee. "I eat oatmeal every morning before I workout."

"Then you must like the taste of bug bootie more than I do." I crack a closed mouth smile. "And...I don't think I want to look like you."

"Ye dinnae?"

"No. Your arms are the size of my legs." I look down at my legs, which are clothed in a pair of tight, black yoga pants.

Last night, I'd slept the best I have in forever, and when I woke up, Lachlan was drinking his morning coffee in the kitchen. I was kind of surprised he wasn't out in the barn working those muscles, or, you know…that other horrific thing that we've still not fixed.

As soon as I had greeted him, he'd told me that Bonez had called to check in, and when doing so, informed Lachlan that he thought I should start working out to help my leg and overall health. I don't like the idea for reasons I've explained before. Jiggling…need I say more?

After a ten minute tug of war, Goliath vs Tiny Female style, I surrendered to two weeks of Lachlan torture. If, in those two weeks, I don't feel better or like the results, I'm allowed to go back to living a delightful, no workout life. I can't wait for the two weeks to be over with. Although, I can't deny that spending more time with Lachlan does sound appealing, even if I am doing it heaving for breath as I sweat my butt off. Not that losing a few inches on my behind would be a bad thing. I've got plenty to spare.

"I dinnae want ye tae look like me either." He leaves the table to put his own bowl and cup in the sink. Then he stops next to me. "Ye done?" He grabs my bowl before I reply, removing the grossness from my sight.

I change the subject. "How'd you sleep last night?"

"All right after my problem went down."

"You mean your erection?" I tease, and he grumbles, not liking me speaking it aloud.

Bridget opens the basement door, entering the kitchen with a huge smile. "Hey, you two."

Lachlan kisses her forehead, and she gives him a hug before she moves to me and we hug, too. "Morning." I pat her back before releasing her. "You sleep well?"

She goes to the fridge and steals the milk. "Yeah. Cas and some chick crashed at Whisky's last night, so I came home about five."

"Why does it matter if Cas crashes at Whisky's? You can still stay there," I comment.

Bridget walks over to the basement door, milk jug in hand. "I'll bring this back later." She descends the stairs, not even bothering to answer my question. I dart my eyes to Lachlan, who's leaning against the kitchen counter, fixing his post workout shake like he does every day.

"What was that all about?" I ask, thumb pointing to the door.

"Aboot the milk? Or Cas?" He shakes the container, sloshing the liquid and powder inside.

"Cas."

"Pip used tae be close with Cas's daughter. Then his daughter started runnin' in the wrong crowd. Pip kinda lost her best friend, and her connection with Cas at the same time. Like ye know, she's a caretaker and his daughter's always been the wild child, kinda like him. So when Pip would stay there, she'd take care of things. Help him with his leg if he needed, do house shit, basically bein' a part of their family. Then that got blown tae shit and Pip got sad. That's when Whisky started bringin' her in tae help more at the bakery."

That's sad, and how did I not know this before? Bridget and I talk all the time about her life, yet this was never mentioned.

"How come I know about Tommy, the boy who flirts with her in class, yet, I don't know about this?" I quirk a brow at Lachlan, and he shrugs, setting his shake in the fridge.

"I dinnae think she wants tae stir old feelings." He pulls out my chair and grabs my hand, bringing me to my feet. "It's time tae get ye sweaty."

It's not lost on me when Lachlan's fingers wrap around mine as he escorts me outside, but not before he grabs two bottles of water and tucks them under his arm for our impending workout.

Oh, joy.

"I don't feel good or numb. *Rob Zombie* is lying," I whine as my legs object, burning like hell itself, as I try to get through this final set. Then I'm going to murder Lachlan for bringing me out here and turning me into a sweaty, grunting, jiggly pig.

Lachlan chuckles, grinning as he does bicep curls with giant dumbbells. "Ye're almost done. Ye're doin' great, my leannan," he coaches, and I desperately want to flip him off, but my hands are tucked under my bottom, flat on the mat so I don't use them as leverage to do these leg kicks.

"Don't you, *my*...whatever me. I'm dying here," I pant loudly, trying to prove my point, and he just grins, knowing he's won.

"Ten minutes ago yer leg was stiff; now it's workin' better and ye're buildin' muscle," he explains like a true gym rat. I sneer at him and shake my head so the sweat beading on my forehead rolls to the sides and into my damp hair. Everywhere on me is damp, so I don't know why it even matters.

"If I can't walk tomorrow, I'm telling Cas what you did, right after I tattle on you to Bonez," I threaten; half seriously, half not. I'm dying here. I know I'm out of shape, except maybe my arms, but my leg is killing me. It hurts so much I want to cry. The muscles on one side have atrophied so much, it's pathetic.

"That's fine. Tattle all ye bloody want as long as ye listen tae me, and flip over onto yer stomach, place yer hands above yer head, and stretch while pointin' yer toes."

I do all of that, and I groan in satisfaction as the burning in my leg wanes some and the cramp in my back subsides completely.

"Bonez told me how tae work ye." He's suddenly kneeling over me, his butt grazing my back as he faces my feet. He lifts my bad leg, stretching it at the hips and moving downward.

"Ah," I protest when his fingers knead into the soreness. "That hurts."

"I think we're done for the day." Gently, he lays my leg down and helps me up. His shirtless body is glistening with sweat. It's distracting.

We've been out here for close to an hour, and he's been working his upper body since we started. He's only stopped when he needed to instruct me on how to work my legs. I've gotten preoccupied twice watching him move fluidly like he was made to work his muscles that way. Unlike me, who looks ridiculous.

I dust myself off as Lachlan shuts down the music and hands me a bottle of water. Throwing his arm over my shoulder, he kisses my temple, and I peer at him in wonderment.

"Did you just kiss me?"

"Aye." Quickly, he does it again with a smirk.

"On my sweat?" I make a gross face.

"It's salty." He licks his bottom lip, and I stare at his mouth, wanting him to do more than lick there. He notices and adjusts the front of his shorts before escorting me back to the house with his arm still slung over my shoulder, my body bumping his.

Pirate darts outside when Lachlan opens the front door, and I duck out from under his arm. He snatches the back of my shirt, spinning me around. My bottled water drops to the floor as I banish a startled squeak.

"Ye need a shower." He grips the hem of my shirt and tugs it over my head, throwing it on the floor. I cover my chest with my hands, and he bats them away.

"Wh—what are you doing?" I sputter, trying to back away, as he stalks me like a predator across the living room and into the bathroom. He shuts the door behind him, locking it. "Lachlan?" I murmur, bursting with anxiety. He ignores me.

Moving around me, he flips on the water and tests it before turning around and pinning me against the wall. My eyes fly wide, and he grins devilishly before dipping his head and lavishing my neck with his tongue. I groan as he grabs my leg, hooking it around his hip, and his dick pokes me through his shorts.

Dear...Oh...

His teeth nibble my jaw before his fingers tug my pants and panties down at the same time. My leg drops from his hip as he gently kisses and nibbles his way between my covered breasts and over my stomach. He glances up at me to see me shocked and trembling, wondering if this is a fantasy or real life. Without pause, he drops my bottoms until they're pooling around my ankles, then he lifts my feet to pull them and my shoes and socks off.

My body catches fire.

"Lachlan." I find my voice, though it's husky with need. "What're you doing?"

"What the bloody hell does it look like I'm doin'? I'm helpin' ye take a shower," he admonishes playfully, standing up and reaching around my back to unclasp my bra, which he works in expert time. It falls away to be discarded with the rest of my clothes, leaving me bare once more. I try to cover myself, to gain some dignity. It doesn't work; he smacks my hands away, again.

"Na," he commands and takes my hand, leading me to the shower. Where he stops to remove his shoes, then climbs in behind me wearing only his shorts. Shutting the curtain, he then flips the spray. It coats me with a temporary blast of icy water, making me yip, and Lachlan wraps his arms around my naked body, holding me flush to him. Melding us as one.

Resting my chin on his chest, I meet his downcast eyes that are laden with longing. My belly flutters. "You're taking a shower with shorts on," I comment.

"And ye're takin' a shower naked." He kisses my forehead.

I playfully smack his bulging chest. "I know that, silly. And you didn't drink your shake either."

"I'll drink it when I'm done washin' ye."

He reaches for my coconut body wash and squirts some in his hand, before running it down my back and kneading along the way. I relish in the attention. When he reaches my butt, I blush, but he doesn't notice when he kneads the soap in there, too, before spreading my cheeks and running a finger between my pussy lips. Wrapping my arms tightly around him, my nails bite into his back as I throttle a moan by pressing my mouth to his chest and biting my cheek.

Brazenly, he touches that magic bundle of nerves and my legs nearly give out.

"Does this feel good?" he breathes heavily, his own excitement bouncing against my stomach.

"Yes." I struggle to catch my breath and his dick twitches.

Doing something I know I shouldn't do, but want to share in the pleasure, I reach between our bodies and grasp him over his shorts. With a startled roar, he flings me off, throwing me into the shower wall and breaking our connection. My head slams hard, and Lachlan's eyes widen, shining with fear and regret. He reaches out to help me, and I brush him off. I can't believe he'd react like that. I know it's my fault, but still.

"I think you need to leave." I point to the curtain, rubbing the back of my head and trying not to cry at the emotional ache eating me up inside.

Holding his hand up in surrender, his face remains stuck in anguish. It breaks my heart to see. "Mags, my leannan, I'm so sorry. Please, let me fix this…Are ye okay? Can I look at yer head? Please."

I shake my head, still pointing, still trying not to fall apart and go to him. Damn, he looks so lost. What happened to my scary, broody man? He's showing so much of himself now. So much it hurts and feels amazing all at the same time. "I think you need to go, Lachlan. I need some time to myself."

"Dinnae touch," he mutters, lowering his hands.

"Don't touch wha—" My words abruptly stop when Lachlan drops his shorts to the tub floor, revealing himself to me, stripped bare. He screws his eyes shut as mine fall to the source of his biggest insecurity, that's now half-mast and shrinking as the moments pass by. Holding his breath, he remains frozen stock-still.

It's long, thick, uncut, and dripping pre-come. It makes my mouth water just standing here. There's nothing wrong with it. It's perfect.

I blurt the first thing that comes to mind. "It's beautiful, Lachlan."

He doesn't open his eyes or move when he grumbles through gritted teeth, "It's not."

"What's wrong with it?" I kneel, but stay as far away as I can to give him space as I look at it.

His entire body has begun to tremble and his hands are fidgeting. He shakes them out then lifts his dick, revealing the underside that has light brown patches of discolored skin. I also get a better view of his sack, and it's tight, large, and dusted in light red hair. It's absolutely perfect. Just like the rest of him.

"Are you trying to show me the coloration?" I whisper, wanting to reach out and run my finger over the three large spots that look like a large birthmark.

"Aye...and I'm..." he falters.

"Uncut," I finish for him.

"Aye, and I make a mess." He runs his finger over the head of his dick, and it glistens with pre-come. I want to suck it clean, and I've never wanted to do that before in my life.

Pushing off my knees, I stand, and the water pelts my back. "I don't care what you think, or whatever your ex thought. I happen to think it's perfect. You're not cut, which I find sexy. You pre-come a lot, and I also find that sexy."

"And the..." he prompts, obviously needing to hear this.

"And the marks, Lachlan, are probably from birth. They're a part of you, and it makes your manhood more unique than most. Which I also find to be sexy."

Normally, spouting all of this about a man's dick would make me feel weird, blush, or be shy. But I am the one who has to be strong for him, to show him whatever it is that's messing with his head is wrong. He was perfect when I first met him, and he's even more perfect now, with his uniquely sexy parts. And no, when I say he's perfect, I don't mean he's truly perfect. But that doesn't mean he doesn't feel perfect to me.

Bending down, he slides the wet shorts back into place then opens his eyes.

"You didn't have to show me, but thank you for trusting me to see it." I hand Lachlan his *Zest* body wash before lathering my hair with my shampoo.

We finish our washing routines in awkward silence, and I do my best to keep my eyes to myself. Not wanting to ogle him more than I already do.

I leave the bathroom wrapped in a towel before he exits the shower. In my room, I throw on some lounge clothes and plop down on my bed next to Pirate. Bridget must have let him back in. Scratching his ears, I grab my book from the nightstand to drown in some fiction for a while, so I can keep my mind off a certain Scot.

Come to mama, *Kristen Ashley*.

CHAPTER 22

"Mags, what are we having for dinner?" Bridget knocks once on my bedroom door before opening it to find me snuggled in bed. I've spent the last eight hours in here cooped up, finishing a book and starting a new one. Reading is the perfect getaway.

Sitting up, I lay my book in my lap—or in this case, my cell phone because I'm all out of paperbacks so I'm reading on my *Kindle* app. What did the world ever do without digital content? It's ingenious.

"I dunno. Why?" I shrug, running my fingers between a sleeping Pirate's ears as they twitch in contentment.

"You're not cooking?" I'm not sure if she's sad or happy about me cooking or not. She's acting strange.

"Honestly? I haven't even thought about food since that congealed stuff your dad calls sustenance made me gag this morning." I will never attempt to eat oatmeal again. Oatmeal cookies? Fine and dandy. The cooked, wet stuff? Yuck.

Giggling at me, Bridget claps her hands together and bounces on her feet. "Perrffeectt," she singsongs. "Get dressed and I'll meet you out back in ten."

Before I'm able to ask why, Bridget shuts the door and I'm left to get dressed. Rifling through my dresser, I throw on a pink t-shirt and a pair of my unstained coveralls before I meet her out back in five. The sight before me is definitely not what I expected.

Coming to the edge of the grass, my feet meeting the rocks, I stop dead in my tracks. A tent is set up in the furthest part of the backyard, and there's a campfire burning in front of it. Lachlan turns something over the flames and raises a tentative hand in *hello*. I do the same, cautiously walking his way.

"What's this?" I sweep my hand to the checkered blanket in the grass, which has a brown picnic basket in one corner. Yes, just like the baskets *Yogi* used to snatch. That's one cartoon even I watched as a kid. I haven't seen one of these baskets since my grams was alive. She always took hers to the farmers market and came home with it overflowing.

"What's it look like?" He lifts his chin to the blanket.

"It looks like a family campout."

"Wrong," he states.

"Wrong?"

"It's a ye and me campout."

It's a *what*? When did he decide this? *How* did he decide this?

"Bridget's not coming?" I don't know whether to be flustered or flattered; maybe a little of both?

Lachlan shakes his head, pulling the metal from the fire and lying it in the grass. "Na; she's goin' tae Whisky's."

"But she has school in the morning," I argue. "And I haven't gotten a chance to ask her what she needed me to get from the store tomorrow." I put my hand on my hip. "You should have told me she was going to be gone."

"I just did," he notes, looking at the metal thingy and opening it.

Crap, he's got me there.

"Just text her," he adds. "Now, sit and eat."

"It's not oatmeal, is it?" I grimace, and he rewards with a throaty laugh. It's the best sounding laugh I've ever heard. And it's even more special coming from him.

Sitting on the blanket Indian style, Lachlan joins me and pulls utensils from the basket. Inside the metal contraption, he removes a brown, doughy thing. He sets it on a paper plate and uses his pocket knife to cut four sections before cleaning the blade in the grass and flipping it closed. He's such a *Boy Scout.*

"What's this?" I tap a section with my finger, not wanting the bubbling cheese to burn me.

"It's a pizza pocket." He divides our halves, placing them on separate plates.

"What's in it?"

"Cheese, pepperoni, and mushrooms."

"No olives?" I blurt, panicked.

He snickers. "No olives."

Exaggeratingly, I wipe my brow and blow a breath. "Shoot, and here I thought I would've had two ruined meals for the day," I tease. What can I say? I hate olives.

He chuckles and sprawls out on the blanket, lying on his side, his legs extending into the grass. "Ye know, yer sense of humor is much different than I thought it'd be."

I dip my finger into the sauce oozing onto my plate and suck it clean. He curses under his breath, eyes raptly watching me.

"How so?" I raise a curious brow, and dip my finger again, repeating the process.

"Ye were sad and jumpy at first; I didnae know if ye had one or not." He bites his pizza, and I follow suit, taking a bite of my own. I moan as cheese, mushrooms, and pepperoni create an exultant food-gasm in my mouth. This is probably one of the best pizzas I've ever had. It's simple, but the smoky flavor in the crispy crust is heavenly.

I swallow and take a drink of the bottled water Lachlan offers me.

"Thanks for this," I say as I lift my plate and set it back down.

"My pleasure," he nearly purrs. It comes out thick and husky, forcing me to swallow hard. Damn, his voice is sexy.

"As for my sense of humor," I begin, taking pause as he chews with eyes still fixed on me, "you should know that I had just left a man I had dated for a while." He opens his mouth to ask a question, and I raise my hand for him to let me finish. "I had gotten injured, and then you went and saved my life. I was confused and scared, and so much was going on. I got sad, and then as I started to heal, things were a little less sucky. But, I was still worried about what to do with my life…you know…after all this." I gesture to the house and him.

"Yer not leavin', right?" I can't tell if he's concerned or just interested.

"No." I shake my head. "I like it here. And if you ever want me to leave, I promise I won't cause a fuss. Just tell me, okay?" I hope he understands that I'm being one hundred percent sincere about this. If he doesn't want me here, I'm gone. I don't want to ever overstay my welcome. Even though, this feels like home—more home to me than I've felt since Kansas living in my grams's house. It's a godsend.

Lachlan swallows his food and sips on a water. "I never want ye tae leave."

Bashfully, I blush and absentmindedly rub my cheek at his words. I was hoping he'd say that.

"What do you want from me?" I blurt, because I can't contain myself. I know this is the first time I've spoken it aloud, but it doesn't mean I haven't been waiting to ask this for quite some time.

Lachlan finishes his food and throws the paper plate into the fire. It crumbles into an orange, flaky ball in seconds. Dropping onto his back, his ankles crossed, he tucks his arms behind his head as he stares at the near dusk sky, sighing. "I want ye around as long as ye wanna be."

What kind of answer is that?

I snort. "That's a non-answer."

He tilts his head to look my way. "What do ye want me tae say, Mags? I cannae promise ye the world, and I sure as hell cannae give ye what ye need and deserve."

"What is it that I need and deserve? And who are you to tell me what it is? Isn't that for me to decide?"

I hate when people try to make choices for me, thinking they know what's best. I know what's best for me most of the time. And up until I moved here, I knew being alone, casually dating, and not getting emotionally invested was best for me. I basked in the darkness—or maybe I drowned. I can't be sure. Now, I want to bask in the sunshine, or more specifically in the arms of a huge man with an even larger heart. It might be flippin' scary to hold onto something so good, but it's even scarier not holding onto it and having to let it go. *That* frightening possibility messes with my head more than I care to admit.

"Aye, I suppose it is. But ye deserve a good man who can give ye everything," he remarks.

He's vague again. I hate that.

"And what's *everything*?" I finish my own meal and toss the paper plate into the fire. It crackles, dissolving the paper in a few moments.

"For starters...*Sex*."

I fire a comeback. "You can't have sex with me?" There is no way I can believe this. He can't have sex with me?

"Na, not when I puke every time I come. I did it again after ye left the shower."

"You mean you jacked off? Or you threw up?"

"Both," he grumbles, returning his eyes to the sky.

I was afraid of that.

"Were you like this before Meredith?"

"Na. It's only been aboot ten years that I've been dealin' with this problem."

I guess that's better than a lifetime. Nevertheless, it's still too long.

"Have you seen anyone about it?"

I'm guessing I already know what his reply will be. I just hope that I'm wrong.

"What? Like a doctor?" he asks.

"Yeah, like a doctor."

"Na fuckin' way. And tell him what? That I puke when I get off?" he rumbles in disgust, smacking me in the face with the truth, which had been obvious. What's wrong with men and going to the doctors?

"It might help," I offer in a whisper.

He growls, irritated, shaking his head. "Na, it won't. I've pulled dead, mutilated bodies from car wrecks, Mags. And I've seen people burned alive. Sure, that shit bothers the hell outta me, but I get bloody well past it tae do my job. A job I love. But I cannae stop pukin' when I get off. That's not somethin' a shrink's gonna fix."

He doesn't know that! How could he know if he hasn't even tried? Why does he have to be so stubborn and resistant? My life would be so much more fricken-frackin' easy if he'd just relent a tiny bit. Of course, that's a pipedream. He's never going to back down. He's too thickheaded for that. *Gah!* This beautiful man drives me bonkers in my mind *and* in my pants.

"Now tell me aboot this lad ye dated." He changes the subject to one that I am desperate to stay away from. I don't want to talk about Johnathan, or anyone else I've been with.

Hunching, I hug my arms around my stomach, as my loose hair falls forward to drape over my shoulders. "I have nothing to say about him."

"Sure ye do. Did ye love him?"

His mouth pronounces the words, but I can't believe they actually formed the question. Did I love Johnathan? Absolutely not. But Lachlan engaging in a conversation about my past boyfriends is not something I care to speak about. They were inconsequential, anyhow; warm bodies to live out my days—the days when I didn't care about much other than a hot meal and a decent lay. Those days ceased to exist when I nearly met my maker. I'm a new woman now. And as time slips by, I'm stronger, too. Something I never thought I'd hear myself say.

"Why would you ask me a question you already know the answer to?" I counter.

"Did ye or did ye not?" He's relentless.

"No," I huff, then add, "Did you love Meredith?"

Eyes still cast upon the dusk sky, Lachlan shakes his head. "I loved her as the mother of Pip. I didnae love her as my mate. There wasn't enough tae love. She's too selfish, and I cannae give my heart tae a lassie like that."

My heart thuds.

I gulp.

"Wh—what kind of woman…can you give your heart…um…too?" I inquire meekly, my eyes staring at my arms that are wrapped around me, too afraid to look at him.

Moments seem to tick by with no response, my nervousness tripling as each second passes. Then, a rough warmth slides over my arm—his hand. He unlocks me from hugging myself and takes my hand into his, folding our fingers together and squeezing. I think I might pass out; I can't control my breathing. His skin on mine sends a jolt of electricity through my body, heating my core from the inside out. I have to bite my inner cheek to keep from moaning. God, I hate to love, and love to hate that he evokes these emotions. Cheesy or not, they're feelings that I've never felt before. They're all-consuming and too much.

"Mags," he rasps, and I peek up, caught in his gaze. It's hot and tender all at the same time. *Beautiful.*

"Ye-yes?" I stumble a whisper.

Languidly, he samples his bottom lip, then jerks my arm forward. With a squeal, I tumble, landing on his massive chest as big arms engulf me in a gentle embrace and I freeze in shock. With surprising ease, he pulls me on top of him. My legs instantly separate, straddling his wide, muscled hips. His excitement prods me between my thighs, and I squirm.

Cupping his hands on my bottom, he sits up, his fingers deliciously digging in. My chest melds to his chest as my arms loosely drape over his shoulders. He maneuvers my legs so they wrap around him, settling his hardness to my damp core. The urge to thrust and get that friction on my clit is so overpowering that it fogs my brain. I need to get a little bit closer, touch him a little more, smell him, taste him, and curl my arms around him, because I never want to let go. *God,* I need so much.

Gripping my butt to near pleasured-pain, Lachlan's grizzly voice tugs me from my haze. "My leannan," he calls to me, and I shake my head to clear my naughty thoughts. They don't go far.

"Yes?" Shyly, I peer up, meeting his eyes once again.

His head dips, and he brushes his coarse cheek along mine. It sends a shiver through me, and his dick lurches at the juncture between my thighs. Lips brush the shell of my ear, as his hot, ragged breath bathes my skin, making it tingle. "Ye're," he whispers then slowly moves away, his stubble scratching my cheek until he turns his lips to my jaw, peppering soft kisses down to my chin. Then, his attention sweetly moves to my other side, where he kisses up to my ear and mutters, "the," before making a slow descent back to my jaw, drugging me with his kisses the entire journey.

He ends on the tip of my chin, and I tilt my head back further, offering myself. I want him to touch me anywhere he wants. He feels so damn good.

With a possessive growl, Lachlan drags a hand up my spine and cuffs it around the back of my neck, dominating me. My insides quiver when he moves my lips a hair's breadth from his and lashes out his tongue to taste mine. I whimper a compulsory moan, melting into him as he sweeps over my bottom lip before scooping the top with the tip of his wet tongue. "Mmmmm," he groans appreciatively.

Oh my...

My lady parts clench as my nails bite into his shoulders and I rock myself to him, unable to sustain another moment. His hand on my backside grinds me against him, and I gasp with pleasure.

"*That*," he grunts, "is the reason why ye're the only person I could ever love."

Oh...

Without warning, his lips brutally crash upon mine, stealing my breath. I cling to him, taking whatever he wants to offer and reveling in it. He slants, opening his mouth, and forces his tongue into mine. I moan as they collide, tangling in a mess of hot, delirious ecstasy. He groans, battling for more, drinking me in as I drink him in, unable to get enough.

Thrusting his hips in the maelstrom of our passion, his dick hits my clit and I violently shudder, throwing my head back and breaking our kiss as I belt a heady moan to the sky, locked in his embrace. With his hand on my neck, he forces my lips back to his, swallowing the rest of my pleasure. He thrusts again, hitting his mark, and I cry out, his mouth devouring it all; every whimper, every need—everything.

Soon, it all becomes too much and I lose my breath. Lachlan slows, his tongue gently swirling with mine, giving me a moment of reprieve as we both pant for air. Softly, sweetly, we bask in each other's taste. He tastes better than anything I could have imagined.

Lachlan

Fuck! I need tae claim her. I need tae lay her down and take her right here in the grass. I cannae, but my blood is roarin' and there is nothin' I can do tae stop it. *Shit!* Her taste, her sweet, coconut smell, her soft body wrapped around mine…it's more than I can bloody bear.

My hips surge like they belong tae someone else, and she moans against my mouth. My cock throbs, buckin' at the sound, and my balls tighten, needin' more. More of anythin'.

Whirlin' my tongue inside her perfect mouth once more, I slip out and lick the seam of her bruised, parted lips. I meet her eyes, which are as heavy and glazed as mine. Still needin' more, I brush my lips across hers, sneakin' out my tongue tae taste her again. She's my addiction. I'll never be able tae get enough. Not after this. There's na goin' back.

Today, in the shower, she saw me. I'd broken her, and I wanted tae fix it. I wanted tae do somethin' tae make it all better. I couldn't, so I dropped my shorts tae expose my cock. Tae entrust her with seein' it was hard; I could barely muster the strength tae stand there long enough for her tae examine it. I wanted tae run. She didnae need tae see how ugly it is. But what she said…those words…they hit me in the heart so fuckin' hard that it knocked the breath from my lungs and I almost crumbled tae the shower floor. I wanted tae weep.

I wanted tae take her into my arms and tell her how I feel. I wanted tae do so damn much, but I was frozen. I couldn't stop thinkin' aboot her tellin' me *it* was sexy. That *I* was sexy. That the birthmark wasn't bad and it, too, is...*bloody hell*...she said it was sexy.

Once those words came, fillin' a void I didnae know I had; it was clear she owned me, and would be my salvation. The bonnie lass I saved, saved a part of me, too. I cannae give her what she deserves. I can never give her what she's given tae me. I will never be worthy of her or her love. I'm a fuckin' arsehole, and my head and cock are damaged. But she still accepts what I cannae change. She accepts me for me. How terrifyin', yet, bloody grand is that?

When I'd finished comin' in the shower and pukin' in the toilet, I went tae Pip. I told my daughter shit that I never thought I'd admit tae a soul, like how I felt aboot Mags, and how I kept pushin' her away. We also talked aboot me needin' help tae mend what I'd broken so many bloody times. That's when Pip helped me devise this plan tae show Mags a wee bit more of myself. And so I could give her the gift I found in a store window last week when she had lunch with Bonez.

"My leannan," I speak, brushin' my lips over hers, my fingers caressin' the back of her neck, my hand still palmin' her arse.

"Yes?" she whispers, breathlessly.

Bloody hell...that mouth...those words...*her.*

Fuck...I really am owned.

Mags

Lachlan rests his forehead on mine as we steady our breathing. His heart's pounding so hard that I can feel it through my breasts. I wonder if he can feel mine, too.

"That was the first kiss I've had in a long time."

And the best I've ever had, I admit, even though we shared so much more than just a kiss. There was an explosion and an understanding in the way our lips synced, like we were one. I'm sure I never thought that was possible. I'm not one to believe in fairytales or happily ever afters. There's never been a reason to. But, he said that thing to me...those words...their meaning...I feel them, too. Didn't think that was possible either, but I felt it.

"Me, too." Lachlan softly presses a lingering kiss to my lips, and I melt. The fluttering in my belly expands to my whole body, making everything gooey and warm, and absolutely perfect. I feel lighter than air.

Our lips stick like magnets, and as he tries to pry us apart, even our mouths don't seem to want to let go. "I have a present I need tae give ye, then I have more tae say," Lachlan whispers, fanning my mouth with his hot, silky breath.

"Oh...okay...Yes...and um...the gift...it's...not...ummm..." Geeze, I can't even formulate a proper sentence.

"Dinnae even try tae argue with me, lassie." Swiftly and sweetly, he drops an adorable kiss on the tip of my nose, then extends his arm out to the picnic basket and scoots it over.

Inside, he extracts a square, white box. Okay, it's nothing huge and it's not a ring box. All right, so I wasn't expecting anything, let alone a ring box. But, you know even if I'm feeling a little something or maybe a lot of something, a ring...yeah...not a good idea. I already have two on my finger, and a third wouldn't look right. Or that's what I'm going to keep telling myself. It sounds good, right? Geeze, I'm nervous. *And* I'm rambling with soaked panties. I'm an utter mess.

"Here." Lachlan hands me the package and I sit back. Both of his hands securely hold my hips like he's afraid I might try to escape.

Jiggling the box, I attempt to figure out what's inside. It doesn't make much noise.

"Open it." He nods toward the present.

"It's not oatmeal, is it?" I tease and wink, trying to defuse some of this inner turmoil I'm battling deep within. He grins, chuckling with his entire body. The amusement crinkling at the edges of his eyes liberates a fraction of my troubles, making me grin, too.

"Na bloody oatmeal. And I won't try tae feed ye that rubbish again."

"If it's rubbish, then why do you eat it?" He eats it a lot, along with bananas. Heck, he eats a lot in general.

"'Cause I like it...now open the bloody box, Mags." He's getting impatient, but not in his normal growly, I'm *King Kong* kinda way. It's more of a nervous impatience. And it's making me more nervous, too. I don't wanna open it. Maybe I should just keep the box and pretend that's my present. You think that'd jive with Mr. Handsome? No? You're probably right.

"My leannan," he sighs.

"Yes?" I play dumb.

"Open the box."

"I'm nervous...I don't like gifts," I try to delay.

"Ye do tae. Ye're just a stubborn lassie."

"I. Am. Not." *I totally am.*

"Ye are tae. Now open the bloody box." Uh oh, he's moving from nervous growly to angry growly.

Sheesh…fine…I'll open the *bloody* box. Which is white, by the way, and not bloody at all. Him and those words, they get me every time.

Gluing my eyes shut, I lift the lid and toss it in the blanket.

"Open yer eyes." He's getting growlier.

"You said to open the box. *Not* that I had to do it with my eyes open." *Ha*, I win.

"Stop bein' a pain in my arse and look at it."

"But I—"

To shut me up, Lachlan claims my mouth again, delivering a hot and sensuously mind-blowing kiss. I part my lips for him, and moan when his tongue lightly caresses mine before he emits a hungry growl to seize more, and I let him take it all.

My body's flickering flame roars to life once again. Slick heat boils between my thighs and I grind my hips on his erection. I can't wait another second. I need it. I need to come. I've waited too long.

Suddenly, he jerks away, leaving me wanton and breathless. My body shakes and my stiff nipples ache, craving more. I try to attack his lips again, but he moves away, his back nearly dropping to the ground. Pouting, I groan a needy protest, and he grins. He flippin' grins at me! With his lips red and thoroughly used, and his chest pistoning for air, he's grinning. Damn, I love that look. It makes me want to do so much more, like ravage him. But right now, I hate it. It's a grin of knowing. A grin of his retreated desire. *Gah!*

"Now look." He licks his bottom lip, his voice raw. *Fine.*

I peer inside the white box.

On top of a little puff of cotton is a silver bangle with three charms. A circle, a moon, and a tiny, round diamond.

Lachlan plucks it from within, snatches my hand before I get a chance to yank it away, and he slips it on. It fits perfectly on my wrist.

Raising it to eye level, I marvel at the charms. The circle's engraved and says *I love you*. I swallow thickly, trying not to cry. Next to that, the crescent shape that curves around the circle reads *to the moon and back*. A single tear escapes and slides down my cheek, and Lachlan catches it with his thumb and wipes it on his shirt. This is just too much.

"Do ye like it?" He sounds so vulnerable right now. It makes my chest ache.

Timidly lifting my gaze to meet his, I finger my charms and massage my thumb over the beautiful engravings. "Yes, thank you. I love it." My bottom lip trembles, so I suck it into my mouth to stop it.

"I do mean those words, my leannan...my *beloved.*"

His beloved? It...*oh*.

Incapable of controlling myself, I throw my arms around his neck and lay my head on his pec. Another tear slides free, soaking into the cotton of his shirt. "You've been calling me that a long time," I mumble.

"Aye." His hands caress my back, up and down, softly.

"That word means beloved?" Another tear slips down my cheek, and I suck in a sharp breath, my emotions bubbling to the surface.

"Aye, it means beloved. 'Cause that's what ye are, *my leannan*."

"Oh, wow." I nuzzle my nose to his heavenly scented chest as more tears threaten to flow. My nose burns. "You are just too…I dunno…that's a lot to take."

"I cannae deny what I feel. I've tried tae, but I felt somethin' that day when…" His hand brushes my hair to the side, and he traces the scar on my neck. The very place his finger plugged the hole to save my life. "Holdin' ye in my arms, ye're blood coverin' me, it felt different than before. Different than all the others I've rescued. Shit, I dunno how else tae explain it. I'm bloody terrible at talkin' aboot my feelin's." He sighs, crestfallen.

"You're doing a fine job," I encourage through an emotionally clogged throat, knowing that I want to hear this—that I need to.

He continues. "Yer blood on my hands scared the hell outta me, but it also did somethin' else. It made me feel. That's why I wanted tae take ye in. That's why I couldn't leave the hospital. I tried tae stay away, and Pip tried tae convince me tae give ye some space. But I was too fuckin' selfish. I couldn't do it. I needed tae see that ye were all right."

"You freaked me out in the hospital," I admit.

"I know I did. I kept starin' at ye tae make sure ye were still breathin'. And my cock kept gettin' hard when I did."

"It did?" I whisper like it's a secret, my lips pressed to his shirt.

"Aye, it did. And still does. Never had this reaction tae a lassie before."

I hope that's a good thing. I think it is.

"What does that mean?"

One of his hands cuffs around the back of my neck once again, as the other traces designs along my back. It's like he's deep in thought and his hands are subconsciously acting on their own accord.

He clears his throat. "It means that before ye came into my life, I hadn't...ye know...gotten off...in at least five months, maybe longer. I cannae remember."

That's a long time for a man not to touch himself.

"Was that normal for you? Is it because of the puking?" I ask.

"Aye. Since that started, I've tried tae do it as little as possible. Four tae five times a year for the past five years."

"Then I came along and screwed it up," I mumble, internally berating myself for doing this to him.

If I hadn't gone into that freakin' gas station and gotten hurt, then he wouldn't be getting sick like he does. He could have controlled it, and then I wouldn't be here sitting on his lap, my head on his chest, and my arms around his neck. Sometimes life wields a double-edged sword. It's cruel and lovely all at the same time. Because I wouldn't have changed any of that, not even Meredith kicking the crap outta me. Not the damage to Viola. Not even my broken leg and arms. I wouldn't change any of that if I knew that it would lead me to this moment. A moment where the man I know I...lo...*you know*...is holding me and expressing things that I'm sure he's never told anyone else. I just wish that could be perfect. But life's not that simple, and there are still complications that me coming into his life has caused—*sickness.* And for that, I sort of hate myself.

His fingers tighten around my neck, causing my thoughts to pause. "I have tae fuck my fist every day, my leannan," he growls, hostilely. "*But*, me needin' tae do that *is not* yer fault. Ye bein' smart, and beautiful, and bloody sexy *is not* a fault. It's my gift. A gift I would happily die tae keep, even if that meant I had tae puke every day for the rest of my fuckin' life..." Expelling heated curses under his breath and grumbling in his throat, he pauses a beat to reel in his ire. The hand on my neck relaxes, and I snuggle my cheek over his pec.

He called me sexy, beautiful, and smart. What did I ever do to be blessed with such a great man? Another tear slips free, and I blink it away.

Lachlan sighs. "I found the bracelet and thought I'd show ye how I feel all the time. Even if I cannae express it like I wish I could, that's how I feel, ye know."

"I know you do. I trust you."

He really...loves...me...me...me. I can hardly believe it no matter how many times it tumbles through my brain. It feels like a dream. All of it does.

"And I dinnae expect ye tae...ye know...say it b—"

"Lachlan," I cut him off and bring my hands down to clutch the front of his shirt. "I...I need to process. But that doesn't mean I don't feel the...the same. You've just been so unclear. You can't be my friend. You can't give me what I need. You tell me these things, and now you're telling me this...something different. It's...um—"

"Fucked up," he interjects.

I shake my head. "No. I was going to say confusing."

"I cannae be yer friend, Mags, 'cause of these feelings. And even though I know I cannae give ye what you need, it dinnae mean I won't try. I know I dinnae deserve ye, but I'm gonna take what I can get. I'm bloody selfish like that." He laughs humorlessly.

"You're not selfish," I defend.

"Aye, I am. With ye, I am. And I won't apologize for it. That's never gonna bloody change."

"I don't want it to. I like that you like me that much." I rub my cheek against him.

"I dinnae like ye, Mags. I'm fuckin' in love with ye," he states proudly, like he doesn't care what people think, or if I say it back. It feels like the winds have changed and he's no longer going to push me away. I pray that I'm right, and that my gut's spot on.

I sit back and wipe away the tears from my eyes before meeting his gaze. My hands cup his jaw, and the scruff scratches my palm. His jaw tightens, and I feel it flex under my touch. "I care for you, too. Now, why don't you show me how much you care for me, and let me try to show you how much I care for you?" Still holding eye contact, I drop one hand and slip it between us to palm his cock over his jeans. He sucks in a sharp breath, his eyes smoldering. Involuntarily, he thrusts into my eager hand. He wants this, I can feel it. He just doesn't want to want it.

He starts. "If I get—"

"I don't care if you get sick or not. I want to touch you, and I'm dying for you to touch me, too."

Closing his eyes in pain, he dips his head and wraps his arms around my back to pull me in for a hug. My hand slips off his cheek and hooks around his neck, holding him. Laying his head on my shoulder, his lips touch the crook of my neck, and his hot breath tingles my wanton flesh. "I," he samples my skin with the sweep of his tongue, and I whimper, "want tae touch ye. And I promise I'll try tae let ye touch *it*."

Affectionately, I rub his back. "It's not an *it*. It's part of you. And I want to touch that part of you. I want to touch every part." I can't believe I just admitted that aloud. But it feels right to tell him. He needs to know that I find him sexy, and that includes his dick. Because I'd be lying if I said I hadn't dreamt about it endlessly.

Disengaging from our embrace, he sits back and I flatten my palms to his chest, pushing him until his back is to the blanket. With a devilish grin, I reach between us and run my nail over his straining cock.

"He's ready," I state brazenly, trying hard to sound sexy and confident, even though I'm neither of those things.

"Aye," he croaks, swallowing hard, the knot of his Adams apple bouncing.

Seizing my hand, he flips me onto my back, him on top, my legs spread as he settles between them. His thickness nestles against my core, as his hands brace on either side of my head. I wrap my legs around his waist, my heels digging into his firm butt.

"It's beautiful here," I whisper, spending more time looking at my body locked under his, than where we are. It could be Mars for all I care, as long as his delicious weight never moves.

"The tent..." He tilts his head to the side, never taking his eyes off me. "It has flaps that I've unzipped so ye can see the stars. We cannae stay out here; the mosquitoes will bite yer tits and arse. And I dinnae wanna share ye with them."

My pitch squeaks with amusement "You don't want to share me with mosquitoes?"

"Aye." He nods. "I dinnae wanna share ye with anyone or anythin'; especially not those bloody fuckers."

I giggle. I can't help it. It just comes barreling out. He's being serious. This isn't a joke. Therefore, this is probably the sweetest and the most oddly romantic thing that anyone has ever said to me.

Lachlan's eyes narrow, darkening around the edges. "It's not funny, my leannan."

"Yes, it is. It's adorable." I giggle some more.

"Yer not supposed tae be laughin' when I've got my cock this close tae yer pussy," he grumbles, and shuts me right up when he thrusts his hips, hitting my sweet spot on the first try.

My back arches involuntarily. "Lachlan," I breathe, so he does it again, harder this time. Blowing out a needy groan, my eyes roll into the back of my head as I feel his thrust hit deep, making me shudder, every part of me coiling tight, ready to detonate.

"Inside," he growls, and then he's rolling off and standing up. The loss of his weight makes me want to complain, but I don't. Offering me his hand, I gladly accept, and he yanks me to my feet. Stumbling a little, Lachlan's arm quickly curls around my waist, steadying me before he pulls me flush to his side and drops a sweet kiss on my temple.

"Rules, before we go in the tent," he mutters, his lips brushing the side of my head, along the edge of my hair. "I will touch ye anywhere I bloody well want. And ye can touch me, but if I tell ye tae stop, ye have tae stop."

"Okay," I murmur.

At this point, if he asked me to pat my belly and rub my head for three hours just to see him naked again, I'd do it. I'm a fiend, and that body of his is out of this flippin' world. What makes that even more special is the man underneath it all is out of this galaxy. I'm so excited and scared all at the same time that I'm ready to jump out of my damn skin.

Together, Lachlan unzips the tent and we duck inside. The ceiling is practically missing, as a screen exposes the stars trying to breach the dusk sky. It's lovely.

A small battery operated lantern and a layer of colorful blankets is all that lies before us. Lachlan removes his hand from my hip to pull his shirt over his head, uncovering all of those tight ridges of flawless muscle that I can't help but admire. Over his heart, he bears the MacAlister clan crest. My eyes dip lower, really, truly, looking at him for the very first time without blinders; I see the flames rising from his side as clouds of smoke swirl over his chest and abs. I swallow thickly at the glorious sight.

He tosses his shirt to the corner of the tent and runs a hand over his rippling abs. "Do ye like what ye see?" He's not being cocky; he genuinely wants to know.

Oh, I likey. I likey a lot. My mouth waters in recognition, and I bite my lip. "You're perfect," I whisper under my breath, not sure if I'm talking to God, or Lachlan, or acknowledging it aloud to myself. It doesn't matter because it's the truth.

Lachlan flushes red and immediately turns away, slipping off his boots and socks. They, too, join the pile he's started in the corner. I take a step forward and run my hands along his broad, beautiful back, that's inked with scrolling scripture. Goosebumps sprout across his skin, and he shivers under my faint touches.

Wrapping my arms around him, my chest to his back, my palms resting on his abs, I press a kiss between his shoulder blades. His skin is smooth and hot beneath my lips. He turns to steel in my arms, his body frozen in time, as breath ceases to expel from his lungs. "You are beautiful." I kiss him again and glide my hands down to the front of his jeans. I slip my hands into the waistband, feeling nothing underneath but hair-sprinkled skin.

"You're not wearing any boxers," I mutter wickedly, slipping one hand deeper to grasp his thickness in my hand. It throbs, hot and hard, in my palm, coated in slickness from his pre-come. I stroke him, and a tremor rocks through his body as he expels a rushed groan and his hips pitch forward. "Mags," he croaks, his voice wavering with both fear and excitement.

"I've got you." I work my other hand on his button and fly. Thankfully, he's not wearing a belt.

Freeing him, I drop his pants to his ankles and use my foot to help. "Step out, sweetheart," I instruct in a whisper, pressing another kiss to his back. He complies, and I kick his jeans over toward the corner. They don't quite make it, but I don't care. I've got my man naked, and my hands are all over him. More importantly, he's letting me do this, even though this has to be eating at him.

One hand wrapped around his thickness, my fingers unable to touch, I run my other over the head, catching more pre-come. The silkiness feels amazing between my fingers, and I use it to slide up his shaft. His legs nearly give out as he fumbles a husky groan.

His hand seizes mine, stopping me from stroking him again. "My leannan," he rasps in agony and need.

This is hard, and it breaks my heart just thinking about how difficult this has to be for him.

Folding his fingers through mine, I raise our joined hands to lay on his stomach as my other stays wrapped around his dick. "Sweetheart, let's lie down and we can touch each other." I nuzzle my nose to his spine, inhaling deeply to get high on his scent. God, he smells so good.

Then, with difficulty, I let go and take a step back, but he doesn't turn around. Instead, he moves to the blankets with his hand covering his erection. I watch the flex of his glutes as he kneels in the cotton before lying on his side. He pats the spot next to him with glazed eyes staring up at me with uncertainty. "Lay, my leannan." His tone is gruff, but in a good way.

"Do you want me to undress?" I ask, unlatching the buttons to my coverall straps and throwing them over my shoulder. The front flap falls to my waist, exposing my pink shirt and taut nipples as they poke through my thin, lace bra.

"Take it off, slowly," he orders. "Let me watch ye."

Turning red from my ears to my chest with unbridled bashfulness, I bend forward and glide my coveralls down my legs until they pool around my ankles. Stepping out of them, I take my shoes and socks off as well. All bundled in my hands, I toss the ball into the corner and stand before him in my white panties and rising shirt.

I run my fingers along the hem and chew the inside of my cheek, too scared to meet his gaze.

"Take yer shirt off," he rasps, and my hands tremble.

Little-by-little, I drag my shirt up and peel it over my head. I feel too exposed, so I cover my breasts with my arm as I discard the shirt into the mounting pile.

Lachlan groans his appreciation.

"Now yer bra." His voice grows huskier.

Head dipped, staring at my feet, I reach back and unclasp my bra before slipping it down my arms. It drops to my wrists, catching there and exposing my heavy breasts. My nipples pucker as the air hits them, and I fling my bra over with the rest of my belongings.

"Dinnae even think aboot coverin' 'em," Lachlan orders, and I expel a shaky breath, feeling his intense, teal eyes burning into me like hundreds of hot fingers caressing my form.

Goosebumps sprout under his attention, and I try not to shiver.

I can't believe I'm doing this.

My arms hanging at my sides, I feel my palms itching to cover my chest to shield myself. I don't have a body like his; it isn't sexy like his. It isn't muscled like his. Gosh, I'm going to feel like a fool.

"Take yer panties off, too," Lachlan instructs. "Then I want ye tae come lay by me."

"Ar—are you sure you want that?"

"Aye, I'm bloody well sure, my leannan. Ye're sexy, and I wanna touch ye. Now get over here. I need ye."

He thinks I'm *sexy*. I snatch that tiny confidence boost and hold on tight.

Not wasting any time, I shuck my panties down my legs and kick them off before I nearly run to lie next to Lachlan. He doesn't wait a second to have his hands on me. They touch me everywhere, caressing, fondling, and pawing.

Lying flat on my back with Lachlan on his side, I let him explore as his erection prods the outside of my thigh, leaking silken pre-come down my sensitive skin.

Hot lips attack my neck, and his hand trails down the valley of my chest and over my belly to the light dusting of hair on my mound.

"Is this okay?" he whispers between kisses, swirling his fingertips below. His scruff scratching my flesh in the most delicious of ways.

"Yes," I breathe, wrapping my arm around his head and tilting mine to the side, offering him whatever he wants to take. Hoping he'll take it all.

His tongue lashes out, tasting my skin between sensual kisses. "Ye taste so fuckin' good," he groans, thrusting his dick against the outside of my thigh.

Oh god....

Lachlan's finger lowers to my mound, and my back bows off the blankets as he brushes my throbbing clit. Eyes rolling into the back of my head, I splutter a throaty moan, and he growls his satisfaction, massaging my clit over and over with the pad of his finger.

Kissing his way down my neck and over my collarbone, his generous lips travel to my breast and envelop my nipple. Running a tentative tongue over the puckered tip, he sends an overwhelming strike of pleasure down to my toes and back again, where it settles at my clit, making it pulse and swell under his rolling touch.

"Lachlan," I rasp, my body coiling tighter as my breathing sputters out of control. I need more, so much more.

His mouth turns greedy, feasting like a savage as it sucks, nibbles, and pulls my bud between his teeth before his tongue laves the sting away. Then he hungrily launches onto my other nipple, giving it the same attention.

Higher and higher he drives me as his finger lazily coaxes me closer to orgasm. My legs quiver, and I squirm, nearing the precipice as my nails dig into his shoulder and my other hand fists the blankets, making my knuckles hurt.

Oh, it's coming.

Then, everything stops. His hand moves away, leaving my clit neglected, and his tongue swirls my tit one last time before he sits up and crawls on top of me, spreading my thighs apart to settle himself between. I lock my legs around his hips, bringing him closer, and he peels them off, resting them gently on the blankets.

My eyes refocus on him as I try not to frown at the loss of connection. He grins, "Ye're sexy."

He leans down to press a long, beautiful kiss to my lips. I hum my appreciation before he pulls away, leaving his hands planted on either side of my head, and his body covering mine without touching. I need us to be touching. I need his scent to be surrounding me. I don't like this. When he's not touching me, I physically ache. It's like my entire body knows I need him, and it craves him.

"Lachlan, please touch me," I beg, rising my back off the blankets to press my chest to his.

"I—" he starts, but lowers to rest his chest atop mine, and then he kisses me, hard. His demanding tongue delves into my mouth, claiming it.

Battling ravenously, we groan into each other's mouths as I fanatically grasp at his shoulders, his arms—everywhere that I can touch. My legs wrap around him once again and his dick connects with my pussy, sliding through my wetness and brushing my clit before folding between us to press to his stomach.

Tearing his mouth from mine with a grunt, I gasp for air. "Fuck, ye're so bloody perfect." He catches his breath, his lips red and swollen, cheeks flushed. The compliment forces my chest to expand, and something warm and sweet settles there, mixing with the butterflies that are hatching.

Cupping his jaw, I meet his gaze. "So are you, but I'm *so* horny. You've wound me up and left me with just a little taste, more than once. I need you to touch me. I need you to help…" I trail off, unable to make out the words. Unable to express how much I need him right here, right now.

Turning his head, he kisses my palm. "I dunno what I'm doin'."

"You may not, but your hands do. Your," tenderly, I brush my thumb over his lips, "body knows what to do, sweetheart. Just let it show you."

"Will ye tell me what feels good?" His eyes soften with insecurity.

"I will tell you if it hurts. But, your lips touching my hand feels good. You make me feel good no matter where we touch," I encourage, trying to wipe that uncertainty off his face. A place where it doesn't belong.

Kissing my palm once more, he dips his head and pecks the tip of my nose, my cheek, my lips, and slowly makes his descent down to my neck, to my breasts, dragging his lips and planting tiny kisses along the way.

Swirling his tongue around my turgid tip, he flicks it sharply, and I moan, cupping the back of his head, eager for him to do more. He doesn't disappoint when he sucks my nipple into his mouth and plays with me. Soft and tentative at first, then quickly building to a hot pull and tug. Fire boils between my legs as my hips undulate, silently begging for more friction.

Hot air pumping from his lungs wafts across my skin as he nibbles me before kissing his way down my peak to the other, leaving me squirming with anticipation.

I moan, turning ridged when he draws my neglected nipple into his mouth.

Oh…

Growls of satisfaction rumble in his chest, as he, too, starts to roll his hips with the erotic tempo of his hard pulls.

"Yes, that's it," I moan with praise. "Just like that."

Lachlan's head lifts and my hooded eyes meet his. He rests his chin on my breast, his tongue poking out, stealing tastes of my tit. "Ye like it?" He grins shyly before licking across my tip.

Lachlan

Bloody hell, she wasn't lyin' when she said she loves it when I touch her anywhere. She responds tae everythin', and cannae stop moanin' or touchin' me. Not that I want her tae. But, fuck, I'm hard and my mind is focused on her so much that all I wanna do is climb up her body and slip into her wet heat. I can feel the warmth radiatin' from her pussy. I can smell her sweet scent, and it's drivin' me mad. I didnae have a clue that touchin' a lassie could feel like this. That my blood would roar with a need so intense that my hips cannae stop thrustin'… seekin' her pussy—our connection. *Her.*

Fuck.

"I love it," she pants, her chest heavin' for breath. I did this tae her. I made her this way, and it feels damn good.

Slidin' my tongue over her nipple, her back arched in response, pushin' the tip further into my mouth. I take her not so subtle cue and attack it again, suckin' it deep and feelin' the hardness stiffen further under my attention, ignitin' my taste buds.

My hand moves between our bodies to find her soft pussy, and I slip a finger between her folds. She writhes on contact, moanin' for more, and I bloody well give it tae her. The slickness of her heat coats my fingers, makin' it easy for me tae guide two fingers into her tightness. It pulses around my digits, drawin' them deeper.

Bloody hell.

"More, please. More," my leannan begs in a whisper, and my cock jerks at her plea, achin', needin', beggin' for me tae give in. Na. I hold fast. This isn't aboot me. This is aboot my lassie and me makin' her come. It's aboot me showin' her how good she makes me feel by just breathin'. Damn, she's so fuckin' beautiful; all flushed, and on the brink.

I kiss her nipple once more before stalkin' up her body tae her mouth. Where I take it as mine, just as I intend tae do with the rest of her for as long as she'll let me.

Brutally, I fuck her mouth with my tongue. Her breath comes so fast that she cannae keep up with me, and I take that as a bloody challenge. My fingers drag out of her pussy and I thrust them back in, bottomin' out with force. She screams on my lips, and I swallow her pleasure before I do it again and again. Fuckin' her on my fingers, her pussy soakin' them in her slick juices. *Aye! That's it.*

"Lachlan!" she cries, rippin' her lips from mine.

"Ye're not done yet," I growl against her mouth, spurred on by her need and my cock that's pourin' precome all over the blanket. My balls tighten as the primal urge tae come inside her claws down my spine, makin' my cock swell, throbbin' tae the beat of my heart.

"I can't wait." She seizes my shoulders, those nails of hers bitin' into my flesh. My cock bucks. *Hell*, if she dinnae stop, I'm gonna come from touchin' her.

"Ye will wait," I demand harsher than I intend, then kiss the side of her mouth before I trail my tongue down her neck and breasts tae stop and swirl it around her navel.

"Yes, touch...oh yes." She pushes my shoulders down, and I smile against her stomach, kissin' and lickin' everywhere I touch.

"Move, lower," she begs, her legs tremblin'.

Tae prove a point, I leisurely glide my fingers out of her wet pussy and thrust them back in, showin' her who's in control—it ain't her. I might not know what the hell I'm doin', but I know what I want.

She screams my name when I bottom out, and I grin at the sound, feelin' a warm tightenin' in my chest. I love this lassie so bloody much.

Nuzzlin' my nose tae the patch of hair on her mound, I inhale deeply tae remember this moment for the rest of my life. I've only done this once before, and I'm scared outta my bloody mind. But I know this is what she wants, so I wanna give it tae her. I need tae make her happy. That's all that matters tae me.

Lower, I slide my tongue through her engorged folds and run it over her clit. Her body flails on impact; her hands aggressively tug at her hair. Cautiously, I flick my tongue on the bundle of nerves, and she humps my mouth. I do it again, and I'm rewarded with the same reaction as her juices bathe my tongue in sweetness. Indulgent gratification hums through my chest.

"Your." Her legs hook over my shoulders, heels diggin' into my back as she pitches her hips, grindin' herself tae my mouth. "Your."

She's close. I can feel her pussy tightenin' around my fingers. I curl them tae play with her as I take a deep breath tae calm my nerves before I draw her clit into my mouth. It's time tae make my lassie come.

Mags

"O...oh...god!" Thrusting my breasts to the sky, the fire between my thighs detonates. Brilliant white-hot sparks of neon colors burst in my eyes as I'm catapulted over the cliff into radiant ecstasy.

Moans of rapture pour from my trembling lips as Lachlan continues to suck and fuck my pussy, rolling one all-consuming orgasm into another. I writhe and squeeze around him. Sweat forms on my forehead, and I reach down to touch him, to feel his short hair sift through my fingers. It centers me, making me acutely aware of everything: his goatee scraping my inner thighs, his hot breath washing over me, his scent filling me with a heady mixture of lust and contentment, thick fingers plowing in and out of my pussy as it clenches, milking them. Hungrily, he growls, his tongue swirling around my clit. Another spike of pleasure shoots up my spine, forcing a long, luxurious orgasm to ripple through me. Warmth and heat and pure bliss skitters through my arms and legs, making my toes and fingers tingle. My brain fogs with sated happiness. A smile forms on my lips as my garbled moans simmer, and my breathing calms.

As the last of my orgasm fizzles, Lachlan runs his tongue lazily over my clit and removes his fingers. I groan at the loss, and he kisses his way to my empty pussy, his tongue delving inside, tasting and teasing me.

"Did ye like it?" he whispers to it, like he's asking it for an answer.

I scrub my face with my hands and lean up onto my elbows to watch him work between my thighs. Reaching down, I run my palm over his head. "It was amazing," I rasp.

He glances up, his eyes locking with me, lust thundering in the cool teal. "Are ye sure?" His tongue swipes my core up to my clit and circles there, making my legs quiver as they fall to the wayside, turning boneless.

"I am positive." I sigh, caressing the arches of his furrowed brows with the pad of my finger. I don't think he believes me. How could he not? I came three times. I can't remember the last time I came that many times in a row. Not sure it's ever happened. I'm sure I'd remember if it had.

Lachlan suckles my clit for another moment then climbs up my body, his powerful form looming over me. His dick juts out, hard and heavy, spilling pre-come all over my lower belly. "Sorry aboot that," he apologizes, wincing, and I scowl.

"Why would you say that? I like it." I run my hand through the wetness, massaging it into my skin to prove my point. It's a turn on that he makes that much of a mess. It means he's excited. And I want him excited. Just as I want to see the full crown of his dick, that's partially hidden under his foreskin that hugs his plump cockhead.

His gaze drops to my hand. I gather a dollop of the clear pre-come on the tip of my finger and I suck it into my mouth. Lachlan's eyes widen, watching me lick it clean. Delighted, I hum in my throat, reveling in his faint sweet-salty taste.

"Ye...ye just licked my pre-come," he whispers to himself, stunned, his body lowering just enough that his dick runs atop my belly without dispersing weight. More pre-come pools, glistening on my skin, and I smile.

"Yes, I did," I admit, my cheeks heating. "And I wanna do more." Boldly, I wrap my hand around his shaft, and he bucks forcefully into my fist, closing his eyes tight, moaning.

Enchanted by his vocal pleasure, I play with him. Up and down, I grip his shaft and force him to bang my fist, his foreskin sliding in my palm making it easier. *Sexier.*

Rocking his hips in succession with my tugs, his body begins to shake uncontrollably. The raw moans emitting from his parted lips turn feral, rumbling from a place deep within.

My body burns hotter.

His thrusts turn quick and desperate, as his mouth hangs open, panting for air. Knowing that he's close to coming, I stop, and his eyes spring open. Seeking more friction, he lowers himself on me, fucking his dick on my belly.

Grabbing his hips, I force him to stop long enough for me to tip him onto his side and push him onto his back. He falls without complaint, and I make quick work of climbing between his legs and wrapping both of my hands around his thickness.

Frantically sitting up, he wrenches my hands away. "Na…Na touchin' him," he demands, holding my hands outward, away from his straining erection.

I look him in the eye. "Lachlan," his name rolls off my tongue like a sweet caress, "I want to touch you, just like you touched me, sweetheart."

"I dunno." He turns shy. Scared.

I fold my fingers through his, holding hands, and I rest our interlaced fingers in his lap just beside his erection. Leaning onto my knees, I raise up and plant a soft kiss on his mouth.

Hovering there, I whisper, "You almost came when I was playing with you, with my hand. Now I would like to do it with my mouth."

At my confession, he sucks in a sharp breath through his teeth and releases it with a shaky exhale. I love it that I can affect him this way. At least it isn't one sided. I feel the same.

Pressing my lips to his, my tongue demands entrance, and he invites me in. Without pause, our tongues tangle and everything turns hot and heavy.

My hands pull from his to wrap around his hardness. I tug, pull, and play with it greedily until he's groaning into my mouth, his hips punching, as he permits lust and untamed emotions to govern his movements instead of over-thinking.

Slipping my tongue from his mouth, I kiss and nip his cheek, his bristly chin, and his neck as I move south. Over his pecs, I pepper kisses and swirl my tongue around his flat nipples. He trembles, sputtering a moan, so I do it again, reveling in the same result.

Driven by my own desires, I run my nose between his pecs, inhaling the scent of his hair as it tickles my face.

Damn, he's perfect.

With a push to his shoulder, I coax him to lie flat on his back and my mouth travels over his abs. One-by-one, I kiss each defined ridge until I reach that stupidly hot V of his hips.

Lavishing along each groove, he moans and undulates below me, succumbing to my touch.

Basking in the power, I move lower and lick his pre-come beaded tip. Tugging the foreskin down with my fingers, I engulf his head and groan when his flavor bathes my mouth.

I squeeze my thighs together to dull the ache that consumes me, as Lachlan freezes, turning rigid, holding his breath.

Pulling off his succulent cock, I look up at him. He's watching me with equal parts worry and fascination.

I should have anticipated this. I should have known that it wouldn't be that easy for him to relinquish his control and ignore the years of mental abuse from his ex. I have no choice but to battle his demons with my actions and kind words.

Sensuously rubbing my bottom lip over his cockhead, I murmur, "You're so sexy."

Lachlan's face slackens and he releases a repressed breath, the worry slowly dispersing from his eyes, and his darkened need replacing it.

My stomach dips, and I suck on his tip for a second, swirling my tongue around the crown before I pull back and whisper, "I love touching you; every part of you." Then I take him hard and fast. Swallowing him whole until he breaches the back of my throat and I moan around him.

Up and down, I fuck him into my mouth, jabbing the back of my throat until it stings. I go wild, unable to get enough. Enough of his scent, of his gloriously thick cock—of everything that he means to me. I want to give him so much pleasure, he doesn't know what to do with himself. I want to show him how much I lo—care for him. How much I want this. How much I *need* this.

Over and over, I twirl my tongue around his head, sucking the pre-come from the tip before deep throating him again and again, until my pussy is soaking wet and my body is vibrating with molten lust. On my knees, I hump the air in succession with my mouth. My one hand wraps around his shaft, following my lips up and down. My other rests on his thigh, feeling it contract and release over and over again as I drive him closer to climax.

Disjointed words endlessly fall from his lips in quiet tones of pleasure, spurring me on, making me possessed.

I stop again to lavish his crown, and Lachlan's body seizes, his thighs turning to stone. With a sharp jerk, he growls voraciously as hot spurt after hot spurt of his come fills the back of my throat and I hungrily swallow it down.

Suddenly, without warning, I'm being tossed to the side and Lachlan's sprinting for the exit and unzipping it in just enough time to throw up.

My heart sinks, listening to the awful sounds of him retching. I want to go to him and make sure he's okay. But I know he doesn't like me seeing him like that, and I don't want to ruin this amazing moment more than it already has been.

The sounds stop, and I hear him walking back to the tent. He pokes his head inside, his face is matted with sweat, lips wet. "I'll be back in a few." His voice is raw, and all I can seem to do is nod, trying to fight away the tears and the guilt for doing this to him.

Lachlan disappears, but not before he re-zips the entrance. I listen to him walk away, and the basement door sliding open and closing in the distance.

Minutes pass and I roll onto my back, staring at the brightening stars through the mesh screen.

I kissed another man today. Something I'd promised myself I'd never do. As much as I had anticipated the pain resurfacing for breaking that vow, I don't regret a single second of it. I would love to kiss Lachlan every day for the rest of my life if he'll let me. I know it seems too soon, but my heart doesn't agree. It thinks it's time. It's time for me to accept him into my life without worry or fear. And that's what I'm going to do. I'm going to care for him the best way I know how. No matter how screwed up that is. Even if that means I can never give him oral again, or make love. I'll be with him because he's worth it. Lachlan's worth all of it and more. He's my savior and my blessing for a fresh start. A start I would have never had it if wasn't for him.

Some time later, I'm not sure how long, Lachlan returns to the tent just as naked as when he left. I lift my head to watch him come inside. Zipping the tent after he enters, his beautiful backside is left for me to ogle for a few moments.

Turning, he catches me and grins. "Were ye lookin' at somethin'?"

I'm unable to help it when my skin turns tomato red from my ears down to my chest.

"Um...yes?" I smirk timidly and shrug.

Lachlan steps over to the blanket and lies down beside me, resting on his hip, head perched on his palm. I turn onto my side, my body facing his, mimicking his pose. He sets his hand on my hip and glides it down my back, just above my butt. Then, he scoots closer and fits a leg between mine, forcing me to hook my leg over his, locking us together. My breasts mash to his hardened chest. I set my free hand on his bicep.

We stare at each other for a good long moment, soaking up each other's presence.

He's the first to break the pregnant silence. "I'm sorry I got sick. I'd hoped that wouldn't happen with ye."

I cup his jaw. "It's not your fault. I can't expect you to be fixed after our first time."

Blowing out a breath, he looks relieved. "Ye still want tae do that again?"

"Yes!" I blurt without thinking, and he smirks, holding back his laughter.

I clear my throat. "What I meant to say was...Heck yeah, I do. I...umm...liked it a lot." Gosh, I'm pathetic, and blushing again. I wish I'd stop. It's getting ridiculous.

Lachlan leans in to peck my lips, and when he pulls back, he's smiling, flashing a full set of dazzling teeth.

My heart skips at beat at the sight, and I smile, too, unable to stop myself.

"Did ye think we'd ever be doin' this?" he asks.

"No," I answer honestly. "I didn't think I'd ever kiss another man, let alone fall for one."

It's his turn to go shy. "Ye're fallin'..." He trails off.

"For you? Yes. It's kind of hard not to. Underneath all of that hard, broody, I-don't-give-a-damn shell, there's a sweet and caring man. And you're a great father, too." Crap, I'm rambling again.

I keep going. "And...ummm...that's just a smart part of what makes you pretty gosh darn perfect. Sheesh, most men, would love to be you. A badass macho man with a good heart—"

"And ye," he cuts in.

"And me?"

"Aye. They'd want tae be me 'cause I've got ye."

Oh, Jesus, he's perfect. Now he's making my insides go all gooey. Dang him.

Curling closer, I snuggle into his fame and we lapse into warm companionable silence.

Some time later, when the moon and stars are illuminating us from the dark sky, Lachlan rolls onto his back and pulls me on top of him. I settle my head on his chest, listening to the rhythmic sounds of his heart.

We barely speak a word and just *be*, and there's something perfect about it. He's a man of little words, and those he does say are to the point. That's another thing to add to the list of things I adore about him.

Just before my eyes drift off, Lachlan kisses the top of my head and wishes me, *his leannan*, sweet dreams.

And what beautifully sweet dreams they'll be with him by my side, cuddling under the stars, my heart filled with contentment and love.

CHAPTER 23

"Good afternoon to ya," singsongs a pretty, brunette waitress, wearing a floral print dress as she slaps two plastic menus on the Formica tabletop. We're sitting at the little diner down the street, having another friendly lunch after my therapy session. I'm really beginning to love this friendship thing. It's kind of amazing. But not as amazing as Lachlan and last night. Mmmm...

"Afternoon, Teena," Bonez replies, sliding over one of the menus to me. .

"Afternoon." I yawn loudly, covering my mouth.

"Coffee," she pencil points to Bonez, then swings it to me, "and lemonade."

"Yes, and a date for this Saturday if you're free." Bonez reaches out to run a finger over her hip, and she blushes fifty shades of flattered pink.

"I—I can't do that, Bonez," Teena stammers, swatting his hand away. "I have a boyfriend."

"Bring him along," Bonez shoots back, as happy as a toad on a stool.

Sticking out her hip, she shakes her head. "Bonez, you know I can't do that...I'll be back with your drinks in a minute." She pivots on her pink flats, leaves, and is clearly out of earshot before I raise a curious brow to Bonez.

"What was that all about?" I nod to the metal swinging door that the waitress just disappeared behind.

"She's sexy."

"Yes, she is, but she's taken."

He rolls his eyes, leaning back in the red vinyl booth, not bothering to read the menu that's probably been the same for the past twenty years, anyhow. "That doesn't matter. I told her to bring him along."

Resting his elbows on the table he leans in like he's about to tell me a secret. Reflexively, I lean in, too. "Straight men aren't as straight as they seem. Get 'em a little drunk, stick your finger in their ass, and then they'll be whistling a whole other tune."

"What?!" I shout, powerless to control my outburst. All the heads in the restaurant swing my way and I turn scarlet, shrinking down into the seat, praying that I'll disappear. Bonez laughs, his entire body shaking.

Did he...oh my, jeezy joggin' jockstrap, he just said that, didn't he?

"You want to *do* her *and* her boyfriend?" I whisper harshly.

The waitress returns, delivering our drinks and taking our orders. Bonez orders a burger, undercooked, and curly fries. I get the chicken fingers and a side salad with ranch, one of my usual's. There's not much to choose from in terms of restaurants in town. It's the diner, that coffee shop that the rude chick works at, Whisky's, a little dairy bar which isn't open in the winter, a couple chain restaurants, and that's about it.

Once our waitress is out of range, Bonez takes a sip of his coffee before bobbing his head. "Yep, her and her boyfriend. Have you seen Calvin?"

Since I don't have a clue who he's talking about, I ponder if I've just wandered into an alternate universe, and shake my head because a cat has officially caught my tongue.

"Calvin is a bit too pretty for me, but he'd make a good, quick lay." He takes another sip. "Plus, I like to corrupt innocent men. It's fun." He winks at me mischievously.

Are you hearing this? I have zero problems with gays, lesbians, or anyone in between. However, Bonez and corrupting straight men? I'm not sure what to think, much less say. And here I figured he'd be giving me an extensive scolding about not texting him last night. You know, when Lachlan and I slept outside in the tent, under the stars, where we held each other all night long. *Oooo*, just thinking about it makes me melt all over again.

This morning, he'd carried me into the house half asleep before he left for work. Laying me in bed, we kissed until we were both left panting and in need of release. Lachlan used his fingers to give me a glorious orgasm that lulled me back to sleep, and then he left for work still horny.

Speaking of my man... *Eekkkk.* He's texting me.
Enjoy your lunch with Bonez. If he doesn't behave, tell him I'll kick his arse.

I grin.

"Uh oh, Smoke's texting you. And now you're blinding me." Bonez holds up his hands to shield his eyes. "Damn, don't smile so much; I might go permanently blind. And then I couldn't fix your leg if I can't see. I might accidently fondle you instead, then Smoke would really kick my ass."

Now it's my turn to roll my eyes. "Whatever." I reach over the table to smack his bicep. It stings my palm, shooting a streak of pain up my arm, but I pretend that I didn't just hurt myself by slapping a brick wall. Dang, he's solid.

"He just said to have a good lunch, and for you to behave," I note.

"Gotcha. But I never behave."

"True," I tease, and the waitress delivers our meals, setting the big white plates in the middle of our table.

I text Lachlan back before digging in.

He's being his usual Bonez self. Be safe, and thank you for last night and this morning.

I should be the one thanking you, he replies.

No way. I'm the one who came.

On my fingers— which I get to think about all day while working. If you knew what you looked like coming on my fingers, you'd understand.

Blushing, I grin like a love-struck teenager. Who knew life could feel like this? Not me.

I type. *You can't say things like that when I'm eating at the diner.*

Why? Are you blushing?

Yes, I reply honestly.

Good. I love it when my leannan blushes. It's sexy.

Who are you, and what did you do with my broody boyfriend? I muse, hitting send and then immediately regretting it. We never agreed to be together formally. Crap, I really stuck my foot in it this time. *Way to go, Mags.*

I'm not your boyfriend. I'm your man. And I'm right here wishing that I was off work so I could taste those lips again.

My cheeks burst from so much happiness. He's *my* man. Ekkk.

Bonez reaches across the table and yanks my phone out of my hand and sets it on his seat.

"Hey!" I protest, trying to snatch it back and failing miserable. His reflexes are way faster than mine.

"You can live in dreamy, love-land after you eat." He shoves my plate closer. "Your chicken is getting cold, and you're giving me a complex."

I spew an overstated huff, knowing that he's right, and I rip off a bite of chicken with my teeth, glaring at Bonez in mock fury.

"What kind of complex am I giving you?" I grumble.

"One that makes my pants tight and my balls ache."

I choke on my food and quickly reach for my lemonade, taking a large gulp to clear my throat. His eyes smile at my reaction.

"What...the? Where'd that come from?" I sound hoarse, still not believing he said that.

My pants tight and my balls ache. Sheesh, those words.

"Your smile is where that came from. You grin sometimes, and it's cute. But I've never seen you actually smile, 'til now."

"I did not." I cover my mouth. I hate my smile; it's crooked, even though my teeth are straight and white. It's not my finest quality.

"You did, and it's hot. Makes me fucking envious of Smoke for putting it there," he states with conviction.

"It's not pretty, though; it's crooked," I argue.

"So?" He shrugs.

"So? I don't smile because it's crooked."

"You should. You'd give every man raging hard-ons," he states seriously.

"Oh my gosh, can you stop?" My ears and my face are burning. I can't take this. He can't be talking to me like this.

I fan myself.

"No, I'm not gonna stop being honest." He sternly looks me in the eye, challenging me to fight him on this. I won't.

"Fine. So tell me more about your male corruption." I change the subject, not wanting to hear any more about me. I hate talking about myself.

We lapse into a lengthy tête-à-tête about Bonez and his love for both men and women. How he enjoys men's hard bodies as much as he loves women's breasts. He knew he was bisexual since forever and has never been afraid of being himself. That much didn't surprise me; he's always confident in his words and actions. Bonez is sort of like the male version of Whisky. Blunt, honest, and caring to a fault. Except I'm willing to bet that Whisky doesn't occasionally bat for the same team. Pretty sure her panties only get wet for one man—Sniper.

My lunch hour comes and goes before we're strolling out of the restaurant, where I give Bonez my customary kiss on the sidewalk. Then I head back to the shop.

Checking my texts on the short walk, I see two from Lachlan, one from Cas, and one from Bridget. I'd texted her this morning to ask what she wanted me to pick up at the grocery after work. Lachlan's read, *Headed out to a call. See you in the morning. Kisses.*

I reply, *Be safe. Kisses back.*

Bridget's: *I do need some more of that yogurt you got last time. And you're going to need milk. I stole yours.*

I text, *Okay, sounds good. See you at home for supper.*

Cas's is last. *I take it Bonez wouldn't shut up. So before you get back, run to the parts store for me and pick up the order I called in. Please and thank you.*

With a crooked smile and an extra bounce in my step, I head to the parts store. It's a beautiful day out, don't you think?

Whistling and maybe doing a little dancing—*okay*, a lot of dancing—I make my way through Carolina Rose's tiny supermarket to none other than the great *AC/DC*. I'm sorry, but it's impossible to stand still when '*Thunderstruck*' is clearly ordering you to let loose. So that's what I'm doing, letting my proverbial hair down. Even if it's actually in a bun, on the top of my head, since I was hanging over the hood of a Corvette all day.

Tossing the frosted shredded wheats into the cart with some slam-dunk pizazz, I then mosey further down the cereal and candy aisle. Crazy aisle combo if you ask me, but whatevs.

I stop in front of the oatmeal section and try not to wince, grumble, or spout any obscene curses as I unceremoniously toss two brown sugar kinds into the cart. Then I cover them with the sugared cereal to hide the revolting product before I light it on fire. Don't think Lachlan'd appreciate that much, being a firefighter and all. I hate the stuff, but he was low, so I am doing my job and providing what he needs. I'm being a good *girlfriend*. Gosh, that word, I kinda love it. Don't you? Okay, so maybe *his woman* sounds better. Ya think? Oh, who cares, it means the same thing. *His.*

Mmmm…

"Hey," a deep voice calls from behind, tearing me from my reprieve, and skittering a gross, unfettered feeling up my spine. *It's Thor.*

I don't turn around to greet him. Instead, I keep walking, which doesn't matter because he slides up beside me and throws his arm over my shoulder. My annoyance elevates and I shrug him off. So much for my cheery shopping experience.

Thankfully, he lets me go, although he continues to walk beside me, sounding way too friendly for his own good. "Hey, Magdalene. How are you?"

I continue to stride, keeping my eyes forward, my body stiff, lips tight. "I'm fine, Thor."

"That's good. Hey…" He steps in front of my moving cart so I'm forced to stop or I'll plow him over. Not that I'd mind.

I cock a brow at him. "What can I help you with, Thor? As you can see, I am getting groceries before I have to head home to cook supper for Bridget and myself." I sweep my hand to the cart, speaking demurely, which is totally out of character for me. However, I refuse to use my friendly tone with him. He's a womanizing jerk, and must think that I didn't notice him at the party, which I surely did. I saw him with those women. And that just cemented my already poor opinion of him. He's good looking in his tight jeans, man bun, and *Spiderman* t-shirt, I'll give him that. And from an outsider's perspective, he appears to be a nice, courteous gentleman. Nope. That's what he wants you to believe. When deep down, my gut says that he's nothing but, as my grams always use to say—*a no good, dirty rotten scoundrel.* Or as Lachlan would say—a *bloody arsehole.* Take your pick.

Stuck in the middle of the aisle, Thor's beefy hands cuff over the end of my cart, making it impossible to move. "I know you have to get home to Pip, but I was hoping that if you had time this week, we could maybe grab some lunch or dinner?"

Jesus, he's really grasping at straws, ain't he? Did he truly miss my orgasm in Lachlan's arms at the party after I'd handled that chick pawing at him? I doubt it. Whisky has texted me twice about it, and Cas gave me a high-five this morning when I came to work. Even sweet ol' Rosie gave me a hug today, congratulating me for landing *Smoke.* Since everyone in the club lives in this town, and there were outsiders in attendance at the party, I'm willing to bet that everyone in a thirty-mile radius is well aware of my orgasm and minor showdown. And I couldn't care less. Actually, I hope everyone knows. Then maybe chicks will stay away from Lachlan, or I might go buck wild on them, too. Okay, maybe not buck wild. That was kind of a one-time thing. But I wouldn't be happy, and my reaction wouldn't be pretty, let's just leave it at that.

"I don't think that's a good idea," I respond politely, keeping my face blank.

"Why not? You go to lunch with Bonez all the time," he argues like a three-year-old whose mom told him he couldn't have any cookies.

Keep calm, Mags. Keep calm.

I take a deep breath and release it slowly, forcing my tense shoulders to deflate.

"Bonez is my therapist and my friend. I like going to lunch with him." I speak to him like he's that three-year-old I mentioned.

He scowls and rears his head back. I wait to see if I care; and strangely, I don't.

"You tryin' to tell me I'm not your friend now? Is that what you're saying?" His cool demeanor is slipping. This isn't good.

"I'm saying that Bonez is my doctor, then we became friends. I am with Lach—Smoke now, and I don't think it'd be right to see you outside of club functions, or at, say, the grocery store."

Why won't he just take the hint before we make a scene? I don't want to do this. Apparently, I'm the only female who's in this thirty-mile radius who he's attracted to, who's said no to him. I don't think he takes rejection well. It's apparent by the look of disdain he fires my way as he jerks my cart out of my hands and quickly rolls it behind him.

What the...

Shocked and disgusted, I try to take it back, but he grabs my bicep, hard, and maneuvers me so I'm flush against him. His other hand secures at my waist, and I immediately feel the erection poking me through his jeans.

"You need to let me go," I assert.

"No. You need to agree to dinner with me, tomorrow night, when Smoke's off work."

"I can't do that." I try to wrestle out of his hold. It does no good. His fingers only dig in tighter, bruising me.

An older woman pushing a cart strolls by, head down, pretending we don't even exist.

Great. It's nice to know she turns a blind eye to abuse.

"Then what can you do?" His tone is placating, giving me a sense of whiplash. And here I thought only Lachlan was capable of such things. At least he's never put his hands on me in this manner. If he had, I wouldn't be living with him. And I sure as hell wouldn't be in…you know…that love stuff…with him.

Tilting my head back, I leer, making eye contact. "What I can do for you, Thor, is allow you the dignity to walk away without me making a huge fucking scene. I *do not like* your hands on me. If you think this asserts your dominance as a man, *you're wrong*. It's a *turn-off—*"

"It is not," he opposes, still not releasing me. Although his grip slackens some.

"It *sooooo* is." I roll my eyes for effect. "And if you think I'd give you the time of the day after the night I had, you're out of your ever lovin' mind." I don't even care that I've cursed. I'm so damn mad right now I could spit in his face. But I won't. I'm still too nice for that. Go figure.

"What'd ya do?"

Ha, I prompted that one like a pro. Whisky would be proud.

"I had *orgasms*. Lots and lots of glorious orgasms given to me by a beautiful man, with a…*Big. Fat. Dick.* And you know this man well. *Because* if you don't release me this instant, you will become best friends with the bottom of his boots, when he kicks the ever lovin' shit outta you and then lets Bonez finish the job,"

I stress, whispering harshly under my breath, trying not to make a scene.

Granted, I'm kind of lying, because I'm already going to tell Lachlan, and I know for sure he'll kick Thor's hiney for doing this. Afterward, I'm sure Cas, Whisky, and Bonez will want a round, too. Obviously, he's not the sharpest tool in the shed if he thought I'd say yes. And he's even dumber if he thinks he can act this way without repercussions. Life doesn't work that way. *Bloody arsehole.*

Thor takes a moment to contemplate my words, and then he finally releases me with a string of not so nice curses.

"You know," he shakes his head, peering at the ground, scoffing, "it's funny how you won't go to dinner with me, yet your so called *man* is allowed to have an early dinner with Carrie, the chick from the party. Seems fucked up if you ask me." He scratches the back of his neck and gives me a two-finger parting wave before sauntering away.

Lachlan did what?!

I don't even contemplate what I do next as my fingers yank my phone out of my purse and text Lachlan. I'm not sure if I should believe Thor or not, so I go with something not as hurt as I feel right now.

Two things. One: Thor and I had an altercation at the supermarket. When you get time, I'll tell you about it. Two: funny thing is, he mentioned you having an early dinner with the chick from the party. Is this true?

I hit send and throw my phone back in my bag, too nervous about what his response might be. The last time I heard from him was at lunch. And I just got off from work before I drove to the store. I don't know what to think. Thor's one to stir the pot, I know that. But at the same time, I don't think he'd openly lie.

Sweeping those painful thoughts under the rug, I finish my rounds at the market. When I check out, I make small talk with the friendly cashier. The bag boy helps me to the car and loads my groceries into the trunk. I spot him a five, and he thanks me before rolling his cart back inside.

Once I fold myself into Viola, I'm finally able to breathe. And I do. I take a few long, cleansing breaths to wash away all of the crap that happened inside the market.

Then I chastise myself aloud. "Why am I so emotional? It's not like you know what happened."

It's true. I don't.

Turning over the engine, I head home and don't even bother to check my phone, which probably has messages from Lachlan. I'm too much of a coward to read them, and need to wait to do it until after dinner. Then, if I need to break down and cry, I can. But not beforehand.

Right now, I need to put groceries away, fix Bridget dinner, and feed Pirate, in that order.

I just hope I can stop freaking out long enough to accomplish what I need before the truth is unfolded. Or maybe I should pull up my big girl panties and let him tell me what really went down. No, I think I'm all tapped out of my big girl panties for the night. After I had to muster up enough courage to confront Thor, I'm awarding myself this pass. I think I need it.

KENTUCKY-'44 CHAPTER 24

Lachlan

Two things. One: Thor and I had an altercation at the supermarket. When you get time, I'll tell you about it. Two: funny thing is he mentioned you having an early dinner with the chick from the party. Is this true?

Mags just texted me that fifteen minutes ago. I tried callin' and textin' her back, but she's not answerin' her damn phone. Pip ain't home yet, either, so she cannae relay my message.

Tae answer the question, hell fuckin' na I didnae go tae dinner with Carrie. I bumped into her at the diner. And I was only there because I decided if Mags is gonna be havin' lunch with Bonez, then I'm gonna be the one treatin' her tae it. At least I'll be there in spirit. So I handed Maurice, the owner, a hundred and told him tae give me a call when the money ran low. Maurice is a romantic lad at heart, and his old eyes lit up when I'd told him what he was gonna do for me. Easy as pie.

On the way out, Carrie stopped me at the door and we talked for a second. Or, she talked for a second and I listened, tryin' tae be polite. Then I left and hit all of the other restaurants in town with a few bills, so when Mags goes in tae grab a bite tae eat on her lunch hour, it's covered. It's my duty tae take care of my lassie, even if she's eatin' lunch with one of my brothers. One of the few I can stand tae be around for more than ten minutes.

One that I highly respect, even if I dinnae like him fancyin' my lass for any reason. It pisses me off, actually. But I'm gonna shut those feelings down before they come between Mags and me. And I'll tell ye now, there ain't nothin' comin' between us. She's it for me. The best damn thing, outside of Pip that's ever walked into my life, and I sure as fuck ain't ever lettin' it go.

Right now, I'm headed tae confront the bastard that I cannae stand tae even look at. The fucker tried messin' with what's mine one too many times. Now I'm gonna take care of it, and teach the arsehole a lesson once and for all. Then I'm gonna throw a motion tae Sniper, askin' if we can vote this motherfucker outta the club. Ye dinnae mess with another lad's lassie, and the bastard went beyond that. I'm done playin' nice.

Rollin' my *Harley* tae a stop in front of Thor's gym, I see him through the window talkin' tae some blonde bodybuilder named Tiffany. Nice girl. Too naïve, though.

I know he sees me when I kick off my bike and remove my dagger from my side, puttin' it in my saddle bag. This way I dinnae use it and end up in jail for guttin' him.

Stepping onto the sidewalk in front of my bike, his sharp eyes cut tae me before he says bye tae Tiffany and meets me outside.

"We got a problem," I bite off with a low growl, my hands fisted at my sides, my body wound, ready tae unleash all of my rage on this bastard.

"We have no problem, Smoke." Thor crosses his arms over his chest and lackadaisically leans against the brick wall next to the gym's glass door.

"Aye, we do. Ye talk tae *my* lass lately?" I crack my neck side tae side, gettin' ready.

"Yeah." He shrugs, liftin' his chin in arrogance. "So what if I did?"

Such a bloody punk. Ye'd think he would've grown up by now.

"Ye tell her…" Ah, fuck it, who gives a shit if he told her what he told her or not. I know he did. I'm tired of dealin' with him, and I'm sure as hell tired of him messin' with Mags.

Takin' a step forward I close the distance between us. "Ye know what? I dinnae care what ye told Mags. I dinnae care aboot any of it. I've been tired of yer arse for a while now. It's time ye learned some respect, *boy*."

Lungin' forward, I wrap my hands around Thor's neck and quickly take him down in a headlock. His knees crash tae the sidewalk as he struggles, clawin' at my hands. It's a futile effort when I'm twice this bastard's size.

Gatherin' his composure, his fist clips my side, and I grind my teeth, inhalin' sharply, tae move past the pain.

Then, shit gets real and I lose my temper, as all of my past comes crashin' tae the forefront. First, my fist collides with his kidney, then another tae his gut. He dinnae know what hits him as someone else, someone fueled by merciless rage, inhabits my body. I see nothin' but red.

Fist after fist, I pound into his unforgivin' flesh, roarin' my shameless hatred. He doubles over on the concrete, tryin' tae fend me off. Kickin' his legs. Screamin' like a wee bitch for me tae stop. He lands a couple hits, but I cannae feel them. I cannae stop. He's fucked with my lassie; he's threatened tae touch her. I'm so lost that I dinnae notice the blood that bathes my knuckles as I smash into him with all of my strength, over and over and over, until I'm sweatin' and pantin' for air. My arms burn, my legs burn, everythin' burns as ecstasy-laden adrenaline courses through my throbbin' veins, drivin' my instincts tae protect what's mine. Tae take care of what's mine. And tae take out anythin' that might get in the way of that.

Mags is mine!

People gather in a circle.

Thor grows weaker, and his body fizzles out, shuttin' down from my powerful onslaught of wrath. Suddenly, strong arms are yankin' me backward, and someone's yellin' for me tae stop. People are runnin' tae help Thor.

The roar of sirens break through the sound of blood rushin' through my ears, and I glance down tae see my clothes are red, and my knuckles are busted open, stained with blood.

"You're done with him. It's done," Sniper says, rubbin' my shoulders tae calm me down.

I shrug him off with a grunt. I dinnae feel done with him. I feel like I need tae inflict more pain so he'll get the bloody lesson I'm tryin' tae teach. One I feel zero remorse over, whatsoever. He's an arsehole, and I've dealt with him as such.

"He's out of the club, Sniper! He fucked with Mags!" I growl, not givin' him a choice.

"If he still lives, then we'll take it to a vote," he replies calmly, releasin' a heavy sigh.

"I cannae be there, or I'll kill him." I stare off into space, as the redness recedes from the edges of my eyes and my breathin' levels out. I unclench my jaw.

Cops and paramedics arrive in hordes, fillin' the street with flashin' lights. Blockin' the downtown traffic.

A paramedic sees tae my minor wounds as another ambulance carts an unconscious Thor tae the hospital. Then Joey, a cop I've known for ages, takes my statement. He says that I'm free tae go, but tae stay close just in case they've gotta bring me in. Ha, I'd love tae see them try. They do that, and I'll beat Thor again, just for spite. Shoulda done it a long fuckin' time ago.

My phone buzzes in my pocket and I pull it free.

House fire 756 Maple Lane, all hands on deck.

Fuck! It's time tae go fight some fires.

With a sharp nod, I say goodbye tae Sniper and Whisky, who's now standin' with her husband, arm locked around his waist, her eyes of concern pinned on me. Kickin' over and straddlin' my bike I prepare myself for a long night of work, sans Mags. I just hope she texts me back soon. I fuckin' miss her.

Chapter 25

"Yes!" I scream in ecstasy, my nails clawing at Lachlan's shoulders as his mouth devours my nipple, sucking in hard pulls. Closer and closer, he lures me to the point of no return.

AC/DC's 'You Shook Me All Night Long' blares to life, disturbing my imminent orgasm, fading it into the distance.

What the heck?

Closing my eyes, I ignore the noise and focus on his hot, wet mouth that leaves me to sizzle as he swaps to my other nipple, giving it the same love.

For a second time, *AC/DC* wails to life and I sigh, irritated. Where in the frick is that coming from?

Glancing around the room, I seek the distraction. It's killing the moment. Yet, he doesn't seem to notice as his mouth continues his ministrations, trying to pull me under once more.

"Lachlan, we need to shut that racket off." I run my hand over his head to steal his attention from my breast. When he looks up, his eyes meeting mine, the teal has vanished. Replacing the coolness is the terrifying flames of hell as they lick the edge of his irises.

What the...

My eyes burst open and my heart leaps into my throat. I scratch it, trying to breathe, then I force myself to calm enough and inhale a lungful of air to ease the struggle.

Shoot. That was a freaky dream.

AC/DC screams at me again from my phone on the nightstand, and I roll over to grab it.

Jesus, it's still dark outside. Who in the heck could be calling me at this hour?

Without looking at the screen, I accept the call, placing it to my ear.

"Y—yes." My tone is groggy.

"Maggie? You up?"

It's Bonez.

Rubbing the sleep from my eyes with the corner of my fist, I stretch my legs under my blanket, groaning tiredly. "Uh, I am now. What's up?"

"I need you to get dressed, and wake Pip up, too…" He cuts out as he's interrupted by someone else. "Hold on— Whisky, give me a fuckin' minute, woman. Calm down."

Why is he with…?

"Sorry about that," he returns quickly. "I need ya to get up, get dressed, and drive you and Pip to the hospital."

What?!

"What?!" I shout, knifing up in bed, my heart racing. "What's wrong?"

"There was a fire, and Lachlan's been injured. Stay calm and just get here as soon as you can," he explains, his tone soft.

Oh. My. God. This can't be happening. This…Oh. My God. Not to him. Not this. Not to me.

Tears well in my eyes as I climb out of bed, flip on my light, and pull on some clothes in a haze. Pirate perks his head up from Lachlan's side of the bed. I stare longingly at the pillow where his head should be lying. Where his hands should be touching me. Where we should be cuddling after we make love. But he's not there. A sharp pain strikes my heart, knocking the wind out of me. I rub it with my fist, trying to massage away the lingering ache.

Get a grip, Mags.

"Maggie, you still there?"

Gosh damn it, I forgot about Bonez.

"Yes." I try to hide the tears in my voice. It doesn't work.

"You're crying. *No crying.* You have to get it together before you wake Pip."

Right.

He's right. I have to be the adult. I can't cry. I can't be weak. I have to put all my fears aside so I don't alarm her.

Just like I couldn't tell her about the dinner, I thought Lachlan might've had. Which made me insanely jealous and insecure. A dinner he assured me didn't happen when I finally read his texts before I went to bed. All eight of them as well as seven missed calls, on top of the two calls from Whisky and one from Casanova. She didn't leave a message, so I didn't bother calling her back. However, I did text Lachlan, but I've not heard anything since. Until now. Oh. My. God. What if he was out there getting injured while I was concerned about what he might've done? What if he was worried about me being angry with him and that's why this happened?

"Maggie!" Bonez yells into the receiver, tearing me from my morbid thoughts. "You have to stop thinking and do what I asked." His tone is demanding before it lowers, growing gentle. "I know you're worried, sweetie. But can you please do what I asked and wake Pip up?"

"Yes. Yes, I can get her up." I fake my confidence, knowing that my mind won't stop swirling with possibilities and shame until I see him again. Until my lips are on his and I can tell him I love him a hundred times. Why didn't I do that sooner? Why....

Damn it, I have to stop thinking and just do.

"Good. That's my girl," he praises with love, which makes me smile a sad smile. I'll take it. I'll take anything at this point to get to the hospital without having a meltdown. I'm not good at this kind of stuff. "I'll call you in ten minutes to check to see if you're safely on the road, okay?"

"Okay," I murmur vacantly, schlepping to my bedroom door and opening it, hoping to see Lachlan standing on the other side with a hug waiting for me. No such luck.

I wipe my tears away with the back of my hand and forge ahead. Bonez hangs up, and I slip my phone into a random pocket as I make my way downstairs to Bridget's bedroom door. Not bothering to knock I see myself inside and find her sleeping peacefully on her side, with wild hair fanned over her white pillow.

Expelling a depleted sigh, I click on her night lamp and nudge her shoulder.

"Bridge, ya gotta wake up, honey," I soothe, channeling my inner grams.

Groaning, she rolls onto her back, drowsily opening her eyes. They widen with concern when she spots me standing there. "Is everything okay?" she asks, too smart for her own good.

"Yes and no." I give it to her straight. "Your dad has been injured in a fire, but he's being taken care of. So we just have to get to the hospital. I need you to get dressed so we can leave." Apparently, my inner grams works, because Bridget climbs out of bed without freaking and glides on a pair of slippers by her bed. Then nabs a hoodie off her dresser and combs her fingers through her hair, gathering it to secure into a messy ponytail. I stand to the side and allow her whatever space she needs while my own mind runs a billion miles an hour with fear so intense that I might throw up. Despite the fact that, on the outside, I remain cool as a cucumber for her.

On the never-ending drive to the hospital, we don't speak. Bridget spends the entire ride staring out of the side window as I drive Viola, trying not to cry as the violent thoughts in my head overwhelm me. Visions of Brian's dead body surface, as does my grams rocking her last moments on our porch. Coldness seeps into my bones with fear so immense that my entire body aches as it shivers in tormented silence. My fingers squeeze the steering wheel to keep us safely on the road, and I swallow hard every few moments to keep from purging as the bile rises higher and higher, forming a thick knot in my throat.

Soon, the dim lights of town near.

Bonez calls like he said he would, and I make it brief, unsure of what to say at this point.

The hospital arrows make my heart crash into my ribs. My palms sweat as the lights of the ER bay illuminate before us. I reach over to grab Bridget's hand and give it a tiny squeeze for comfort. She doesn't react to my touch and continues to stare blankly out the window, her forehead resting on the pane. My heart goes out to her, wishing I could steal her worry away.

We park in the designated ER lot and exit Viola. My legs fill with liquid lead the closer we get to sliding doors, anxious of what I might find on the other side.

Through the tall windows, I can see into the main lobby where the entire club is gathered, wearing their vests. I spot Whisky tucked under Sniper's arm as the first set of doors retract for us. Taking Bridget's clammy hand into my own, we enter. And when the final door opens for us, all eyes swing our way.

Whisky's eyes rimmed in red meet my gaze first. Then I turn and meet Bonez's stare, one that's stricken with agony and communicating my worst fear.

"I—is," I fumble, and Bonez strides to us, securing his arms around Bridget and me, pulling us to his chest, surrounding us in comfort. I snuggle closer and curl one arm around Bridget's back as my other wraps around Bonez, holding them both tight.

A hiccupped sob tears from Bridget's throat, and I do everything within my power not to succumb to the pain and emotional torture. Not again. Not until I know more. Not until…

"He…" Bonez chokes on his own cry, and then I know. I know it isn't good. I know deep in my marrow what's coming next. And nothing in the world will prepare me for this moment. *Nothing.*

"He died in the ambulance," Bonez forces out, shattering my world into a million little pieces of broken hopes and dreams. Blackness fills my heart and I go numb. Everything I wished for, everything I'd wanted in life, everything I saw in my future is gone—vanished.

Lachlan's dead!

I can't even process that. How can this be possible? This has to be some sort of sick joke, right? I mean...my iron man, my thighs-for-arms, beautifully broken man can't be dead. Can he? This isn't right! None of this is right. This can't happen to me again! Brian and grams, and now Lachlan. The man I knew I could spend the rest of my life with. The man I love.

Oh. God.

He's dead!

Fat droplets of loss spill down my cheeks.

Bonez tries to speak to me through Bridget's endless wails of grief. Nothing registers.

Whisky's arms surround us, pressing us into Bonez. More arms and more bodies curl around our growing ball of suffering, and I feel like I'm being suffocated. I can't breathe. I can't...

Words try to filter through the pounding in my ears, through the pain, through the tears. But I can't hear them. I can't make them out.

Oh god. I can't breathe!

I struggle for air. In and out, air passes through my lungs, but I can't get enough oxygen. I stuff my face into Bonez's chest to make this go away. To make everything right again. To make this nightmare end. To allow me to breathe. To fix this. To do something. *Anything.*

This can't be happening!

"My dad's dead!" Bridget screams beside me as Whisky tries to soothe her, tormented by her own grief.

I can't be here. I can't take this. I need to leave. I need to go far-far away where this pain can't reach me. Where my life can start over. Where I can forget cold lemonade and warm kisses. Where I can forget his face and those teal eyes that will haunt my dreams forever.

Shoving off Bonez's chest and away from the group of bikers, I make a beeline for the exit.

Barely making it past the first set of doors, steel arms wrap around my chest, locking my back to his hardened front. "It's going to be okay," Bonez tries to reassure, but he's lying. I'm *not* going to be okay. I'm *not* going to be anything. I'm going to die alone with another broken heart. One that won't be fixed this time. Never again. *Never!*

Bonez kisses the back of my hair. His arms hold me close as I struggle, twisting and grunting in frustration to make him unhand me. He flips me around and locks his arms around my back, fingers interlacing so that I can't escape. Inclining his head, his lips speak to my forehead as the heat of his breath fans over my scalp. "I know this is hard, Maggie. But we're your family. We are going to get through this."

"No," I croak. "No, we're not. I was in love with him, Bonez. Brian died...a boy that I loved *died*. Then my grams...*died*. Then I went and fell in love with him, and he *died,* too. Why does everyone I love, die?" I press my nose to Bonez's chest, seeking comfort. Unable to sustain any longer, my resolve to be strong fades fast and I let it all go.

Pain, fear, anger, love, and agony flow freely as I cry in Bonez's arms, and he whispers tender words of reassurance to me.

I'm never going to get over this.

This is the beginning of my end.

Please pray for me.

CHAPTER 26

My tears, fears and forgotten dreams skip like a child around a barren merry-go-round. Around and around it goes. Where it'll stop, nobody knows.

I exhaust an extensive sigh.

In the cool breeze, bagpipes play for our fallen firefighter, spreading love with their bittersweet farewell song. Another tear trails down my cheek, and I brush it away, smearing the wetness into the black cotton of my dress. Who knew this day would be like this? Not me. It feels all too surreal.

Gathered around the cemetery plot, hundreds of people say their final goodbye to a shiny, black casket draped with an American flag. The wooden box hovers above its final resting place as a faux grass tarp covers the excavated hole. More than twenty people spoke kindly about a man they barely knew as many others openly mourn, tears teeming down their cheeks. Their show of sympathy and support hits deep in my gut as I swipe more than a days' worth of tears from my puffy eyes. I can't believe this happened this way. I'm still in shock— numb from the aftermath of truth. This is all too much to take as memories from my other life are trudged up, stripping me raw.

A preacher I've never met before speaks his peace, providing his condolences as a pillar of the small community. Stoic men in dress uniforms gather around the casket to show their utmost respect for their fallen hero—their brother.

My lip wobbles at the sight, and I suck it into my mouth. Bridget squeezes my hand in support, her own fingers trembling in mine as she sniffles.

It's almost over. It's almost over.

I release a shaky breath, watching as they carefully fold the flag and present it to the leader of the family—his sister. The finality of this moment settles like a rock, deep in the pit of my soul. He lost his life trying to save an elderly woman who refused to leave her old, rickety farmhouse because her three cats were still trapped inside. Sadly, that's something I could've seen my grams doing if she were still alive.

Walls caved, beams fell, and firefighters were trapped. That woman died, along with her cats, when the kerosene heater in the kitchen exploded into a fiery ball of death, simultaneously bringing down the roof and the floor beneath it.

Stories of his heroism have been whispered throughout the crowd today. First, they spoke of it at the church where the wake took place. I tried to listen. And now, as fellow friends and neighbors drape flowers on the closed casket, they speak of their pride in hushed tones. Not that I think he can appreciate their words. He's gone. Off to a better place where angels sing. Or that's what I have faith in. Something I have to believe in, or those that I've lost would have been for nothing.

Thick fingers startle me as they begin massaging my shoulders. I tilt my head back just as he bends at the waist to kiss my upturned forehead. "It's almost done," he soothes, kissing his way down my cheek, to my lips. "Just a few more minutes, then we can go home," he whispers, hovering his mouth above mine. Those words wash over me with a gentle wave of elation, and my bottled stress scatters.

Going home. We're going to go home.

My shoulders relax as his fingers continue their love.

Home.

With Lachlan.

Us.

Yes. He's alive. Still alive. Thank God.

The past three days have wreaked havoc on my already sensitive emotions. At the hospital, I'd spent nearly an hour crying in the waiting room, while Bonez held me. Then, when it came time to identify the body, Sniper did his duty and went back with the nurse. To our bittersweet surprise, the man on the table wasn't Lachlan. It was Steve. Steve, who was tattooed, and big, but looked nothing like Lachlan. From our fuzzy understanding, the four ambulances that had carted seven of the fallen firefighters away had gone to three separate hospitals in the county and those neighboring. Among the chaos, there were multiple wires crossed, which resulted in mix-ups with the patients locations. How that's possible in this day and age, I have no clue. I'm just relieved he wasn't the one lying on the table.

Sniper went wild on the doctors and nurses for putting us through hell. Whisky had to hold her husband back, and the cops were called to restrain him. Afterward, Bonez drove me to another hospital to see Lachlan since I was in no shape to drive. Bridget rode with Cas in his truck.

Arriving at the hospital, I'd sprinted inside and demanded to see him. They had already been informed of the mistake, and immediately showed us all back to his small ER room. It was packed like sardines, but the hospital didn't complain about the noise or the ten plus bikers. Smart choice, if you ask me.

Without thought, I threw myself at him, and he pulled me across his lap, his lips claiming mine in haste. The world phased out as we made love with our tongues, his hands roaming all over my body like he couldn't get enough. His erection poked me from under his blanket. I was close to stripping all my clothes off to be with him right there, until a haughty nurse went and ruined our little bubble when she came to check his vitals.

In the end, after all of the tests, Lachlan sustained two cracked ribs and a sprained wrist. While we waited to be released, he described what had happened to the group of us. Evidently, he was the one who had tried to save Steve, but the roof had come down, trapping them both. He'd freed himself, and by the time he'd dug Steve out from under all of the flaming debris, the man was unconscious. I'm almost thankful that the poor guy didn't have to endure the last few moments of his life in agony.

I'd stayed with Lachlan in the ER, cuddled right next to him in his bed, my leg strewn over his, until they released him. Ever since then, I've been eyeing him like a hawk to make sure he's safe and still alive. That hour was one of the hardest moments I've ever had to endure, and because of that, it's excavated all of those ugly memories from when Brian died. I've been obsessing over Lachlan because of it. He's been understanding of my internal struggle, and more than accommodating with how clingy I've been. I can barely stop touching him to go to the restroom. I'm too scared that if he leaves my sight, he might vanish forever. I know it's stupid, and I'm acting crazy. But I can't help it. I've regressed. Thankfully, though, I have the most amazing man to hold my hand through it. And for that, I couldn't feel any more blessed. I knew when I'd began to love him that it wasn't going to be an easy road for us, but he's made it worthwhile.

Lachlan rounds my chair and pulls me to my feet, his arm snaking around my shoulder, holding me to his side. "Let's say our goodbyes." He propels us closer to the casket, and my legs lock up. I don't want to do this. I hate funerals and caskets. Even if I'm grateful that Steve passed without any pain and didn't leave anyone but his sister and brother-in-law behind. It doesn't mean I want to move closer, to replay my past again and again. I just want to go home.

Lachlan stops and turns to me, his front to my front. Tapping his finger under my chin, he coaxes me to make eye contact. "My leannan, I know this is hard for ye. But I'm here." He leans to place a tender, lingering kiss on my forehead. "We need tae say goodbye. Aye? This man was my brother for the past three years. It fuckin' blows that he's gone. But I need tae say farewell tae a friend, and I need my lassie tae do it with me. I *need ye* with me."

He needs me. He's asking me to help. I can do that for him. If not for me. For him.

Straightening my spine, I take a deep breath and nod. "Okay."

He dips to kiss my forehead once more. "Thank ye."

With his arm locked around my shoulders, Lachlan saunters up to his fallen brother's casket and lays his hand on the top. Quickly, he whispers a few kind words, and I say a silent prayer for Steve before Lachlan escorts me back to the Tahoe. Cas is waiting for us next to the rear passenger side door, speaking to a teary Bridget.

Cas raises a hand in greeting and steps away from Bridget. "Hey, sorry about Steve," he says, offering up a man hug. Lachlan disengages from me to do a quick pounding, and I stand back to watch with a small smile, warmed by their affection.

Then Lachlan's arm is secured around my back again, my body glued to his. "Aye, it fuckin' kills, but that's what we gotta live with," he remarks.

"I suppose it is." Cas bobs his head, moving to stand next to Bridget's door, and reaches inside to grip her headrest. "Hey, I was wonderin' if I could take Pip for a ride? I'll drop her back tonight sometime. You know, she's pretty torn up. I wanna take her mind off this shit." He flicks his free hand toward the row of cars lining the edge of the cemetery road.

"Do ye wanna go?" Lachlan addresses Bridget, his eyes keenly watching her every move.

Bridget shrugs. "I don't care, Dad. I just..." She dabs another tear from her eye and leans into Cas when he hooks his arm over her shoulder, bringing her into a side hug. She buries her face into his chest, desperately clutching at the cotton of his shirt with her hands.

"Take her, and get the bloody hell outta here. But ye better be fuckin' careful with my daughter. Aye?" Lachlan thumps Cas's bicep with his fist, his expression firm.

"You know I will." Cas nods affirmatively to Lachlan and me, then turns to Bridget and wraps both of his arms around her as she locks her legs around his waist and he hoists her out of the Tahoe. Carrying her to his bike, her face stuffed in the crook of his neck, Cas's hands hold her bottom. Hum...that seems a little too intimate to me, but hey, what do I know?

I turn to Lachlan and open my mouth to say something, but he's grinning at me so I don't. "I know what ye're aboot tae say," he teases a little too happily, since we're standing at a funeral.

"What?" I tilt my head to the side, and he steps closer, his front melting to mine. I groan in delight.

Sifting his fingers through the side of my hair, he observes, "Cas touchin' Pip bothers ye."

How in the frick does he know that? I didn't say that. Even though it does. I'm like a mama bear when it comes to Bridget. Cas being my boss or Lachlan's club VP, doesn't factor into that equation at all. I'd be a mama bear to her even if the man were a saint. And he's definitely not that.

"I never said that!" I defend.

"Ye didnae have tae. I saw yer face. Ye were close tae kickin' his arse," Lachlan muses.

"Doesn't him putting his hands on her butt bother you? I mean, that's sort of inappropriate."

"Cas is a horny bastard, my leannan, but he's not gonna mess with my daughter. He knows that I'd kill him. Ye have nothin' tae worry aboot." His fingers tighten on my scalp, and the feeling burns in my belly, turning my blood hot with want.

I wish I could believe that, but I don't. Bridget looks up to Cas, and if he takes advantage of her, I'll be the one to kill him with all of those wonderful tools he bought me.

Sighing, I lean my head into Lachlan's touch. "I dunno—" I begin, but he doesn't give me a chance to finish when he claims my mouth in a searing kiss that makes my toes tingle as my pussy dampens. I grab his dress shirt, seeking more, and hitch my leg over his hip, grinding myself against him.

He rips his mouth from mine, leaving both of us struggling to breathe.

My lips sting with his addictive taste. Dreamily, I run my tongue over them and flick my eyes downward to catch his dick tenting in his kilt. Reaching out to touch it, he seizes my hand and wrenches it behind my back. My breasts jut upward, firmly pressing to his stomach when he locks my hips to his thighs, his hardness rooting my stomach. My nipples pebble on contact, and his mouth dips, hovering over mine, his warm, minty breath teasing me.

"Time tae go home so we can put all of this shit behind us. I need tae put my mouth on ye." His lips faintly brush mine, igniting goosebumps down my curvy frame.

My eyes grow heavy, lidding with desire. "Yes." I smirk wickedly.

His mouth on me. Shoot, I want nothing more than that. Lachlan's mouth kissing me. His tongue licking me. His body covering mine. My pussy quivers at the thought.

Releasing me, Lachlan moves to open the passenger side door and spanks my hiney when I climb into the bucket seat. Before I know what's happening, he's strapping me in with my seatbelt and pecking me on the lips. He slams my door and rounds the front of the SUV, then he coolly slides in and turns over the engine.

On the ride, he reaches his hand over the console and rests it on my thigh. The touch brands me with tenderness and lust. Squirming in my seat, my hand settles over his and our fingers link together.

God, I can't wait to touch him and wash away all of this misery once and for all. No more regression. I need to take life for what it throws at me. And right now, it's throwing me something quite remarkable.

Lachlan lifts me under my arms and throws me onto the bed. Squealing with surprise, I bounce a little, and he pounces on me, covering me with his deliciously naked body. Laughing and smiling at his eagerness, I spread my legs and wrap them around his waist, my arms going around his neck, pulling him closer, right where I need him. His erection nudges itself between my folds, and nuzzles it's dripping head to my equally wet entrance.

"It's time, my leannan." He shifts his hips a fraction, slowly breaching my core, stretching me around his thickness.

Oh yes...

When we'd arrived home, he didn't waste a second to shuffle me into the house and start stripping me. I knew what that meant without him saying a word. I knew he wanted this. Ever since the day we left the hospital, he's been touching me constantly just as I've been touching him. We've played with each other anywhere and everywhere we can, without making Bridget uncomfortable. We can't get enough.

It's *never* enough.

Yesterday morning over breakfast, he'd sat me on the kitchen counter, tore my pajama bottoms and panties down my legs just so he could go to town, giving me three glorious orgasms with his mouth. He's frickin' insatiable, and I'm giddy as all get out because of it.

This morning in the shower, we'd washed one another and I brought him to climax with my hand, which ended the same as always—him retching into the toilet. A little while afterward, he found me standing in front of the bathroom mirror, crying, consumed by guilt and the memories of Brian and Grams. Since Lachlan's death scare, the only time I can seem to put those feelings to rest is when he's touching me. And that's exactly what he did. He'd lifted me onto the bathroom sink, rolled my dress so it pooled around my waist, and kissed me as he told me how much he loved me, while his fingers forced me to come, twice.

Lachlan's lips on mine bring me back to the present. "Do ye want this?" He rolls his hips, his cock sliding in further. I clench around him, and he growls, plunging his tongue into my mouth without awaiting an answer.

Wickedly, we kiss, until my mouth aches and my pussy is grinding against him, my legs squeezing around his hips. He moves in slowly, sheathing himself in my heat as we groan and wrap our tongues together, breathing heavier and heavier the deeper he seats himself inside me.

When he bottoms out, we both moan, swallowing one another's pleasured cries of connection. I can feel him, everywhere. His hefty body resting on mine as his chest scrapes across my sensitive nipples. The way my pussy stretches around his girth, hugging it like he belongs there, *forever*. We fit perfectly.

My heart gives way to the glorious sensations and emotions that fill me up inside, making my heart warm and full and my stomach gooey with happiness. It's perfect. *This,* is perfect.

My nose burns as I fight off a wave of unshed tears as Lachlan pulls his lips from mine, swiping his tongue over my battered lips. "Ye…" He groans, his body quaking above me. "Ye…" He chokes this time and swallows hard, his Adams apple bobbing in his throat.

Gently running my hand over the side of his rugged face, I whisper, "I know," and softly press my lips to his again, melding us as one. I know this is it for me. He's it for me. Having thought that I'd lost him showed me more than what I already knew. That I love him deeply. That he's the one, deep down, that I know was made for me. We fit seamlessly. It's easy to love him after I got over how much my attraction scared me. After I accepted the one thing I couldn't change—my feelings.

"I love ye," he rasps to my lips, and my heart expands as tears of happiness drip down the sides of my eyes and into my hair.

Caressing the side of his face, I breathe him in as my bracelet jiggles, reminding me of him—of us.

"I love you, too, sweetheart," I whisper, and he shudders, resting his forehead to mine, his cock swelling inside me. "Now make love to me."

He shudders again, exhaling a shaky breath, his stomach quivering against mine.

"It's okay, sweetheart. It's okay. I want to be with you. I want this." I speak gently to him to move him past the emotions that I know we're both feeling.

"Ye," he gulps, "ye feel so fuckin' good."

I peck his lips and hug him tighter, trying to convey how much he means to me. "You feel good, too," I mutter. "So good, Lachlan. So good."

"My leannan." He nuzzles his nose to mine and glides his cock out, leaving just the tip inside. Goosebumps race down my arms and legs.

"My leannan." He breathes reverently and rocks his hip forward, gliding himself back in.

"Yes." I dig my nails into his shoulders and my heels into his hard glutes.

In and out, he gently drags his dick, hitting me in all the right places. Leaving me writhing and whimpering under him.

Tortuously slow, he revs me up, turning me into a growing ball of fiery lust and indescribable need.

"Mine." He rumbles a husky growl, punching his hips forward and hitting me deep, before gliding back out slowly, agonizingly.

Arching my neck into the pillow, my eyes rolling back, toes curling, I sputter a long, heady moan.

"Always mine." He thrusts again, rougher this time, and I hang onto him for dear life, worried that if I let go, I might float away from the sheer euphoria of it all.

Harder and needier, he slams into me with jerky thrusts, his body trembling fanatically the faster and deeper he makes love to me. His heart beats so hard that I can feel his pulse blending with mine. My pussy tightens around him, feeling every inch of his thickness plundering me in the most delicious of ways. A voracious mixture of our combined grunts and moans echo off the walls in our bedroom as we consume each other.

Sweat beads on his forehead, dripping onto me, and I grasp the back of his neck, forcing him to kiss me. Our tongues tangle and fight like we're possessed as my body coils tighter, the heat at my core rising me to a place I never knew existed. Bright colors burst in the back of my eyes, and I stop breathing as a searing orgasm crashes through me.

"Lachlan!" I cry, gasping for air as my body rides the wicked peak of unadulterated ecstasy.

"My leannan," Lachlan growls to my lips, his body thrusting wilder. Then he suddenly stops, going still, and pours himself into me, his liquid heat coating my insides, making everything perfect in my world—everything.

Lachlan releases a breath and melts into me, settling most of his weight atop me, going boneless, with his face resting in the crook of my neck. I caress his back up and down, waiting for him to make a run for the bathroom. Only, by the grace of God, it doesn't come. Overcome by hope and love, I send a silent prayer, saying thank you to the man upstairs for giving me the chance to live and love again. And for allowing Lachlan that same chance, too.

A single tear drops from my eye, and I smile happily.

Seconds, minutes, tick by as I draw lazy circles on his back with my fingers, both of us catching our breaths, our bodies recovering.

Then, he pushes himself up and kisses me, soft and tenderly. "Ye're mine forever?" He sounds unsure.

"Always," I whisper. "Always."

Beaming, Lachlan smiles, and I kiss him again, expressing all of my emotions and love, beyond my words.

The End

To My Readers

What else can I say other than thank you so much for taking this wild and painful ride with Magdalene and Lachlan. Now that you're finished, I'm sure you're either ready to hug me for loving the story or scowl at me for hating it. If it's the former, I want to send you a virtual hug right back. And if it's the latter, I want to send you a virtual hug, too, just for finishing the story even though it wasn't your cup of tea. And if you're reading this note before the book...as Mags would say—"Quit cheating and start on chapter one, you silly goose."

Beyond Her Words was a journey for me to expand my horizons as a writer and truly tap into a set of characters that kept nagging at me. Strangely, they came to me in a dream. And for six months, I poured my heart and soul into this beast of a novel. A novel I had no intention of writing in the first place, since I told myself I was taking a summer off to spend time with my family, but the characters wouldn't listen.

So here's a bit more about these people I hope you've come to adore as much as I have.

Lachlan: He was inspired by my love for Outlander. Not that he's anything like Jamie except for his Scottish ancestry, but the Scottish dialect really appealed to me. And let's face it, it's sexy as hell. Plus, let's not forget the kilts... *Swoon.*

Magdalene: She was inspired by no one, actually. Except maybe she has bits of me in her, parts of her darkness that I don't want to shed light on. But as a character as a whole, I thought her up.

Most of the other characters in the book weren't inspired by anyone else either...

However, Casanova being an amputee was not only inspired by all those men and women who lost their life and limbs fighting for our freedom. But it went a little more personal for me. I have a sister in my clubhouse, whose beautiful daughter lost her leg to cancer, and I wanted to instill a part of that into my story, just as her story of triumphant inspires me every day.

And.... The last but not least....

Bonez: I am sure y'all wanna know more about him. Bonez was never a character I even dreamed up until half way through the book. Honestly, it came to me after I'd been seeing my chiropractor for weeks on end, working on my hip, which meant he was touching my ass pretty regularly. After one session where I left sore as hell, I called Pixie in my truck and told her that in one of my books I needed to write a perverted and loveable chiropractor. She agreed right away. And there you have it, Bonez was brought to life.

Okay, I'm going to stop now, because I'm sure I could talk about this book all day.

In the end... even though you and I hate to see Mags and Lachlan go...know that they'll be back in future Corrupt Chaos novels, possible MC Chronicles novels, and a special novella that I will be publishing with a little more of their story.

In the words of Lachlan, "I hope tae see yer bloody arse soon. Thank ye for readin' aboot me and my leannan."

Peace, Bink Cummings

P.S. I hope you will consider posting a review. It would mean a lot to me.

Playlist

1. Whitesnake: Here I go again
2. Eric Clapton: Tears in Heaven
3. Thousand Horses: Smoke
4. Everlast: Broken
5. Brantley Gilbert: Fall into Me
6. Limp Bizkit: Behind Blue Eyes
7. Pop Evil: Footsteps
8. Blake Shelton: God Gave Me You

Bink Cummings Social Media

Email: BinkCummings@yahoo.com
Facebook: www.facebook.com/BinkCummings
Pinterest: https://www.pinterest.com/bcummingsauthor/
Twitter: https://twitter.com/BinkCummings
Facebook Clubhouse:
https://www.facebook.com/groups/BinkCummingsClubhouse/
Website: http://binkcummings.weebly.com/